WARRIORS
AND
WIDOWS

By

William T. Gleeson

First Printing January 2006

ISBN 10: 1-933817-03-8
ISBN 13: 978-1-933817-03-3

Published in the USA by Profits Publishing of Sarasota, Florida
http://profitspublishing.com

DEDICATION

To my friends and comrades of the 1/16, 1st Division, who fought so bravely and died so well. A special dedication to my good friend George Adams who died in April of 1966.

I would not be alive today if it weren't for the American Military Medical Doctors, Nurses and Corpsmen who so diligently put my broken body back together those many years ago. And to the Veterans Administration who has kept me in prosthetics these many years. With a final note of gratitude to the United States Air force Academy's 10th Medical Group for their 37 years of kindly care.

INTRODUCTION

I served with the 1st of the 16th, 1st Infantry Divisions, in 1965 and 1966. I was wounded twice, once in January and again in February of 1966. Our unit trained at Fort Riley and was shipped over by boat in September of 1965 to search out the enemy and destroy them. We built a base camp first and then set out on our missions. Generally, we would be taken by helicopter to a designated place in the jungle, dropped off and begin hunting the enemy. We carried three days supply of C-Rations and ammunition, and would be re-supplied every third day by helicopter. In most cases the mission would last for 25 days after which we would be picked up and taken back to our base camp for rest and recuperation. Many times we were sent out on patrols during this time, even though we were supposed to use the five days in camp to recover.

When I was wounded the second time, the 18 men remaining out of the original 44 that I was sent over with, were also wounded. One man, my grenadier, was killed. Of the remaining 18, three of them lost two legs above the knee and one arm above the elbow. Both my automatic rifleman and I lost a leg and I received broken and compound fractures of my other three limbs. This is our story.

GRATITUDE

I was fortunate to have many people help me write this book: My sons, Sean, Troy, Brett and Brock, my daughter Renee and her Aunt Linda. Niki Miscovich and Ann De Stefano did the editing, and the cover was created and produced by Constance Pharr. And to Joanne, perhaps she is most responsible for giving me five reasons to readjust to this society - a thing which needed very good reasons. With out the children I probably wouldn't be alive today. Not suicide, just a lack of concern for living.

TABLE OF CONTENTS

1

Symptoms

Betty Cambel stood at the podium, looking over an auditorium containing more than two hundred women. The need for all of them to be there was as close to an order as army wives received.

She would have liked to open with a joke but couldn't think of one.

"Wives of American soldiers. Our men have gone to Vietnam." After a pause of about six seconds, she continued. "They are there." She paused again for a noticeable breath. "Things will happen over there. Woundings, maimings, and deaths. Before those things begin to happen, we've got to have a good support system in place and functioning. We are late in getting it set up. We must do it today."

After another slight pause to let her strong words sink in, she continued in a louder voice. "We must hurry and develop friendships. An organization of friends set up to help us deal with the tragedies that war always produces. God knows I've been through this before." Her voice rushed a little to recognize other wives who had been through it, too. "As have some of the other wives here today. Experience shows, ladies, that it works best if every woman has a job in a committee. When a tragedy takes place, a wife will have many needs. We must know ahead of time what these needs will be and be prepared to meet them."

Getting the feel of it now, all nervousness gone, she continued. "First, we need to have an interview committee. This committee's job will be to interview each wife and list her individual situation. A form has been developed to log the individual family's profile and possible needs. It is a well-constructed, tried-and-tested form that will assure consistency. The committee to fill out the profile forms must be fully functional today. No woman should leave this building today before her particular situation is recorded and filed with the interview committee. I will lead this committee and will be assisted by a couple of the more experienced women. I repeat, we must start gathering the information right away. From everyone."

Like an athlete warming up before an event, Betty purposely intensified the reality of their situation. "We must have all the information about you and your family before a tragedy happens. I hate to sound morbid but I, and some of the other women here, have been through this before. So please trust me when I say, all that must be known needs to be known before a tragedy occurs. When a tragedy does occur, that, ladies, is no time to be asking a woman what support she needs."

She paused for a full minute, letting her stinging words soak into the hearts and minds of the wives in the musty, old, wood auditorium. When she did continue, it was with a commanding voice. "We must have a clearly defined plan, one that can be implemented immediately upon an occurrence. Don't worry about there being enough jobs for all of us. We will divide ourselves up so that each woman has a position on at least one committee. Each position will have at least ten women to back it up. Every woman will have a job. We will need to mix the women up from the four companies, the twelve platoons, the forty-eight squads, and so on. We will mix them up so that we do not end up with a large group of women serving on a committee whose husbands are in the same unit. We do that because experience has taught us that, when the wounding and dying starts, it happens in units. Thus, the more our committees are not clustered in the identical groups that our men are clustered in, the more likely we are to have unaffected people in each committee to help the affected ones." The room was morgue-quiet as each woman considered these words. Not wanting to hear them, but not being able to avoid it. Words that said her husband might be wounded or killed. Words that said it probably would happen and could at any time. The room stirred as the message penetrated. Some whimpered, some cried, and some held it in. All felt it.

Affected by her own words, sadness compressed Betty's heart. *There's no time for that; you have to go on.* Mustering her reserve strength, she continued. Her voice rang out, clear and strong. "If something should happen to your man, be it death or wounding, you will be given a telegram—a short, impersonal note, delivered by a stranger—from the Department of the Army. Let's talk about the damn telegram boy. That Western Union kid on a bicycle or in a car can ring your doorbell and ruin your life. Every woman here will become afraid of her doorbell. We'll become afraid to answer our door, afraid of seeing that young man in a plain, unattractive uniform holding a telegram of sorrow and pain for us.

Then she shouted into the microphone, startling them and offending their ears: "WOMEN OF MEN AT WAR, LET US MAKE A DEAL. Others, outsiders, may ring our doorbells, but we won't. No! If you want to visit a neighbor, call her first, shout at the door, but do not knock or ring the bell." Then, more quietly and softly, relieved that it was over, with compassion and kindness she said, "For those of you who don't know, we are all we've got who cares. Thank you. There are tables and forms available at the rear. Coffee and cake are also available, compliments of the U.S. Army."

The women cried, talked, drank coffee, ate cake, planned, filled out the forms, and organized. They made plans for and discussed all aspects of their new possible life changes. They discussed and agreed about many things, such as what the men should be told and what they shouldn't be told. They agreed that the letters must be kept flowing to the men and that they must be optimistic. The group leaders emphasized the need to send care packages, and a list was made and distributed on what were the best things to send. They would write about the small, good, and peaceful things. To write about the fun they were having, even if it wasn't true. To tell them about the kids and the things they were doing. To leave all other male friends out of the letters, no matter how innocent the friendship might be. To write about anything, as long as it was optimistic.

"Don't tell them about problems," the older women said. "They have enough to worry about. Do not burden them with things that they have no ability to help you with. Be tough. Be army women. Strengthen your men. If you don't give him strength, he won't have the will necessary to survive. The problems that your man would ordinarily share with you, we will share with you. We women will run this post and take care of our own problems." There was a committee for everything from child care to the best way to get the car fixed. They set up a network of women, a detailed and working support group.

Betty watched them. The women chattered as they left the auditorium. Feeling better. *We're lucky, we women at Fort Riley, lucky to have each other. From now on, men won't go over as a unit, like our men did. They'll be replacements for the wounded and the dead, and they'll be sent from posts all over the country. Their poor women won't have the chance to set up organizations like this. They'll be all alone waiting for the doorbell to ring. All alone, waiting for their lives to be destroyed. God, I hope this is a good cause,* she prayed silently. *I'm afraid, though, it's already starting to have an odor to it. Of course, what I didn't tell the wives is that if their husbands are killed, they will lose their income and their homes, too. Once he is no longer in the army, she isn't either.*

Betty suddenly felt fearful again. It was dread, a horrible feeling of heaviness in her heart that she had never experienced before, and it worsened as she drove home. Then it began to affect her breathing. Shutting down her throat until she feared it would kill her. Through sheer willpower, she stayed conscious and turned off at the post hospital, which was on the road to her home. Once in the driveway, she honked the horn until help came.

2

NEW REALITY

Sanchez was smoking a nonfiltered Camel while occasionally wiggling his toes. Sometimes the smoke drifted under Hart's nose, causing it to twitch. He hated the smoke, but was afraid to say so. "That was hell this morning. I damn near jumped out of my skin when Sergeant Leary's rifle fired. My ears are still ringing." As if soothing a pain, he rubbed his palm over his ear. "At first, I thought I had been shot. Sergeant Leary just kept shooting. I had to roll away from him to get away from the explosions." Sanchez responded with another puff of smoke. "I don't remember much after that. Except for that other sergeant screaming. I'm never going to forget that."

He paused a minute and seemed to think as he flicked the ashes off his Camel. "Sometimes I think one of us should've shot him. Finished him. Hell, he ain't nothin' now."

"I didn't even fire my rifle."

Sanchez turned and looked at him condescendingly. *Weak, spoiled man.*

Hart shrugged and said, "I made it a whole damn year in the army. Went through all of that training. I've never been that physical, but I made it, and now this."

Sanchez never would have associated with Hart back home. "So you didn't shoot, who gives a shit? You think these people give a damn about us? Look at where we are, stuck on the side of a hill, two men living in a one-man tent." Then Sanchez inhaled a deep breath of hot, dusty-smelling air. "Sergeant Leary is the only one who hit anyone anyway." It was quiet for a moment while Sanchez stretched out his leg muscles. Wiggling his cracked toes, he pushed his palms in the fine dirt at his sides and raised his body a couple of inches, reveling in the strength of his muscled arms.

"I fell asleep."

"Well, you were supposed to sleep," Sanchez replied. "Leary is awake, you sleep. You're awake, Leary sleeps: that's fifty-percent guard. That's what this shit place is about."

"I slept when I was supposed to be awake."

Last week, Leary had caught Hart sleeping on guard. Hart was pulling his guard while lying on his air mattress on the top of the bunker. Leary walked up on him, found him sleeping, grabbed him by the hair, and gouged the thumbnail of his other hand across his neck in a mock throat-cutting. He had then tossed Hart, air mattress and all, over the drop at the front of the bunker. When Sanchez, awakened by the commotion, stood up and yelled at Leary to leave Hart alone, Leary had punched him in the jaw, knocking him on his back.

They had both gone and complained to Platoon Sergeant Cambel the next morning. At first, Cambel had reprimanded Leary, but then Leary reminded Cambel what he had said when they arrived in Vietnam. "Men, we'll take care of our own problems in the platoon. If it only affects the platoon, we won't go to the captain." To that, Cambel had responded, "You're right, Leary. Sanchez, you and Hart do your damn jobs and act like soldiers." Though Sanchez and Hart had cursed Leary afterwards, they hadn't mentioned it again.

Sanchez came from a tough neighborhood in Los Angeles and had a reputation for being good with his fists. He felt resentment now as he thought about it. *Damn, Hart is weak, but Leary better watch it.* Then he said, "Yep, you got a problem. They were sure hell on us in training when we didn't stay awake on guard. Then it was practice, here it's for real."

"What do you think they'll do?"

Still angry and thoroughly sick of Hart's whining, Sanchez said, "I don't know, Hart. What can they do? Send you to Vietnam?"

They looked up to see Sergeant Leary coming towards them. Leary was a brown-haired, blue-eyed, twenty-one-year-old, tanned white man. He had a strong, athletic build and a very tired look on his face. He moved with dexterity as he traversed the hillside without once looking at the ground. He wore fatigue pants and shower thongs and carried his ever-present M-14 rifle.

Sanchez flipped his cigarette down the hill, sending sparks flying as it hit the ground and, as he looked at Leary, he realized he couldn't remember seeing him without his rifle. He shook his head.

Leary squatted down in front of the two men. It was a full squat like the Vietnamese did. He nodded his head. "Sanchez, Hart. You men doin' all right?"

"Sure, Sarge," Sanchez said. "Could use a bottle of whiskey and a woman."

Leary shrugged, smiling tightly. The look he gave Hart demanded an answer. "Sure, Sergeant Leary, doing fine, except I'm a little shook about last night."

"Yeah, well, maybe if you stayed awake a little more, you wouldn't get so shook, Hart. Huh, ya think?" His intense glare shot a sharp pain to Hart's stomach.

"I'm sorry, Sarge, I try. Really. I don't know why I can't stay awake. Must be the way I deal with my fear and the stress of this place."

"Hart has stress and fear in the middle of Vietnam. God almighty. Because of your candy-ass attitude, I don't dare sleep when we're out on an ambush. Why, Hart? Why? Because I need to stay awake and pull your damn guard."

"Sorry, Sarge, maybe you should put me with someone else."

"Goddamn, you're brilliant, and that's typical of your selfish thinking. I put you with someone else, say Sanchez here." Sanchez's body stiffened. "Right, don't blame you, Sanchez. But say I put you with Sanchez, he goes to sleep when it's his turn, and soon after he falls off, you go to sleep, then no one's guarding that position. Right? That jeopardizes the integrity of the defensive circle we call a perimeter now, doesn't it, Hart?"

"I'm sorry, Sergeant Leary. I really am. I tell myself to stay awake, but it never works. Even being miserable, with bugs crawling on me, rocks sticking in my back and sides, doesn't keep me awake. I've tried everything I can think of." Lowering his head, he said pensively, "But I still fall asleep."

Sanchez felt an urge to speak up for Hart. Leary's tone of voice and body language were offensive to him. Not that he didn't agree with the sergeant, but Leary was authority. Authority had always meant punishment to him. He said, with a hardness in his voice, "Hey Sarge, back off. Hart is doing the best he can. Cut him some slack."

Leary paused, still squatting, and slowly turned his concentration to Sanchez's perfectly featured, olive-brown face. Staring into Sanchez's black eyes, he said, "I'll cut him some slack. I'll put him with you from now on. I'll do that, and you, Sanchez, big man that you are, you keep this in mind when he falls asleep. You remember when he is supposed to be guarding you, that poor Hart can't help it. You remember as you're dying with a gook knife in your throat that Hart needs some slack."

The mental picture was too real for Sanchez, and he blurted out, "Hey, Sarge, I didn't mean that. Shit, I got him a lot of the time now. Give him to someone else."

Frustrated and helpless, Leary struck back at Sanchez. "Tough shit, smart boy, you got him. Live together, die together, the tough East L.A. boy and the sleeper."

Sanchez started to protest. *That dumb Mick can't talk to me that way. But even in training, he was a tough son of a bitch. He showed the whole battalion how to stick a bayonet into the base of a man's skull, and the look on his face said he would do it, too. No, don't need any of that. Leary will kill ya.* Sanchez said meekly, "Okay, Sarge."

Leary's facial muscles relaxed as he said, "Good luck." Then he stood, stretched briefly in the hot sun, and walked down to the bottom of the hill where their squad leader was cleaning his rifle. Staff Sergeant Carson was sitting in the shady part of the only bunker with a tree in their area. The bunker was thirty meters down the hill from Sanchez and Hart's tent, and just above the old rice paddy elevation.

God, Leary thought, as he got closer to him, *I thought Carson was black before, but all of this sun has made him even blacker. He's almost blue-black.*

Not looking up until just before Leary stopped in front of him, Carson continued rubbing the operating rod of his rifle with an old T-shirt soaked in oil. "Having a talk with your men?"

Leary smelled the gun oil. "Yeah, Sergeant Carson, something like that."

"You really think making Sanchez responsible for Hart will do any good?" He spoke quietly so that they couldn't be heard up the hill. Leary moved close to him and squatted in the shade between the bunker and where Carson was sitting. He spoke quietly, too.

"No. Just wanted to make a point with Sanchez. I know Hart is worthless."

"He's having trouble. The beating you gave him last week didn't help. I'll speak with the platoon sergeant and Lieutenant Tooley, see if we can't just not expect anything out of him. Not count on him for anything."

"You mean give him a free ride?"

"No such thing. Just on guard. We've got to deal with the reality of the situation. Do the best with it, always. That's our job as NCOs."

"Screw him. He needs to pull his weight just like the rest of us." Leary's anger rose.

"I've seen men like him before."

Leary nodded.

"We could use him as a company clerk or some kind of clerical worker. God knows the army has plenty of jobs like that. But this isn't the States, this is war and we got him. We never depend on him for guard or any kind of warrior duty-ever."

"Won't that encourage some of the others to try the same thing? You know, encourage goldbricking?"

"They won't try to pull any crap." Then as he smiled a little, "Hell, the rest of them are too scared not to stay awake. Hart has given up somewhere deep in his mind. Just look at him as a man who will always have extra ammo."

"I tried shaming him, but it didn't seem to work. Sanchez can get mad and fight you some, but not Hart; he doesn't have anything in there to pry against." Leary shook his head in disgust.

Carson said, "He carries a hundred and twenty rounds of 7.62 ammo, food, and water. He's probably not going to shoot any of his ammo, may never shoot, and so we'll always have that. It isn't much but it's all we've got."

"Okay, Sarge. But I'm going to leave Sanchez thinking he's responsible for Hart. Let him sweat it. Maybe it'll cool his mouth a bit."

"You did good this morning. You okay with it?" Sergeant Carson spoke gently.

"Didn't like what happened to the boys from weapons squad, but killing those gooks was okay."

"Just don't let it make you mean, Leary. Meanness can only lead to a man's distraction. Distraction leads to self-destruction."

"Sergeant Carson, we've got twelve months and two weeks left to do here. Seems to me that meanness is all it's about."

"Don't let yourself like it. If you let it take control, it might make you forget who the enemy is."

"The enemy is quite clearly all the slant-eyed little Vietnamese bastards that I see."

"Leary, you are already forgetting that some of the Vietnamese are on our side."

"No, sir. I haven't seen anything that would make me want to trust even one of these gooks. Not one."

With that, Leary turned and trudged back up the hill toward the tent he shared with his automatic rifleman, Specialist Fourth Class Folger.

Sergeant Carson watched him walk up the hill and then lowered his head and mumbled a prayer, "God in heaven, help save that boy. He's a good boy. I'll do what I can. But You've got to help, too." Then, depressed, he remembered: *Hell, Hart isn't the only can't-do-it problem I've got. Yep, my other fire team leader has a little Hart in him. It's just that boy and me for leadership. Leary is smart and talented, but so young.* "You don't always make it easy, Lord."

Just as his prayer was finished he heard the radio operator shout from the door of the command post bunker: "Sergeants, report to the platoon CP."

3

RIGHT TO FEAR

The noncommissioned officers of the Second Platoon were gathered in front of the platoon command bunker. The bunker was dug into the ground seven feet and walled with sandbags. Logs from the nearby jungle supported the ceiling, which was sealed with ponchos and held in place by two layers of sandbags. The platoon's leader, Lieutenant Tooley, Sergeant First Class Cambel, and radio operator Specialist Fourth Class Nash lived in the CP bunker. It had only one entrance and no port from which to fire.

Tooley sat on top of the bunker with his feet dangling over the doorway. Cambel was on his right sitting next to him, and Nash was next to Cambel. The other sergeants stood or squatted, facing the three men on the bunker. It was the first time they had met since the ambush that morning, the men were tense, shocked and tired, and the lieutenant wanted to keep the briefing as light as possible. He would be informal in his speech too, because much of the army's protocol was dropped in Vietnam, like the salute. It was no longer desirable to salute officers, since it made targets out of them. Furthermore, all indications of rank were removed from their clothing. For the most part, low-ranking officers and men shared the same food and accommodations.

"All present, Lieutenant Tooley," Cambel said.

"Thank you, Platoon Sergeant. Men, we have two matters to cover this afternoon. The first is our mission tomorrow. We fly out tomorrow morning at 0900 hours. Let's synchronize our watches." Tooley turned his wrist over, staring hard at his watch. Like almost everyone's, it was a simple, cheap windup with a leather band worn backwards on his wrist to keep the glitter down. "I'll have 1637 in five seconds, thousand-one, thousand-two, thousand-three, thousand-four, thousand-five, and mark." Most of the NCOs adjusted their watches, looking up when they were done. "Okay, Sergeant Cambel will provide most of the details, such as how much food, ammo, and grenades to carry, how and when to get them, and the order of march to the choppers. We will be gone for twenty-five days or until the colonel decides we should come back. Our mission is to hunt the enemy and destroy him. We will be walking north up the Ho Chi Minh Trail along the Cambodian border. The whole battalion will be going, but I don't know the order of march at this time. In fact, that's all I have. Any questions concerning logistics and such, Sergeant Cambel will answer."

He paused until some of the sergeants started fidgeting. When he spoke again, his voice was clear, but tinged with sadness. "While the ambush this morning was a success, it was also costly. The high cost, as nearly as we can figure out, was due to a mistake. Action taken in haste." No one moved. Tooley cautioned himself to be careful with his words. *They are all feeling loss, and fear. They can probably all still hear him screaming. I damn sure can.*

"This hasn't anything to do with blame, but we all need to become more aware. The training is over." Slightly louder now, "Some of you may have already heard through the enlisted grapevine what happened to Sergeant Beldair, Specialist Jackson, and Private Gregory early this morning." He paused again to let his words sink in. Still no one moved. *Like talking to a bunch of statues.* "As near as we can piece together, it went something like this. Just before the shooting started, Sergeant Beldair was already on his way to check on the gun crew. He was probably close to their position when Sergeant Leary opened up, and soon after, seconds probably, Specialist Fourth Class Jackson opened up with his machine gun. It becomes less clear after that.

"Maybe Sergeant Beldair saw something that no one else saw, or maybe he was just caught up in the firing like the rest of us. We're not sure, but what we are able to figure out from his movements is that he crawled up behind Jackson and Gregory, who were so busy shooting that they didn't know he was there. We know he tried to throw a grenade and evidently either Jackson or Gregory unknowingly kicked it out of his hand. Like I said, the rest isn't completely clear. Sergeant Beldair is, or was, still alive, but hysterical. Why he couldn't retrieve the spitting grenade and throw it in the four seconds after losing it, we don't know but, when we got to them Beldair would occasionally stop screaming and say, 'He kicked it out of my hand. It wasn't my fault. It wasn't.' That's all we know."

"Sir, how seriously injured is Sergeant Beldair?" Carson asked.

"Somehow he got it in the groin. Needless to say, he won't be back." Lieutenant Tooley stopped talking for a full ten seconds, exhaling while his light-brown eyes lost focus, leaving him staring blankly, lost in his own memories. It was dead quiet, then his freckled face twitched and he seemed to be back in the present again. He had a bright red, almost orange, head of hair. Along with the red hair, he had skin that didn't tan but just burned. Burned to blistering, especially on the back of his hands.

The men were all a little cautious around the lieutenant. In the few months they had been under his command, signs of his hot temper had surfaced more than once. So far, he had been able to keep it under control but still, on more than one occasion, they had all seen his face turn bright purple with rage. It was no secret that they expected him to blow sometime soon, and no one wanted to be the cause of it.

There was still no movement or noise from the sergeants. "As you probably already know, Jackson died immediately. Both legs were severely damaged and he had multiple abdominal wounds. They believe he might have scooted or somehow moved onto the grenade. Gregory died on the way to the Ninety-Third Evacuation Hospital in Ton Son Nhut, and I've told you all I know about Sergeant Beldair's condition."

Almost as an afterthought, Tooley said, "Not surprising that he's mad, though, his privates are gone as well as his legs." He regretted his words immediately. Silence hung in the air like a thick fog, smothering the breathing and suffocating the scene. Finding himself short of breath, his throat trying to close down, Tooley's voice rasped, "That's all I have. The platoon sergeant will work out the details of tomorrow's operation with you." Then he jumped lithely down into the entrance and pushed the blanket aside to enter the lantern-lit bunker. The entrance, also lined with sandbags, was a dirt ramp running down into the bunker. A blanket hanging at the bottom of the ramp served as a door. Inside the bunker was a small field desk and a folding cot for Tooley. Cambel's and Nash's cots and gear were also there. The bunker space, which measured twenty feet by twenty feet, was divided up among the three men with the larger portions going to the lieutenant and the platoon sergeant, as was proper, commensurate with their rank. Each of the three men had a wall behind them. The entrance and a small table where the platoon radio was kept took up most of the fourth wall.

Snakes and bugs continually invaded the bunker. The snakes especially liked the logs of the roof, and the scorpions found comfort under the sandbags. Keeping them out was a constant problem, a problem generally left up to Nash who, because of his proficiency at it, was referred to as "Killer Nash," a term to which he only pretended to take offense. Each level of authority—platoon, company, and battalion—had bunkers similar to this one. The higher the rank, the more elaborate the bunker, but all were primitive. There was a shortage of soap but not sandbags. Better alive than clean.

Sergeant Cambel will be able to communicate more freely with the men if an officer isn't present, Tooley thought. *Sure as hell could have gone all day without making that last statement. I'm not one of them and can never be. There's an officer's wall between us, yet I have to live with them, separate from the other officers. Gonna be a lonely tour.*

By 1800 hours, a light rain was falling. The rain was a warm one, and it seemed to refresh everyone. The men kept their equipment inside their tents in an effort to keep it dry. Most of them were sitting in the rain, wearing their boxer shorts; a few were completely naked, letting the rain wash their soiled bodies.

Leary and Patkins were over at Carson's tent. They were outside in the rain sitting on a log, and Carson lay inside the tent on his air mattress. He had one of the few mattresses left that still held air. Since he was squad leader, he also had an extra shelter-half, giving him his own tent. As he lay on his back, his head on his pack in the rear of the small tent, he stared blankly at the beads of moisture slowly running down the inside of his tent. The mattress was almost too large for the small tent and his feet were getting wet which didn't seem to bother him.

They had long since quit wearing the army boxer-shorts they had painstakingly dyed green before coming to Vietnam. Now the underwear was used for shorts during their rest period or as rags to clean their weapons. It hadn't taken long after their arrival in Vietnam to find out that wearing underclothing caused a severe rash. All three men wore their boxer-shorts with a large black safety-pin to keep the fly closed. The safety-pins came with their ammunition bandoliers, and this was the most popular use they had found for them. The three of them were silent for a while, enjoying the feel, smell, and sound of the light warm rain. Carson was waiting. He knew it would come out. It had to surface. It was like a boil ready to explode. The silence lasted for a full five minutes. *Too damn long*, Carson thought. *I'd better push it a little. Squeeze the box and force it out. Need to get it over with, that's for sure.* As an icebreaker, he chose to start with the other problem, hoping that it would be a transition to this problem.

"Leary, I spoke with the platoon sergeant and the lieutenant about Hart, and they pretty much agree."

Leary's rifle lay across his knees with water splashing off of it. Patkins had left his in his tent where it would stay semidry. Since arriving in Vietnam, Leary never went anywhere without his rifle, locked and loaded. "What's that, Sergeant Carson? Sorry, my mind was seven thousand miles away. You talking about Hart, not counting on him for anything except carrying ammo?"

"Yeah, pretty much."

"They both agree then. I mean, the lieutenant and Sergeant Cambel?"

"Sort of, the platoon sergeant for sure. The lieutenant had the same argument you had. But now he agrees with sergeant Cambel and me, though not wholeheartedly."

"It still seems wrong—somehow."

Carson was the leader of the second squad, which consisted of ten men. There were five men in Fire Team A and four in Fire Team B. Patkins was Fire Team A Leader, and Leary was the Fire Team B leader. As Fire Team A leader, Patkins was second in command, leaving Leary as third. The squad leader, Carson, was the tenth man. There were three rifle squads and one weapons squad in each of the three platoons. The weapons squad was made up of two machine gun crews and one weapons sergeant.

"Sure, it does." Carson had a calm, deep, and steady voice that rarely showed any urgency. His father was a Baptist preacher and, after listening to his father urgently shout at his congregation several thousand times, he had made up his mind to never communicate that way. "It goes against every movie you've ever seen, every book you've ever read, and everything the army has taught you up until now. Maybe it is wrong but, based on who and where we are and what we've got to do, it seems like the right plan."

"What are we talking about?" Patkins asked, more anxious than curious.

"It's Hart. You know how hard soldiering comes for him. Seems he can't stay awake on guard, never fires his rifle, and generally is so scared that he's worthless for anything except carrying extra ammo for the rest of us. Leary and the lieutenant want to punish him, kick his ass, and humiliate him into action. Try and force him to be a man. Make him live up to his duties. The platoon sergeant and I have seen this sort of thing before and don't have much faith in it working. We don't think anything can be done to make him be anything more than what he is. Some men won't do their duty, don't worry about anyone but themselves, and they are worth punishing, beating. They are worth it because they fight, cause trouble, and have a spirit, a force that can be redirected. Hart and men like him have little life force in them. Beat a man like him in a place like this and you'll just drive him in deeper. He's like a rag, scream at it, beat it, doesn't matter, the rag will never stand up on its own. Does that pretty much sum it up, Leary?"

"Sure does, Sergeant."

"Maybe he can't help it," Patkins said, his voice slightly strained.

Leary turned his water-streaked face away from Carson and gave Patkins a "what-the-hell" look. Patkins wouldn't look at Leary, but he could feel his look, and he shrugged his shoulders sheepishly.

Riling, Leary said "And maybe I can't help beating his useless ass…"

"You want me to take him out of your team? I can't get rid of him. Have nowhere to send him, but I could give him to Patkins." Carson nodded his tightly curled black head towards Patkins. In a deep, easy tone, he asked, "What do you think about that, Patkins?"

Defeated, Patkins answered, "If that's what you think should be done, then it's okay with me." Leary had difficulty concealing his disgust.

After an hour-long minute of silence, Leary said, "Just the same to you, Sergeant Carson, I'll keep Hart. It's my problem and I'll handle it the way you and the platoon sergeant want." Then, sarcastically he mumbled, "No fussing from me."

Ignoring Leary's sarcasm, Carson maintained his fatherly authority. "Good. Thank you, Sergeant Leary. So, this is the way it'll work in the field. Hart will be assigned to the nearest machine gun team at night. He'll never be told that he isn't expected to stay awake-it just won't be mentioned. The machine gun crews, however, will be told to never let Hart or anyone else but one of them man their gun. They'll be told that one of them must be awake and behind their gun at all times while in the jungle, and that, if anyone is assigned to them for the night, he should pull his guard with one of them. Of course, the third man will always be Hart. Hart will inevitably go back to sleep, and eventually they'll probably quit waking him. It may not work exactly like that, but it's a plan. We don't believe for a minute that we're fooling anyone, but we still believe it is the best plan, considering everything."

Leary reluctantly agreed.

"Got it," Patkins replied in a lackluster voice.

Without pause, Carson responded. "You all right, Patkins? You know, about everything?" *No way out, I gotta push it harder.*

"Sure, Sergeant, everything's okay."

"Well, Patkins, I was just wondering how you're doing over here. You seem a little taken aback by everything. You were a good, damn good in fact, sergeant in the States, and I just wonder how you're doing here, where it's for real. You know, combat? Like this morning? The killing and all?"

"What do you mean, Sergeant Carson?" A false bluff was evident in his blush-red face as he said, "What are you referring to?"

Very slowly, his lips barely moving, his neck locked in its bent position on his pack, and his hands serenely folded on his bare, black, hard stomach, Carson said, "Well, I have nine men I'm responsible for. Nine. You are one of the nine and the next in command if anything should happen to me. Now, Sergeant Patkins, I need to know to what degree I can count on you. Sergeant Leary needs to know, and everyone in the squad needs to know. Am I getting clearer?"

"No, Sergeant."

Damn his ass, no wonder he's like he is, he won't even help kick it loose. "Well, let me put it another way for you, Patkins. We all know that Hart can't be depended on to shoot his rifle. Since we all know this, we will, hopefully, never depend on him to do so. In short, we'll know that, if he's the only man facing or guarding a particular direction, then that direction is not guarded at all, but open. So where do you fit in this guarding thing?"

Bent double by a sudden flash of nausea, Patkins said, "Just what are you trying to ask me, Sergeant Carson?"

Stay cool, he's hanging onto something he's probably been hiding all his life. Try not to be too brutal, but you have to get it out. "You don't make it easy, Patkins, but it will be said. Why didn't you fire your weapon this morning?"

That goddamn Branden must have told him. My own damn man must have talked. "I didn't see anything to shoot at."

Smart, but I can't let him get by with it, not totally. He probably knows Branden ratted him out. Can't have that either. We have to know these things. This is no game. "You're the only one besides Hart who didn't need to replenish his ammo. The only one who didn't need to run a patch down the barrel of his rifle." Carson's voice, though still low, was steely hard. "You didn't need to clean your weapon, Sergeant Patkins. Did you or did you not fire your weapon at the ambush?" Patkins started to respond, but Carson pulled his right hand off his stomach and held its white palm out, a sharp contrast to the blackness of his stomach, halting him. "And if you didn't, was it because you didn't see anything to shoot at or was it because you froze? I need to know. We need to know."

There was a long silence as the rain fell and the smell of burning wood drifted by on a slight breeze. The rain on the tent canvas was the only noticeable noise. Leary was staring down at his wet feet. Patkins finally said, "No, I did not fire my rifle. Yes, I froze. Bust me. Put me in charge of Fire Team B, do what you have to do, 'cause I don't know why. Nor what I'll do next time."

More gently now, but clear and strong, Carson said, "Well, I am not going to bust you or anything like that. In fact, it needs to be kept among the three of us. Maybe, hopefully, it's nothing. It could be a one-time thing. Anyone could freeze. Can freeze. Buck fever. Whatever. Until we know, when we hit the jungle tomorrow, Leary and Fire Team B will be in the lead. Leary, you take point, then myself, then Folger, and so on. That will put Hart farther back in the formation, the place where he can do the least harm."

Puts me in the middle too, Patkins thought. *Where I can do the least harm too.*

"Sergeant Patkins, you take care of the logistics. Sergeant Leary, you double-check the men after Sergeant Patkins has inspected them. We need to do this right and we can."

"Now, I've been thinking about how to keep those hard cans of C-rations from digging in our backs. We'll all be carrying an extra pair of socks and, if we fill them full of cans, we can tie them to our front suspenders."

"Okay, Sergeant, that seems more comfortable than putting them in our packs. I just hope I don't get shot though one of those cans of ham and lima beans. I'll bet that shit is poison if it gets into your blood."

Carson smiled and said, "You just might be right, Sergeant Leary."

"Why don't we, in addition to the socks thing, take our packs off the belt at the small of our backs and tie them to the top of our suspenders? Carrying the weight high up on our shoulders should be more comfortable," Patkins said.

"What will we use to tie them with?" Carson asked.

"We could use commo wire, it's plentiful, strong, and easy to tie knots in," Leary added.

"Good, it's settled then. You men see to that and the night guard, and I'll talk to you when you're done."

They set that night's guard so that one man from the squad was up at all times until 0600 hours, when it would be full daylight. Hart would pull his guard duty with Sanchez.

Around midnight, Leary dreamed about his girl from back home. She was right there with him. It was scary. She was in Vietnam, and he was fearful for her safety. He kept insisting that she leave, but she wouldn't hear of it. She said that she was only there in his dream and in no real danger. She said he was the only one in danger. She worried about him all the time, but it was nice to be with him again. Still, he was fearful for her. He wanted her womanly warmth and comfort but was afraid for her to be there. And he forced her to leave. He woke up feeling alone and knowing that he would never let her come back again, not even in his dreams.

Consciousness that Folger was talking to him seeped in. "Sarge, you all right? You were upset as hell about something."

"Yeah, sorry, dream."

"I can understand that."

But that was the last time that Leary, or any of the men of Charlie Company, would allow their bodies to move while sleeping.

4

SISTERHOOD

After a thorough examination, the doctor told Betty it was nothing physical. When he offered her an antidepressant. She refused. She had a responsibility to the ladies of the Eighteenth, and she would not set a bad example by getting help from drugs. Though the pain seemed to diminish, it never completely went away. Not ever. Soon she would know intimately that the Tragedy Relief Organization hadn't been set up any too soon.

She sat in his easy chair looking at the phone on the small, doily-covered table to her right. She often sat in this chair when he was away, but she never did it when he was home. It was his chair and he sat in it every evening after supper as they discussed their day. It had formed itself to his body and still retained his smell. Sitting in it was like having some bit of him at home.

She knew that she had better call soon. Still, she didn't want to call until she not only knew what was bothering her, but could also explain it to Anne, her sister. It was hard to pin down, this vague knowing or feeling. Whatever it was, she knew it had to come out. Lately, she was frequently on the edge of tears and that wasn't like her. She was not normally given to loss of control. Certainly not known as the blubbering type. She looked away from the phone and down at her hands, clasped in the lap of her summer dress. She liked the dress and thought she looked good in it. It was a blue cotton dress covered with small yellow and white flowers. *I hope I haven't wrinkled it*, she thought as she realized her sweating hands had been clutching the soft material.

Yes, of course, it's a pretty dress and I'm still a nice-looking woman. After all, I'm only forty-three, she reassured herself as she covered a brown spot on the back of her left hand with her thumb. *Oh, I better*

*get off it. It's an age spot and covering it isn't going to do any good.
I'm getting old, so what. My hair doesn't need coloring yet. Well, not
much anyway. But the truth about the dress is I have to wear it. It's
the best-looking one that fits. Every time Mike leaves on one of those
remote assignments, I start eating more. It's happening fast this time.
I'm already into the clothes he never sees, the fat rack. I'm not going
to worry. I'll take it off just before he gets home—like always. Now I'd
better call Anne and stumble through it. Maybe she can help me figure
it out. Anne's always been good at that.*

Betty May Cambel was married to Sergeant First Class Mike
S. Cambel, the platoon sergeant of the Second Platoon, Charlie
Company, Sixteenth Infantry Battalion. It was a battalion of the First
Division, formed, trained, and shipped out of the old cavalry post
at Fort Riley, Kansas. She had helped all the newly arriving wives,
young and old, who had been assigned to the post over the last five
months. Soon after moving into their house on post, she had installed
an information booth at the Post Civic Center. She sat behind a table
and provided information about Fort Riley to newcomers. Betty kept
her information booth open every morning, nine to noon, Monday
through Friday. She had maps explaining where everything was,
from the hospital to the movie theater. She liked doing it. It made
her feel worthwhile, plus she remembered her days as a young wife
and mother and how scary they could be, especially coming to a new
and strange place. It was something that had happened often in her
husband's career. When she was young, the older, more experienced
women had always helped her out. She felt the least she could do
was to help out now.

Betty and Mike had been some of the first to be transferred to
the Sixteenth. Previously, they had been posted to a mechanized
infantry company at Fort Carson, Colorado. They were only in
Colorado for two months, barely enough time to make the army's
family housing duplex a home. Before that, they had been posted
in Germany. At least in Germany, they had stayed in one spot for a
blessed three and a half years.

In the twenty years she had been married, she had moved
fifteen times. To be uprooted again, so soon, was a burden. But
Betty considered herself as much a member of the army as Mike.
In the past, she had always just done what the orders said. "Why
question or complain about something you're going to do anyway?"
she responded when Mike asked once how she felt about moving
again. Then he had told her how much he appreciated her love
and strength to which, after a moment of reflection, she replied,

"Sergeant Cambel, in my own way, I'm just as damn tough as you are. I'm woman-tough, Mike, different kind of tough, but tough just the same. So, you're welcome. I love you, too."

Fortunately, in the past when he was away, she had had their daughter, and that had made his absence bearable. Now Mike was gone and so was their daughter, Beth. Beth was married to a nice man, a soldier she met when they were stationed in Germany. *Gratefully,* she thought, *Beth's man has two more years to serve in Germany. Then his enlistment will be up, and they're planning on going to his hometown, where he'll work in his father's business. Mainly, I don't want him to have to go to Vietnam.* But she was alone now, and she felt it. Really alone and it hurt deeply. *Going to be a lonesome tour,* she told herself, as the tears tried to break through.

Chin up, Betty, you're in the army, too. She chastised herself. *Well that is the problem, isn't it? It's the army! There's something wrong with the army.* Knowing she was on the right track, close to the root of what had been bothering her, she probed her mind for the answer. *It's definitely the army, but what about it? Was it because they sent him on another overseas tour so soon after Germany? Yes, that is definitely part of it. Mike shouldn't have had to go off on another hardship tour after his Korean tour. In fact, he shouldn't have had to go out of the country at all, not for four years after returning from Germany. That's always been the rule. It was a rule that valued the man and his family. It was an agreement. It's one of the things that kept men reenlisting. How could they take us so lightly? Yes, that's one thing that bothers me. It's a big thing, too. But there's more,* she told herself. *What else is wrong?*

How dare they treat our men like they have recently? "They," she asked herself, *who exactly are "they"? Well, "they" are the powerful people at the top. And the top is all high-ranking commissioned officers. It's definitely those order-givers from on high. The unseen. Who do "they" think they're fooling? Can "they" be so dumb, or is it that "they" just don't care? Or maybe "they" just figure we're too dumb to know what's going on. "They" are dumb not to care about quality people like us.*

First, sending Mike overseas when they promised they wouldn't and then this big secret thing. My good God, it was so obvious that it makes them look silly to try and hide it. Her anger built until she was outraged. *Those idiot men who run the army and government would not say where the Sixteenth was being sent. No, "they" could not utter the words, big "non-secret secret," yet everyone knew it was Vietnam. I would rather have him back in Korea than off to another war.*

This was the third war for Mike, and she was feeling used up. She had only been his girl when he went off to fight in World War II, but it was still hard. He was still her man. *It doesn't get any easier,* she admitted to herself. *Seems to take more out of me each time. God, I feel lonely and bad about this one.* She dialed her sister's number as her mind kept probing and analyzing.

"Hello," a woman said at the other end of the phone line.

Fighting back her despair and fear, she said, "Hi, Anne. It's me, Betty."

"Betty, how are you? Is everything all right? Mike okay, Betty?"

"Yes, yes, near as I know. I mean, I haven't heard anything." Betty could hear Anne rattling pans in the background. "But I'm really upset all the time. More this time than any other time in the past."

"Betty, I'm sure it'll be okay. It's always turned out okay."

"Hope you're right, maybe it's just my age and being alone. Beth gone too, and all. Still, I have such a terrible feeling about Mike and this Vietnam War."

"Mike'll be all right. This is his third war, and he came through the other two just fine."

"But this time it seems different. You know, little things are different. Little dumb things are happening. Something is wrong with the army."

"I don't know what you mean, Betty. What's wrong?"

"I mean the whole thing has a strangeness to it. I've never said anything about it to anyone before. Don't think I really knew what it was. I'm not sure I know what it is now. You know, maybe there's a method or purpose to the way things have been going, some method that I don't understand. Maybe being a woman, I just can't see the right, the workings of it."

"I don't believe that. Betty, you've always been real clear about things. If you see something wrong, then there's something wrong. I might be a little slow on some things like this, but you aren't, so please try and explain it to me. I'm trying, Betty. But I still don't know what you're getting at. To most of us the army hasn't been a way of life, but it has never seemed strange. You know, it's been cut and dried, march, shoot, and practice war games. Stay ready to defend our country."

"I know, Anne, I'm not being clear. It just seems strange, the things they've been doing lately, especially the last six or eight months. They're doing things that don't make sense. For example, why train men in ranger training and then send them over to a jungle war? This Sixteenth Infantry Mike helped put together and train is a ranger battalion. Oh, they spent a lot of time training for the jungle, but why waste time on that ranger stuff? They did a lot of climbing cliffs and sliding down them again. Rappelling and things like that. You know how I'm a geography buff. Well, I have been reading all about Vietnam, and I don't see where they will ever use such training or equipment. And Mike says the same thing in his letters. He's not complaining, mind you, he won't really do that. He tells it as a joke, but it isn't. He says they've been there two weeks and haven't seen one cliff that they could climb. He says everywhere they look, even from helicopters, there's nothing but jungle and rice paddies."

"Well, Betty, maybe they made a mistake. Didn't know that there wasn't any need for cliff climbing and the like."

Betty's free hand twisted the fabric of her dress—this was getting to be a nervous habit. "That's it exactly, Anne. How can you train men to go to a war and not know what to train them for? It would be like training men for jungle fighting just before sending them to the arctic to fight in the snow and ice. Who's making the decisions? What group of men is passing down the orders? I tell you, Anne, it's a pattern, and it scares me. Something is very wrong at the top in this country."

"Now, Betty, hon, everything will be all right. I'm sure it will. We don't know much about the rest of the world here in this small town. You know, just what we see on TV, and that can't really be trusted to tell us how things truly are."

"I gotta go in a minute, Anne. The phone bill this month is going to be a bunch as it is. But one more thing makes me think something is wrong. Mike, in his first letter after getting off the boat, wrote and said that when they landed in Vietnam, they got in landing crafts and hit the beach just like in the Second World War. Well, besides the fact that the men didn't have any training in amphibious landings, they were led to believe that the beach was hot, too."

"A hot beach? Betty, what's a hot beach?"

"I'm sorry, Anne, it's army language for a place that the enemy has occupied and is going to fight to keep. You know, shoot your way in and fight-to-the-death sort of thing."

"Oh, and it wasn't?"

"No. Mike said that they came all the way in to shore, nervous, with guns loaded, waiting for the enemy to open up any second. But nothing happened. There was no enemy. Mike's platoon was with the first wave and, when the door dropped and they came running out of the boat, looking desperately for the enemy, all they found was a very scared Vietnamese band. A band meant to welcome them to South Vietnam at the secure American air base of Da Nang. Guess the air force had a good laugh over it."

"What a dirty, thoughtless trick, Betty. Why would anyone, ever, do such a thing to their own troops?"

"Well, there was a camera crew there, too. It was in the news, the pictures looked good. The commentator said, 'American troops land in Vietnam today to hunt out and destroy the enemy.' Guess 'they' didn't tell Mike and the rest of the men so the pictures would look good. Look real."

"Betty, that's sick. I agree with you, hon, it does sound like there are some strange decisions being made around the running of this war. I just can't understand why. What's happening here? What's there to gain from such treatment of our own troops?" With a rush to her voice, she hurried to say, "But Mike will be okay, sis, honest he will. He's a smart guy and an experienced soldier. And maybe, I pray, someone with integrity will take over the direction of this thing."

"I hope so, too, Anne, I gotta go now, though, and I love you and yours. Give my best to your family."

"Love you all too, Betty. Talk to you later."

"Anytime, sis, really. I'll call you next week."

Betty hung the phone up and felt heavy as she pushed herself out of the easy chair. She stopped and looked at herself in the mirror that hung under the clock on the wall. Pulling a pinch of brown hair out away from the rest, she looked at herself in the mirror. *Thank God the gray is holding off. I hope I don't age too much before Mike gets back. I would hate to have him come back and find me a wrinkled fat old hag. 'Course, I do take pretty good care of myself, except for the weight, and, hey, fat people don't wrinkle like skinny ones do. My best feature has always been my blue eyes. Yeah, have to get real old before the eyes lose their appeal. By the time my eyes lose their looks, Mike's vision will be too poor to notice.* She chuckled at the thought.

5

SEARCH AND DESTROY

"**M**en." *Thank God my voice isn't squeaky,* Tooley thought, then continued. "Today we go on our first large search and destroy mission. I don't know how long we'll be out, but time doesn't matter over here anyway. This is the way it will go. We'll board helicopters in the grassy area located on the south side of the base camp. That is the clearing next to the road to Ben Cat." He paused to let that sink in. "The Fifth Mechanized Company will be responsible for our security during our loading of the choppers. We will load eight men to a chopper. Since most of you have ten-man squads, break the squads down into groups of eight. Do this before the choppers arrive. We must be there, waiting, organized, and ready to load when the choppers arrive. The choppers are scheduled to be on the ground for troop loading at 1000 hours." Feeling better now, nerves settled, he paused again while he made eye contact with the men nearest him. Looking into their eyes to make sure they were with him.

"Keep your groups together in an orderly fashion. We won't have time for confusion once the choppers land. The choppers will not shut their engines down, so make the loading safe, efficient, and speedy. Our destination will be War Zone C. We need to land and deploy south of the Lo Bo Woods. We have no idea how hot the LZ is or might be. The LZ is at the extreme southern end of War Zone C. From there, for as long as it's deemed necessary, we'll work our way north along the Ho Chi Minh Trail. Our mission will be to search out the enemy and destroy them, all of their equipment, food stores, and the trail itself whenever and wherever possible. Each man will carry his basic load of ammunition and three days' supply of food.

"On the way past company headquarters, each man will pick up and pack nine boxes of C-rations. How he carries them, and the rest of his equipment, I leave to you in your individual squads to work out." After another slight pause, he said, "You men are the best-equipped and most well-trained soldiers in the world. You are American soldiers. Like your fathers before you, and their fathers before them, you will do well. You did well in our first encounter, the ambush yesterday morning. I have full confidence in you and your abilities as soldiers and look forward to a successful mission."

Then turning to Cambel, Tooley nodded and said, "Platoon Sergeant, if you please."

"Thank you, Lieutenant," Cambel said. "Men, make sure that all of your equipment is in working order. Check and double-check it. No supply where we're going. Be sure that every man has his basic load of ammo. That is 120 rounds for each rifleman, M-79 and machine guns as much as you can carry, but I caution you not to overload yourselves. I do not think we will have a resupply problem and, with the C-rations and heat, we're going to be heavily loaded as it is. I warn you again against overloading. One case of heat exhaustion or sunstroke can cause the whole battalion to come to a standstill, not to mention what it can do to the man who gets it. Make sure, sergeants, and check each man yourself.

"Water," he shouted. "Water is everything. Without a large and continuous amount of it going through our bodies, we cannot function over here. Squad and fire team leaders, see that each man has two canteens full of water on his belt when we board the choppers. Men, try not to drink out of your personal canteens while waiting for the choppers. Water yourselves up at the water bag in the company area when you get your rations. Try to drink all that you can. Force the water into your system. All NCOs should carry an oversupply of salt tablets. Each man should have at least one tablet in the morning and one in the evening. Take the salt tablets with your meals, or they will eat a hole right through you. We will not be able to carry an extra set of clothes or any bedding except ponchos. Every man will wear his helmet and have no other head covering with him—no soft caps. If I find a soft cap, I will throw it away."

"Check and see that you have enough cleaning patches and oil to maintain your weapon. It must be enough to keep your weapons clean under continuous combat conditions and rain for at least thirty days. I trust that all of you are using the thirty-weight motor oil on your weapons and have thrown away that light gun oil we brought over with us. Even though the monsoon season is supposed to be near its end, it can and probably will rain anytime and possibly for long periods of time. Each of you must check your bandage pouch. See that it has an unopened compress bandage in it and not a package of cigarettes." The men laughed since the pouch was just the right size to hold a pack of cigarettes and, whenever someone harbored a package of Lucky Strikes in his pouch, the leadership threw a fit.

"The question has been asked of the lieutenant and myself, 'Who is not going?' and the answer is that everyone in this platoon is going. We have no physical profiles that will exempt any man of the Second Platoon from going. What other platoons are doing, or not doing, like the weapons platoon, does not interest us. While I'm on that subject, welcome Williams and Franks, who have been recently assigned to our platoon from the weapons platoon. They will replace two of the three weapons squad men we lost at the ambush. Welcome to the Second Platoon, men."

"Poor bastards," Sanchez said.

"You boys have had it now; write your last letters home," Branden almost shouted.

"Knock that shit off," Tooley shouted back angrily.

"Damn right, knock it off," Cambel said, so forcefully that a few of the men in the front jumped back. Then, more normally, he continued as if nothing had disturbed him. "Now, the mechanized boys will guard our equipment, personal things, and the perimeter while we're gone." He stopped, inhaled deeply, and let the air hiss out before asking, "Are there any questions?"

After scanning the men and seeing no hands or other signs, Cambel said, "Good, we don't have much time. It is now 0833 hours." A few of the men adjusted their watches. After pausing for effect, Cambel continued with the clear, precise, military communication of an experienced professional soldier. "We have less than one hour to get this done.

"As Lieutenant Tooley explained, the platoon will form in groups of eight, by squads. This will bust up the squads during transport. It cannot be helped, and squads will reform on landing as soon as conditions will permit. We will start with the first squad, and we will be ready to go, at company headquarters, no later than 0930 hours. This will give us only thirty minutes to get to our positions for chopper loading. It is enough time, but just enough. No time for dawdling around or grab-ass. If there are no questions, then we will see you at 0930 hours. Thank you all and good luck to all of us."

Very little was said as the men went back down the hill to their positions. By 0915 hours, the Second Platoon had gotten their nine cans of C-rations apiece. As Patkins had suggested, they'd filled their extra pair of socks with the rations and tied them to their front suspenders. When this was done, it looked like they all had two large black sausages tied in front. Looking ridiculous, they decided, was better than major discomfort.

It was time for their final check. Hart stood in front of Leary as the sergeant checked his equipment.

"This is a lot of stuff to carry, Sarge," Hart said.

"Yep. But it'll get lighter."

"How's that?"

"Well, Hart, as you eat, shit, smash the cans, and bury them, your load will get lighter. Lighter and lighter until the end of our third day, the day when the choppers, if they can find us, bring us a whole new supply of food to carry. Then, Hart, it will seem heavy again. But once again, it will get lighter again each day, until the fourth day. And so on until the mission is over."

"I just don't know how they expect us to fight carrying all of this stuff."

"Come on, Hart, it's not like you're going to fight or anything. The least you can do is not bitch about carrying a few things. Think of it as a picnic and your servant has the day off."

"Hard, Sarge, real hard," said Sanchez, who was standing next to Hart.

"Nah, it's not 'hard,' Sanchez. 'Hard' is when we have a perfectly able-bodied and trained soldier right here with us. A man whom we should be able to depend on to help us do our job and stay alive. But he won't, Sanchez. No, he won't fight, so we can only hope he's carrying something we might be able to use. Something useful to help the rest of us do his and our jobs. We need to see that Hart here is carrying things we can use to stay alive and keep him alive. But even then, when his only contribution to our situation is to carry things, old Hart here gripes about it." Leary patted him on the top of his helmet as he spoke. Hart didn't move. "Old 'hard' Hart here is so selfish that he even complains about the one thing that he might be able to do to help. Yes, he gripes about having to carry his own food and ammo. Now that, Sanchez, is 'hard.' Hard to take."

Tooley and Cambel were watching all of this closely. How the squads were handled and how they dealt with the preparations would tell them much about both the men in the squads and their leaders. Experience had taught them—especially Cambel, who had much more experience than Tooley—that they could not know too much about the men under their command.

Nash, the radio operator, was near them. It was his responsibility to keep tabs on these two men. His job, no matter the situation, was to provide immediate radio communication for them. He stood behind them, watching them, listening to the rush from his radio receiver, which was hooked to a loop in his right suspender at the place it went over his shoulder. Occasionally, his lips moved soundlessly as he practiced call signs and radio procedures in his mind.

While watching the men, Tooley became distracted by his own thoughts. How could he be standing here, in this place, doing this job, having these responsibilities? *It was just one year ago last June I graduated from college.*

His father worked at the CF&I Steel Mill in Pueblo. Tooley had four younger brothers, and money was never abundant. Tooley had put himself through school with the help of a football scholarship and the Reserve Officers Training Corps.

ROTC had made good sense. He would have been drafted after completing college anyway, so he figured that he might as well do his time as an officer. Furthermore, the money that the ROTC program provided for school had proven to be invaluable. Right after getting his degree in business administration, he had been commissioned a second lieutenant. And it had been perfect. He was stationed with an infantry battalion at Fort Carson. Fort Carson was just forty-five miles from the front door of his home, and he could not have imagined it any better. He could visit his family and see Sally, his fiancée, on a regular basis. Sometimes, he would even drive home at night. Most weekends, Sally would come and stay at his apartment in Colorado Springs.

They were officially engaged and had planned to get married September 9 of this year.

Tooley had called the wedding off.

"I know we're going to Vietnam. It isn't ever said, but the message is clear. I couldn't go over there married, knowing that I might not come back. I can't leave you a widow. I can't leave you pregnant. I just can't."

She'd spoken with a sadness that almost made him change his mind. "I would hate not to have been Mrs. Tooley. I would have a baby, too. It would give me something from you, something that I could keep forever, no matter what."

Fighting hard for strength, trying to do what was right, he said, "I just can't worry about a wife and staying alive at the same time. I just can't."

Sally cried all night but never mentioned it again.

She chose you to love. God knows why. I guess you have your moments...

He remembered all the films from World War Two and smiled to himself. The soldier about to go overseas is supposed to talk the girl into bed, not out of it. This act of selflessness comforted him. Made him remember the better parts of himself. Unfortunately, he would soon have trouble remembering those things.

Fifteen minutes later, the men of the Second Platoon walked down the road in a calm, orderly fashion, joining the other platoons as they went. They waited for the choppers, which were fifteen minutes late, and then boarded the air-beating slicks. There was no rain, but the air was laden with moisture, forming a haze that could be seen in the distance. The sun was a barely discernible glow in the east, and the smell of hot fuel was heavy in the air.

The choppers, now loaded down with men and equipment, inched their way into the sky, forming a narrow V-formation as they headed west. It wasn't long, traveling at seventy-five miles per hour, before they reached the LZ.

The closer they got to the LZ, the more anxious the crew became. The obvious nervousness of the crew filtered to the passengers. The crew, especially the pilots and copilots, knew the destination and had intercom communication with their two door-gunners. The choppers were much too noisy to talk normally; even shouting couldn't always be heard. So, when the gunners started straining to see over their machine gun sights and the copilot pulled against his safety restraints to try to look farther ahead, the troops knew they were close. They always thought the chopper ride to an LZ would never be long enough, and the ride from an LZ never short enough.

6

HUNTING

The landing zone was in an abandoned and dry rice paddy. Most of the vegetation was sun burnt down to brittle rice plants. The old paddy was just large enough for the two parallel rows of sixty choppers to land ten at a time, five per row. As soon as the first chopper's skids touched the ground, the heavily encumbered soldiers frantically bailed out. Their legs were already running as their feet made contact with the dry, hard ground. Though some stumbled and tumultuously struggled to regain and keep their balance, none stopped. With fear pushing them, they all hastened to get away from the rotating machines as quickly as possible. They ran at full speed to cover at the edge of the paddy. They were scared and desperate men, trying not to hold their breath as they ran, heading for the nearest jungle around the clearing. They tried not to think of the bullets or explosions that could tear into them at any moment.

Before the second set of choppers had touched down, the men from the first wave had already formed a protective circle around the LZ. Though most of the men had never ridden in a chopper before coming to Vietnam, their training together at Fort Riley had paid off. They all knew their jobs and carried them out with very little instruction or confusion. By 1200 hours, the entire battalion had landed, formed a protective perimeter, eaten lunch, and been given instructions on their part in the search and destroy mission.

"The order of march is," the colonel said, "B Company, take the point and have one of your platoons cover the right flank. The flank platoons will maintain a distance of no more than three hundred meters away from, but never more than one hundred meters closer to, the battalion formation. B Company's flank platoon will work the area to the right, or east. C Company will follow B Company.

C Company will maintain a one-hundred-meter distance behind B Company, but C Company's point man must always be able to see B Company's last man. C Company will likewise deploy a platoon to the battalion's left flank, or west, staying within the one-hundred- to three-hundred-meter range."

The colonel paused for a minute looking at his company commanders, all dripping sweat and kneeling in the dirt at the center of the old rice paddy. The colonel was worried. *I hope we aren't too exposed here. Should be plenty of soldiers between the enemy and us, though. However, a good mortar team could wipe out most of this battalion's officers. The lieutenants would have to run this operation then. I had best get on with it.*

"Men, it's not necessary for your flank platoons to stay in sight of the main body. The flanker platoons are only meant to prevent a surprise attack on the battalion's flanks. If your flanking platoons make contact with the enemy, then they are to stop and fight until I can bring the main body of the battalion to the fight. A Company, you will be our drag and reserve battalion. You will not need flanker platoons out since B and C flankers should cover your sides."

Again, the colonel stopped speaking and looked at each officer in turn, man to man, making sure that each understood. Every man nodded as the colonel looked in his eyes. *Now is the time for the pep talk. Time to restate the attitude of our mission.* In a more commanding voice, he said, "Men, do not think in defensive terms. Be smart, remember your training, but remember above all, that we are here to do a job. We are the aggressors, the hunters. It is a search and destroy mission, and we are American soldiers. We have never lost a war. Is there anyone here who does not think he can do his job with the attitude I've just described?"

The colonel looked again from man to man, as each nodded consent, just as the colonel expected. Even if they didn't believe what he was saying, the colonel knew they wouldn't admit it. *I'm not doing it merely for their consent. Hell, I don't really care what they think, not really. I just want them to know what my attitude is. Want them to know what I expect from them. Yes, I'm your colonel. Christ, it feels powerful. My battalion is going to march up this trail and kick ass all the way. We're going as far north as they'll let us. Japs couldn't stop us in the Second War, and these little gooks aren't going to stop us, either. This battalion will go north destroying the enemy, leaving only graves and burnt places behind it.* "Nothing? No questions or comments? Good, then back to your units. Let's do it and do it well."

The company commanders went back to their companies and briefed their platoon leaders who, in turn, went to their platoons and briefed their squad leaders. All of the briefings took an hour. The men on the perimeter lay behind what cover they could find and under such shade as was available to them. They sweated and smoked, but rarely spoke. When they did speak, most cussed the army.

Carson, after a briefing by Tooley and Cambel at the Second Platoon CP, headed to where his men were located. Second Squad members lay in the prone position—facing outward—in their part of the large perimeter. As it turned out, they were in the west part of the circle. It had not been a hot LZ and, for that, Carson was grateful. Now, however, he had to brief his squad about their position in the coming search. *Maybe I should be flattered that the lieutenant and platoon sergeant chose my squad to be the point for the platoon.* The Second Platoon was assigned as the left-flank platoon for the battalion, and his squad would lead them. It would be their responsibility to find, read, and move down the trails, protecting the battalion's left flank. *It's my job not to let the platoon get closer than one hundred meters from the battalion or farther away than three hundred meters. I've no idea how I'm going to do that. I don't know shit about this jungle. Could be impossible keeping up with the battalion while at the same time not walking into an ambush or booby trap. Will take some doing, if it's even possible. Oh well! Time will tell.*

As he knelt down, about twenty meters from his line of men, he knew that he'd better display a positive attitude. *I can't allow my fears and doubts to show. I need to set the attitude. It's my job.* With this determination at the forefront of his mind, he sounded angry as he said, "Patkins and Leary, back for a briefing."

Both men immediately moved out of their prone positions on the hot and sun-bleached paddy and rose to their feet. While occasionally glancing over their shoulders to check the ground, they backed up until they could both kneel down, one on each side of Carson. Except for a couple of glances while moving backward, neither man took his eyes off the jungle to their front. *Pretty smooth,* Carson thought, *and scared enough to be alert. Good!*

Patkins spoke first. "What's up, Sarge?"

"This is the way it is. The Second Platoon is going to flank the battalion. The battalion is going to follow that road there." He pointed with his right index finger at a two-track road that headed north, disappearing under the canopy of the jungle. "We're point squad for the platoon. The Second Platoon's job is to stay as parallel as possible with the front of the battalion. We are not to get more than three hundred meters away from them or closer than one hundred meters to them. It'll be our job to find trails that allow us to do that while, at the same time, safely moving north with enough speed to stay up with the battalion. Any suggestion about where to start?"

After a considerable pause, Patkins said, "There's a trail just to the left of the road. It's the only trail I can see from here. Maybe that'd do for a start." He didn't need to point. He knew they had both spotted it. Leary said nothing but kept looking ahead at the jungle.

"Okay," Carson said. "Seems like it heads due west, but maybe it'll swing back to the north. Anyway, it looks like the only trail this side of the road." He paused for a minute and noticed the belt area of his pants, as well as the front of his shirt, was soaking wet with sweat. *The only good thing about having wet clothes in this weather is it helps make even a slight breeze cool.* In a voice that allowed for no discussion, he continued, "Here's what I want. Leary, you take your fire team in first. I want you on point. Have Folger follow you with his automatic rifle. Folger is a good man and can be counted on to back you up if you run into anything. The rest of your men can follow in their natural order."

Turning slightly towards Patkins, "Sergeant Patkins, you follow with your team and prepare to give flanking cover for Leary if he runs into trouble. I want you at the head of your fire team, too, but put your automatic rifleman—what's his name?—oh yeah, Branden, on drag. That'll give us some firepower to the rear in case an ambush lets our point go through before opening up. Tell him to be sure and not shoot the rest of the platoon if we get hit. Also, Patkins, make sure the men keep their intervals. I don't want them to bunch up. Keep an eye on Leary's men, too. He won't be able to do anything but maintain the point." He paused to catch a breath and could smell the dry dust from the rice paddy. "On the other hand, don't let them straggle. Above all, don't let them lose sight of the man to their front or their rear. Be sure and remind them that the penalty for screwing up, from now on, will be death or wounding. I know it may seem silly to remind them of that but, in spite of what happened at the ambush, I think a couple of our men still don't believe that they are in this game." His voice relaxed a little. "So humor me and remind them, okay? Well, enough of that. The time for talking is through, it's time to do." Somewhat embarrassed at the little rhyme, he continued, "I'll move up and down the formation until I'm sure that everyone in the squad is awake and doing their job. Then, when I feel it's right, I'll relieve you on point, Leary. When I relieve you, though, stay behind me, don't move back in the formation—let Patkins keep them straight behind us. We'll have our hands full trying to spot booby-traps and ambushes and picking trails that serve our purpose. Any questions?"

He looked first at Leary to his left. Leary pushed his lips tightly closed and shook his head no. Then Carson looked to Patkins, on his right, and Patkins said dejectedly, "No, none."

Well, Patkins' feelings are hurt because I didn't put him on point. Tough shit, Patkins. It's the only decision I can be comfortable with. Not my fault he's weak. Training's over, this is real. As their leader, I damn sure will put men where I think they belong. To hell with what any or all of them feel like.

"Okay, no questions? Good, then we move out in fifteen or when the battalion does. Tell your men, no talking once we move out. No one talks—all hand signals. We know 'em. Use 'em. Good luck to us all. God help us all."

Fifteen minutes later, the battalion moved out and was moving at a cautious pace down the road when Leary first stepped onto their trail.

The colonel's helicopter pilot was just heading back to Lia Kae to park the chopper when he took one last look down at the battalion moving north through the jungle. *It looks like a large green snake making its way north*, the pilot thought. *North down a cleared path in the jungle just large enough for the green snake.* When looking closer, he noticed the flanker platoons on each side of the battalion. *And, they look like two little snakes, one on each side of the big one. Momma and two babies*, he laughed to himself. *I'm sure as hell glad I'm not with them. Back to clean sheets and whiskey for me.*

The small man in black pajama-like clothing was watching the large green men move out. He was proud to be the one chosen to lead the four-man reconnaissance patrol. It was his first such responsibility, and it was an honor. His orders were to watch and report, to see everything but not be seen. *It should be easy. These men are so big, so loaded down with equipment, and they come in with such an obnoxious attitude. They will be easy to defeat. Like the French, they are a bunch of strutting roosters.*

He moved carefully, his rifle held out in front of his chest. The muzzle was always moving, pointing at what his eyes saw.

With the safety off and his finger on the trigger, Leary stepped from the old paddy onto the trail. His M-14 rifle felt heavy, a good and powerful heavy. The coach in Leary's head talked to him, *You must see everything for what it really is or what it could be—never what you wish it to be.*

The squad slowly picked their way down the trail, their pace picking up slightly as they became more familiar with the jungle. Still, it was slow going, and they didn't dare rush. Leary found it even more difficult than he thought it would be, keeping up with the battalion and, for the first hour, he believed it was impossible. But by noon, he had found that they could keep up. And, for the most part, the smaller trails ran parallel to the larger one that the battalion was on. Thus, they found that there were many Ho Chi Minh trails under the canopy of that jungle. The trails all generally headed north and south.

It was hot in the jungle and they smelled, saw, and sensed many things. The jungle odor could change from the sourness of rotting vegetation to the sweetness of wildflowers by just rounding a bend in the trail or a shift in the breeze. The many shades of green and brown, dark and light, were so variegated that it was impossible not to be distracted by them. The weight of packs and ammo belts, along with stinging sweat and aching arms, legs, and backs, was a constant drag. But more than all of that, the knowledge that they were walking, step by step, into inevitable violence created a palpable anxiety. They all knew that what they were doing now wasn't much different from what the enemy had been doing the night of the ambush. When would it happen to them? Was there one or more than one of them at this very moment lying somewhere in the thick vegetation pulling the trigger of his weapon? It wasn't a question of if, only when.

7

TRAPPED

At 1700 hours, the Second Platoon rejoined the battalion to set up a defensive perimeter for the night.

"Isn't it a little early, sir? We still have plenty of daylight left," the A Company commander asked.

"No, Captain," responded the colonel. "Much better to let them get numb to the discomforts of war before they have to engage in it. This battalion has safely loaded, unloaded, and traveled a few miles without any losses—I'm willing to let it go at that. Tomorrow we can do some serious search and destroy."

The men quickly and gratefully set up their individual campsites. They segregated first into company, then platoon, and finally into squad areas. The guard would consist of two-man groups, twenty meters apart, forming the outer protective perimeter. It would be fifty-percent guard tonight and every night while hunting in the jungle.

Every man, from squad leader down, would be paired with someone else from his squad or platoon. All except Hart, and he would be put with the nearest machine gun crew. During the night, one man from each pair would always be awake and prepared to fight. Usually, the squad leader paired up with one of his fire team leaders; the other fire team leader would pair up with his automatic rifleman.

Carson, Leary, and Patkins were gathered around a small fire talking. Patkins was heating water in C-ration cans for coffee and hot chocolate. He knelt with his back to the lush, grassy clearing behind him and continually wiped sweat off his forehead, trying to prevent it from falling into their hot water. Carson and Leary were both on the other side of the fire with their backs toward a creek lined with bamboo. Leary sat on his helmet, and Carson lay in the grass on his left side supporting his head with his left hand.

Folger was just outside the circle. They were used to, and didn't mind, Folger's presence on the outskirts, about four feet north. Folger, who rarely joined any socializing, was on his back in the grass as he inhaled a Pall Mall cigarette, then let the smoke drift out of his mouth, watching it disappear into the humid air.

"So far, so good," Patkins said as he poked in the fire, more from nervousness than to help the fire.

"Yeah, no 'big bunch of enemy' waiting for us. No signs, really. Except those punji pits," Leary said.

"Those wouldn't fool anybody. The stakes were there just waiting for someone's foot. Probably had dung on them, too. Fortunately, they weren't hard to spot."

Carson rolled over onto his back, then spoke. "No. Those were old. The vegetation covering them had long since dried up. Does make ya wonder who they were intended for. 'Course, could've been meant for us. They could've thought we were coming yesterday. Fresh-cut vegetation doesn't last very long in this heat."

Leary chuckled. "Nothing lasts very long in this heat unless it's alive. And staying alive over here could be a problem, too."

"Speaking of staying alive," Patkins said as he fished a can of boiling water out of the fire and handed it to Carson, who had his pack of instant coffee ready. "I feel kinda naked and alone over here on this side of the creek."

No one said anything. Carson just stirred the coffee in his water with a section of his rifle-cleaning rod, and Leary waited for Patkins to fish his can of water out of the fire. He had his hot chocolate opened and waited patiently. Though the can's lid was bent back as a handle, it was still hot, and Patkins moved quickly to set the can down at Leary's feet. When the can was safely placed, Patkins said, "Well, it's just that the bamboo following the creek to our rear is as thick as a fence, and it separates us from the rest of the battalion." Carson and Leary still did not react. "Well, it's so thick we can only cross it in two places and can only see through to the other side in about three places. I just think, if we get attacked, we'll be hung out in left field. Like we've been all day." He was into it now and he rushed to explain what he perceived to be an injustice. "I mean, there could be—hell, probably is—a large force of enemy soldiers out here just waiting for the right opportunity to wipe us out. And it wouldn't be that hard to do, either. Not during the light of day or the dark of night. Being on the flank during the day, if we get hit, we

could be wiped out by the time the battalion could get to us. Now
this stupid bamboo separates us from them again, thick as a fence
and going from one end of this clearing to the other. Shit. It just isn't
right."

"Sure is thick, all right," Leary added, as he borrowed Carson's
cleaning rod and stirred his chocolate mix into the hot water at
his feet. "I agree the bamboo does isolate us from the rest of the
battalion. Hell, I bet a man would have trouble crawling through it.
Has anyone checked it out?"

"I am sure the battalion did before we got here," Carson said.
"Surely the lieutenants made sure. As far as us being isolated from
the main body—we're not that far. The creek can be crossed in two
places, and that's sufficient for them to back us up. I wouldn't worry
about it."

But Patkins did worry about it. He worried about everything
and was hoping that Carson would say something that would make
him feel safe. He needed something that would make the knot in
his stomach go away. That heavy, brick-sized, lump of fear hurt and
sucked all of the energy out of his body. *Shit, I'm scared and close to
freezing up all the time. It'll probably get worse, too. We should be over
there with the rest of them,* his child's voice whined in his head. *How
can I even get any sleep out here? I mean, four hours of sleep a night is
not enough for anyone. Even those who brag about only needing four
hours a night ought to try it over here, under these conditions. Jesus,
even then the sleep isn't continuous. You guard your partner for two
hours, then he guards you, then you guard him and he guards you
and then it's time to be awake. That just isn't enough to survive on.
Especially in a place like this where everything is out to get us, snakes,
fire ants, poisonous bugs, scorpions and Vietnamese, all trying to get us.
We just don't have a chance.*

Carson was sipping his coffee and watching Patkins' lips twitch.
*It's getting worse. When Patkins gets scared, which is all of the time
now, his face starts twitching. I wonder how long it'll be before he has
a permanent tic? Hell, we've just started over here and he's already
showing signs of cracking up. I got one sergeant who is just a kid and
the other one who's scared into helplessness. I'd better keep an extra-
close eye on Patkins, though. Leary will be all right. He's got a lot of
steel in him, but I hate to see the responsibilities of this place harden
him too much. Got nine men and two of 'em are scared into inactivity.
Going to be a long war, or a short one, depending on how it goes. We've
been lucky so far. God, keep the luck up. Please.*

"Well, I personally don't give a shit," Leary said. "The battalion doesn't mean shit to me. More men would just get in the way. Folger and I, we need a clear field of fire." Laughing and turning to where Folger was trying to get the last drag out of a very short butt, he asked, "Ain't that right, Folger, me boy?"

"That's exactly the way it is, Sarge," Folger said without humor.

"Well, I tell you all, this is the good time. Now, before dark. Hell, this is the only time we can stop and laugh and be reasonably safe. 'Cause, the closer to dark, the more nervy it'll get. We all know that the night belongs to Charlie Cong and his northern buddies. We're all on our own after dark. Each of us is alone, individually and as a group, too. I mean, we might be able to get artillery support after dark. That is, if they don't drop it on us. Still, after dark we sit out here in the blackness by ourselves. Waiting for daylight. We won't get any wounded out, or any ammo in, or any reinforcements—not at night. Like the boogeyman from our childhood, we wait for him. Charlie Cong thinks the night is his time. And, of course, he's right. The little bastard can come out of his hole in the ground and attack like a beast in the night. He can maybe kill a couple of us with a grenade or mortar round and then do nothing else the rest of the night but let us sit in our fear hoping we don't shit in our pants. Or he can just plant a couple of booby-traps so that we leave in the morning thinking we've made it...then wham! Yep, this is his damn country, and he knows it like the back of his hand. Well, screw him. He wants it at night, he can have it—same as in the day. Screw Charlie and screw the battalion. Let the little bastards do their thing. Folger and I are going to get as many of 'em as we can, when and where we can."

"You're right, Leary," Patkins said. "That's the only attitude to have. Bring the little bastards on." But they all knew he didn't mean it.

The place chosen for their first night was a seemingly ideal campsite about four miles from the LZ. It was a large hilly area covered by brilliantly green grass, which grew over a foot high. The grass had a sharp edge that would cut if handled improperly. This area was surrounded by jungle and punctuated with occasional clumps of healthy bamboo. By far, though, the most arresting feature about this clearing was the bamboo-lined stream running out of the jungle in the north, across a grassy valley and back into the jungle south of the clearing. The water in the stream looked clean and drinkable. The banks of the stream sloped gently, and the bamboo was thick and lush. The bamboo followed the stream separating the valley like a large green fence at least thirty feet wide, with the creek running right down its middle. There were only a few places where the water could be seen through the thick bamboo.

Though the battalion had already been in the meadow for more than an hour when the Second Platoon came into the clearing, no one had checked out the bamboo. It had just never occurred to anyone. Maybe because it seemed so thick that, in their inexperience, they assumed no one could be hiding in it.

The four Vietcong soldiers who found themselves trapped in the middle of the American force could not believe that the Americans hadn't checked the bamboo either. They did worry about when the Americans would realize their error and check the area. *Surely*, the young VC leader told himself, *someone in this large group of men will soon think of it and then they will find us. If that happens, when it happens, you will kill as many of them as you can. But we will all surely die. There are only four of us and we don't stand a chance against so many. Even as dumb as they seem to be, there are too many. Be careful whom you call dumb. You are the one caught. These big dummies have trapped you and your men. I can't believe you have failed in your very first assignment. You worked diligently for five years to become a leader in the People's Army and now you have failed in your first duty as a leader.*

The harsh, criticizing voice in his head chided relentlessly. *Your orders were clear. Observe the American unit, learn all that you can about them—number of men and weapons, and make a judgment concerning their competence as a fighting force. You had all of that information.* He was beginning to feel sick to his stomach. *You are stupid. You should have returned to your underground base and reported before this. If you had, you and, more importantly, your men, men who trusted you, would be safe now. But no, in your arrogance, you stayed for one more look and got trapped. You had done well all day—pacing it so that you and your team could observe and fall back just before detection. And now this. You are an arrogant dumb peasant, and you will die from such stupidity.*

He continued this self-criticism as he had been taught to do for the past five years. It was five years ago that they had taken him, at twelve years of age, from his village of Ben Cat and brought him north for training as a Vietcong guerrilla. He had learned many things in the last five years: how to shoot, how to booby-trap, and how to be self-critical. *If you ever get out of this, you will confess your stupidity and unworthiness to your comrades at the next confession time.*

Where did you go wrong? You did so well until a few hours ago. Even with the Americans' obvious inexperience in the jungle, it was no easy task. Yes, it was dangerous but you led well. The jungle was dense, forcing you to stay dangerously close to observe. But even though this was your first time leading, it shouldn't have happened; the four of us are experienced in reconnaissance. The technique you used always worked with the South Vietnamese Army. In fact, then, and he grinned in memory, *you could almost stand in plain sight of the ARVN troops and not be detected. These Americans are different though. They are so rudely overconfident. They are very big, and either very white or very black. And equipment,* he laughed, *they do have equipment strapped all over their big-ass bodies.* The grin widened on his face as he remembered the big joke in camp, *"Did these elephants come to fight or to set up a store?" Furthermore, they are the clumsiest bunch of humans I've ever seen.* But the humor ended when the critical voice inside his head took control again. *If they are so incompetent, then, how come you are the one trapped? Your complacency towards the new enemy is largely responsible for your staying too long. You are guilty of overconfidence, too. You are an idiot for forgetting about their flank platoon.*

At first, they hadn't been trapped. Not until the Second Platoon came drifting out of the jungle. Leary and the second squad led the Second Platoon out of the jungle on a trail west of the bamboo fence and south of the clearing. They had been moving on a trail parallel to the battalion's. When that trail opened into this meadow on the west side of the bamboo fence, the battalion was on the east side and the Vietcong soldiers were stuck in the middle. They couldn't move up or down the fence. The bamboo was too thick to crawl through for most of its length. They were in one of the rare pockets that allowed for human penetration and cover—a small clearing in the middle of the thick bamboo hedge.

The young VC reconnaissance leader tried to calm himself with the knowledge that it looked like rain and would no doubt be a dark night—they would make their escape then. The VC never spoke as they lay huddled. Each man in his own hiding place at the base of the bamboo plants, each drawing comfort from the closeness of his comrades. They waited for dark and hoped that the Americans were as incompetent and weak as they had so far appeared to be. The

VC had no intention of doing battle that night. They only wanted to escape.

Night fell early. It was close to the end of the monsoon season and, by 2100 hours, it was pouring rain and pitch black. Everyone was soaked. About half of the men sat with their ponchos covering as much of their bodies as they could, especially their weapons. The others were lying down, most on their backs with their weapons on their stomachs. Weapons protected first. They all knew that they would be soaked the whole night through, and there wouldn't be any drying out until the morning came. It would be long hours of wet clothes and clammy skin.

Everyone was nervous. The rain was not only uncomfortable but also dangerous. It was especially dark, with the clouds blocking the moon's light and, to make matters worse, the noisy rain made hearing anything else difficult. Not only were their sight and hearing gone, but the rain's moisture wiped out their sense of smell too, leaving them with only the touch as a means of enemy detection. And touch would be too late. Touch, they feared, could be the feel of a VC knife buried deep in their throats.

The young VC leader decided to break his four-man team up into two teams in an attempt to increase their odds of someone escaping. Through a series of gestures and sign language, he explained where each team would attempt to crawl out through the American perimeter. He would touch them in the night to signal when it was time to go. Until then, they would stay clustered together in the small clearing.

What is a curse for the Americans is a stroke of luck for us. The rain and darkness combined are our only hope of getting out undetected. Getting out alive. With any luck, we can all crawl out of here and return to camp safely before sunup. Timing will be everything. We need to wait until they settle down, become less fearful and uncomfortable. Yes, at their maximum numbness we need to move quietly out between their positions. It would be great if they would fall asleep, but that is too much to ask for. Cannot wait too long, though. It is a gamble—the moon could pop through the clouds at any moment and then we are stuck. Or, worse yet, it could show itself when we are exposed. Quit thinking.

Two hours later, he decided that the time was right. He was mostly sure, though part of him wanted to wait until later, wanted to wait until a better time. But he knew they could wait no longer. The time had to be now. They had been wet for hours and, without any covering, they were cold. Their bodies had already become sluggish and painful. *Besides, they were very late getting back to camp. It is very important to your superiors that you be on time. And there is always the danger that it might quit raining and the moon might come out. Then it would be too late. Maybe we could just stay here until morning, and they will take off and never discover us. Don't be any more of a fool than you already are. It is unbelievable that they have not found you before now. Quit procrastinating. Give the signal. Get your men out of here, now.*

He held back the critical voice in his head for just a moment to play, again, a favorite fantasy. A fantasy quickly adjusted to the current conditions in which he would get his men through this and be a hero. Become known as a great recon leader. Be the man who was invisible to the stupid, big Americans. He would, of course, do more great deeds and become a national hero. He would then have a high position in government practically forced on him. This would allow him his pick of the fine young women available. All would want to be his wife. Of course, with the position would come a good place to live, good food, clothes, and other privileges.

Yes, based upon my fine work this day, my commander will plan a large and successful ambush of these big old dummies.

Stop that, you idiot. No true hero allows such child-like dreaming. Give the damn signal. It was 2105 hours, and he lightly touched the men on each side of him.

8

SALLY TOOLEY?

Dear Greg,

It's after seven here, the day is done, and I'm doing my favorite thing—writing to you. I've got our picture in front of me, you know, the one taken at our graduation. It is my mood enhancer and always makes me feel warm inside. Even if I've had a bad day, this picture of us brings me up.

Mom and Dad are fine; I think Dad is getting kind of tired of working at the mill. Can't blame him, he's been going there for twenty-seven years. He keeps saying, "Three more years of hell and then I'm all about fishing." Hope he makes it. He sure deserves to. Mom doesn't say much. You know Mom, she just shrugs and sometimes pats him on the shoulder.

I saw your mom yesterday at the store. She says your dad and brothers are all doing fine. She's worried about you, though. Of course, aren't we all? And she says she hasn't heard from you in quite a while. I told her I hadn't gotten a letter in a couple of weeks either, and that sometimes the mail is slow. I also said, "No news is good news." I don't mean that, though. I know you try and write as often as you can and that you live under primitive conditions and all, but I so love to hear from you. Your mom and I have agreed to share any and all information that we might get from you. Well, not everything.

I understand why we had to put the wedding off until you return from Vietnam, but I still would have liked to hear my third-grade students call me Mrs. Tooley. Speaking of which, my teaching is going well and I love the children. Cannot wait until we have our own.

They will be pretty children, too, with my natural beauty, ha ha, and your manly handsomeness. I am very proud of you and have been for longer than we have dated. It's a good thing I got us together. If I hadn't made the move we would have just missed each other for the rest of our lives. Well, honestly, Mom put me up to it. I guess I was as scared to ask you out, as you were to ask me. Seems silly now. We had known and liked each other all of our lives, but just hadn't dated. Once we did it was the most natural and warm thing this world has to offer.

I do love you, Greg, and miss you so. I believe, though, that you will come back to me and we can have a fine life. I never cease to be grateful for the good things in life that God has given me—Mom, Dad, school, health, and, most of all, you. Write when you can, but make that soon.

Love you always,
Sally

9

BLOOD TRAIL

It was not a pretty sight, those three Vietnamese bodies. From time to time during the long night, one or more of the men would think that he saw movement from one of the dead VC and fired. When this occurred, as if a mutual trigger connected all four of the positions with dead VC in front of them, the other three positions would open fire, too. Even Carson and Leary got caught up in the fear-firing frenzy.

It was a full thirty minutes after sunup before anyone moved. They just sat there and looked, some smoking and many cursing everything from life in general to the Vietnamese in particular.

"That was some night, huh, Folger?" Leary broke the silence.

"Yeah, some night. One of those little shits is missing. Wonder where the fourth little bastard got off to."

"Don't know. Must have crawled off right away. I can't believe it, but you must have missed him."

"Nah, Sarge, I didn't miss the little shit. He just didn't get it as bad as the other one. I had a little trouble with balancing and getting out of my poncho. You can see a trail through the grass for a ways. And there's blood in the grass. He was hit, all right. We should run him down now and finish him."

"No. We've got orders to sit where we are until the battalion sorts itself out."

"Yeah, I heard. I just can't figure out what they have to sort out. Seems cut and dried to me. We ought to get on that little rodent before he gets back to his hole."

"By the looks of the blood, the darkness and clots, he's not going to go far. Not today, not ever again. I bet he's lying out there dead now." Leary squinted his eyes, trying to see farther. "Somewhere out there, dead in the grass. As for sorting things out, there was a lot of firing last night all around the perimeter, and the colonel is trying to see how much of it did anything. You know, who else has bodies."

Folger said nothing, but just continued to stare ahead, over the VC body and out across the meadow. "Jesus, you and Branden sure made a mess out of 'em. I wonder what those little gooks were doing crawling out from behind us. Maybe they crawled in and planted booby-traps in the middle of our perimeter?" Leary wondered.

"Nah, Sarge, I figure they had to already be there when we came into this area. Probably trapped them when we came busting out of the jungle yesterday afternoon. You know, the battalion on one side and us on the other. Could be more in the bamboo. I doubt they're booby-trapped. They look to be traveling pretty light. Look at them. They just have a little extra ammo, no canteen, and no food. Their hole is close by, that's for sure."

"Probably a reconnaissance patrol. Might have been watching us all day. Could've left most of their equipment in the bamboo. I don't think so, though. You see that squad from the Third Platoon checking the bamboo earlier this morning?"

"Yeah, I saw 'em. Just don't trust them."

"Why is that? They're C Company men."

"Well, Sergeant Leary, any army that would let a man like Hart come over to a place like this will put anyone in uniform and call him a soldier. There could be another Hart, or maybe lots of Harts, everywhere in this army. The army can't be trusted, and the Harts of the world can't be trusted. Since I don't know how many Harts there are in the Third Platoon, I don't trust any of 'em."

Leary was silent as Folger looked at him and asked, "Tell me I'm wrong, Sergeant Leary."

He waited about fifteen seconds, then looked Folger in the eye and said reflectively, "Wish I could. Can't." Then Leary laughed, an almost hysterical laugh that originated deep in his belly. Folger grinned a few times but didn't give in to Leary's humor. When Leary finally managed to calm himself, he blurted out, "And Sergeant Carson thought I was mean. Folger, I can't hold a candle to you. Going to be a long war."

"Short for some. Flies already all over those gooks."

"True. We could get it any time."

"Well, personally, I don't care. Got nothing at home to go back to. I just want to kill as many of these gook bastards as I can before I go. That's all I ask out of life."

"Damn, Folger, that seems like a sad sort of thing. I'm here to kill as many of these Commies as I can, too, but to keep them from harming my family and friends back home. I'm willing to die over here, but only so they can live without the threat of Communism."

Folger's laugh was dry and empty. "You think that you can stop the threat of Communism by killing Vietnamese?"

"No, I'm not naive enough to think that Communism can be stopped here. Not unless it makes Russia and China know that we will fight. We take their threats to our loved ones seriously. I guess I'm sick of them threatening us and am willing to get the fighting started."

"For me there's nothing at home to fight for. But I'm tired of the Communists' bull, too. So being over here killing them is okay with me. I just don't care that much either way. I'm not naive either. It's rough over here, and it's going to get worse."

"Yeah, looks like we're stepping in it regularly. Believe we've been lucky so far. Well, most of us. This is their ground, though, and they have the home field advantage. Only reason we aren't dead or wounded yet has a lot to do with luck. It all boils down to right time, right place—that sort of thing. But not wanting to get back home again seems fatalistic to me."

"Wanting to get back home or not doesn't mean anything. I have no one I want to go back for. Here or there, it's all the same to me."

"How could there be no one back home? No father, mother, uncle, girlfriend, school friends, someone to care about? Surely you weren't raised in a monastery, were you?"

"Yeah, I had all that, but my life fell apart three years ago. You notice I never get any mail," Folger pointed out to Leary, who nodded. "Well, that's the way I want it. Screw those people. Anyway, it's a blessing over here. You want to go home too much, and you think about it too much, and it gets you killed. Only way you can hope to go home is to not want to."

"I see that." Leary nodded as he said, "I want to go home, but not if I have to listen to any more of that 'Commies are coming to get you' crap. Can't stand being threatened. Only way to handle a problem is to go after it and get rid of it. So, here I am getting rid of a lifelong problem. Who the hell are those people who make it their life's goal to destroy our country or our way of life? Killing these little bastards is the right thing to do, and I don't want to go home until I've done my part. If I come home in a box, so be it. But, I just can't imagine not having anyone back home that I love and want to see again. I've got good parents, a brother, a sister, and one hell of a girlfriend back in Montana. I love thinking about seeing them again, being back with them. They are the reason I'm over here. They are worth protecting, worth fighting for."

"We're doing this for different reasons, you for your loved ones and me. 'Cause I don't care. I agree with you on one thing, though, I'm tired of their stinking threats, too. Still, you and all the rest of them," he gestured with his hand to include the battalion, "would be better off without any thoughts of home. Thinking of any place but here is dangerous. It makes you want something you can't have, but more importantly, it will get you killed. Oh, we're all probably going to die over here anyway but, if our minds are here, our concentration is on the jungle and the fighting, then maybe we can take more of these little slant-eyed Commies with us before we go."

"Damn, Folger, you're a good man, the best. I wouldn't wish to have anyone else with me in this thing, but your way of looking at life is depressing."

"No, Sergeant Leary, I'm real. I'll tell you what is real and you tell me where it isn't. Stop me at any time and tell me when I'm not describing the reality of our situation." Leary didn't respond. "First, this army, our government, the powers that sent us over here, they don't give one shit about us."

"Why do you say that? I mean, what are you talking about? We're soldiers sent to fight a war. Sent to stop the spread of Communism. We're making a stand here in Vietnam, so we won't have to stop them on our home ground."

"Well, Sergeant, that is the first big lie. If they want to stop this war, they need to go attack the north. That's where the source of their problem is. Without the source of their supply and leadership, the Vietcong wouldn't be any threat. There wouldn't be any fight."

"Well, sometimes it does seem like we do things backwards," Leary agreed, "like coming clear over here to War Zone C to find the enemy, when we all know there's a big nest of them not seven miles from our base camp."

"Right, exactly. Look at the stupidity. Is it blind ignorance or maybe the lack of interest in really winning this thing? Hell, they pulled that boat trick on us just for the pictures. They don't even care if we're clean. We don't have showers or even soap. I'll bet there isn't one enlisted man who has any soap."

"Well, we haven't been over here long enough to build showers, and soap has always been sold at the PX, which we don't have."

"I've been out of toothpaste for two weeks. When I do brush it's with water."

"Yeah, Folger, it's strange here. At least, it's not how I thought it would be. Not that that means anything, really, but I'm still trying to figure it out. It's like a real measurable plan is not in place. I mean, the way we're doing it, how will we know when we're done? How will we know when we've won?"

"I don't know what winning will look like either. Maybe you're right, and we're only over here to hunt down and kill Communists."

"Sure," Leary nodded, "how'll we know when we've killed enough? Will they surrender and promise to quit threatening us?"

"Hell no, they don't have to do anything. If they want to quit, they just have to go back to their rice paddies or back north. We don't even know who they are when they're not trying to kill us. So we'll never know and can never know when we've won. There is no winning for us, only staying alive, and if a man doesn't forget about home he can't live. This place won't allow it."

Leary looked at Folger, puzzled.

"The jungle we fight in is worse than a jealous woman," Folger explained. "If you don't have your mind on it all the time, every second, it'll kill you. Simple, don't be here—be dead."

"You're right, Folger, never thought of it that way."

It was 0930 hours when Company Commander Haps, Platoon Leader Tooley, and the colonel came to the death scene. Just before first light, Tooley and Carson had crawled from position to position questioning and checking each man. They then crawled back to their CP and reported by radio to the colonel back at Lia Kae that they did have enemy dead but none of their men had been hit. The colonel wanted them to call in artillery illumination but Tooley asked that it not be deployed. He was afraid that there might be more VC within their perimeter, and the light might make targets out of his men.

Tooley had instructed everyone to stay put and hold his position. "If you have to urinate," he told them, "roll away from your position a couple of times and go in the grass."

Though other positions and companies around the perimeter had reported possible enemy sightings and killings when daylight came, none were able to produce any bodies. Only Charlie Company, Second Platoon, had bodies.

At dawn, Tooley checked the bodies as well as the bamboo fence and then reported to Haps. The captain wanted to go see for himself before he reported to the colonel. After a brief look at the dead VC, the two of them reported to the colonel, who had flown in at first light. Then the three of them went to the killing grounds.

Tooley was feeling a little guilty and a lot angry for the chewing-out the colonel had given him. The captain had stood there and nodded his head, as though he completely agreed, as the colonel pointed out Tooley's lack of military competence.

"You neglected to check out the bamboo bushes to your platoon's rear. That is basic military reconnaissance. What in the hell kind of a platoon leader are you? It is unbelievable and, if I had a replacement for you, I would relieve you of your command." *Screw both of you Regular Army sonsofbitches*, he thought, as the colonel continued his tirade. *These officers consider themselves above me. They are Regular Army officers, graduates of West Point, and I'm a United States officer, a product of college ROTC. In their minds, I can never be as good as they are. I should have seen that the bushes to our rear were thoroughly checked, but at first sight the bamboo looked so impenetrable that a snake would've had a tough time getting into it. Second, I damn sure wasn't the only platoon leader, officer, or man in charge who had an opportunity to check the bamboo fence—including this stupid-ass captain standing here nodding his head. He was here in this clearing at least an hour before we got here. He should've had the area secure. Screw both of you. You, Colonel, are nothing but a West Point mouth with his bootlicking captain shaking his hypocritical head in agreement. My stupid-ass cowardly captain who, until you, Colonel, started in on me, hadn't even mentioned that I should have checked out the bamboo. Hadn't so much as hinted that the bamboo was my sole responsibility.* But he didn't say anything. He just clenched his teeth. *Haps has the nerve to insinuate by his actions that the colonel's ass-chewing is the second one I received this morning. He acts as if he's already chewed me out. Rank-grabbing ass-kisser*, he told himself, feeling better, even if it was only said in his mind.

Tooley was right on the edge of going insane with rage when the colonel finished chewing him out. A red face, a few head shakes, and some "you worthless shit" looks displayed themselves in Tooley's body language but were not acknowledged by the colonel. *Not once,* he assured himself, *did either of these two big shots mention what a good job my men did. The only thing these two pompous asses are interested in is their damn careers. How will it look on paper, that's all they care about. And that "first kill" thing. Yeah, the badge goes to the one who gets the "first kill" on this operation. That's what they're selling. It's like some kind of hunting party. Trophy hunting. Well, since it is so damn important to them and since my platoon got it, where is our goddamn trophy?*

Looking straight into the colonel's eyes, calmness now coming over him, Tooley made up his mind about a few things. *From now on, they can kiss my ass. It's their army. I'm only here to do my duty, for God and country and, when my time is done, I'll gladly go back to civilian life. Get away from pricks like these. Yes, I can get away, but these assholes will have to stay together for the rest of their lives; they can't fit anywhere else.* He laughed to himself. *It serves them right—they do belong together.*

Now the colonel was talking with Carson at Folger's and Leary's position. Tooley stood to the right and to the rear with the captain in a secondary position, where he could monitor what was going on but not be a part of it. He was only half listening anyway. He had gone through the interview twice already, once for himself and the second time with the captain, so now he just listened to see if his *brilliant colonel* could find out some new earth-shattering details. Get something from his men that he had failed to do. He was slightly relieved that the story was the same one he had heard and told. Finally, the colonel asked Carson to show him where he thought the enemy was hiding. Carson gave the colonel a professional, "Yes, sir," and they both headed to the bamboo bushes, leaving Leary, Folger, and Tooley with the captain.

"Sergeant Leary," the captain said, "have your men drag those bodies," he gestured with his left hand, "across the creek and to the battalion HQ where they can be viewed by the rest of the battalion." The captain, seeing by Leary's face that his order wasn't being received well, rushed to add, "Congratulations, Sergeant, you and your men got the 'first kill.' "

There it is, Tooley thought. *Gonna be a backfire.* The captain must have felt he should clearly mark his territory, Tooley would later muse to himself. But instead of claiming territory, he would lose face. Even though what happened next was potentially tragic for Leary and the platoon, it gave Tooley great satisfaction to hear it.

Leary raised his eyebrows questioningly towards Haps.

"Sir, these bodies were men yesterday," Leary almost whispered to the captain. "I helped kill them. I will bury 'em but I won't drag them over to the battalion area. Not for some kind of sadistic viewing."

The captain's face turned bright purple-red. He wanted to interrupt, but Leary held up a hand to stop him and continued. The captain's mouth hung open as Leary went on, his voice filled with sarcasm, "What is this 'first kill' thing, sir? Is this a hunting party we're on? Are we going to stuff and mount our enemy?" Leary paused, then added, "Will there be awards for winning, sir?"

Tooley turned his head, trying to suppress the smile on his face. *Going to be hell to pay for this,* he told himself, *but it's worth it.*

The captain, trying to change the direction of the conversation, only made it worse by saying, "Sergeant, I didn't say you—you don't have to do it. I said for you to have your men do it."

"Sir, I don't ask my men to do anything that I am not willing to do myself."

Wow! Tooley thought. *The fur is going to fly now. Leary has just explained a code of leadership to the captain. For our West Point captain, that's a major slap in the face. Things are going downhill fast. I should jump on Leary for his insubordination, but I just can't bring myself to do it. The shit's headed for the fan, probably for both of us. Leary, for sure.*

It was quiet as the captain gathered his attitude and analyzed his options. Leary continued to glare at the captain. Tooley didn't move, and Folger seemed unaffected, even uninterested. It was a long, full minute before the captain responded. When he finally spoke, he was back in control, calm, with lightness in his voice.

"Sergeant Leary, I have requested that you do something. You have refused my request. Now I make it an order. Have your men drag those VC to the battalion command post area. Do you understand, Sergeant?"

"Yes, sir, I do understand. You don't understand, sir. I will bury them, but I will not, nor will I have any of my men, drag these dead men anywhere." Then, with determination, he added, "Not anywhere for display purposes, sir."

At first, the captain's brain refused to comprehend what Leary had said. With comprehension came anger. *How dare this young, punk sergeant disobey a direct order? By God, I am his commanding officer. It cannot be allowed to happen.* He had never considered that anyone under his command would dare disobey him. *But I'll try one more time. He's young and a civilian in military clothes.*

"Sergeant," he said, pausing for effect, "perhaps you are not aware of what could happen to you if you do not obey my orders. I am your company commander, and to disobey a direct order will surely get you busted to private at best, and maybe even a jail sentence."

Leary said nothing for a long, uncomfortable period of time. Finally, not being able to stand it any longer, the captain broke the silence. "Well, Sergeant, let's hear from you. What is your choice?"

Leary was as still as he could be without being rigid, and his flat voice held no compromise as he said. "Captain, go ahead and bust me. It makes no difference to me. I can be a private. I don't need to be a sergeant. The food is the same. The accommodations are the same." Though he paused for a moment, it was clear that he was not through. It was also clear that these threats were nothing to him.

"As for the jail thing, sir, does Leavenworth have showers, bunks, hot food?"

The captain didn't know what to do. His mind was blank. And then, suddenly the way out became clear. The thought brought him relief and made him almost happy enough to smile. He knew what kind of order Leary would not refuse, and he gave it.

"You're right, Sergeant, the dragging of bodies is not what you and your men should be used for. You have killed these men, and you and your men should be exempt from having to do anything with their bodies. I do have a job for you and your men, though. A job that you've proven to be good at." He became quiet to let what he said sink in. "I want you and your men to check out every clump of bamboo in this clearing."

They all followed his pointing finger to three large clumps of bamboo plants to their left, front, and right. The nearest clumps were about two hundred meters across the open grassy clearing.

The captain continued, "Since there were VC in these bushes, in the middle of our perimeter, then there could very well be more hidden in those clumps to our front. Of course, I realize that to approach those islands of bamboo, you and your men will be completely exposed," he said, allowing amusement to creep into his voice. *God, I got him now, and it makes me very happy, the self-righteous little punk.*

"There is no cover for you or your men between here and the objectives. It could be dangerous. We certainly cannot adequately cover you from this distance. Even if we could cover you, we wouldn't dare. No, since you and your men will be between us and the target, we dare not fire. However, I think that those bushes must be checked out. We cannot have any more stupidity like what happened last night, now can we, Sergeant? Make sure, Sergeant," he grinned, "that you thoroughly check them out, just you and your fire team. All three of those bushes." He flippantly pointed. "That is all, Sergeant, right away."

Turning to Tooley, he said, "Lieutenant Tooley, be sure and report the fire team's findings to me upon their return."

With that, he joined the colonel and his radio operator as they came by on their way back to the battalion headquarters. The captain was feeling proud of himself as he thought, *a dead soldier is no disgrace to his leader. In fact, his death may even bring credit to his commander. A soldier who refuses to obey a commander's orders would cause a court-martial, an investigation, etc., which could damage a leader's career, especially if the orders are a little tacky. A dead soldier, though, that's different. No inquiry. The end. And the chances of there being VC in those bushes are good. The VC cannot escape without being seen either. They must fire, too. They'll be forced to shoot at Leary. So long, you asshole.*

No one commented after the captain left. It seemed wrong and everyone knew what the captain was trying to do. They also knew nothing could be done about it. If Leary disobeyed this type of order, then the captain would be supported in making an example out of him. Furthermore, everyone knew Leary would go.

As they moved out towards the first bamboo bushes, Hart wished he could be assigned to another fire team. He would have preferred to drag out the dead than walk into death. *Leary is going to get us killed,* he thought, as his fire team spread out on line, walking point-blank toward the first clump of bamboo.

10

JUST WAR?

About two hundred meters from the first clump of bamboo, Leary told Sanchez to fire three grenades from his M-79 grenade launcher into the cluster of bamboo. Sanchez accurately placed the three grenades into the bamboo, making it improbable for anyone hiding in the bamboo to survive unscathed. Leary, Folger, Sanchez, and Hart then checked the clump of bamboo, finding no humans alive, dead, or wounded. They repeated this procedure in the remaining two bamboo clumps that the captain had ordered them to check out. Though Leary and his men found two dead rabbits and one dead snake, they found no human bodies or any other signs that the bamboo had been occupied by their enemy.

The platoon, including Tooley and Cambel, smiled with relief at Leary's solution. The captain was furious. He did not laugh and secretly vowed to try again at the next opportunity. *Time is on my side, and there'll be more opportunities in the future to get rid of that smart-ass punk. Leary, you've just earned every dangerous job at my disposal. Sooner or later, the last laugh will be mine.*

It was camping time on their second day in War Zone C, and the men gathered in small groups near their assigned positions in the perimeter. It had been a long, hot, and humid day. There was no more live enemy contact for the platoon that day, and they saw no booby-traps or other offensive signs. They had managed to stay parallel with the battalion, but they could care less about doing so. Their sore, slow movements were the only signs of their extreme fatigue. Their clothing was more sweat stained than the day before, and they were now numb to their strong body odor. No one complained. Being tired and sore was becoming normal. Normal wasn't worth complaining about.

Even the young were beginning to take on the slow, achy movements of old men. Few of them, especially the enlisted men, had slept a full night since their arrival in Vietnam more than thirty days ago. What little sleep they did get on the hard, uncomfortable ground was interrupted by guard time and nervous fears, often causing bad dreams that would haunt the survivors for the rest of their lives.

Leary, Patkins, and Carson sat in the grass around the small fire that was becoming an evening tradition. Carson heated three C-ration cans of water. It was the same ritual they had engaged in the previous night. Folger, who had politely refused hot water, lay down a short distance away, as usual.

"Wonder what it felt like to bleed to death like that gook we found this morning," Carson winced at his own use of the word *gook*. *Where did that come from,* he asked himself. *If my father heard his son use that kind of language to describe a human being, he would be very angry.* It was definitely out of character for preacher's son Carson to use ethnic slang in describing any human. Carson felt a little out of sorts, and he saw that Leary and Patkins had also noticed his breach of character. He was disturbed and felt a bit of shame. It was not that he just didn't use those kinds of words out loud. No, more than that, up to this point in his life he hadn't even allowed himself to think words like "nigger," "spic," "wop," or "mick," yet now he referred to a dead enemy soldier as a "gook." *Damn, Carson, forget your father. You have always been a well-controlled man. Right is right, no matter who says it. You are a professional soldier. You have breached your own code of conduct.*

Seeing that Carson was nonplussed and wanting to get past it, Patkins said, "I heard you just get weak, then go to sleep, but that's just what I've heard. No one's really come back from the dead to let us know." He sort of smiled at his last remark. For him, it was a rare attempt at humor. But the other two men's sober looks wiped the smile off his face, and he added, "I wonder if he was part of that patrol that got caught inside our perimeter last night? I still think we should have buried him or something. Not just left him there. He didn't have a weapon either."

"His own people no doubt came and got him," Carson said. "Better for him to be taken back and buried with his own. Sure, he was part of the bamboo boys and, as for his weapon, he probably ditched it in the jungle when he knew he wasn't gonna make it. Probably got to be too much to carry, especially after he became weak."

Leary rubbed at an imaginary spot of dirt on his rifle with his right hand. He sat facing the fire with his rifle between his knees, barrel pointing toward the sky, and holding a canteen cup of hot chocolate in his left hand. He took a sip of chocolate and then, slowly, unhurriedly, looked up and in a quiet but clear voice and said, "Yeah, I am sure of it. When the captain sent me bush-checking this morning, we spotted the blood trail coming out of our perimeter and heading north towards the trail we took today-the trail we found him on later this morning. He was tough, I'll give him that. He was shot up pretty bad, his stomach ripped open. Poor bastard was trying to hold his guts in with his hands. Even dead, his hands were still there, frozen, trying to keep his insides from spilling out. Then the leg wound, and the shoulder wound, no obvious bones broken but, still, it's surprising that he made it as far as he did."

Carson sipped, then spoke while looking into his can as if he were reading something in the coffee. "I wonder how close he was to his base camp? Maybe even his home?"

"Don't believe we'll ever know that," Leary said. "This jungle is so thick most of the time that we could have walked by a whole nation of 'em and not known it. The only things we're going to find and destroy out here are things we happen to stumble into. That, or things they leave out for us. Shit, these VC not only have the home advantage, but they have a lot of it, too."

"Yeah," Patkins said as he blew on his hot coffee. "These people are great diggers. Finding them, much less digging them out, is a major chore."

Carson, professional leader that he was, feared letting his players give the opposing team too much credit, so he said, "Well, it may be true they have some advantages, but they aren't perfect. Not perfect by any means. They've been screwing up regularly, and if you'll count, you'll see we've taken out quite a few of them in the last couple of days. And we're just ten men. They're probably hundreds more just like us out in this jungle, too. Men out there hunting and killing them. It looks to me like they're in trouble. The American army is making sure that a lot of them never get home again. Wherever their homes are."

"I hope it continues to be like that," Patkins said. The other two men nodded their agreement. They were all silent for a couple of minutes. They could hear the other men talking, punctuated by occasional shouts and the sipping of their drinks. Folger just smoked, lying with his head on his pack. The men who smoked did a lot of it in the morning and in the evening before dark because there was no smoking while hunting.

Fighting a wave of depression, Leary said, "Speaking of home, I wonder where those guys lived. They could be from a rice paddy or village around here. Maybe even from the north, except they were wearing the black pajamas of the Vietcong."

"I don't care," Carson said. "To hell with all of 'em. I'm starting not to care about anything." Then, afraid that his words might bring their morale down, he said with a hint of remorse, "I'm sorry, must be tired. It's my job to hold up our attitudes—not bring them down. Won't happen again."

"No sweat," Patkins said, surprisingly pleased at what he perceived to be a potential weakness in someone else, no matter how small. Up until now, he felt that he was the only one who showed weakness, except for Hart, but then, no one expected anything out of Hart. Among men, Hart no longer counted.

"Well," Leary said, almost to himself, his eyes looking at nothing but the grass between his boots, "we can call what we're doing over here anything we want to, but it'll always be just what it is. And we'll always know what that is."

Both Carson and Patkins grunted, "What?" simultaneously. And even Folger turned a puzzled face towards him. Leary slowly raised his head to look each of them in the eye, first Carson, then Patkins, and finally over to Folger. "It's more of what we kind of covered yesterday. It's bugging me. We call what we're doing over here protecting the freedom of South Vietnam. We say it is keeping the Communists from taking over here and then going on to the Philippines. Then, according to the theory, going from the Philippines to Hawaii, and so on right into the continental U.S. It's called the 'domino effect,' or 'domino theory,' whatever. Really, I've been told all my life that the Communists are after all of the free world. Christ, we had a kid in the neighborhood who continually pointed out that the Communists were after us. And then, as things would have it, turns out that little shit was exempt from the draft, was physically unfit for military service. Damn, I still can't believe after all of his yakking, he didn't have to go in the damn army. Oh well.

"So anyway, all my young-ass life I've believed I'd have to go somewhere, hopefully not in my own home state, but go somewhere and fight the Communists. I don't know about you guys, but for me it was everywhere. The TV, the goddamn school, everywhere, stupid atomic bomb drills. Making bomb shelters in the basements, the whole screwy works." Remembering ignited Leary's anger, and his body tensed. "So here I am, you Communist bastards. I'm here to kill your ass before you kill mine." Then he relaxed again and continued quietly, easily. "So we can call what we're doing over here whatever we like. Protecting freedom, stopping Communism, protecting our home, our God-assigned duty, etc."

"Sure, that's true," Patkins said. "That isn't just what we're calling it. That's what it is! What the hell are you trying to say? I must have missed something because I don't understand."

Carson nodded, "Me, either." Folger just returned to gazing at the few clouds in the powder-blue sky.

"I know I'm not explaining it very well. Shit, it's not totally clear to me either. It's there, the explanation, below the surface in my mind, but it's not clear. I mean, there's something wrong with what's going on over here. Hell, I'm young and maybe all wars are this way. Maybe all soldiers feel this way in a war, but something is bad-wrong over here." Leary raised his right hand, a palm-up gesture, indicating frustration and a plea for patience before speaking again. "I mean, what can we win here? We take ground. We kill for it and then just leave it. There are certain areas here in South Vietnam that we know belong to the enemy. These enemy areas are behind us and around us. Goddamn it, we all know that they're enemy strongholds. Shit, we know exactly where the enemy is and yet we go looking for him where we guess he might be. Think about that, goddamn it! Christ almighty, we pass right over, or by, areas where we know for sure the gooks are. It's more than just frustrating. It's just wrong. Dead wrong. We're more like hunters than warriors. I mean, we come out for a period of time and hunt men. Then, after a time of hunting we go back to our hunting camp, called a base camp. At base camp, we rest up for a time and then go hunting again."

"Seems like we're damn poor hunters, too. By Montana standards, we sure can't hunt. You know, we're here now, looking for the enemy in this big-ass War Zone C. We're here only because we suspect that they might be here. Maybe we even know that they are here, somewhere in this huge area. But someone, anyone, explain to me why the fuck we flew right over an area where we, and everyone else, knows for damn sure they're at. Flew right over a smaller, known enemy area more concentrated than this huge-ass place. Shit, this war zone is just a hunk of the Ho Chi Minh Trail, which goes all the way to North Vietnam. Of course we won't go there. Hell, no. That would make too much sense. Maybe even give this stupid shit a purpose. Screw the dumb bastards, including the colonel and his shit-for-brains captain. It's true and you all know it."

The other three men were silent. It was obvious to them that Leary wasn't through. They were silent and still as they waited for his tirade to continue. When it did, his face reddened and his voice cracked from anger. "Christ, the damned Iron Triangle is only about seven or eight miles from our base camp. It isn't a guess, either. It's a known and admitted large enemy base. It's their damn home and we fly right over it to come way the hell out here." His right fist gripped his rifle hard, his knuckles white from the strain. "Tell me something doesn't stink here. I say it's rotten to the core. Something is wrong with the people giving the orders." He paused for a deep breath. His face was beet-red. Leary gulped air and released it slowly. "So, what we say we're doing is going after the Communists. Going after them and destroying them. What we're really doing is not going where we know they are, but looking for them where someone said that they might be. I just can't get over not destroying the Iron Triangle first—completely. Then when it's eliminated, I mean the damn thing is right in our back yard, then come into this War Zone C bullshit.

"Even forget all that if you want, but even here we pass areas we should thoroughly check out. It's like not covering your rear or something. It smells and it's wrong. Damn wrong. Where I come from, they would laugh at our hunting abilities. When they hunt, they know enough to look in the area where the game is known to be before going to an area where they think they might be. Furthermore, I just don't think hunting men is right. What will hunting and killing men do to us? What does it make us? This isn't a damn war; it's a hunting party, and man should not hunt his own kind. Even animals don't do that. I mean wolves might fight over territory, that's war, but they don't hunt each other just to kill each other. One thing for certain, this isn't a war. There is winning in a war and there's no winning here." He stopped to take another deep breath, hissing it out again. Suddenly spent and feeling a little foolish at losing control, Leary attempted to lighten things up by saying, "Hell, maybe I'm wrong, maybe this is just the starting phase and it will all become clear later. What do I know? Maybe this is a good and righteous thing to do."

Whatever efforts Leary had made to improve the atmosphere things up were soon dashed, as Folger decided to speak, while still staring straight up. "Everything is what it is. This place, us here, is no different than what's happening everywhere else in the world. The world is nothing but the doing of things and then the leaving of it. The doing and the dying, that's all this world is and has ever been. No one gets out of this world alive. No one. At least, we get to face that reality and kill a few people before we go."

"May God help you, Folger," Carson said.

"Thanks, Sarge. He will and I'm going to help Him, too, as long as I can. I'm going to send as many of these little 'gook' bastards to Him as I can, for as long as I last."

That ended the conversation. In silence the three sergeants went off to see their men and set them up for the night. Each man was alone with his own thoughts. Each felt empty inside.

That night was uneventful from an attack standpoint, and the men, though dirty and tired, felt noticeably better with the dawn. Better than yesterday. There was a subtle "good mood" evident that morning. A mood owing, partly at least, to the fact that their whole second night in the jungle had passed without a shot being fired. Also, it was the beginning of the third day. The day that their food was almost gone, making the load on their backs at its lightest, and tonight would be resupply night—mail and new rations—and they would have to quit early.

Yes, Carson thought, *the good mood prevails because of these things. It's a welcome change from the obvious depression last night. Thank God. It will be a short day for us and we need it. The colonel will be looking for a place to camp early this afternoon. He has to find a clearing large enough for the whole battalion and choppers. Not like this cramped place. It'll have to be a place that has clear visibility all around. Clear enough so that we can see the enemy coming in time to defend the choppers as well as ourselves. Yes, and mail, our one lifeline to the world, a faraway world that once held warmth for most of us. A place that we all came from and hope to go back to. A place called home, a place called America. God bless America, God bless home.* He hollered, "Saddle up, get ready to move out in ten minutes. Ten minutes men, get your minds right, get your thoughts where they need to be."

Ten minutes later, they were on the trail again. Slowly, carefully, they moved out, nervousness diminishing with each step. Routine and purpose brought a sense of security. It was a false security, though. For some, this would be the first day of the worst days of their lives, and, for others, it would be the last day of their lives.

11

MARY

Her father died on a Friday night, days after coming home from Fort Harrison VA Hospital in Helena, Montana. Though she couldn't remember him ever being in good health, she was aware that he had become progressively weaker and frailer with each passing year. By the time of his death, he weighed only ninety-eight pounds. *Then, mother and I could easily lift him from his wheelchair to the bed, couch, and toilet. Poor Dad, he was so embarrassed at his helplessness. What a man he was, though. What a spirit he had*, she reminded herself, in a futile effort to hold off the sorrow.

He never seemed to give his illness any credit as a force in his life, except that one time shortly before he died. *Yes*, she remembered, *he did acknowledge it then. Not from any self-sorrow or pity, but from a need to explain it to her. When he did speak of it, it was from somewhere deep inside him. Yes, even his voice sounded different, distant, as if it were coming from another person. A person I never heard before.* They were sitting together on the front porch. It was a perfect spring evening, with a fresh smell in the air from the flowers edging the front walk.

"Mary, this illness I've got, it's just a 'thing,' " she remembered her dad saying. "Everybody has some 'thing,' that's what this life is about. It's not what you've got that's so important, but what you do with it. That's what counts, Mary. Some people might look at me, know my condition, and say, 'Poor man, what a shame,' but I don't feel that way. Not now. When I think about this condition I've got, I figure it's not me. Not the real me. The real me can't be touched by it. It's kind of like the sickness is something separate from the real me. Different from who I am and, as long as I keep that in the forefront of my mind, then it can't really get to me. In truth, strange as this may sound, that disease sitting out there always waiting to try and destroy my body, well, it's a blessing. I know how it sounds. I can see by the look on your face that this is hard to understand. Don't get me wrong. One part of me wouldn't wish this affliction on anyone, certainly not myself, but another part of me knows the affliction is necessary, even if it's killing me. See, Mary, this strange disease, sitting out there, fighting with the doctors and medicine for my life and winning, too, well, it keeps me in my place. It keeps me in a better place than I would be without it. Yes, I'm afraid it's true, that sick I'm a better, more loving person than I would be if I were healthy and strong.

"This disease takes more and more of my energy every day just to stay alive, just to fight it off. But in this struggle to keep it from killing me, I seem better able to remember who I really want to be. Everyone has more than one side to him, and certainly I am no different. I won't horrify you with the details, but the years I spent in the jungle forced me to develop my bad side. I couldn't have survived without it. I became one with the jungle. I killed to survive and became very good at it. There, in that Burmese jungle war, there was no room in one's mind for love. Love and concern for home quickly became an unrealistic fantasy. And in that world, fantasy would get you killed. Reality in that time and place was to kill first and often. It wasn't that I didn't want to feel love, hope, and other better emotions—it was just that after a short while over there, I couldn't. Didn't know how anymore. Killing became my reason for living and, after the war was over and I was sent back to your mother and my family, I didn't know how to act. I couldn't make the transition from jungle fighter to loving husband and father. I was feeling violent toward everyone and barely able to keep this hostility in check when the disease hit me. It weakened me and seemed to drain the violent energy out of my body. Oh, at first, I would still feel the rush of killing anger, but nothing would happen. And slowly, not being able to act out my violent urges, I started to lose them. As I lost my anger, love began to replace it. So always think of me as that father who loves you, Mary. That's who I really am and want to be. The disease is not me. It's just a 'thing.' Like a car is a 'thing.' It serves a purpose, but is still just outside of the real me. Do you understand, Mary?"

She had said yes and, to a degree, she did understand, at least the attitude of it, but she didn't really understand it, not entirely, not until just before he died. He was very weak then, and she needed to know more. Though she hated to face his impending death, she couldn't let him die without trying to fully understand. Part of her didn't want to ask him because she was afraid of the answer; still, she certainly couldn't go through the rest of her life wishing she had asked him. She needed clarification.

Her memory of that day was forever etched in her mind and she'd spent the major part of it working up her courage to finally talk once more about the disease. By three o'clock, a determined Mary came straight home from school, avoiding all distractions, and walked with purpose into their living room. There she found him sitting, slumped and drooling, in his favorite wicker chair. She took the rag kept on the small table by his chair and wiped his mouth. He woke with a start, and she could see from the look in his eyes that he had been somewhere else in his dreams. It was somewhere not good. *That brown wicker chair, with blue soiled cushions that Mom could never seem to get clean, was more of a basket, really. A form-fitted, chair basket with matching footstool, always placed right in front of the TV.*

With his eyes wide, fully awake, he said, "Mary?" It was more of a question than an acknowledgment.

"Yes, Dad, it's me." *Oh, I felt horrible at having awakened him. Waking up seemed to take so much energy from him. Energy he scarcely had.* She remembered she apologized for the intrusion, but as always, he managed a big smile for her, and slightly embarrassed, he took the rag from her hand while asking, "How are you, Mary?"

Then there had been a pleasant moment of silent love that passed between us before I asked, "Dad, remember what you told me a couple of months ago, about your illness being a 'thing' outside of yourself? That it wasn't really you, but in a strange way it helped you be what you want to be? That the unknown jungle disease you have is a good thing even though it's killing you?"

"Sure, Mary. I remember."

"Well, you said the disease was a good 'thing' because it helped you to remember that what you really are is a man who loves Mom and me totally and the rest of the people in the world, too, though not as much. Something like that, right?"

"Right, Mary. That 'thing' is good as well as bad. In my case, it's good because of the limits it places on my body. Although I don't think I would ever need it now that I can freely love again. But still I'm not sure. I mean, you know, if I had my strength again would I return to the person I had become then? I know I'll never know. It's too far along. I know in my heart that it will end my life in the near future." The tears increased as she remembered his exact words.

Those were words she hated to hear. "So Mary, don't feel bad and don't waste any time hating the disease that is killing me, or the conditions, or people that seemingly put me in a place where I got the disease. Just remember that this affliction has kept me focused on the truly good things in life. Love, Mary, love is all that is worth anything in this life. Only love. Nothing else matters."

"I guess I understand, Dad. The war had made you something you didn't want to be, and the illness forced you to be something else, something better."

"Right, Hon, it can kill me but it isn't me. It only takes away the bad so I can concentrate on the good."

"So this disease is good because it kept you loving. Right?"

"Right."

"And you said that everyone has some 'thing.' Right?"

"Right."

"Well, but Dad, I just can't see how a debilitating sickness like this could ever possibly be considered good. I mean, wouldn't you be better off without it?"

"Maybe, I don't know. I'm not sure I would want the cure if they happened to find it. I'm afraid of what I once was. I can never be that way now, weakened like I am. I'm just not sure what I might become again if I were to get well." He'd laughed weakly then and said, "Sort of like that story of the troll under the bridge, I got across the bridge and back, but the disease or troll will never let me cross again. Never."

"You've lost me again, Dad.'

"Sure, Mary," he said, hesitantly. But then, he nodded yes and she knew that he was about to explain more than he wanted to. And she intuited that he hoped she wouldn't think less of him after he told it. "Guess if you're old enough to ask, you're old enough to know. I joined the army when World War II broke out. Everyone did—it was our understood duty. Not to brag, but like most young bucks, I had inexhaustible strength and no real fears. I was the exact opposite of what I am now.

"The army recognized my talents and gave me special training. Then I was assigned to a special jungle unit. I don't want to get too graphic, but let's just say that I did my job very well. The jungle, the killing, the war, it gets to a man if he does too much of it, if he does it for too long. He changes into what he does. The more he kills, the more of a killer he becomes. He can't help it; he has to become what he does—to survive. I was good at it, and I became it. I became a Japanese killing machine. I guess a person likes what he's good at, and I was good at killing. When the war was over, I never told anyone this, not even your mother—although somehow I believe she knows. She could see it in me right away, I'm sure. Thinking back on it, maybe everyone could." He stopped and she was afraid he wouldn't continue. But he raised his head, looked gently at her, and spoke again.

"When it was over, I was sorry. I was sorry that I couldn't go on hunting them down and killing them. I didn't hate them for anything except quitting. I hated them for that. Like I mentioned earlier, to survive in an atmosphere like that you have to become that atmosphere, and I couldn't remember who I was before. Couldn't remember and didn't want to be anything else. Just wanted to stay in the jungle and fight the Japanese and, if not them, then anyone else I could wage war on. Crazy, huh? Well, I don't see how anyone could be there like that, day after day, month after month, and not become crazy. But we didn't think we were crazy. We just were what we were. I can see now that we were crazy, but I couldn't then.

"Of course, they sent me back. Gave me medals and all, thinking I would be relieved to be home, safe. But the ones who gave me the medals hadn't been where I'd been, hadn't done what I'd done, hadn't lived like I'd lived. How could they understand? Maybe I don't really understand it. Maybe no one ever understands it because it's crazy." He paused, looking at her kindly. He tried to read it, hoping that what he was seeing was still the girl who loved her daddy.

"I told several of the doctors earlier, when I first came home, how I felt, but they just said I'd get over it. They didn't really know either, can't blame them, how could they?"

Rushing now, wanting to finish. He was rapidly becoming weary and weak and hating the memory of it all. "So I came back here, still wanting to be what I'd become, not wanting to be here, but not knowing where else to go. Your poor mother, she's such a wonderful woman. She stuck by me. I was moody, would lose my temper over any small thing. Thank God, I never raised my hand towards your mother, but I was hell on any man who got in my way. Your mother hoped I would, in time, return to the man I was before the war. She was half right.

"I wasn't back long. Fortunately, I hadn't done anyone any real harm, before the disease started taking over. Its weakening effect forced me to forget my warrior ways. It would not allow me to consider finding another war to participate in. That side of me, the evil side, was dominant, and it wanted to go on warring. It still craved the feelings that war can produce in a person. But the disease made it impossible for me to act on my feelings. It kept me on the other side. It put waging war out of the question. The 'thing' forced me to find my loving self again and it forced me to stay there. Truthfully, if it hadn't been for the 'thing,' I hate to think where and what I might have ended up. So, the disease allowed me to redevelop the self I was before the war. Of course, the cost was the physical health I once enjoyed and misused."

The recollection of that conversation made her heart feel as if it had to struggle to pump its blood. As if it were wrapped in a covering of lead. She was fearful that it might stop and not start again. *The parallels are frightful, unbelievable. My love, my future, is now in a foreign jungle, fighting a foreign war, too. Furthermore, my dear Tim Leary is much like what I picture my father must have been back then. God, will he come back the same way, too? Will he need a "thing" or disease to keep him civilized? Will he need some "unknown" to force him back to the loving man he was when he left? What, God, could we Americans possibly owe those Vietnamese people? What kind of threat could they pose to us that we risk our loving men in such a way? Will I be doomed to live with the "unknown" like my mother was? Can I accept it if Tim comes back that way? Do I even* want *to? Could I even get out of it if I wanted to? How can I live with myself if I break up with him while he's over there? What kind of a person would I be then? God help me. If he comes back needing a disease to keep him sane, maybe it's better that he die over there.*

Totally upset by that last thought, she shrieked, "God no, don't let anything happen to him. Send him back no matter how he is. Please God. I didn't mean that."

Assured that her plea to God was heard, she made efforts to reassure herself. *How could her loving man ever be anything else? Was it even possible? He was so good, and they had a good life ahead of them. They deserved a good life. They were good people. Surely, no stupid war could ever change that. Men had been going to war, defending their countries, homes, and families, since the beginning of time, and this was just another stupid war. Yeah, just another stupid war that men went to and came home from. No big deal. Her father's war was different. Sure, I'll be a biologist in two short years. He'll come back okay, and we'll get married, have children, and enjoy our lives. We love each other too much for anything to happen to us. Heck, Tim may not even see combat. And even if he does, it doesn't mean that it will affect him like it did Dad. He doesn't have to like it. It's difficult to see how Dad could have grown to like it. Still, they're a lot alike.*

She knew that she needed to get control of herself. She was almost scaring herself to death. *Get your mind off it. Use your imagination for something better. Quit your crying. Your nose is probably already red as a tomato, and everyone will know that you were crying. Especially Mother. You need to think about good things. Yeah, that's your "thing" not to let in. Keep those bad thoughts out. Concentrate on the love, the good in your life.*

It was working. *Just takes a little discipline, a little strength of will.* She could feel the smile begin to appear on her face with the warm recollections. *Tim* had been her best friend. Oh, she had close girlfriends, but her friendship with him was deeper, more special, much more than two people of the same sex could experience. They had lived less than a block apart ever since the first grade. She always felt that they had an indescribable, deep understanding of each other.

From time to time, when growing up, she had heard the other boys rib him a little about having a girlfriend or about playing with girls, but he never seemed to let them embarrass him over it, and no boy ever pushed Leary too far. On some things he was just unmovable, and she was happy to know that she was one of those things.

She liked remembering those young days growing up in Helena. She especially enjoyed remembering the look on his face whenever he saw her. She could see it every time. *God, it was great.* Seeing it now, clear in her mind and strong in her heart, the way he looked at her. He was a powerful man, and a man obviously full of love for her. *No man like that could ever be anything but good. It is impossible to believe otherwise.*

You're lucky, Mary, you had two strong good men to love you in this life. Sure, Dad was physically weak, but he was not a weak man. No, you'd be hard-pressed to find another person in this world who could take what he did from life and still remain loving through it.

She didn't know what war was like but surely it didn't have anything that could replace who *Tim* is. He had a smile so warm it could melt anyone's heart. And his touch warmed her whole body. It was impossible for her to ever imagine his touch being anything other than loving. That he could ever use such power to hurt anyone or anything was just plain silly. *Couldn't happen.*

She felt better again. *Yes, I'm lucky to have him in my life. He's the best and, besides being the love in my life, he's an honorable man.*

"Please God," she said aloud, "bring him back to me undamaged."

Now a small, persistent, negative voice began nagging from somewhere deep in the back of her mind. As it grew in strength, it relentlessly claimed reality. *Are you sure, Mary? Is all that love stuff real, and if it is, at what cost? You know Tim is much like your father was. It's true—Tim's loving, strong, and good like your father was. Fate seems to have dealt them a similar situation, though. Your father was sent to a jungle war, and now Tim is in a jungle war.* The voice went on, destroying her good feelings.

"My God!" she cried, unable to suppress the agony of realization. As a child hides its eyes from what it doesn't want to see, her hands covered her tear-soaked face. But covering her eyes wouldn't stop the voice from lecturing her. It gained in power until it seemed to be shouting at her. It was unstoppable as its harsh pronouncements echoed in her head: *Get real, Mary. Your father, by his own words, came back with a "thing." A needed disease, which kept him crippled, hobbled like an uncontrollable animal. He was physically held in check because he could no longer do it himself. The truth is, he no longer wanted to do it himself. He admitted that it forced him to stay away from seeking the killing, unloving side of life. He was held against his will in a place that he said allowed him to find love again. All true, and you know it.*

The voice continued, slower now and more certain. *What if your Tim's jungle war affects him the same way? What if he becomes like your father admitted he'd become? Maybe he already is an efficient, dedicated killer. He could already be a monster who has lost his ability to love and only feels the need to kill. What if he comes back and must have a "thing" to force him to live back here? You would be his second choice then, wouldn't you, like your mother was to your father. She was chosen only because the "thing" wouldn't give him his first choice. Think about it. Could you take it, Mary? Do you even want to take it, twenty years or more with a cripple for a husband? Think about it. It could happen. Then that look of power and love you saw coming from his eyes will change to either the look of a killer or that of a spiritless man.*

I don't know, I don't know.

12

GOODBYE AMERICA

In platoon headquarters, located to the rear of the platoon's place in the defensive perimeter, the horrible sixth day in the operation was over and Platoon Sergeant Cambel was watching Tooley. It had happened earlier that morning when the platoon was, once again, on flank guard for the battalion. Tooley had, in fairness to Leary and the second squad, placed his first squad on point and they had run blindly into a huge booby-trap, which leveled their portion of the jungle and completely obliterated the squad. The death and maiming was so horrible that Tooley had thrown up and then passed out. They would have sent him to the hospital with the dead but Sergeant Cambel talked them out of it, saying that he would pull him out of his shock. Now, he wasn't sure, it had been several hours and Lieutenant Tooley hadn't shown any signs of normalcy. He tried not to be obvious as he looked slightly away from the lieutenant. Years of standing in formations, needing to see what his men were doing while keeping his eyeballs straight ahead, had developed Cambel's peripheral vision to a spectacular degree, and he used that skill now. If Tooley was aware of his vigilance, he did not show it. But then Tooley wasn't showing much recognition of anything and hadn't moved since throwing his unopened letters into the fire. Cambel knew that he would have to take over leadership if the lieutenant didn't snap out of it soon. He'd already tried, on several occasions, to make conversation with him, but the lieutenant had not responded. He had not moved—he just sat there watching the small dying and impotent fire.

I'll protect him as long as I can, Cambel thought. *I know that the men are all aware of their platoon leader's condition, and it's up to me to stay sane and in charge. I can't afford the luxury of going off the* deep end. Got some good men to help me, though, that Carson and his squad are good. Carson immediately took over radio communication with the captain until I could get there. He also protected the lieutenant as much as he could. Kept most of the platoon from seeing that their platoon leader had puked, fainted, and soiled himself. Yeah, Carson's a good man, I'll never forget his yelling, "Platoon sergeant up, everyone else hold positions." What a mess. He can be counted on under the worst of conditions, good to know. This was bad. He handled it all, the communicating with the captain on the radio. Even called the dust-off chopper in for medical evacuation.

Leary didn't have to be told what to do either. He and Folger immediately pushed ahead to scout for the nearest clearing that would support a chopper landing. The speed with which he'd moved ahead and down the trail, while knowing that there might be more booby traps, seemed too risky, but they made it. That's all that really counts anymore. Once they'd found the clearing, he sent Sanchez back to tell me and to lead us to it. Yeah, Leary will be okay. He even thought to take a yellow smoke grenade out of the lieutenant's pack with him to signal the choppers in.

Yes, some of my men are real good, and Carson, Leary, and Folger are three of them. It's too bad about Leary's trouble with the captain. Guess it just comes with the territory. We'll have to see how it plays out. Can't have a man like Leary without having some trouble. The best warriors can be defiant and a little crazy. Hell, it's what makes them what they are, do what they do. Sure as hell can't be passive and be a good warrior. We got some passive ones, though. We'll just have to see about them. Back to my big problem—one that must be solved right now.

"Lieutenant Tooley, sir," Cambel said in a low, no-nonsense tone of voice, "we need to talk." The lieutenant did not respond. "Sir, damn it, you had better get yourself together and come out of your self-pity. Damn you, Lieutenant. You better goddamn answer me!"

The lieutenant turned his reddened face towards his platoon sergeant slowly, as if he were just awakening, and said in a strained but firm voice, "Platoon Sergeant, you do not talk to me that way—ever. I am the officer here, and you will stay within your designated bounds of respect. Is that clear?"

"Very clear, sir, and quite welcome too, but let us get it all out on the table. Sorry as hell about what happened to you. I can tell that some damage was done to your pride and possibly to the confidence that the men might have in you." Using well-developed clear military language, the experienced NCO continued. "But it can all be repaired, for both you and the men. Most important, we need to get back into our designated roles and assess our situation. We've got to weigh our options and plan some strategies, like the soldiers we are, in the place that we are. So let's be real about everything that has happened." His military classroom voice and manner did much to bring Tooley back to the present, back to being a platoon leader in Vietnam.

"Yes, Sergeant Cambel, we'd had better do that, but right now I feel worse than I can ever remember feeling. It's a failure in my duty, a loss of pride in myself—hell, loss of everything I ever was, or ever thought I was. I've disgraced myself, and the thought of that fills me with sorrow.

"I don't know how I could've done it," he said less formally. "Damn it, I'm not just off the truck. I've been around. I've experienced injuries and even some death before this shit today, and never has it caused me to lose it before. Our first real test and I failed it. I not only failed my men, but myself as well. Tell me, Platoon Sergeant, how do I deal with that?"

The sergeant spoke softly, forcing Tooley to concentrate as Cambel looked directly into his eyes. His tone was concerned, knowing. "Sir, I enlisted in the army in 1942 when I was eighteen. I am now forty-one years old and will soon be forty-two. I fought in the jungles of the South Pacific with the Marines against the Japanese. I reenlisted in the army during the Korean War and have been in ever since. I have experience in war. So, let me tell you what happened today and why."

"Okay." Tooley's shoulders slumped and he hung his head.

"What happened to you when the first squad hit that booby-trapped artillery shell this morning was twofold. First, no matter what you think you have prepared your mind for, it is never enough. Furthermore, what you saw when you came around the bend in the trail was the worst. It was more than just that visible human pulp lying around. That's a sight that, although I don't know how since it was so bad, you might prepare your mind for—at least to some degree. A mind that is prepared will be less likely to go into shock—which is exactly what you did. So you might have been able to handle the visual picture, but there was the smell too. The sense of smell is very influential in the animal world. There is nothing that can prepare a man for the smell of pulverized, burnt humans. So the look of it and the smell of it were big factors in the effect it had on you. But others saw and smelled it too, and they didn't react the way you did. So, what really got you today? Sir, what paralyzed you was the responsibility. It was the responsibility, that's what threw you into shock."

"I appreciate your pep talk, Sergeant, but I think you are stretching it all to hell. I'm the only one not wounded who is screwed up by what happened today. The men seem okay."

"Sir, if your mind was with us here in Vietnam, you would see that your men are not in the best of shape either. Sure, they didn't react the way you did, and they managed to do their jobs, but they're in bad shape, too."

"They look normal to me, Sergeant. They're sitting around their small fires bullshitting and doing the things they do every morning and every night. They can't be too upset or they wouldn't be visiting like they are."

"I've made my rounds and, believe me, they aren't talking like they did yesterday. They're quieter, they're not interested in their mail, and they are very low on morale. Their conversations are strained, bitter, and depressing. Of course, they have established their fires and free time. They're still human. They go all day without talking, smoking, sometimes not eating, and always being quiet. That time in the morning before we move out and the time in the evening, before dark, are the only times they can speak, relax, or make any noise at all. They're in bad shape and they need leadership now more than before."

How can they trust me as their leader after today? How can I trust myself?"

"Lieutenant, you're failing to take into account the one load that you alone have. The burden that no one else has, the extra burden of responsibility."

"Many people over here have responsibility, all of us, one way or another, and I'm the only one who reacted that way. God help me, even Hart didn't make a fool out of himself."

"No sir, you have just failed to really look at it. The way I see it, no one has more responsibility than you do. As a commander in chief once said, 'The buck stops here.' "Which for you, sir, is here." He shoved his right index finger at Tooley.

"Hell, you're responsible for the men too, and you maintained a dignified military presence."

"Sure, but take into account that I had time to prepare myself for the horror, and I've seen it and smelled it before. But more than that, ultimately it was, and is, your responsibility. They are your men, Lieutenant Tooley. And only if something happens to you do they become mine. Then, mine only until you are replaced. Which wouldn't be long. But they are yours, Lieutenant. Yours until they are carried out of this country, and deep down you know that. I'm a good soldier and a damn good NCO, but I am not an officer. I depend upon an officer to take the total responsibility. I just take responsibility for the small things, like ammo, proper gear, proper formation, and the like. You, sir, say who goes where and who takes the most and the least risks. It's an awesome responsibility—especially for someone like you."

"What do you mean, 'like me,' Sergeant?"

"Well sir, the world is made up of all kinds, or so the story goes. You are not like the captain. We all know that the captain cares about his career and that everything else in his world is secondary, including his men. If the captain thinks losing a few men would further his career, I don't think he would hesitate to sacrifice the men. Men are things to be used by him for his own purposes. You, on the other hand, are someone who sees your men as humans. You would never sacrifice or jeopardize a man's life for your career. It just doesn't come out that way for you. Consequently, when you lose men, especially in such a god-awful manner, it hits you right in the core of your gut. It almost killed you to see what had happened to your men. I am glad, sir, that you are in charge and not me. In spite of my experience in war, I do not believe that I would have handled myself any differently than you, had the 'buck' stopped with me."

Neither man knew it then, but the lieutenant would need to have all of his confidence and leadership back by tomorrow, if anyone in the Second Platoon were to survive the day.

13

BUSINESS FOR
WESTERN UNION

It was 1000 hours when Leary raised his closed fist into the air, a signal to those behind him that he was going to stop. After each man made sure that the man behind him received the signal, he went down on one knee, facing the direction in the formation he was expected to protect. Leary seemed to take an inordinate amount of time looking to his front. Fear and curiosity began to set in, and the men had trouble watching their own area; they all wanted to see what had so grabbed Leary's attention.

As the seconds went by, the lieutenant could feel his anger rising towards Leary's failure to signal his reason for stopping the platoon. Then, finally, he saw Leary signal a mock salute with his left hand while still staring straight ahead.

About time for a saluting gesture, the hand signal requesting the ranking man to come to the point, Tooley thought, as he looked back at Cambel and his radio operator and repeated the signal. To Cambel, this meant that the lieutenant and Nash, the radio operator, would be at the extreme front of the formation and that Cambel as the next ranking man should stay to the rear.

After cautiously moving up beside the now prone Leary and Carson, the lieutenant spent a few minutes observing what Leary had been staring at, wondering if he was seeing everything that Leary saw. Even though it did not take the lieutenant long to spot what Leary had found, he needed to be sure they were all seeing the same thing. Perhaps there was a hidden bunker that he didn't see. He couldn't take anything for granted. They would need to pull back and compare what they had seen, but first he would carefully examine and memorize everything his eyes revealed.

It isn't that obvious, not at first glance. It's well tucked into the jungle and has a lot of natural vegetation surrounding it. And the guard pits, well, they're quite obvious once you've identified them as such. But from the air they probably look like bushes, especially if they keep fresh bamboo boughs on the roofs. Then Tooley felt a stab of fear, wondering for a moment, *If I'd been on point would I have spotted that for what it is, or would I have blundered into the clearing? That's enough self-doubt. Who knows? Be the leader; get on with the job.* The muscles in the back of his neck were already starting to cramp from holding his steel-helmeted head up as he turned his face towards Leary and Carson and signaled for the three of them to crawl back out of sight. His fears and doubts were now gone, and he felt good being in charge again.

As the three men crawled to the rear, Folger automatically crawled up to watch the front. They crawled single file back down the trail about five meters and stopped just short of the place the lieutenant had told Nash to wait with the radio. Tooley then turned around. Carson and Leary managed to squeeze together on the narrow trail. They were side by side facing the lieutenant, their feet towards the enemy. Once they were settled, the lieutenant said in a low whisper, "I'm going to draw what I saw." He cradled his rifle in the crook of his left arm and started drawing on the sandy trail with his right index finger. Like a faucet with bad gaskets, sweat continually dripped from the three men's foreheads, splashing on their folded arms, rifles, and clothing. They tried to ignore its itching. They knew that scratching was a fruitless thing to do—better to get used to itching, though sometimes the urge to scratch was unbearable.

While drawing in the fine sand of the trail, Tooley gave a whispered verbal rundown of his sightings. "Looked to me like a large warehouse complex, eight covered structures, no sides, filled with some kind of goods. There were two sandbagged areas visible on each corner of the complex. A road, probably the one they brought the stuff in on, took off to the right or east of the complex. I counted two men in the east sandbagged area with what looked like a machine gun. They were smoking and talking and didn't seem too alert, but then they have a large open area in front of them. That's plenty of time to spot and shoot anyone trying to cross the paddy.

"They don't seem to be concerned with what's behind them. Might mean there's something behind them so big that it makes them feel safe. Something I saw no signs of." He paused a minute to think as he watched the sweat dripping out of his helmet and onto his left shirtsleeve. The pain in his neck from supporting the

heavy steel helmet was just too much and, in what seemed like an
angry impulse, he quickly jerked it off his head and sat it roughly in
the grass to his left. He looked at Carson and Leary, who remained
expressionless, and quietly said, "Heavy bastard." Then, Carson and
Leary both removed their helmets as well, setting them off to one
side.

Tooley continued to whisper calmly, "I also saw two men in
the sandbagged area on the west corner of the warehouse complex.
They didn't seem to be overly alert either. It looked like they have
an automatic rifle, one of those with the magazine on top." In hopes
of providing some relief to his cramping neck, he stopped and let his
head rest on his right arm for a full ten seconds. It was silent—even
the jungle was quiet—then, he raised his head and asked, "Sergeant
Carson, what did you see?"

Carson made the index finger of his right hand available and
started to draw while whispering, "I saw eight warehouse-like
structures under the canopy of that thick jungle. Three sides, opening
up here on this large rice paddy, the one between them and us. I also
saw four soldiers, in what looked like North Vietnamese uniforms.
There are three dikes that cross the paddy. The one in the middle is
wider than the rest, and I believe the shortest distance to both the
gun pits. It doesn't look like we can get to where they are without
crossing the paddy. The jungle on each side is very thick, and we
don't know the area.

"The battalion might be able to find this place and come in on
that east road, which looks more an ox cart trail, since it appears
to head off in their general direction. I didn't see any barracks for
billeting their soldiers or any other such type facilities, which might
let us guess how many of them there are. I agree that those men
in the gun pits don't seem to be worried about anything, especially
about what's behind them. Their guns are pointed our way, and they
don't look back. So what is behind them? What makes them feel
protected from that direction? Some of their people must be back
there, somewhere.

"With warehouses that large, there must be a whole support
area behind them. Maybe everything back there, barracks, mess,
hospital, the works. I mean, we can't see back there. I figure those
warehouses to be about thirty meters wide by sixty meters long.
Four of them are facing us in front of the paddy, and four are directly
behind them. All lined up in perfect rows with about ten-meter-
wide paths crisscrossing between the warehouses." Then Carson
wiped his forehead on his right shirtsleeve and nodded to Leary.

Leary whispered, "I don't have anything to add to the drawing. I agree that there could be these four men or that there could be several thousand in the jungle around the warehouses. We've got to figure on there being a lot of them around here somewhere, or they wouldn't need so much storage. With the exception of that large trail heading off to the east, the jungle surrounding the warehouses looks impenetrable. From here it looks like they hacked a square chunk out of the jungle and built warehouses in the cave-like opening. I doubt that those warehouses can be spotted from the air."

Tooley said, "I'm sure the colonel won't want us to try and take this by ourselves. Could be thousands of them over there, but just in case, sergeants, how would you take the complex if he orders us to?"

It was quiet for a few seconds, then Carson said, "If we have to take them by ourselves, then I suggest we have the two machine guns and two grenade launchers each take a gun pit and pour fire into both of them at the same time. Hopefully, they can kill them right away, but barring that, maybe keep them ducking while a squad runs across the paddy. So while they're dying or ducking, two fire teams run across the center dike and take the gun pits. We'll have to make sure that we set the shooters up undetected. Once they're alerted by anything, we'll have to run for it."

After a short pause, Leary said, "I hope the colonel gives us time to scout for a couple of trails that would allow us to flank the complex before taking it straight on like that. If we could scout it, we might be able to find out what's behind it, too. There could be a whole North Vietnamese regiment back there. If he tells us to wait, we might have a tough time staying here undetected. Someone could come along any time. If that happens, the choices are over. That's all I've got, except that a lot of somebody's stuff is in those warehouses. There has to be a lot of the enemy around here somewhere."

Carson nodded and said, "I hope he lets us just call in an air strike on it."

Tooley, a worried look on his freckled face, nodded his agreement. "Anything more?"

Carson and Leary both shook their heads no.

"All right, I agree with everything we've all said. First, let me see where the battalion is and what they want us to do. You two crawl back up with Folger and watch. I'll brief the platoon sergeant and speak with the colonel. If the gooks do anything that might affect what we know at this point, have someone crawl back and let me know. I know you'll remember that if they spot you, it'll cost us in

lives." Both men soberly nodded. "Okay then, Nash and I will move
back to where the platoon sergeant is so we can't be heard. I'll brief
all of the men before I pull you two back. Send Folger back in about
five minutes for the general briefing." Nodding his head and putting
his helmet back on, he said, "Let's do it."

Without further communication, Carson crawled to the
front of the formation with Leary right behind him. They crawled
competently, almost gracefully, cradling their rifles and helmets in
their folded arms. Tooley crawled farther than he really needed to
before standing up and, with an exaggerated stealth meant to let the
rest of the platoon know that they should be quiet, made his way to
the rear where Cambel was anxiously waiting.

Then the lieutenant spoke with the captain, who also contacted
the colonel at battalion, until all three were on the radio. Neither
Tooley nor the colonel knew where the other one was. The colonel
believed that the battalion was south of the Second Platoon's position,
and, hopefully, still east.

"Surely," he said, "we haven't crossed your path and are now west
of you?" Then after a brief pause, "No, Lieutenant, I am sure we're
still east and south of you. We stopped to destroy some hooches and
tear up a few gardens. No people around. Looked like they left just
ahead of us. It took longer than I thought. The rain last night made
the hooches hard to burn." The colonel had no idea where the road
they spoke of was, nor did any of the other company commanders—
who were by then all listening on their radios.

The B Company Commander suggested that Tooley throw
down a smoke grenade and let a helicopter identify their positions.
The colonel quickly rejected that. "No! No smoke. First, there are no
helicopters in the area, and second, even if there were, I'm not sure
we want to alert an obviously lax enemy."

"Let's have them pull back and wait for the battalion to circle
around behind the enemy," Captain Haps suggested.

The A Company Commander said that they should call in an
air strike.

The colonel become frustrated at the free-flowing advice from
his junior officers and stopped all suggestions with his order, an order
that Tooley could only label as hasty. "Lieutenant Tooley, you and
your men attack and capture that warehouse area. That's just exactly
what we're out here to do. We'll reinforce you as soon as we can find
you. We'll try and find you from the sounds of your firing."

There was a long moment of silence from Tooley that the colonel
correctly interpreted as a need for encouragement. "We can't be that

far away. We're probably just a couple hundred meters to your right."
Then the final command, "That is all. Good luck, Lieutenant. Out."

"Yes, sir, Colonel, we will attack. Out," Tooley responded. *This
is one hell of a risk. He'd better be right about how close he is.*

Tooley briefed his men, expanding on the plan Carson had
suggested. The jungle was thick on each side of the trail right up
to the place where it entered the clearing. The trail was just wide
enough for the two machine gunners and the two grenadiers. The
assistant gunners would have to lie behind the gunners. In fact, they
were so close to each other that there was little room left on the trail
to walk or run between them.

Getting into their positions was tedious and, if their enemy had
been more alert, they probably would have been detected. *Good
thing I reminded them that the eye can easily spot quick movement,*
Tooley thought, *and that the camouflaging of their helmets looks good.
I guess we're as prepared as we can be. Still, I hate this plan, far too
risky with my platoon.*

They had agreed to leave Hart behind. Leary was going to lead,
and he was impatient to get it going. There was no conversation about
it; Carson hadn't even cleared it with the lieutenant. He had just told
Hart to stay with the third squad. Hart's face was as full of gratitude
as Leary's was of disgust as Carson gave the order. Hart had been
given the M-79 grenade launcher that had been Sanchez's. Carson felt
that since the M-79 was quieter, only making a popping noise, firing
it might not scare Hart into freezing. Leary didn't believe it would
make any difference and hated to see such a valuable weapon put
into the hands of a selfish coward. He tried to console himself with
the knowledge that they could always take the launcher away from
him. *Of course, now it wouldn't be with them because the shit was
being excused from the charge. Screw the bastard,* Leary thought.

It seemed to take hours for the lieutenant to get those gunners
ready and in place. He wanted to get going before he had time to
think about it, before he had time to become afraid of it. *Well, it's
damn sure time.* He was just out of sight behind the prone gunners
and grenadiers, trying to figure out how to get past them, when the
lieutenant gave the signal.

Just as Leary began to run between them, one of the gunners
nervously moved his leg, causing Leary to step on part of the man's
thigh, twisting his left ankle. Leary felt a sharp pain and cursed under
his breath as he came out of the thick jungle in a stumbling run.
Fighting to gain balance and not lose his forward momentum, Leary
welcomed the adrenaline-induced rush. He dared not look back, but

he knew Folger was hot on his trail. He could feel it. The North Vietnamese soldiers looked up and were momentarily stunned at the sight of the white soldier stumbling out of the jungle, trying to catch his balance, as if he had jumped off of a moving truck. They watched in disbelief as they wondered who Leary was, just as he regained his balance and began to run with some grace and speed. The enemy, as if on cue, came out of their stupor and dove for their guns. Their peaceful duty was over.

Cutting his mind off from any ankle pain, Leary headed straight down the dike that halved the large water-filled rice paddy. Carson was in the middle of the squad just in front of Patkins and his fire team.

Down the center of the large rice paddy they ran. Their options were limited. They couldn't go left or right, not until they had crossed the full length of the paddy. This was no time to think about what ideal targets they were; there was only time to think about running and hoping. Hoping that the machine gunners and grenadiers behind them would do their job. If the weapons men couldn't kill the Vietnamese, they needed to keep them ducking until the squad got across. To a man, they knew their chances for success and for survival were dependent upon their speed, their machine gunners' accuracy, and their grenadiers' ability to put the 40mm grenades into the North Vietnamese gun pits.

Shit, Tooley felt the fear as he thought, *run, damn it run. God, let them make it. Even then, we don't know what's waiting for them over there in that jungle behind those warehouses. There may be several hundred, or even thousands, of highly trained North Vietnamese regulars waiting for them to get across. That goddamn colonel. Christ, where is his head, that old goat? If I lose one man, I'll get him. Sure as God's above. Damn stupid shit. We're attacking a jungle cache that obviously supports hundreds of men. We're alone, lost, and damn few of us. Jesus, what kind of fool order did he give us, and I didn't even protest it—like a puppy.*

As Leary pushed for speed down the dike, the stress sped his mind up, forcing it to run at a super speed, which slowed down the world around him. Leary could feel the blood pumping through his brain, swelling it, plugging his hearing and making the sounds of firing and explosions seem like they were miles away instead of a few hundred meters. He desperately forced his mind to concentrate on running faster. The shooting and explosions seemed like they were late in starting, and he couldn't tell if it was his people firing at the enemy, the enemy firing at him, or both. *Be prepared—at any moment you might feel enemy bullets knocking you to the ground. Maybe hitting you in the head and that would be it. One second you're here and the next, nothingness. Expect it to happen, and then maybe it won't be so bad if it does. In fact, they're probably just missing you now. Shit, there goes your damn helmet. The strap wasn't tight enough. Well, to hell with it. It was heavy and wouldn't have stopped one of their bullets anyway. Run, legs run. Am I really running? I know I am but I can't feel my legs anymore, I can't even feel my body. Maybe I'm dead and don't know it. Maybe I've been killed already. Doesn't feel like I'm really here anymore. There's no pain, and I'm running full out. I can't feel anything. Well, if I'm already dead, how come I'm almost across the paddy? It's about time to turn towards my target. I must be alive, unless a person keeps going after death. Maybe you have to keep doing what you were doing when you died. Then I'd have to run forever. Quit thinking. Get to the east gun pit. I have to take the gun, stop its firing, nothing else. I'm across the paddy, now make a right-hand turn, come on, turn shorter, my ankle's not cooperating. It doesn't hurt, it just isn't working like it should. Jesus, that's too wide a turn. I'm exposed longer than I should be. I should be running straight at the pit now. Not making this wide arc, this easy target. Turn man, turn. Ah, there's the pit, Christ, the boys are sure pouring the fire on them. Yeah, but they're still alive. At least one of them is. Don't forget to shoot him. Shit, he's turning to shoot me. Hell, shoot him, quit running, drop to the ground, anything but quit running right into his sights. What's the matter with me? I'm still running. Stop it. Stop running towards him. He has a perfect shot at you. Damn it, legs, quit running, fall, turn, anything, but quit running towards him. Shit, my legs won't listen anymore, my own legs are going to kill me. I'm a dead man for sure. He can't miss.*

Folger, though close behind Leary, had made his turn tighter and was running right on the edge of the paddy when he saw the wounded Vietnamese trying to get his rifle sighted at Leary. Even in the turmoil, Folger recognized the weapon as a Chinese-made weapon, a Chicom, or a Russian bolt-action rifle and that his chances of saving Leary were slim. He was out of breath and silently cursed the cigarettes he'd been smoking. Struggling against gravity and fatigue, he pulled his heavy automatic rifle up and pointed it towards the enemy who was almost completely behind the sandbags. There was no time for anything but a bouncing hip shot. With the selector on full automatic, Folger fired four rounds that surprised both him and the North Vietnamese at how close they came to the wounded but determined enemy soldier. He had to try again. His second burst was five rounds, and they seemed to go over the Vietnamese's head.

Folger could now clearly see a bloody area on the enemy's right shoulder. His wound was slowing him down but he was going to fire. Folger tried adjusting his sighting for another burst as he saw the enemy's rifle kick back and up as a light puff of smoke came out of the barrel. Folger wanted to see if Leary was hit, knowing he must have been, but was afraid to look lest he lose his hard-earned rifle sighting.

Holding the trigger back, firing the remaining eleven rounds from his magazine, Folger screamed something incoherent as he fought to keep the powerful bucking rifle on target. In less than a couple of seconds, the magazine was empty, leaving the bolt locked back in the open position, and the hot barrel smoking as it burned the gun oil off. It's a foul smell, Folger thought, just as he reached the pit.

Leary saw his death coming. *It's simple. Wounded or not, he's going to kill me dead. He's lining up on me now and he's going to pull the trigger and kill me. I'll keep going, can't seem to stop anyway. Shit, there it is, the rifle bucking and the puff of smoke or dust, whatever. Maybe I'm hit and don't know it. His bullet should have knocked me down, or something. Damn, he must have missed. Christ, there goes his head. Bullets hitting all around him and his head explodes. Looks just like someone's thrown a watermelon.*

As Tooley watched anxiously, Leary got to the pit just ahead of Folger and ran point blank into the sandbags as if he had no intention of stopping or of even slowing down. Holding his rifle across his chest, he flipped over the low wall and into the pit, landing facedown on top of the bloody corpse of the man who had been trying to kill him. Folger came sliding to a halt in front of the sandbags just south of where Leary had pitched over the wall, with Sanchez skidding up on Folger's right. All three men were desperate for breath. Leary's chest heaved as he used his rifle as a crutch on the dead man's chest and painfully pushed himself to his feet. He looked down in disgust at the blood and brains now stuck to his sweat-soaked right side. Folger, coughing while gasping for air, ignored Leary's finicky reaction to the enemy soldier's misfortune as he fished another loaded magazine out of his ammo pouch and inserted it into his still-smoking rifle. Satisfaction showed on his face as he heard the click of the magazine locking into place and, without looking, he reached down and unlocked the bolt, chambering another round. Ready for more.

Leary stood there a moment, trying to normalize his rapid breathing. Sweat was pouring from his head as he stared down at the faceless soldier who had tried to kill him. Then, in a ragged, strained voice he said, "Tried to kill me, didn't you?" and started firing into the small chest. Slowly and methodically he fired, causing the body to move with every shot. "You shit, how do you like it? I got more for you and your prick buddy, too." After firing five times, he turned and fired five bullets into the other man's already very dead body. When he had fired his tenth round he stopped, defiantly looked up, challenging anyone to disapprove of his actions.

Sanchez had no words, but Folger did.

"Christ, Sarge, you're making a mess out of the gun pit. Shit, we got to occupy it and you're tearing pieces of these gooks all over the place. The goddamn flies will be everywhere. The place will start to smell."

"Screw you, Folger," Leary said, while shaking his head in an effort to clear it. A slight smile, hardly noticeable, appeared at the corners of his mouth as he said, "Don't blame me, Folger, you're the one who blew these brains all over the place."

Folger managed a strained grin as well when he said, "Too true, too true, sloppy shooting, I'll admit, but in the end effective, wouldn't you say?"

Elated that they had survived, Leary was reenergized. "Yeah, thanks, Folger. Damn, that was close. Awful close. Oh well! Let's get these bodies out of here and scoop the guts out the best we can. There have to be more of them around here. Somewhere. We could get hit anytime. Plus we need to get in this pit so we can protect the rest of the platoon as it crosses."

Then, all squeamishness gone, they frantically threw out the enemy bodies and used the enemy's pith helmets to scoop out the majority of the blood and guts. By the time the bodies were out lying by the rice paddy's edge, the flies were already covering their many bloody wounds. In a matter of minutes, though, both gun pits were set up and nervously watching north, expecting at any moment to see a large contingency of enemy come charging out of the jungle near the warehouses. As soon as they were all in a reasonably comfortable firing position, Leary waved his arm, signaling Tooley.

In the west pit, Carson's fire team was ready, too. They had received no enemy fire at all and, upon reaching the pit, found one dead and one dying Vietnamese soldier. Though Carson used his own bandage on the wounded enemy soldier, the man had a severe chest wound and never regained consciousness. As soon as Carson finished tying the bandage, the little man quit breathing and died. *Quietly,* Carson thought, *as if he's gone to sleep.*

Fortunately for the second squad, the accurate long-range machine gun fire had mostly neutralized the enemy. It was early in the war and the machine gunners were still carrying their heavy but effective tripods. They had set up and fired their guns in perfect textbook fashion. Their fire on both gun pits was so sudden and accurate that the Vietnamese had little chance to believe what they saw running out of the jungle before they felt the mule-like kicks from bullets punching their bodies. Neither of the grenadiers had managed to score a direct hit, which was unusual since both had made harder shots in the past, but their rounds were close enough to be distracting.

As the two fire teams in the gun pits caught their breath and watched for other enemy, Tooley and the rest of the platoon came running across the rice paddy. True to the plan, they split up after crossing the paddy. Half the platoon went right, following Cambel, and half went left with the lieutenant. Machine gunner and grenadier crossed with the platoon, while the other two stayed with the weapons sergeant to provide cover while the platoon crossed. Once Tooley, Cambel, and the platoon had safely occupied the two gun pits, the weapons sergeant, machine gunners, and grenadier moved across the paddy. One gun was set up in each of the two pits. The weapons sergeant went to the lieutenant's position. Once everyone was reasonably settled, Tooley called the colonel.

"We heard the sounds of shooting," the colonel told Tooley. "There seemed to be a lot of it. We're still not sure where you are or how to find you. Oh, I know we're east and south of you, but just how far in either of those directions, or what trail to take to you, I don't know. However, I'll send a platoon from the drag company to scout for a trail west of us and, more importantly, I'll see if I can get some choppers up from Saigon. My chopper is in Saigon standing by. So at the worst, I can have him in the air within ten minutes, but it'll take another thirty minutes to get over your area—wherever that is. So, lieutenant, throw yellow smoke after you hear that the chopper has spotted us. After that, finding you and getting to your position should be elementary. Out."

"Elementary," Tooley said sarcastically, as he handed the radio's handset back to Nash, "the colonel says finding us will be elementary, Dr. Watson."

"What, sir?" Nash asked.

"Nothing, really, not important."

"Okay, sir," Nash said, still not getting the joke.

The sound of the single shot in the new calm was a violation to them all. It seemed to have come from the east. Tooley strained his eyes trying to see more clearly the other half of his platoon, which was now crowding into the east pit. He could see a lot of commotion there. *What in the hell is going on? Why are they all trying to crowd into that pit? Shit, it's not big enough for half of them. What is going on? Christ, if they only had a damn radio, or a phone, some goddamn thing. They're too far away to command from here. Of course, Cambel is over there, but still there's a big gap in between us. They're all ducking but no one is firing. I don't like it here one damn bit but, still, we have to stay here. "Hold the complex till we get there," the colonel said. We're so exposed here, and we can't all get in these two pits. Well, we shouldn't be clustered up in them now, not like this. One RPG or mortar round could wipe out half the platoon. Goddamn it all. I'd feel safer in the jungle. At least there we could spread out and have cover.*

Tooley took his eyes off of the east gun pit and anxiously looked at Carson and the weapons sergeant for a nervous second. *What the hell is the weapons sergeant's name? Christ, get hold of yourself. You can't even remember his name? He came out of the mortar platoon after that poor bastard blew himself up. Shit, I can't remember his name now, either. Oh, well. Screw it, this guy is new and doesn't really belong with us yet. Get off of yourself.*

"Good job, Weapons Sergeant," Tooley said. "That was damn good fire from your guns. Now, Sergeant, watch the front, please, and get everyone lower in the pit. Something is going on in the other pit but I can't tell what. Damn, we need more radios."

Then it hit him, the realization moving him physically. He jumped up and waved his arms as he yelled, "Sergeant Carson, get all of those men, except the machine gun crew, out of this pit and spread them out in two-man positions towards the east pit. Have them use whatever cover they can find. Hurry it up, Sergeant! We're bunched up in these pits. One damn grenade can get us all."

Pausing to inhale the hot moist air, he continued, "Do it and do it now. As soon as they're set up in their positions, cover half of the distance between this pit and Cambel's pit. Have Sergeant Patkins go to Cambel and tell him to do the same, but make sure Patkins places his men in their positions first—on the way. We don't want to be exposed like this any longer than we have to."

"Yes sir," Carson said, "you all heard the man, now move."

Already, the sweat-soaked Patkins was making haste to get his equipment on and scramble out of the gun pit.

"Sergeant Patkins," Tooley said, "have a couple of your men face back across the paddy. We don't want to make the mistake of not watching all areas. And Sergeant Patkins, find out what that shot was about, then report back to me, and Patkins," Tooley's voice was strained, his red face full of anger, "make damn sure they get everyone but the machine gunners and the platoon sergeant out of that pit. Have we lost our minds? We're bunched up like two groups of idiots waiting for death." Then, still yelling, "One more thing, Patkins, tell the platoon sergeant we won't be found for at least forty minutes and then only by the colonel's chopper. In truth, it could be hours before the battalion gets here, so we have to hold this ground. We have no other choice. Is that all clear to you, Sergeant?"

"Yes, sir, it is."

"Okay, let's go, hurry it up, all of you."

In the east pit, Leary had just decided that there was no use holding the bandage against the hole in Cambel's chest any longer. He was dead, and except for a jerking left arm, some slight facial twitching, and eye rolling, he hadn't really moved much at all. *Poor Cambel, he didn't even get time to protest losing his life. No time to say those last few words, the ones they always get to say in the movies. Damn it, after all of our training, we never even considered it. Not really. It was so basic, too. I wonder if we know anything? I mean, train and train for all the possibilities and then forgot to pay attention to the first principle of combat, stay down and stay covered. Cambel's whole body was exposed to the obvious enemy area and he was the most experienced of us all. What could have been going through his mind? If he could forget like that, how will the rest of us less experienced survive?*

It was such an easy shot from that jungle out there. It's a spooky jungle for sure, very close and spooky. A man could hide a thousand places in that thick foliage, shoot us dead, and never be seen. God knows I liked this old man. Those bastards are going to pay for this one, I promise. I'll kill a bunch for you, Platoon Sergeant. And God, it was so fast too, poor bastard. The sudden smack in his chest forced out a yelp, much like a hurt dog, and then he flipped right on to his back and right on top of our worthless Hart, who's still lying under him like he's been killed too. "Hart, you worthless piece of crap, get the hell out of there. But stay low." *The noise came right behind the shot. Sniper must be close. Now we're all crowded into this hole like sardines in a can, but getting out of here is getting killed.*

We're all crunched as low as possible; it's suicide to stick our head up for a look. Some of the men have parts exposed. An ass here, a leg there, hell, my back is probably hanging out a mile. Well, no use holding this bandage in place anymore. I can get flatter if I don't, but don't want to lie on him, not really. Must have gotten him right in the heart, and he's still lying on Hart, who hasn't moved yet. "On second thought, Hart, stay right where you are, at least for now. Until we sort this out." *No exit wound. Must have been light on the powder or couldn't make it through his rib cage on his back. It was probably a soft-nose carbine round. Those lead bullets can fragment and tear one's insides up. Bastards aren't supposed to use those kinds of bullets. Shit, I'm still thinking like there are rules. Stupid me. Did sound like a carbine, though. It was more of a pop, really.*

Well, Hart is finally doing something worthwhile, being a pedestal for Sergeant Cambel's dead body. It's about the best thing he's ever done. Goddamn Hart is making no attempt to move. He's just lying there, probably feeling safe with Cambel's body covering him. He'd use his own mother's body to protect his worthless life. Well, I guess I'm in charge now, nothing I can do for Cambel.

Leary looked at the jungle between two sandbags he'd pried apart, then said, "Everyone keep down. Did anyone see where that shot came from?" Without waiting for an answer, he went on. "We shouldn't have been caught bunched up like this. We should have moved into the warehouses. Set up a larger perimeter there."

Leary's voice grew in volume until he was almost screaming as he said, "Start passing the sandbags from the front of the pit to the rear, stay low. Just expose your hands, nothing more. Sanchez, you don't have to see. Damn it, just feel what you're doing. We've got to get some more cover here between the jungle and us. Too many of us in this hole and the sandbags are on the wrong side to protect us all. Hart, get your sorry ass out from under the platoon sergeant, and help Sanchez drag those two dead gooks back into the pit and put them on the wall by Folger."

"Sarge, it isn't right to use them like that, and they're a mess," Hart whined.

"Damn it, Hart," Folger said. "Get them over here. If that sniper wants another one of us, let him shoot through his own men. I hope he fires again too, cause I'm gonna get him if he does."

"Go on, Hart, stick your worthless arm over the wall and help Sanchez drag that gook up here. And then push Cambel's body out on the east side where it will be protected. We need the room, and he doesn't feel anymore. You gunners stay close to the gun."

As the men frantically moved the Vietnamese bodies, the sandbags, and Cambel's body out of the pit to the east, Leary, as cautiously as he could, looked at the other gun pit and, to his horror, watched as the other half of their platoon, directed by Carson and Patkins, moved out of the east gun pit and started coming towards them. They were staying relatively low, running crouched towards them, stringing out and setting up new positions as they went. It was obvious they didn't know the east pit was under siege. Leary tried waving and yelling, but they seemed not to hear or see him and kept coming. *Damn, they're cautious but not cautious enough. They don't have a clue about the sniper. What did they think that shot was?*

Now that the side of the pit towards the jungle was higher with sandbags and bodies, they all turned their attention to what the rest of the platoon was doing. They watched, waiting, breaths held, as the new positions were formed. In order, they strung out, two men to a position, twenty meters apart, bridging the gap between the two pits.

Some of the positions were adequate. Two men were placed behind the cover of an old tree stump. Another position was set up behind the dike facing out across the paddy, the men's backs protected by the height of the east pit. The next two took up position behind a small rise in the ground, and two more behind the dike facing south. They seemed somewhat exposed, depending upon where the sniper was. For the most part, it looked as if the east pit and the warehouse complex protected them from the danger of the jungle wall. Patkins and the last two men, though, had no cover at all. They just lay down on the grass—flat, but exposed.

Thank God, Leary told himself, *no more shots. Looks like they're all placed and that they've covered half the distance between them and us. What the hell is Patkins doing? He's gotten up on one knee at that last position. Didn't that shot mean anything to him? What the hell is wrong with him? What does he want from us? Hell, he expects us to cover the other half of the gap between the pits. Shit, none of them have a clue about what's happening over here. Good God, how to tell them?* He screamed, "Patkins, get your ass down." *Oh hell, look at him wave, like we're in Scout camp or something. Why the hell can't he hear me? Shit, it's not that damn far. Well, we can't leave this pit. Not with that sniper out there. I'm surprised the bastard hasn't taken a shot at one of them. Especially that damn Patkins who's just kneeling there. Maybe he's pulled out. More likely, he's just waiting for the perfect shot. Sure, why waste rounds or give away his position? He knows with all of us bunched up like this, he's in charge. Sooner or later, we'll give him another good shot. Like with Cambel. We were butt-kicking hotshots before, and now we're the butt-kicked. War is some great stuff.*

Feeling more helpless by the minute, Leary and the men in the east pit watched from the safety of their pit as Patkins rose to his feet, turned towards them, and started walking. He was bent forward in a half crouch, carrying his rifle at high port arms about eighteen inches in front of his chest. He was reasonably cautious as he walked into the sniper's sights.

Leary tried, once more, to wave him back, but Patkins just kept coming. Soon most of the men in the east pit were waving and shouting also, "Run, Patkins, sniper, run." But Patkins didn't seem to be capable of understanding them. In fact, he acted as if he thought they were welcoming him.

They must be feeling victorious, Patkins thought as he pumped his rifle into the air—returning their salute. Just as he raised his rifle into the air for the third and most vigorous time, the sniper fired. Patkins mind worked quickly as it spat out one last thought, *Some powerful force is crushing my head.*

14

AMERICAN CARE

Patkins' legs kept running briefly after the force hit his head. He flipped onto his back faster than if he had slipped on ice. He landed hard, with the rifle flying out behind him. All those watching felt anger and sickness knowing he had been shot dead in the face. For some seconds, the whole platoon was mesmerized at the sight of Patkins lying there, flat on his back, limp and lifeless as a rag doll.

The spell and silence were soon broken by the violent noise of gunfire. Folger's automatic rifle fire made them all look first towards him and then to the jungle wall at which he was aiming. Cool man that he was, Folger had not watched Patkins but kept his eyes on the thick cover of the jungle, waiting for a sign, any sign. He hadn't seen that much—just a little movement in the jungle foliage, a puff of smoke, but it was enough. He put five four-round bursts into and around the area he had spotted, then calmly and quickly reloaded and fired another twenty rounds using a slightly larger shot pattern. They all watched, stunned, as a pronounced movement in the jungle followed Folger's firing. Without looking around or taking his eyes off that spot in the jungle, Folger stood up while putting a third fresh magazine into his weapon and then scrambled over the wall and headed toward the jungle.

Leary screamed, "Stay down, and damn it, Folger, where're you going?" Then, realizing that they were committed, that they had to follow Folger's lead, he gave the order. "Machine gunners, provide cover. Everyone else, let's go." And the three men of Fire Team B and the five men from third squad, Fire Team A, scrambled after Folger. The machine gunners pushed Hart out of the pit, and he followed the others in their disorganized charge to the jungle wall.

They raced desperately after Folger while fearing what awaited them in the thick jungle ahead.

It was raining so heavily that visibility was down to five feet; everything was soaked. Several hours had passed since Folger's charge. The lieutenant had the platoon in a large, egg-shaped protective perimeter. Using fifty-pound sacks of corn, beans, and rice from the warehouses for protection, the men built two- and three-man positions connecting the two gun pits. Cambel's lifeless body had been put in the center warehouse, out of the rain. He was laid out on top of the sacks of dried food and covered with his poncho.

Tooley, after speaking with the colonel, was not happy. Following the chain of command, he had initially made contact with the captain but, once contact was made, the colonel had broken in and told Tooley to take all future orders directly from him until they were joined by the battalion. The colonel had also informed him that the choppers were held up because of the lack of visibility and that the Saigon weather report called for heavy rain until morning. "Bottom line," the colonel had said, "we probably won't be able to get to you until morning, and then only if the weather clears. No choppers either, of course. You'll have to hold until then. Whatever happens, Lieutenant, hold that place. It's important."

Now Tooley had Leary and Carson in the west gun pit, which he had designated as his command post. Both gun pits had thatched roofs, which provided some protection from the rain. Those men not in one of the gun pits had stretched ponchos over their food bag forts.

The lieutenant was obviously about to lose it. His breathing was shallow and high; he kept rubbing his hands together and staring off at nothing. *You've got to take blame for this yourself, you lost control of the platoon. Leary followed right after him. I could throttle the whole bunch.*

I've got to stay on top of this; we can't afford any more screwups. I have no idea what's in store for us over the next many hours, but I know this—we are alone. We can't expect help from anyone until this rain lets up. What ammo and food we have now will have to last until tomorrow sometime, hopefully. And I'm alone, really alone. Sergeant Cambel was my wise old mentor, and now he's gone. God rest his soul.

It's going to be lonesome and scary without him, but I have to go on. It's more important than ever that I be the man I need to be.

Carson and Leary sat inside the gun pit, barely out of the heavy warm rain, their backs resting against the sandbags on the east side of the pit. The lieutenant was sitting with his back against the sandbags on the south side of the pit. He faced north, and Carson and Leary faced west. No one man looked directly at another. The three of them still had all of their gear on, including their helmets. Each held his rifle between his legs, pointing up at the rain-soaked, thatched roof. The smells of wet clothing, straw, canvas, and dirt rotated through their noses. They had the weary look of young men who are tired but not beaten. Their clothing and gear was wet, and Leary had brown bloodstains on the front of his shirt, suspenders, and sleeves.

"Sergeant Carson, how's Sergeant Patkins?" Tooley asked.

Carson calmly looked around Leary, who continued to stare blankly ahead, and said to Tooley, "He's still out, sir. Medic says he has a bad concussion. He needs a doctor, sir, could die anytime. He also has a broken nose and a few splinter wounds. We've already taken his and Cambel's ammo, and redistributed it. Folger needed the most. Cambel's rifle is over there by Spec 4 Nash. We threw Patkins' in the rice paddy with the gook weapons. It was ruined."

Tooley glanced over at the M-14 rifle leaned against the sandbags by Nash, who was monitoring the radio at the west side of the pit. The two machine gunners were there too, lying behind their gun and quietly looking out towards the warehouse area—listening while pretending not to. "Well, we'll medevac him with Sergeant Cambel's body in the morning—that is, if this weather clears."

"Lucky he had his rifle up in front of his face when the sniper fired. It was a miracle, really. I mean, think of the timing. Act of God—for sure."

"Yeah, well, we need more of those miracles if we're to survive. And Patkins isn't out of the woods yet, either. You gonna leave him where he is?"

"Unless you think he'll be better somewhere else. He's with the medic in the center position. They made it a little larger to accommodate him."

"Guess it's as safe as any."

Leary knew it was his turn. Tooley's voice was strained as he said, "Talk to me, Leary, what was that crap you and Folger pulled? How in the hell could you let them all run off like that? It looked like a damned panic, every-man-for-himself thing."

Except for the rain and the slight noise the radio made, the silence was total. And Leary didn't move or respond.

Instead of furthering his anger, Leary's lack of response seemed to calm Tooley as he said, "Look at it from my perspective. See what I saw from here. Cambel gets it, Patkins gets it, Folger starts firing and then you all bail out after him in an action that is totally disorganized and, well, damn it, you all disappear around the corner of the east warehouse. Then there's more shooting, a few grenades go off and, after what seems like hours, you all come running in a line around the west warehouse right toward us." Leary still did not respond; he seemed to be in a trance. "Damn you, Leary, I've got to have some answers and I hope to God that they're good. They'd better be."

Leary cleared his throat, looked at the wet ground between his feet, and then abruptly turned his head up, looking Tooley straight in the eye. He said, "Well, sir, to explain what happened, I need to tell it as it happened, the way I remember it."

"Okay."

"Well, I was just starting to realize that we were all bunched up in that gun pit, that one RPG round could wipe us out, and I think Sergeant Cambel was realizing it too, just when he was shot. I wasn't in charge until I'd realized that the platoon sergeant was dead. It probably wasn't long in real time but it seemed like it. I tried to stop the bleeding and all, just wasn't anything I could do."

"You're right. He was in charge until then and there was nothing you could do for him. Nothing."

"Anyway, when he got it, I guess it threw me into shock for a bit. It happened so fast. I believe Sergeant Cambel was about ready to give orders to spread the men out when, wham, he was driven backwards into Hart. I pulled his bandage out and applied it with pressure to his chest, but it must have hit him in the heart because he just looked strangely at me, gurgled a few times, then went limp, and I knew he was dead. Then I and several others started yelling for everyone to get as far down in that pit as far as possible. Getting out of the protection of that pit was unthinkable. Where would we go? We weren't even sure at first where the shot had come from. I mean we're talking seconds here, not minutes."

"Sure. Go on."

"Give me a minute. I have to think. I have to replay it in my mind. Well, then we all became desperate to make the walls higher around the pit. I was consumed with getting that done and gave no thought to anything else. Then, some of the men started hollering and I turned to see Sergeant Patkins coming over towards us. We all tried to warn him but the sniper hit him. Of course, from where we were, we thought he was dead."

Tooley nodded as Carson said, "Yeah, so did we."

"I didn't know it then, but all this time Folger had been watching the jungle for movement. I guess he'd counted on the sniper not being able to pass up Patkins as a target. He's a cool one. Smart too." Tooley and Carson both nodded their heads in agreement. "Anyway, when the sniper fired, Folger fired at smoke and movement. He fired in brackets of four, at the movement and around it. We could all see the bushes move as the sniper fell. I thought that would be the end of it, but then Folger just hopped over the sandbags and took off. We had to go with him. We couldn't let him go out there alone. And he was going—hell, he was gone. So we all went except for the machine gunners. I told them to cover us." Then, relieved, Leary looked back down at the green muddy water forming a puddle around his boots and took a deep breath of the wet air.

"Okay, I commend Folger for shooting the sniper but he had no orders to go charging off across that damn clearing," Tooley said. "We can't just have everyone do what they want when they want." He swung his arm out in an angry sweeping gesture at nothing. "Folger just shoots, then jumps over the wall, and takes off. Then the rest of you take off right behind him. Now that's what I recall. That's what I saw. You all looked like a bunch of schoolchildren let out for recess. I had no idea what you were doing or why."

Leary exhaled noisily. He held out a hand to stop the lieutenant as he said, "Lieutenant, let's get real. In the first place, we shouldn't have been bunched up in that hole. Second, we were sitting ducks for any fire from the jungle, and third, we needed to check out the back of the warehouse area. That should've been one of the first things we did when we got over here. You should've had the rest of the platoon check it out just as soon as they crossed the paddy." Now, the lieutenant's face was dark purple with rage, but Leary still held him off with his halting hand. Consumed with his own rising anger, Leary forced his breath in and out before rasping, "Anyway, when we got around behind the northeast warehouse, we saw two more Vietnamese soldiers run out the back of what looked like their sleeping and cooking quarters. They were heading for a road-sized trail going due north, behind this complex. One had a carbine and the other an AK-47, but at first they didn't make any attempt to fire at us. If they'd held their position and fired, they could've gotten a couple of us, but they just ran towards that road."

"And then?" Tooley asked. His face was now bright red, the rage appearing to subside.

"Well, then we all tried firing on the run, but we were all missing, so we stopped and fired. Even then, we were all out of breath and were still missing. Finally, when they were almost to the cover of the jungle, we started hitting them—most of us, anyway. When it was all over, we'd shot them up pretty good. They're both dead. One fell right on top of the other." Leary stopped, shook his head to clear it, and then turned back toward the front and lowered it. It was obvious he was through.

It was silent in the pit for a full minute. Every man was left with his own thoughts and the wet smells. When Tooley spoke, his questions were rushed and demanding. Everyone was tired of playing soldier and just wanted some peace, and his voice irritated everyone in the pit, even those who were not involved in the debriefings. "Where was Folger and what were those grenades we heard? What is your analysis of that area and our situation? How many men were likely housed in that barracks? Damn it, Leary we need more information. Let's have it. We may not have much time."

Leary looked up, tired and weary, and said, "You'll have to ask specific questions one at a time, Lieutenant. I'm through reporting."

Swearing under his breath, Tooley said, "Okay, all right, start with the three enemy. Are you sure they were dead, and did you have to kill them?"

"Ha," Leary exclaimed in disgust, "I'm damn sure of it. Dead, you bet. Now, I'll admit that Folger gave the sniper a couple more when he got to him, even though he was obviously dead. But I wouldn't fault him on that. If the man had been alive, we would have finished him after what he did to the platoon sergeant—well, to hell with him. But as for those other two, well, even if we'd had the inclination to, which none of us had, they didn't give us a chance to ask. Lieutenant, there was no time for analyzing and asking questions. It was move and kill and try to stay alive. This what-if stuff we're doing now is only because we have time to waste."

Tooley's anger shot off the charts immediately, but he was too tired to maintain the rage Leary's lack of respect called for and was only left with half-hearted sarcasm as he said, "Sergeant Leary, I hope I don't trouble you with my questions, I sure wouldn't want to put you out or anything."

Leary's coldly detached response was immediate. "No, sir, not put out. Tired, wet, worried, pissed off, yes. I'm doing the best that I can. The facts are the facts. I call them like I see them. I run after them like I feel I have to. I shoot them when and how I can. After I shoot them, sir, I prefer that they be dead." He stopped for a few seconds, obviously dealing with spent anger of his own, and continued clearly and steadily. "You can jump my ass or do whatever is in your power to do to me, Lieutenant, we did right today and I won't apologize for it, no matter what you do or say to me."

The only noise for the next two minutes came from the dripping of the rain off the thatched roof and the radio's soothing static. Tooley realized that he was spiritually exhausted and that his anger had dissolved. He just didn't have the energy for it anymore. *Leary's had it. Hell, I've had it too. We've all had it, and there's no relief in sight. He's told all he knows. He doesn't have the information I want. He can't tell me if my platoon will survive until help gets here. That's what I need to know, and that will only be told by time. We need to rest when we can. He's right about Cambel, too. They shouldn't have killed him. He was a good old soldier. I'm going to miss him, feel very alone without him. Now I'm really in charge and don't have that experienced old warhorse to guide me any more.*

"You're right, Sergeant Leary, we're all tired and weary, you and your men did a good job, tell them so. I'm proud of all of you. Just tell me one more thing, if you will. What do you think about our situation here, about how many were housed here? We need to make plans."

Leary stared at the muddy water around his boots and spoke. "I would guess, judging from the hammocks hanging in the hooch, that there were ten men housed here. Maybe five soldiers and five workers, or maybe all ten were soldier-workers, I don't know for sure. If the sniper was one of them, then we killed seven of them, so three could be out there in the jungle waiting for another good shot. Or, they could've gone for help and there could be a large number of men ready to attack as we speak. I do think we're deep in it. It's on the way. How can it not be?"

Up to this time, Carson hadn't said much. A well-balanced black man who had found some equality in the army, it was his belief that staying on task while maintaining balance was one of the highest attributes of a strong man. He knew, now more than at any other time in his life, that the platoon needed him to stay purposefully balanced. *The values are changing. From now on this group, a recently formed family, really, will not attempt to apply the standards of the United States in making their decisions. The rules of conduct in this war will be made over here. It's more than a little sad that, to survive over here, we'll have to become like our enemy. We are simply two forces*

trying to kill each other in the jungle. I'll do the best that I can, Lord
with your help, to try and not let these young ones go too far over the
edge. I'll make every effort to try and help them keep the good in them
alive. At least a seed, something they can re-grow, should they survive.

It was quiet again for another minute. Everyone seemed to be
lost in their own thoughts, then Carson looked past Leary to the
lieutenant and said, "Sir, when do you, in your best estimate, expect
the battalion? I know that is dependent upon the weather, how close
they are now, and probably a couple of other factors. Just your best
guess, something to tell the men."

Tooley spoke quietly, but firmly, "Sergeant Carson, what I'm
going to say is a blind guess, but I will say that the battalion should
reinforce us by ten o'clock in the morning. That's the best we can
hope for. I think that's a safe guess and it'll give the men a time to
hold out for and yet they must know that we have to take care of
ourselves."

"You know, sir," Leary said without looking up, "the food in this
warehouse complex all came from the United States of America.
The food of our enemy came from our own people. The symbol on
those bags of food is the American Care symbol. Two hands shaking
over a flag, our American flag. Someone from our home is feeding
our enemy."

Radio operator Nash blurted out, "Sir, couldn't the Vietcong
have stolen the food?"

"I wish," Tooley said, "but there are tons and tons of food
here, too much to steal and cart off. It would have taken days,
even with trucks, to bring all this food here. This much food must
support thousands of troops. There's a large bunch of men out here
somewhere, and they can't be too happy about us taking their food."
He paused and rubbed his chin with his hand. He was calm now.
"Gentlemen, I would say that we are in it up to our necks."

"Wouldn't that be something?" Nash said. "Get wiped out fighting
over a boatload of food that was supplied by our own country."

As they stood to return to their positions, Leary said hesitantly,
"Oh, sir, there's a hog in a pen back there. The men were wondering
if we could kill it, cook it, and eat it."

Tooley responded, "For God's sake, not now, Leary. Let's just
stay in our positions and try to stay alive."

"Okay, sir. I just said I'd ask."

15

RENEE PATKINS

It was a small two-bedroom duplex among many rows of duplexes that made up family housing at Fort Riley, Kansas. All were simple red brick dwellings with hot water heat, window air-conditioning, and hardwood floors. They were very well maintained. Once inside the front door of the Patkins' residence, the bland conformity ended, and it was clear from the early 1960s decor and cleanliness that this home belonged to a dedicated housewife.

Renee Patkins was sitting at her kitchen table having coffee with her lifelong friend, Marge. They were raised in Fort Riley, Kansas, where Renee's father and mother owned the local hardware store.

"So how you doing, Renee? How's Peter doing in Vietnam? Any word?"

"Not much, really. He writes when he can, but it's not a good place for him."

"Yes, he's a nice quiet sort of man to be going off to war. Of course, he is a soldier and all, but you know he's kind of timid, even though he's a sergeant."

"Oh, he's a good sergeant. But you're right about him and the war thing. He's a good peacetime sergeant, good with logistics and all. Pretty good with the men too, but just not very aggressive. Which is just the way I like him. He's so kind to the girls and me."

"Yeah, I don't know how you two would have ever gotten together if it hadn't been for me."

"Yes, I have you to thank for that. And when we saw him at the skating rink, at first I thought he was interested in you."

"Of course I could see right away that he had eyes for you. Kind of funny, though, how your dad would let you go to the skating rink, thinking that no soldiers would go there."

"Funny how life can be, turns out he was right. Only a man like my Peter would go to the skating rink."

"Well, even then I saw his interest in you, and I had to make him sit with us. Then I found an excuse to get out of there, and somehow you two managed to talk and eventually even get married and have two beautiful girls."

"Yes, we were both pretty shy, which, thankfully, you weren't."

"Yeah, no one has ever accused me of being shy."

"Good thing, too. For us."

"Of course it still amazes me how reserved Peter is. Scared almost."

"Yes, he's a gentle man. Under-confident, really. His father, whom you don't want to ever meet, is a horrible, verbally abusive man. He's badgered Peter all of his life. And he still does. Peter can never do or say anything to him that doesn't get a verbal put-down."

"That bad, huh? What about his mother, does she put up with that crap?"

"Oh yeah, she gets it, too. She's a scared little rabbit around him. I tell you, Marge, he's criticized everything Peter does and has done all of his life. I won't let him around the girls. He still calls Peter stupid and dumb. He's a terrible man and Peter seems helpless to do anything about it. I've actually seen him cringe before his father's verbal bashings."

"How did he ever get promoted to sergeant with that shyness?"

"Well, like I said, he's really good with the organization and such. The sergeant stripes seem to give him courage, too. Them being on his sleeves seem to remind him he has some worth. I've seen him look at them many times and could tell wearing means a lot to him."

"Yeah, seems like I hardly ever see him without his uniform on."

"I've wondered how he feels over there where they don't wear any stripes."

"Did you sew them on his pajamas?" They both laughed.

"No, of course not. You think I should."

"Couldn't hurt. But how are the girls doing with his being gone?"

"Oh, they miss him, but they believe he'll be back and they are such good little girls."

"Yeah, they seem to be quite content to color there in the living room."

Then the doorbell rang. Renee jumped, and Marge wondered why she should be so startled by the doorbell.

"I'll get it, girls," Renee said as she got up and headed to the door.

When she opened the door, her heart seized as she recognized the uniform of the Western Union delivery boy.

"Is this the Cambel residence?"

Renee's heart released its grip on her chest as she said, "No, this is the Patkins residence. Mrs. Cambel lives next door, to the south."

"Mrs. Patkins, is there another adult in the house with you at this time?"

"Yes, my friend Marge, why?"

"I'm sorry, Mrs. Patkins, I have a telegram for you, too."

16

KILLING THE MESSENGER

A few nights later, Jimmy was parked at the drive-in. He had just ordered a hamburger, fries, and a chocolate shake. He was hoping that Jen would bring it out. He liked her and, for weeks, he had been working up his courage to ask her out, but he doubted he would find the nerve today.

He was feeling sick to his stomach. Before placing his order, he thought it might be the fumes from the valve cover leak on his '53 Chevy, that and the smell of hamburgers, mixed with the occasional whiff of garbage from the full cans at the back of the drive-in.

He knew what it was. It had started after he drove by Mrs. Cambel's house this afternoon while making his deliveries. She was moving out and, as he drove by more slowly than he needed to, he had seen her directing the movers and crying. Other women were there too—trying to comfort her. They were all crying. He didn't even know her—he wasn't supposed to know. He had his instruction in the window at the top of the envelope, and her instructions had said: "MRS BETTY MAY CAMBEL, REPORT DELIVERY DON'T PHONE (DON'T DELIVER BETWEEN HRS OF 10:00 PM AND 600AM). He wasn't to read any further. But he didn't have to. He knew that, when it started like that, it was never good news. Not at Fort Riley, Kansas. A short time later, Mrs. Cambel was moving off the Fort. The sudden cruelty of it is what really turned his stomach. Was that how the Army took care of its own?

And now the women looked at him, the fear and scorn in their eyes as he descended on their camp like the Angel of Death. He thought to himself, *Is this what the Grim Reaper feels like? Just a kid with a summer job?* That's how the Fort saw him. Circling slowly in his '53 Chevy, taking the weak and the unlucky and destroying their lives. It didn't matter to them that he was just the messenger. It didn't matter a goddamn.

Under normal circumstances, Jimmy could eat a side of beef at one sitting. Now he stared at his food, his only comfort the girl who brought it to him. She smiled at him the way a girl does who wants to be asked out and he was as surprised as she was when he did.

17

DEATH

Folger was alone, surrounded by the food bag walls they had built from the warehouse they captured. It was constructed four feet from the east gun pit. Though it was futile and he knew it, he had stretched their ponchos over the bags in an effort to keep the rain out. The heavy rain beat its way through every crack and crevice in and around the ponchos. Keeping dry was just not possible. He had considered not covering the hole at all but the flimsy shield made the pit feel safer, even though it was only an illusion. More unsettling, perhaps, was the mud forming around him. It was getting deeper, and it just didn't seem right to let it freely cover his boots and legs.

Leary came back an hour before dark and shared with Folger most of his conversation with the lieutenant and Carson. He told Folger that he hadn't really gotten an ass-chewing, though the lieutenant had not been happy about their taking off. And that, regardless of what anyone else thought, Leary believed Folger's action was the right thing to do.

"I appreciate that, Sergeant Leary, but I was out of line. I knew our orders were to defend and protect—nothing else."

"I trust you, Folger. I respect you like no one else, and I'd like to ask you some questions. You don't have to answer and, if you don't, I won't ever ask them again."

"Fair enough, Sergeant Leary, I trust and like you miles more than anyone else in this world. Ask away. I warn you, though, I might shut down at any time. It's just the way I am."

"Sure. Have you always been this way? Don't you have loved ones back home? I mean, you don't seem to care about anything, not even life."

"Well, I care. I'm just very damn careful about what I let myself care about. I won't any longer just care about someone, or something, just because it's said I should."

"What about your family? You had one, or have one, don't you?"

"Well, they think I do. I lost my mother to breast cancer my senior year in high school and then only after years of operations, chemo, then more operations and more chemo until she wasted away and died without hope."

"I'm sorry to hear that. Must have been rough."

"Yeah, I hoped with her for the first couple of years, and then I just watched her die. 'I think we got it all this time, Mrs. Folger,' 'Oh, I'm so sorry the cancer has recurred. I'm sure if we remove the other breast and treat with chemo we've got an excellent chance of getting it all,' the doctors said. She was just a shell of her old self then."

"I'm lucky, I guess. My mother, father, brothers, and sisters are all healthy, and the only death I've really experienced is over here."

"Well, the goddamn doctors just milked her for insurance money and then she died. They just harvested money off her body like a farm animal, and then after she died they asked my father if he would donate her body to science so they could get the last value out of her. I stopped that, though—said I'd kill anyone who even suggested anything but cremation, which was her wish."

"I expect that stopped the donation, right?"

"Yeah, that stopped everyone cold. I shouldn't have had to threaten like that. I was young then."

"Sure, what was that, last year?" Leary said ironically.

"A little over a year—seems like twenty years, though."

"I know what you mean. What about your father? Was he around then?"

"Oh, the bastard is still around, still living in the same town, the same house, but with a different woman. Married her right after my mother's funeral."

"Did he know her long, you know, before your mother died?"

"Yep, she was my girlfriend's mother."

"Christ, Folger, what a shit deal."

"Yeah, it was bad. My girl knew about it, too. I'd caught them in her house when I went over to get her a sweater. Caught 'em in the act and then my girl denied that she knew, but I could tell by the look on her face that she knew."

"What happened then?"

"Well, Mom died, I went to the funeral, finished high school, joined the army right after graduation, and here I am."

"How did you leave it with them?"

"Never spoke to any of them again. Still haven't. They've tried, but what's left? Everyone I love and cared about either betrayed me or died. So here I am."

"Out of the frying pan and into the fire."

"No, this is the only true place. It's the only place where truth and reality must be the same. You always know where you stand here."

"How's that?"

"Well, everyone over here with us had to prove who he is. You can't bullshit over here. You will be tested constantly concerning your willingness to be honest and stand by your beliefs. For example, take Hart. Hart cannot be trusted, not even a little bit. Hart is so concerned about himself that he cannot force himself to even be here with the rest of us, much less try and help us live. Sanchez now, well, he's grown over here and has proven himself to be a worthwhile man. He isn't overly aggressive, but he will be there when you need him. The captain can be depended upon to do whatever is necessary to further his career. He's dependable in that. The lieutenant will give his life for his men and worries so much about us that he will probably get himself killed trying to protect us. Cambel was a true, unselfish, human being, and now he is truly dead. Patkins cannot be depended on for fighting but he's good at heating water and building a fire."

"Well, I can't argue with that, Folger, but aren't people real back home, too?"

"You never know. They rarely have to stand up under hardship so one can truly see who they are. Back there, you're supposed to believe they love you and will stand by you just because they are your relatives or because they say they will. Try and ask someone back home to prove their concern for you by risking his life for you and see what happens."

"You can't ask loved ones to risk their lives to prove themselves to you. I mean it just wouldn't work."

"Oh, I agree. Thus, this is the only truly real, no bullshit place. That's why it's so great."

"I guess I really can't argue with any of that. Gives cause for thought, though."

⌘

The dawn was just breaking through. Earlier in the night, Leary and Folger had made attempts to keep their shallow hole dry. Despite bailing with their steel helmets, the watery mud always ran back in. Later, after mucking for a while, they quit, surrendering to the rain's persistent power, letting it thoroughly soak their equipment, clothing, and bodies. Fortunately, the rain was warm.

Leary was sleeping as Folger watched the sun slowly illuminate the ground in front of him. He was anxious. He wanted the sun to shine on the jungle wall where the sniper had been yesterday. It didn't feel right to him. Something was wrong over there. Earlier, he thought he'd heard a rustling noise from that black and threatening wall. But, with the rain hitting his helmet and poncho, he couldn't be sure. Now, because of its angle, the sun was doing a good job of lighting up their position, but not the jungle wall, not yet. *Damn you, sun; come on up.*

Easy, Folger, he assured himself. *Stay calm.* He didn't move but watched vigilantly, with the same restrained impatience one has for an old person driving slowly in traffic. The sun's rays moved slowly rose slowly towards the dark jungle. *Just watch the wall. It will be lit up soon and if there is trouble you need to be ready. Of course, if they're there, you need to be ready to open up.*

Folger became slightly hypnotized as he watched the dark shadow creep towards the jungle. In his benumbed state, he wondered momentarily how long he had been looking at it before really seeing it. He was so pleasantly tired and relaxed, he regretted having to move and had trouble seeing the reason for doing so. *It feels so good here, just lying here.* The sun shining on the wet grass sprinkled thousands of sparkling diamonds about. It was brilliant but calming. *It's too bad that this beauty has to be mixed with that ugly reality moving into positions there in the jungle. But there they are, rude little bastards.*

Still, Folger's mind resisted, not wanting to accept what his eyes were seeing. He felt no desire to take action. His mind was not acting normally—self-preservation, usually so strong in him, seemed to be shut off. *This must be how a mouse feels when mesmerized by a snake which is about to kill it. It's not so bad. Not bad at all. I think I would rather look at the diamonds than those "gooks."*

Suddenly his body jerked violently, and a strong voice within him commanded, *Get with it. Mr. Death is trying to lure you in.*

Reality is there; it needs to be dealt with. Though it seemed like much longer, Folger had only been stunned for a few seconds. *Christ, they must have been visible for a while. How long? Seconds, minutes, what? How the hell come you're not shooting? Mr. Know-It-All, you're acting just like Hart.* That did it.

Hello, Mr. Death, I see you brought some gooks with you. His mind cleared fast, and he could now easily discern rifle barrels pointing at him from the jungle wall. More became visible as his eyes believed they were there. It wasn't a wall of rifles, fortunately, not like that picture he'd seen of the Battle of Bunker Hill. No, not that many, but a lot, and more appearing all the time.

The spell was fully broken, and the Folger he had come to love and feel good about was back. The slow and sneaky movement of the Vietnamese angered him. *Sneaky little bastards. Well, two can play . . .*

He moved slowly too, not wanting to alert them until he had a chance to get ready. They were pointing their rifles at him, strange little men shifting and settling in an effort to get a better aim. Behind each rifle he could make out part of a face. Just one eye, one side of a face. He knew the other side of the face was pressed against the rifle stock, and the other eye was looking through the sights-lining up to shoot him. *Why don't they fire? Why haven't they fired before now? Dumb bastards were waiting for someone to give the order. These are men, but they look like boys dressed in black pajamas. Little VCs are doing some work for Mr. Death. Well, Mr. Death doesn't care-he will let anyone die.*

"The dumb bastards must have just gotten here," he said as he snapped the safety off. "Get ready, God, I'm sending you some—as many as I can." It was more the harsh noise Folger made when he pushed off the safety of his AR-14 rather than his words that brought Leary to consciousness.

Folger, cool as he was, quickly looked for the best targets. His search led him to notice the three men kneeling just behind the prone men with rifles. "Ha," he laughed quietly. "You dumb bastards in the rear, all bunched up like that, you must be the ones in charge. You first then."

His firing was controlled, skilled, and precise as he manipulated the three-round bursts out of his weapon. He was an artist perfecting his art.

Leary felt as if he were swimming, struggling against the current while desperately trying to get back to his body. He had been sound asleep, had been somewhere else, a better place. As he forced himself back to full consciousness, his startled eyes opened, frantically searching for the danger. He commanded his half-functioning ears and mind to interpret Folger's mumbling words. He ordered his hands and arms to ready his rifle as he begged his bloodless legs and torso to position his body as a firing platform.

The time lapse from Folger's safety snapping off to Leary's full consciousness could have been measured in heartbeats, but his frenzy made it seem like forever. His eyes hurt, struggling with the light and he rushed to clear his vision, he felt the strain would surely damage his eyes. And the explosions made by Folger's weapon, especially under the drooping poncho, made his ears scream with pain.

Leary forced his reluctant body to an angle from which he could fire next to Folger. Both men were small targets behind the bags of food they had stacked around them. As he settled into a good firing position, his eyes were able to see one of Folger's targets do a spin and flip to his right. The small NCO's shoulder went first as the bullet tore through it, followed by his twisting legs and torso. The man lying in front of the NCO dropped his rifle, too. His contorted face was clearly visible now as he reached back with both hands grabbing his buttocks and began rocking back and forth on his stomach. It looked strange to Leary, almost like he'd stopped to exercise. The rocking ended with Folger's second burst, which blew his head apart. Leary was seeking a target of his own when all hell broke loose. It was their turn.

Damn, Leary thought as he ducked, *are they only shooting at us? Don't they see the other positions? What are the rest of our men waiting for? Are they all sleeping? Was Folger the only one awake? The sons of bitches better start returning fire, and soon. Where in the hell is that damn machine gun? They've got the best location and they haven't even started firing yet.* He rose back up and fired. Everything was on automatic, and he was losing awareness of his actions. A bullet creased the top of his helmet, which he couldn't remember putting on, causing him to duck down and compress himself into their position farther than he would have thought possible. The enemy fire was now relentless.

Smokeless power, my ass, it looks like the Fourth of July at the park, he thought as he struggled to scrunch himself ever deeper into their small fort constructed from bags of food. As the dried corn spilled out of the top of the bags and rained down on Leary, he realized that they wouldn't have protection for long. Folger was down now too, and they could feel the bullets penetrating deep into the dried corn and beans. The dried food wasn't like sand. It was much lighter and oilier. The acrid smell of burned corn and bean dust assaulted Leary's nostrils. With every bullet hole, more food poured out, deflating their protection like the hole in a rubber raft. How long could they last before all their safety drained out on the ground? They were shoved down face to face as a bullet coursed its way through one of the bags, just missing Leary's shoulder. They both scooted closer and deeper, trying to make themselves smaller.

They were there cheek to cheek and Leary thought, *Christ, this is a dumb time to notice how bad Folger's breath is. We're dying here, we'd better do something and fast. At this rate, it won't be long before the bags are just empty sacks lying in front of us. We'll be easy targets, then dead easy targets. It's a good thing we didn't take the lazy way out. That extra row of bags we put down in front may just save our lives. Still, one bullet did get through. Hell, it's just a matter of time. We've got to get active. Got to return fire.* Determination and anger rose in his mind. *I'm not just going to lie here and die. Not me, screw 'em, Charlie Cong has to pay for my life. Where the hell is that machine gun? They have real sandbags. Fire, you bastards.*

Then the opportunity arose, but they weren't conscious of it. The now-dead Cambel had trained it into them. "We are going to do this until we all do it automatically. That means, for you slower ones, that we can do it without thinking. I don't care if we do it until we puke, we'll all learn it, fire and maneuver and fire and load. When A Team moves, B Team fires at the enemy. When B Team moves, A Team fires at the enemy. Got it? Good. Remember we take turns. Now when defending a position, staging an ambush, or fighting in goddamn general, one man fires and one man loads. It worked during the Revolutionary War and it will work now. So once you get the offensive, be smart, use teamwork, and keep the offensive. For God's sake, don't everyone run out of ammo at the same time. Furthermore, if ambushed, identify your enemy's load and fire patterns, or his lack of them. If they are foolish enough to all run out of ammo at the same time then, that's when you take the offensive away from them. So, when he stops to reload, then you start killing him. Remember, a battle is always fire and load, fire and load. Now we begin to practice." And they did, over and over again, until they had developed an unconscious ability to discover the lull in an enemy's firing. Any team that ran out of ammo at the same time was severely chastised by Cambel. "You must always know how much ammo you have expended and how much your supporting team has left." Now his diligent training would save their lives.

It wasn't long before Leary, Folger, and most of the rest of the platoon recognized their opportunity. It didn't take any thinking. It was a trained reflex in the heat of a serious game. The enemy did not have a Cambel and had started running out of ammo at about the same time. Though some of their weapons held more bullets than others, they had no obvious fire and reload training—their automatic rifles could go through a magazine as quickly as the others could fire their bolt-action rifles.

As the enemy's firing came to a near stop, like popcorn being nearly done, the men of the Second Platoon came up out of their small deflating forts and opened fire.

First Leary fired off his twenty; then Folger began his twenty while Leary ducked and reloaded. Other positions did the same. It was like Cambel commanding them from the grave, dead but still effective. Then the machine gun crew kicked in, a little late by Leary's thinking. Their guns' metallic sound continuously hammered out destruction. Leaves and small branches fell in and around the enemy soldiers. From their launchers, the grenades popped, then burst, at the jungle's edge. Some of the small men kicked, jumped, and died while trying to reload. Others tried desperately to back into the jungle, hoping to escape the murderous American fire. A few tried to play dead—a fruitless effort because the heavy metal-covered bullets had no mercy as they tore through bodies and vegetation without prejudice. *Thank you, Sergeant Cambel,* Carson thought as he clicked a fresh magazine into his rifle, *may God rest your soul.*

By the time the Second Platoon felt they could quit firing, those Vietnamese who hadn't been hit had backed into the cover of the jungle, leaving many of their comrades bleeding, dying, and dead in the blood-soaked grass.

There were a quiet few moments. No screaming from the platoon for the medic, although a few men had received flesh wounds. No talking, no commands, just a group of American fathers, husbands, and sons feeling glad to be alive as they watched a few of their wounded enemy trying to crawl away. They watched them over the smoking barrels of weapons, as the hot metal burned off abundant gun oil. The whole battle had lasted only a few minutes but it seemed like a life times. It was a noticeable and welcome pause.

"Shit," Leary said as he laid out his two remaining full magazines, "the little bastards are back. I see movement through the foliage, down that road."

"Yeah," Folger took a long drag on his cigarette. "Well, I see movement on the other side of the paddy, too. Looks like they're getting ready to hit us from both sides. I'm about out of ammo, too. I'm going to crawl over to the pit and take Hart's. No doubt he still has all of his."

18

MISSING IN ACTION

"**C**olonel, why don't they just blow this whole warehouse complex up?" Captain Haps asked.

"We couldn't be sure of destroying it all, and we don't want any left for the enemy," the colonel replied. "The men have to get this done and soon. The whole battalion will be working on it, not just your men. Your Second Platoon can be exempt from the manual labor; they'll act as guards. God knows they deserve a rest."

"Yes, sir, it'll be done, but two days, sir, I don't know. A fresh, peacetime, work party of battalion size might be able to do it in two days. But they're not a normal bunch of soldiers anymore. The men resent having to fight the war and do manual labor, too. They have no incentive to get it done. Threats don't work anymore. They have no privileges that can be taken away and nothing to look forward to when they get done. Most of them can't see how their life can get any worse."

"You know, Captain, you're a good officer, a West Point graduate. I'm not worried about the men, but I'm beginning to worry about you. You've never been anything but go get 'em, and now you talk this way. I think the men, if they are suffering lack of morale as you say, are getting it from you. They're reading you, Captain, and you're failing them. Get your attitude in order and get this damn food destroyed. Understand, Captain?"

"Yes, sir."

"Your men enjoying the hog?"

"Yes, sir, it was good of you to give it to them."

"Well, they deserved it and, besides, it was crazy anyway."

131

"Yes, sir, guess it was all the shooting, killing, and all, but it was definitely nuts. Running back and forth between the warehouses over and over again without stopping."

"Yeah, I'm surprised it didn't run itself to death, but the screaming it made, I was tempted to shoot it myself."

"Yes, sir, I didn't know a hog could sound so much like a human screaming."

"Maybe like a human, although that might be a matter of opinion, but I'll give you this, it was loud, distracting, and irritating. How'd it taste, Captain? I hope it tasted better than it sounded or looked. It sure smelled good when it was cooking."

"Didn't you have any, Colonel?"

"No, there wasn't nearly enough to go around, I limited its ownership to your platoon as a reward for taking this place and thought I shouldn't have any, either. I hope the shit doesn't poison them. Are they cooking it thoroughly?"

"Seem to be, sir. Two of the men in the platoon are farm boys and they took right to it. Made a pit, spit, scrubbed the hog down, burned the hairs off of it, and started roasting it. It's got the rest of the men mad at them, though."

"Yeah, same old story. They can't have any so they're jealous. It's a human weakness. It's a lesson for you, Captain. I knew it would cause trouble for them, but they wanted it and they'll have to deal with the anger."

"Yes, sir, the men haven't had any fresh meat since they've been here. So that makes it a little worse."

"Fresh meat is hard and expensive to get and keep over here. We get it in the convoys of course, but by the time they get back it's usually eaten up or spoiled. Not much we can do about it in these times. In the future, though, it'll be better. If there's nothing else, Captain, that'll be all."

"No, sir."

"Good. Then go see to your men. Push the men all you can. I estimated two days to destroy all of this food, and we've been at it four days now."

"Yes, sir, I know, but each bag weighs fifty pounds, the bags are dusty, and they cover the men with the dust."

"Well, Captain, I'm aware that it's a hard job. I also know that the American Care symbol on each bag doesn't make the men happy. I don't know how they got all that food from our country. Hell, I don't even know how they got it here, must be a shipload of it."

"Yes, sir, I think the men would have mutinied if they had anywhere to go."

"Yes, yes, I know all of that. It's a hundred degrees, the dust off it gets in their eyes and noses, they're cranky and disheartened, but that's where you come in, Captain, you and all of the other company commanders. You and your fellow officers have had a lot of money spent on you so you can handle your men in any and all conditions. You just need to get out there and see to it. Is that clear?"

"Yes, sir, it is."

The men were tired, sore, and sweaty, and knew that they could be dropped at any moment by rifle fire from the jungle around them. Some were so fatigued that death and wounding were starting to seem like viable options, but waiting for it to happen stripped their nerves raw.

By the fifth and final day at the warehouse, the whole battalion had developed a new and ugly attitude towards life. The Second Platoon, though down in strength by a third of its original number and filthy of body and mean in temperament, was physically better off. They'd been given the hog to eat, a day of rest, and then assigned to guard the battalion, which allowed them to stay in the shade and exempted them from the heavy labor. With every step the soldiers took to carry the bags into the rice paddy and then throw them into the water, their rage at the Second Platoon's barbecued hog and day of rest increased. But the Second Platoon ignored them.

It was little consolation to the workers that the water would destroy their enemy's food and, by the time they were done, the large rice paddy was almost completely full of soaked food bags. Sore, blistered, and exhausted, the men's irritation heightened because no one seemed to know where they were going next. Usually, the enlisted man's rumor mill was fast and accurate, but now it didn't seem to be working at all. All it would tell them was that no one below the rank of captain knew where they were going or what would be expected of them once they got there. They had been told that it was a very urgent and important mission, nothing more. These were shallow words to the weary men.

"The morale is bad, Colonel, the men want to know, and maybe it would help," the commander of A Company said, "and who would they tell?"

"Captain, the answer is still no. One of them might slip and say something on the radio. The enemy monitors it, you know. Better that they are left in the dark until we get there. It has to be that way."

"We're losing our power over the men," Haps said. "They used to jump when we showed up. They would listen intently to our every word and obey it without hesitation. Now they give us hard looks or ignore us altogether or, worse yet, after we give them an order, they look to their platoon leader or NCO to see if they should obey us."

"Captain Haps," the colonel said, "the time has come when we have to be leaders. You can only push a man when he has something to lose by not obeying you. These men have nothing to lose. They've been in the shit since they got here. You officers need to be sure you do your best to make the risky duty fair, evenly dealt out. If you don't, it will affect the whole company. They need to know that we, as their leaders, are fair and out front, now more than ever."

"Yes, sir."

At 0900 on the morning of the fifth day at the food fort, the choppers came. Moving like decrepit old men, the Sixteenth Infantry boarded the choppers and headed northeast, thirty miles to the rubber tree plantation of Phu Duc.

The Phu Duc plantation, although not occupied by its French owners, reeked of opulence. As they flew in to land on the asphalt runway, which was long enough to accommodate a small jet, the wealth was clearly visible. After the choppers lifted off, the clean smell of fresh flowers and cut grass floated in on a light breeze. The main house was large and had several fine outbuildings, including a gymnasium.

Downwind and mostly hidden by bamboo bushes stood a village with the standard Vietnamese dwellings of mud and straw walls with thatched roofs. The plantation was as clean and freshly dusted as if it were occupied. The underbrush was cleared away, and the rows of trees looked healthy and productive. Clearly, it was a working plantation that still harvested rubber and, though many Vietnamese were in and around the village, none seemed to be working. Most intently watched the landing, unloading, and dispersing of the Americans troops.

When the landing was complete, a group of Vietnamese approached the Americans' perimeter, asking to see the colonel. The head man, they told him, was the mayor of the village as well as the chief caretaker of the plantation. He and most of the people in the village were salaried by the plantation's absentee French owners to see that the rubber was harvested and the place properly maintained.

There were also forty South Vietnamese soldiers on duty. These boyish-looking soldiers with their ill-fitting American uniforms and Korean War vintage American weapons had been trained by the South Vietnamese Army and appeared to have little structure or discipline. They were housed, fed, and supported by the village. They contrasted drastically with the, dirty, smelly, mean-eyed American giants who had just landed. "Their responsibility," the mayor said through the colonel's interpreter, "is to keep the plantation out of the hands of the Communists. For the most part, they are homeboys in that they come from this village or other nearby villages. Their fathers, mothers, and grandparents have built this plantation. They know little else."

The colonel's military mind automatically appraised the situation. *They are small, clean, calmly content, and only slightly curious. Seem lazy or low on energy. Don't act like they're in a war. Don't seem to be concerned at all. The mayor definitely acts like he's in charge. He smiles a lot and does a lot of pointing as he speaks to the interpreter—I think most of it's for my benefit.*

The Second Platoon was in the grassy shade just east of the runway. It was almost noon and some of the men were eating C-rations. Others were smoking and talking, but all were wary and only their exhaustion made them seem relaxed. Leary and Carson were under the shade of a large old tree. Leary was cleaning his teeth with a straw pulled from the grass, and Carson's measured words were barely audible. Just talking, really, speaking slowly, coherently, sort of talking to himself, with the unspoken understanding that Leary could join in, comment, or keep quiet, as he wished.

"Looks like the French had it made here." He paused for a second and Leary didn't respond. "Fancy shacks, if the insides are anything like the outsides and I hear they are. Some of the men of B Company went through the place—it's in their part of the perimeter. They said the mayor raised hell with the colonel about it, and he told them to stay out of the buildings. But they are plush." Leary, who was sitting on the grass with his back against the large oak tree, shrugged noncommittally.

Satisfied, Carson faced the front again. He lay on his stomach, arching his back with his chest on his pack for support, trying to take some of the pain out of his aching back. His movement caused the sweat rolling off his head to change direction and run into his eyes, stinging them, but the muscles of his back hurt so much that he didn't care. "These fancy-ass plantations," Carson said reflectively, "remind me of the plantations back home in Virginia."

Leary grunted an affirmative answer, while thinking, *It's a good thing I like you, Carson, or I wouldn't bother to listen. You're going to say something that will make me think and I don't have the energy, or the desire, for thinking. But okay, you want me to respond? I'll bite.* "How so, Sarge? I've never been to Virginia but from the pictures it seemed like rolling green hills with an occasional white mansion with pillars and a large circular driveway."

Carson repeated his back-arching exercise and groaned from the effort before saying, "It's the richness of a place like this that tells the tale. A plantation is usually a single-family dwelling so large that it could easily provide shelter and protection for a multitude of people. Close to the plantation, in some cases in the rear of the main house, but always smaller, and out of sight is the place where the real people live."

"Huh?" Leary managed.

"Well, Leary, understand that I've never been to Montana either, but have likewise seen pictures. Anyway, I suppose that most everyone has a house, yard, and garden, and that they pretty much maintain these things themselves. You know, they don't use servants much in Montana, do they, Leary?"

Leary grinned as he replied, "No, not much, although there are some pretty big mansions in Helena, left over from the gold boom days. But, no, Sarge, I don't know any people who have servants. Generally, everyone does their own house and yard work in Montana."

"Right," Carson said. "In Montana, there isn't a group of people generally expected to be poorly paid, live in small shacks, and spend their time doing the house and farm chores for other folks who live in houses too large for them to take care of themselves. I mean, these dwellings in the South are so big that no one who didn't have slaves would ever consider owning them. They are statements more than dwellings. Statements that say, 'I have a place so big that it can only be maintained if I have people who do it for me.' Basically then, if you have a place as big as this rubber plantation, you've got to have slaves to maintain it for you."

His face expressionless, Leary asked without enthusiasm, "Sergeant Carson, are you talking about slavery or employment? I mean, don't those people who own plantations pay those who don't

to work on them?" Carson turned toward Leary and waited for him
to finish. "Of course, this slave master stuff, what do I know about
it? Nothing really. I'm just a Montana boy."

"I can understand that, Leary. You probably don't have many
black people in Montana, either."

"Nope, don't know a one."

"Well, the South is a black-white place. You are one or the other,
and everything about your life depends on which one you are. Black
is poor, white can be poor but doesn't have to be. Because of what
blacks are paid in the South, they are slaves."

Leary paused, looked up while still flossing his teeth with the
straw, thought for a minute, and then continued. "I don't doubt what
you're saying, it's just that I've never heard you even acknowledge
that there is a black-white thing. You seem to be less affected by
racial prejudice than any man I know. Of course, I know you're black
and I'm white, but I have to really think about it to realize that our
skins are different colors. Although I must say, regarding that, we are
both getting darker every day." They both grinned. "Mostly, I don't
know that Sanchez is brown, either. Doesn't matter to me and you've
always seemed like it doesn't matter to you."

"With God's help, I do try to stay away from that crap," Carson
replied. "But it isn't always so easy. I joined the army because it was
a community where, generally, I could make my own way without
having to spend my time maintaining some white man's monument
to himself. My father, mother, sisters, and brothers all work for
peanuts on a plantation, live in a shantytown, and are called, and are
considered to be, niggers. That is not to say that some of those KKK
types haven't made it into the army. The army is usually a good place
for a black man to spend his life. A large percentage of the white
people in this man's army may not think black is beautiful, but they
don't hate it either. So, a black man in my age bracket in the U.S.
of A. can have some respect as a man in the army. Not back home,
though, no respect for a black man there, no matter what he does.
There, they still believe we're their slaves and, for the most part,
they're right. Damn it, Leary," he spoke, loudly now, and seriously,
"how did I get off on that subject? It's a subject that I don't even like.
I prefer to stay where I'm at in life. Live the moment I'm in and that
moment is here. And what I want to say has to do with here. Us,
now, in this country."

"What we are fighting for? Is it this plantation here?" He paused
for a breath and waved his black hand around to indicate the whole
plantation and village. "It's sure too big for anyone to maintain by

themselves, so they have a whole town full of people to do it. A whole village full of slaves to make sure everything at this monument stays perfect. I mean, think about it, this place isn't even owned by a Vietnamese. Yet it's maintained perfectly by them. And even though the French guy that owns this place isn't here, probably because it's too dangerous, the Vietnamese slaves continue to work the plantation and send him money back in France. No wonder there's trouble here, the little slaves are revolting." He shook his head in mock disgust. "The people have gotten tired of being slaves and have the audacity to try not being slaves. Narrow of them." Then he laughed, and Leary laughed too, though neither knew why.

The humor pleased Leary as he said, "Well, 'Vive la France.' Our forefathers fought the Civil War to free the slaves in our country. The least we can do is see that they stay slaves over here. I mean, who'd work these plantations if we weren't here to see that the Commies stay away? It's the least we can do. We owe it to someone, I just can't remember who right now." He paused for a minute. "When you think of it like that, this whole thing is kind of a joke. A bad joke, true, with severe consequences, but the irony does have some humor in it."

"Yeah, getting hard to blame the Vietnamese for their part in this mess. If I do, I might have to look at my own family back home and figure they're suckers, too. I mean, they don't live much differently than these people do. Then, of course, I'd have to start questioning us for dying over here and then blame the French and the white plantation owners back home for following their nature. The truth of it for me is that I'm here because I'm a professional soldier." Carson paused, shifted, and grunted as his back muscles finally relaxed. "I do believe that what we as soldiers fight for should be a just cause. I will go so far as to say that this war is beginning to smell some. But all of that aside, I'm still a soldier, and I follow my orders to the best of my abilities. Being a soldier is what's best for me. Being a plantation owner is probably what's best for the Frenchman who owns this place. The mayor feels like being the mayor is best for him, and on and on. Being a plantation owner, a mayor, a slave, or a soldier is all a matter of what works best for the individual, I guess."

"You mean the slave wants to be a slave." Leary's comment was actually a question.

"Well, sir, some of them obviously no longer wish to be slaves over here." He smiled, showing perfect white teeth. "Thus, the war. I believe everyone has a choice. You have to be prepared to die in defense of your choice, to keep the choice, but you always have a choice. I chose the army because it serves me well. It allows me to be many things: a teacher, a father, an athlete, to provide for my family, but most of all it keeps me from being a nigger. In short, here I'm Sergeant Carson, back home I would be nigger Carson. So if the U.S. Army, my chosen profession, wants to go fight for slavery and call it fighting for freedom, I'll go. I'll go because it's my job to go. I chose this job. Let the politicians do their job and choose what war to fight. It's not the army's job, or mine for that matter, to say what war it should fight and what war it will fight. Anyone who wished to make such decisions should choose to go into politics. And politicians should be prepared to take full responsibility for their decisions."

Leary nodded and said, "Guess me, too. I'm a soldier. Not a professional soldier like you, but I've been made a soldier because I've chosen to do my duty, to fulfill my military obligation. And I'm prepared to die, if need be, because of that choice. I just wish it could be less tiring and make more sense."

"Amen."

Tooley was on his way from the briefing on the south side of the runway when he motioned for the platoon NCOs to start walking toward him. Leary and Carson saw his signal, and Leary threw in one last comment as they forced their weary bodies to stand, "One thing I know for sure, Sergeant Carson, the longer I am over here, the easier it is to piss me off." Carson agreed.

Tooley knelt down at the edge of the Second Platoon's position, which was at the west edge of the runway. The sergeants gathered in front of him. They all knelt on one knee with rifle butts on the ground and waited for Tooley to speak. The sweat streaked down their foreheads, and they had large dark areas under their arms. The smells that they ignored were weeds, hot asphalt, and stale bodies. The constant sweating caused by the heat and heavy clothing kept them wet most of the time. Their bodies were like living radiators with water oozing from every pore.

When they were all present, Tooley began his briefing. Gone was the military rigidity and enthusiasm that had punctuated his briefings a few harsh days ago. "Well, here it is. We've been pulled from our jungle hunt to find a lost company of South Vietnamese soldiers." He put his hands up to quiet the grunts and groans that burst from the sergeants. "I know how everyone feels. To hell with 'em; they're part of the problem. However, if it helps, there were three American advisors with them. One captain and two NCOs. So, regardless of how we feel about this, we are going." He paused to let this sink in. "Their last known position was about five miles east of here. They had one lightly armored personnel carrier, equipped with at least one fifty-caliber machine-gun. It and the company were last seen traveling down that road, day before yesterday." He pointed to Highway One heading east out of the village. "Due east. Information received from them by radio said that they'd come under heavy North Vietnamese attack about midday yesterday. The last radio contact with them was at 1300 hundred hours yesterday afternoon. Their track had been blown up with an old French seventy-five gun, and they were in serious danger of being overrun.

"The South Vietnamese flew over with choppers and a fixed-wing airplane but couldn't determine much. The pilots had seen both South Vietnamese and North Vietnamese troops firing and moving around on the ground, but nothing else. They were afraid to land, fire, or drop bombs without any contact from their own forces on the ground. So, no word, nothing, since yesterday afternoon at 1300 hours. Our job is to find the lost company and determine its fate. Simple, huh? A little walking, a little looking, and back to our base camp at Ben Cat for a rest." He chuckled sarcastically and added, "Oh, yeah, the terrain is mostly rubber plantation trees. I guess it's all part of this plantation and goes for miles. It's mostly clear under the trees, broken up by scattered patches of jungle. Tracts of rubber trees are on both sides of the pavement all the way to the next village, which is about ten miles northeast of here. That village northeast of here is an admitted enemy-occupied and controlled area." Tooley stared hard at his NCOs.

None of the NCOs said a word or moved noticeably; they just stared at him. Their discomfort was palpable as Tooley asked, "Any questions?" He paused, then said, "Men, this looks to be bad, maybe the worst we've been in on yet. What information we have says that there are thousands of North Vietnamese troops out there. They are supposed to be well trained, well supplied, and well motivated. We move out in ten minutes."

19

BRUTALITY ESTABLISHED

After Tooley finished the briefing, his sergeants rose and returned to where their men were positioned. They paraphrased what the lieutenant had said and then saw that the men were as ready as possible for the hot day's march. In fifteen minutes, they were spread out along both sides of the paved road in a typical road-march formation. They suffered as they waited, standing in the sun, not moving but getting hotter, and using up their bodies' vital fluids in sweat. A Company was to lead, followed by B Company, and then C Company. B Company would handle both flanks.

The Second Platoon was in the middle of C Company. It was as safe a place as the battalion had to offer. Leary was point man for the platoon, followed by Carson, Folger, Sanchez, Hart, and Branden, with Tooley and Nash in the rear third of the formation. Leary and Carson stood closer to each other than good safety would dictate and talked quietly. Carson had not bothered to put anyone in charge of Fire Team A.

Patkins was expected to return soon. They had heard that he was still unconscious but had been operated on to relieve the pressure in his brain and would hopefully regain consciousness at any time. However, the doctors were quick to report that full recovery could not be predicted. Only after he was conscious again could they fully determine the effects of the head injury. Probably, though, they had said, he would recover completely. Carson remained adamant that Patkins would come back, and the men knew that nothing more needed to be said.

Everyone worked smoothly together. Carson would take direct control of Patkins' men if the situation called for splitting up the

141

squad, but most of the time they just followed behind Leary's fire team and did everything the way they should.

"Standing and waiting in this heat. Damn, Sergeant Carson," Leary was irritated, "don't they give any thought to the water we lose while we're burning up on this damn road? You don't see the gooks standing in this heat. They have better sense. They respect the heat. They carry very little equipment and don't usually travel far during the day. Mostly, they just hang out in cool caves during the day and come out at night when we're exhausted from doing crap like we're doing now so they can screw with us. You just don't see many canteens on them. Look at us, we all carry two apiece and have to drink four full canteens a day just to stay alive. Just stupid, that's all."

"Yeah," Carson said, "have to agree with you. It's their ball game, really. They live here and don't have to be in any hurry about anything. You know we're the aggressors here. We're the ones on the hunt. They rest when they want to, attack when it's to their advantage. They don't really have to hold or occupy any particular area or place. And they can always just go into Cambodia, Laos, or back to North Vietnam if they don't like it here. Tactically speaking, we are in the worst of positions. They would have flunked me out of NCO school had I proposed a strategy like the one we're operating under. Yeah, the advantage is clearly theirs. Old Charlie Cong can rest coolly in his underground tunnel during the day, come out at night, and poke us full of holes. Not good, Leary, not good."

The sweat ran out from under Leary's helmet and without even trying to wipe it off, he spoke slow and quietly. "I am getting used to living like this, though. Continual physical misery, being dirty and smelly, sore and tired while waiting for the shots or explosions of death to come and claim me. I'm beginning to think that this is the real life. Any other way of living was just a dream."

"Me, too," Carson said as he scratched the bumps on his neck caused by heat and beard growth, "I am starting to doubt the reality of my life back home, too. Sometimes I doubt that life before Vietnam ever really existed. My wife, my kids, the good life are all starting to seem like they weren't real, just a fantasy, something that I've created in my mind to make my existence here more bearable."

"Yeah, as if it never existed. At times, it does seem like there was never any small town in Montana, nor any parents, no Mary. It's like I made all of that up in my mind and that my whole life is and has always been this heat, soreness, and destruction. It's like nothing ever existed before Vietnam and nothing will exist after it. We were put on this earth to participate in this hell, and we'll never know any other place. This is it, everything that's happened before now was just an illusion. A mechanism made possible by our mind's need to escape. We are, and have always been, in hell and are just now realizing it."

Carson looked Leary right in the eye as he said, "That doesn't explain the letters from home."

"That's true," Leary said, nodding his head.

"Well, all joking aside, Leary, more and more, day after day, this life does seem normal. I mean, it's harder and harder to believe back home exists."

Leary nodded again, grinned, white teeth contrasting with his rapidly growing brown beard, and said, "Who's joking? Not me."

Carson grinned too as he picked up his rifle and took his place in the battalion march, which was finally under way.

The battalion moved slowly down the road toward the last known position of the lost company. When the second squad passed the home guard standing outside their small guard shack on the outskirts of the village, a three-wheeled motorcycle came putt-putting by on its way towards the village. It was the kind commonly seen in Vietnam, a combination rickshaw and motorcycle. The man in the back seat had a South Vietnamese uniform on, or what was left of it, and had his hands clasped together in front of his lacerated stomach, in an effort to try and hold his intestines in.

The men of the second squad were shocked when the two guards, supposedly on the wounded man's side in the war, began pointing and laughing at him. They made fun of him like a couple of cruel children as he slowly passed their position. Though his wounds were serious and his intestines were clearly visible, he was a man of great spirit and was very much alive as he cursed the two guards. Leary was only a few feet from the guard shack when this exchange occurred and it enraged him. *Dirty stinking gooks, how could they laugh at their own man like that? Good God, they're supposed to be on the same side. These are the people we're risking our lives for?*

The soldiers of the Sixteenth Infantry moved east and north down the paved road for three hours before turning south down a dirt road. It was a good dirt road, smooth, hard-packed and red, and it was wide enough for two vehicles. The jungle was back from the road on the east side about one hundred meters, but the west side of the road was a larger, flat, grassy area that held the thick jungle off for at least three hundred meters. It was a nice-looking meadow with a clear creek running through it for about fifty meters from

north to south. The creek flowed swiftly and was at the bottom of
a deep narrow gully. The lush grass grew right up to the edge on its
east bank, but the west bank had an area about eighty meters long
by six meters wide that was bare of grass.

They set up a perimeter in the clearing and it was hard to
imagine anything violent having happened there. Except for a couple
of burned spots and the shell of a destroyed personnel carrier, it
was a picture of tranquility. After a sweeping search, they had found
one American helmet with a bullet hole right above the visor, but
nothing else, no expended ammo brass, no weapons, broken or
whole, or any other evidence to suggest that, just twenty-four hours
before, a battle had taken place in that verdant clearing. Still, there
was an occasional whiff of death in the air.

Leary, Folger, Branden, Sanchez, and Hart were relaxing around
the small fire they'd built to heat water for their coffee and hot
chocolate. Carson was back at company headquarters with Tooley
for a briefing. Since Patkins had been dusted off to the hospital,
Branden, Sanchez, and Hart had joined their nightly coffee socials
whenever good defensive strategies allowed. Folger had completely
joined them since the food bag fort. Neither Carson nor Leary had
mentioned it. Branden had taken over Patkins' job of watching the
cans of water. It just happened that way. No one knew or cared
why. He looked up from moving a can to a hotter spot in the fire
and asked Leary, "Does this mean that Sergeant Carson is now the
platoon sergeant?"

"No. Not that I know of. Nothing has been said about it."

"Well, it's bound to come out that way," Folger said. "No one
else could do it better, and someone has to."

"Hell, he's pretty much doing the job now," Branden added.

"True, it's bound to happen. The platoon is getting small enough,
though, that we'll all be together anyway," Folger said.

"Yeah, it'll all work out," Leary said. "I'm more curious about
what that commotion has been over at the creek. There's been
something going on over there for the last half hour."

Branden looked up from the fire again. "Here comes Sergeant
Carson now. I hope he says we're going to stay here tonight."

Carson, his bearded face and walnut-brown eyes blank, walked
quietly up to the three men at the fire and squatted down, letting
his rifle butt rest on the grass. Everyone waited. No one spoke; they
knew he would start talking after he had gathered his thoughts.
"They found the lost battalion in a trench next to the creek. They're
all there, or at least most of 'em. That guy that came through on

the back of the three-wheeler this morning was apparently the only survivor."

"Shit," Leary said. "At least they buried them."

"Not really," Carson replied, shaking his head. "Seems like they dug the grave themselves. Seventy-five of them were shot in the back of the head."

"Christ," Folger said, "executed after digging their own grave?"

"What now?" Leary asked.

"Well, the South Vietnamese are going to come and take care of the bodies, including the three American advisors. We're to get our gear back on and be ready to move north in fifteen minutes. That's," Carson paused to look at his watch, "about 1650 hours by my watch."

"Going where, Sergeant Carson?" Branden asked. "It's getting dark and surely we're not going to chase them in the dark. I mean, the dark is their time and there are a lot of them."

"Look, it's not my decision, but going after these guys makes more sense to me than anything we've done over here so far. This bunch murdered men who had surrendered to them. Now, by all that's right and just, is there any more important thing for us to do than to hunt them down and kill 'em?"

"Not by my thinking," Folger said. "I don't give a shit about the South Vietnamese they killed, but I do care about the way they killed them. They shouldn't have let them think they could surrender. They should have at least shot them where they stood. There's something bad about making men dig their own graves and then walking along behind them and shooting them. Something wrong with men that would let anyone do that to them, too. Did the three Americans have holes in the back of their heads?"

"No, they were all shot in the front," Carson said.

"Well, that's something, anyway," Leary replied.

"I just don't like the night march into strange country. Into enemy held territory." With a note of resignation in his voice, Branden asked, "Where to and how far, Sergeant Carson?"

"Ten miles north of here, up that paved road is a huge mountain. Some of you may have noticed it from the choppers when we flew into the plantation." All three men nodded their heads. "Well, at the bottom, south of that mountain, is a village. It's a large village, supposed to be larger than Ben Cat, and known to belong to the North Vietnamese."

"What, another damn place that belongs to them? This war is so full of that garbage," Folger exclaimed.

"Amen," Leary added.

"Let's get going, put the fire out, saddle up, it's going to be a long night, but I'd just as soon go and get 'em than to wait for them to hit us," Carson replied.

"Yeah," Leary said. "When we get them, I'm going to punish them big time too. Not just for killing these men, although that's bad enough, but for making me walk all night, for ruining my hot chocolate time, and because they're so damned evil."

Twenty minutes later, they moved out. There was a full moon with no heavy rain, only an occasional sprinkling that quieted the underbrush and refreshed the men's hot bodies. They worked their way northeast down the asphalt road from Phu Duc and toward what they had been told was VC Mountain. Some of them remembered the large mountain that poked incongruously out of the flat jungle canopy. From the air, it was as obvious as a pyramid in the desert. Before, it had been an awesome thing but now, knowing to whom it belonged, it was an obnoxious symbol of the enemy's power. Word had passed through the ranks that military intelligence had learned that a battalion of North Vietnamese regulars had wiped out and buried the South Vietnamese soldiers and were last seen in their sanctuary at the base of the large mountain.

Two days later, the battalion was back at the Phu Duc rubber plantation. It was 1000 hours, and the six of them were drinking coffee and hot chocolate around their position north of the runway, just in the rubber trees. They had staggered back to the plantation yesterday afternoon completely exhausted. Folger and Branden were hung over from drinking hot beer the night before. After seeing and hearing them, Carson and Leary were glad they hadn't had any of the beer abundantly provided by the villagers.

"I hope the choppers get here soon. I just want to get back to base camp and take a dip in the spring's pool," Branden said.

"Yeah, well, you better get in quickly," Carson said humorously. "It gets muddy mighty fast, and there are a lot of men with the same idea. Too bad it only holds one man at a time."

"Well, I don't give a shit. I'm going to run for it and just sit in it with my clothes on. I don't care. I'll take my clothes off, which need washing anyway, once I've claimed the pool."

"I'm not fighting for anything," Folger said. "I'd rather stink and itch than have to run from the chopper to get to that damn poor excuse for a bath. Shit, I'll wait until early in the morning and pull my guard sitting naked in that pool."

At the thought of Folger sitting naked in the moonlight, his automatic rifle in his hands, they all laughed.

"It's been hell the last couple of days," Leary said.

"Make it the last couple of weeks," Folger said. "What happened at VC Mountain was the biggest screwin' they've given us so far. How in the hell do they think up these things?"

"What happened wasn't planned to make you mad, Folger," Carson said.

"Oh, I don't know," Folger said. "Think about it. We sneak all night. We come across those civilians they shot just for fun. Killed, old men, women, and children, and left them draining their life out on that asphalt road. It takes us till just before dawn before we get in a position to attack that damn village. Then, when the light does come, do we attack? No, of course not. Why, they start pulling us back and then march us the fifteen or so miles back to here. That's so much bullshit and you all know it."

"I agree," Branden said. "I didn't think at first that any of us were going to pull back. I gotta admit, though, it felt good to pass that 'fuck you' back to the colonel when he first told us to pull back. Of course, finally, we did pull back. Then back and back, until we got here."

"I obey orders. You men know that. And I intend to obey them in the future. I'm a soldier and that is what I have lived my life to do, but I was willing to disobey those orders," Carson said.

"Yeah, we would've attacked if we'd known why he was pulling us back," Leary said. "Who would've guessed that a chopper would bring a damn reporter in during the night? They must have clout. I didn't give a damn if we had artillery support. Hell, we were too close to use it anyway. But even if we'd been able to use it, I wouldn't have cared. It was the last thing on my mind. I just wanted to get those bastards. I felt killing 'em was our right." Leary dumped out his hot chocolate in disgust. "We never would have pulled back had we known why. I damn sure know I wouldn't have. After we all refused, the colonel lied to us. There wasn't any air strike. That would have been okay though. Would've burnt that village to the ground. But it was just another lie. He was worried about what that reporter would say about him; that's why he didn't let us attack. We just walked away after what they did."

"Those fuckin' reporters. I can see the headlines now, 'Colonel outruns artillery--loses his men,' " Sanchez added.

"One thing's for sure," Branden said, "he sold us out. That's why he provided the party for us—beer, bananas, and French bread."

"That gook village chief was gonna refuse to let us rest here," Folger said. "But the colonel knew we were in no mood for any crap. He told him to be here in one hour with bananas and beer, or he wouldn't be responsible for what we might do."

"The colonel was right, too. We were in bad shape mentally and physically. Right. Sergeant Leary, I thought you were gonna shoot those two guards," Branden added.

"Yeah, Leary, what was that about? I was back a ways in the platoon. Something happen at that guard shack?" Carson asked.

"Not much, really," Leary said.

"I've been avoiding this, Leary, but I really have to know. I need to assess our mental attitudes as well as our physical condition," Carson said seriously.

"I don't know. I mean they were the same guards who laughed at their own man who was holding his guts in the back of that scooter. I know we were looking pretty beat, but they shouldn't have started laughing at us. They were speaking in Vietnamese, pointing and laughing, just like they had with their own man. I guess I just lost it."

"What did you do, exactly?" Carson insisted.

"I don't know for sure. I sort of blanked out. I remember I'd built up my anger pretty good, the Vietnamese buried in that mass grave, the dead civilians on the road, and then not attacking because the colonel was afraid of the press. Then seeing those two assholes again and them laughing at us, well, hell, I just lost it."

Carson's look said to go on.

"You tell us what happened next, Branden, you seem to know," Leary said.

"Wait a goddamn minute. I'm not a rat or anything. I'm worried about us, too."

"Just tell, it Branden," Leary commanded.

"Okay, okay, but don't be pissed at me," Branden said as he looked at Leary, who shook his head no. "Well, when they started laughing, you were a few steps away from them. Then you stopped, snapped the safety off of your weapon, and started cursing and jabbing it at them. I thought you were going to pull the trigger, but you didn't. Then the one started to point his carbine at you, and you knocked it out of the way with your rifle and bashed him in the side of the face with the barrel. Shit, he went down and the blood started flowing from the side of his head. Then you damn near stuck the barrel in the eye of the other one and you were motioning and cursing and, with the barrel almost in his eye, you forced him to lie on top of the other one. And then you said, 'Now I'm going to kill you both.' "

"Well I didn't, did I?" Leary said.

"No, but only because Folger slung his AR and came up behind you, reached around, and snapped the safety back on your rifle. Then he held on to you and talked you out of it. I'll say this, those guys will never laugh at anyone again. I was on the other side of the road, and I just knew you were going to kill 'em."

"My God, Leary, what's happening to you?" Carson asked.

"I don't know, Sergeant Carson. At some place in my heart, it seemed so right. But I don't quite remember all of it. I only remember the laughing, then getting really mad, then Folger having a bear hug on me from behind, telling me 'no, Leary, no' and the gooks on the ground, et cetera."

"Well," Carson said. "The word is out on you. The colonel laughed at first and said, 'It helped assure the village chief's cooperation.' But then he got serious and said, 'Let's keep an eye on him. That boy is losing it.' The captain, of course, agreed. Then the colonel went on to say that our good men are fighters and that they are the most susceptible to losing it. It's a two-edged sword. We need them to be willing to kill in a second, attack in a flash, but the better they become at it, the less it takes to set them off. They develop a hair-trigger, he said and, though we use it for our purposes, we can't let them kill people who laugh at them. The colonel told the lieutenant to keep Leary off point for a while. You know, let him settle down in a safe place in the formation. Give him time to get that trigger of his tightened up a bit. We are going back to Ben Cat to rest and maybe that will help. That's what was said, as near as I can remember it." There was silence for a moment, and then Carson said, "I appreciate your stopping Leary, Folger, but your name came up as a shooter, too. They're also worried about your hair-trigger."

"Excuse me, Sergeant Carson, no offense to you, I respect you, but screw them," Folger said.

"I know, Folger, but we've got to stay civilized. We have to be better than our enemy."

"Fight fire with fire," Leary said.

"Men, I'm older than all of you," Carson said, "and I tell you that you may return home someday, and you will be expected to act civilized. If you become too much of an animal over here, they won't tolerate you back home. You'll end up in an institution or dead. That's just the way it is. What is acceptable over here will not be tolerated back home. You can't kill the mailman for laughing at your fat wife."

"Yeah, you may be right, Sergeant Carson, but we need to decide how we will act over here. We can clearly see that we aren't fighting for our country or the freedom of these people. Hell, they aren't a threat to our homes and they're already slaves to the French. These people won't be any better off if we win. So what are we fighting for over here? What're we going to die for?" Leary asked.

"I tell you all this much," Folger said, "after what we've seen the last couple of days, I will not be too fussy about killing these bastards."

"That's for sure," Branden exclaimed. "Look what happens if you surrender. They kill you. Shoot you in the back of your head after making you dig your own grave. And I understand those are the lucky ones. If they decide to keep you alive, it's just to torture you."

"No," Leary said. "We can't afford to be taken prisoner. I say we make a pact right now to not leave anyone, anywhere, dead or alive. We have to make sure the body is flown off, so that we're sure they're safe."

"Yeah," Carson agreed, "making sure that the body gets aboard one of our choppers is the only guarantee that they won't get one of us alive."

"Then we all agree," Leary said, "we leave no one anywhere dead or alive. If we get hit, no matter how large the force, we stay and fight. That's it, period. No exceptions. It's a solemn oath between us."

Carson, Leary, Folger, Branden, Sanchez, and Hart were startled to find that the rest of the platoon had joined them. Everyone was crowded around the dying fire, except Tooley and Nash, who were over at company headquarters. As their conversation had gotten serious, it had become louder and the platoon had migrated to the area. It wasn't good tactically for the men to bunch up like that, but it was open country and they were reasonably safe.

"What about them?" Sanchez asked.

"Them, who?" Carson asked.

"The gooks, that's who," Sanchez said. "Why should we take any of them prisoner? Why should we even consider it? I, for one, am going to shoot every one of them I can. I have no feelings for them after what we've seen the last couple of days. If I can't be their prisoner, then they can't be mine either. Those are the rules of this war."

"That's it then," Leary said, "we all agree not to ever be prisoners and not to take prisoners."

Everyone either nodded or said yes. "Okay, then, that's what we'll be," Carson said. "But remember this, we have to make sure that they are combatants. We don't want to kill civilians. We just can't kill civilians."

"Not always an easy thing to do," Folger said. "I don't trust any of them. They've proven, time and time again, they play both sides of the road."

"Well, we have to try. That's all I'm going to say about it. We have to try."

Then they heard the noise of choppers in the distance. Choppers coming to take them back to their base camp at Ben Cat.

Their captain heard the choppers too and, as he was searching the sky for sight of them, he thought, *Leary is getting close to losing it, huh? Colonel says to take it easy on him. Let him rest up. Fat chance. I'll figure out a way to push him a little further. Dead or nuts, either one will work for me.*

20

THE LIEUTENANT AND THE COLONEL

Tooley had just reported to the colonel's bunker at their base camp, which was on a hill a couple miles east of the village of Ben Cat. Often, when the men were on operations in the jungle, the colonel would stay at the less primitive base of Lia Kae. At Lia Kae his helicopter was parked and serviced and, though it hadn't been announced yet, he knew that soon his battalion's base camp would be moved there, closing down this one near Ben Cat. His bunker was located in the center of the camp and was larger than all other command bunkers. There were two bedrooms as well as an office and a radio room. The colonel was sitting behind his desk, relaxed. Even in the field, his fatigues were pressed and starched, and his boots were spit-polished. His red face was clean-shaven, as usual, and his hair was thinning, short-cropped, and gray. The smells of aftershave and army canvas were in the air.

In contrast, Tooley was standing in front of the desk with his feet a shoulder-width apart, his hands clasped behind his back in the parade rest position. His fatigues were dirty and were wrinkled as if they had been tied in knots. Sweat stains showed under his arms. His boots were almost white from lack of polish, his red hair was shaggy, and his face was unshaven.

The colonel gave Tooley a fatherly smile. *Boy is looking pretty rough. Of course, they're all starting to look like that. I like this boy, though—reminds me of what I wish my hippie son was like. Oh well, better get started.*

"Sit down, Lieutenant, relax." Tooley stiffly sat in the folding chair. "I suppose you're wondering why I called you up here to meet with me, you know, without your captain being present?"

"Yes, sir, it's a little irregular. I wouldn't want Captain Haps to think I've jumped the chain of command."

"Don't worry about that, Lieutenant. I've spoken to your company commander. Told him I wanted to talk to you alone. In fact, I told him to have you report here."

"Well, sir, you know, I just don't want to make him any more upset with us than he needs to be."

"I am the commander here. So don't worry about it. But what were you hinting at when you said, 'Any more upset with us than needs to be'?"

"Nothing, sir, just trying not to make things any rougher over here than they have to be."

"Right. Let's cut the bull, Lieutenant. I'm not stupid. I know what the hell is going on in my command. You and your men have been in it since the start. You have lost more men, been in more action, and done more damage to the enemy than all the rest of the battalion put together. Your platoon is already down to two-thirds strength, and you've had two replacements from the mortar platoon."

"Yes, sir."

"Well, that's what we're over here for."

"Yes, sir, if that's the reason we're over here, then we're real successful at it."

"Just the luck of the draw? Right, Lieutenant?"

"Sure, Colonel, just the luck."

"Cut the sarcasm, Lieutenant Tooley. You believe your captain is out to get you all killed, isn't that so?"

Tooley looked puzzled.

"You wonder how I know these things?" Tooley shrugged a "maybe." "Well, it's my job to know everything about everyone in my command. That's what makes a good commander. Nothing else is more important in commanding troops." Tooley didn't respond. The colonel leaned forward, lowered his voice, and spoke in a conspiratorial tone. "It's the enlisted man's pipeline." Tooley nodded. "You've heard of it, of course. It's not in any of the books and is rarely spoken about. That's because you can't set up anything like that. It's out of our control. If it's good, accurate, bad, et cetera, we have nothing to do with it. It makes sense; I mean, they do everything. They drive the trucks, load them, unload them, operate the radios, cook the meals, fire the weapons, and basically do it all. So, they talk. We're like the parents and they're like the kids who keep things from us. If we don't see it, they don't point it out. However, if you have a good relationship with your radio operator, he will keep you informed." He pointed to the radio room. "I have a good one. I take care of him, too."

"Yes, sir."

"Thus, we get to the problem. The word is out that Captain Haps is out to get Leary killed, and he doesn't give a damn if he loses the whole platoon in the process."

"Yes, sir."

" 'Yes, sir,' what, Lieutenant? This will be a conversation, not a lecture. So speak up like the man I know you are."

"Yes, sir, I agree with your radio operator. The captain is out to get us."

"What do you think I should do about it?"

"Nothing, sir, we don't want you to do anything about it."

Uh oh, just as I thought, he's bonded with them and that's dangerous. "Lieutenant, your use of the word 'we' tells me you're starting to identify yourself as one of the men instead of as their leader. They don't need another enlisted buddy; they need an officer. They need a man elevated to a higher status. A man who can give an order that they're afraid to refuse. They need something above their own self-interest to believe in. That's what a leader is, Lieutenant, not someone in sympathy with them. Their mothers sympathize with them, worry about their well-being, and so on. They don't need another mother. They need an ass-kicking father. So, be the father. Am I making sense here?"

"Oh, I understand what you're saying, Colonel. I'm just having trouble agreeing with you."

"That's OK, Lieutenant Tooley, you're young. If you live, you will understand."

"Yes, sir."

"Don't start that 'yes, sir' shit with me again."

"I just don't have much more to say about it, Colonel. You've said it all."

"Let me approach this another way. Let's say that the captain is trying to get Leary killed. What can be done about it? I could transfer Leary to another company. Of course, everyone already knows about the situation, and his new company commander would be resentful." Tooley looked at the colonel quizzically. "I mean, think about it. The officers have their pipeline, too, and no officer wants a troublemaker—a soldier who refuses orders, an aggressive man carrying a weapon that he is very proficient with and who is already half brain-fried. Besides, say we move him, the platoon gets it, and he survives, hell, he'll feel guilty the rest of his life. A fate worse than death, believe me. And fate is a bad thing to interfere with. I am the commander of the battalion, Captain Haps is the commander of Charlie Company, you are the commander of the Second Platoon, and God is the commander of fate."

"Right, Colonel. We're back to the place we were at when I came in here. There is nothing we, or I, expect you to do about it."

"Yes, you're right, Lieutenant. However, I will say this. I will see that you get two weeks' rest. We've been guaranteed that from Saigon. I'll interfere enough to see that your platoon has no extra heavy duty until we go back out. And, I'm glad we had this talk. I'll watch for anything obvious in your assignments, but keep in mind that your platoon is good, maybe the best, and it's natural to want to put the best players in."

"Thank you, sir, is that all?"

"Yes, Lieutenant, that is all. Have a good rest."

Tooley turned and started to leave the bunker when the colonel said, "Oh, Lieutenant." Tooley turned around to face the colonel. "Your Sergeant Patkins, in the hospital." Tooley nodded. "Well, he's regained consciousness."

"That's great, Colonel. When will he be sent back to us?'

"Well, Lieutenant, he's conscious but not well yet. He had a pretty bad concussion; they had to drain his brain to relieve the pressure. So, it'll be a coupla weeks at best. They say he woke up eager, though, ready to come back to the unit. Said he wants to fight and is impatient and verbally crude, even with the nurses."

"No, sir."

"Pardon me, Lieutenant?"

"That is not Sergeant Patkins, sir. He was a timid, polite, nonaggressive man. He was one of the last men I'd expect to request coming back to combat. They are reporting on the wrong man, sir."

"I'll check on it, Lieutenant, but when I spoke to them, they were pretty damn sure. However, I'll let you know. That's all."

"Yes, sir, thank you."

At the Ninety-third Evacuation Hospital in Ton Son Nhut, Patkins was sitting up in his bed with a turban-like bandage around his head. It was one bed of many that lined the walls of the half-round Quonset hut. The hospital was large and consisted of many such buildings.

His watch on the nightstand said twelve o'clock and, though he had been conscious for six hours, he still believed that the dream he'd had just before waking was real. He was sure that he had killed his father. It was very real to him and very clear. His father had been standing over him, pointing his finger at him and telling him what a worthless boy he was. Over and over again, "You are a worthless, spineless son. I wish you had been a girl, then I could understand why you are so worthless." And on and on he had ranted, as he had done so many times in Patkins' life. But then Patkins had changed right in front of his father and he'd become a full-grown man like he was now. A soldier with a beard, a uniform, and a M-14 rifle.

It had been so effortlessly simple. He had just pointed the weapon at his father and pulled the trigger. Over and over again, he pulled the trigger, punching holes in his father's body, knocking it to the floor. Patkins did not stop then. He kept pulling the trigger until the twenty-round magazine was used up. Then he woke up, feeling good.

When the nurse spotted his movement, she summoned the doctor. They were both visibly delighted with his new status, as he coherently conversed with the doctor about his condition. When the doctor had finished his medical inquiry, he asked Patkins, "Is there anything else you would like to say? After all, you've been out for quite a while."

"Well, no doctor, not really, except that I have killed my father and I am happy about it."

The doctor and nurse looked shocked for a moment, but they had seen and heard many strange things since coming to Vietnam and quickly regained their composure. The doctor asked, "When did you do that, Sergeant?"

"I don't know, Doctor, must have been before I came to Vietnam, because I had my uniform on, it was sweaty and I was dirty and needed a shave. I had my rifle, too. I shot him with it."

"No, Sergeant, you only dreamt that you shot your father."

"No, Doctor, I shot him. I killed the son of a bitch and I'm glad. Of course, I can't go home anymore. They'll find the body, or already have, and are looking for me. So I'll just stay here and die. I need to get out of here and back to my unit."

"I'm sorry, Sergeant, but you didn't kill your father and you're going to have to stay here for a while."

"Listen, you piece of crap, you and the bitch here get me some clothes and a rifle, and I'm going back to my unit."

"I'm telling you right now, Sergeant, that kind of language is uncalled for."

"You're right, Doc, go to hell. Now get me my fighting equipment."

The doctor relaxed and said easily, "Sure, Sergeant, we just have to give you an antibiotic, and we'll get you on your way. Nurse, go get the shot and call supply for new clothes and a rifle." The nurse nodded and headed quickly towards the nurse's station a few steps away. They had a lot of emergencies, and the medicines used most frequently were handy.

"That's better, Doc. I'm sorry about the language, but you didn't understand that I need to get back to the unit."

"You bet, Sergeant. I understand now. We'll have you on a chopper within the hour. You'll have to take some fresh bandages with you and have your medic keep the sutures clean and sterile. In about two weeks, maybe sooner, have the medic take the stitches out. Probably won't be able to wear the helmet for a while."

"No sweat, Doc. I don't like the damn thing anyway."

"Good, the nurse is back, we'll just stick this right in the IV going into your arm, and then we'll take it all out and you can get your gear and go." He bent over and stuck the needle in the intravenous tube and pushed the plunger, giving Patkins a major dose of morphine.

Patkins felt the rush immediately and knew he was fading rapidly. It felt so good though that he had trouble being mad at these two. *Hell, I love them both*, he thought, as he said in a slurred voice, "D-o-c, y-o-u-u-u..." And he was out. Peacefully asleep.

"What now?" the nurse asked.

"He's got a problem. We'll get Jakes up here. He's the psychiatrist."

Hours later, when Patkins returned to consciousness, the psychiatrist was standing over him. "How are you feeling, Sergeant?"

"I'm a little foggy, but feel fine."

"I'm Doctor Jakes, and I'm worried about your wanting to get back to your unit before you're ready, and I'm especially worried about this idea you have that you've killed you father."

I'd better play this out. They'll give me another shot if I don't act the way they want me too. I need them to help me get my equipment and get back to the unit, so I'll be patient and go along with them. "I'm sorry, Doctor, what's that about my father? Is he all right?"

"Yes, sure, we've heard nothing about anything being wrong with your family at home. And, believe me, they would have told us if anything serious had happened to any of them."

"That's good, Doctor, I would hate for anything to happen to Mom or Dad, or my wife and girls."

"Well, you've had a bad blow to your head, and you need to rest. If you need anything or feel like you've done something that is horrible, have the nurse get me. I'll be checking on you daily, just to see how you are."

Stupid ass, he doesn't know, the body must not have been discovered yet. Wish I could remember what I did with it. Oh, well. This quack is gonna be watching me. I'd better play the game till I get out of here. Then screw them all; I'll never take any crap from anyone again. Never. "That would be great Doctor, thanks." *And to hell with you.*

21

AMBUSH AT BEN CAT

For two pleasant weeks, the battalion sat around, smoked, read, joked and, for brief moments, almost forgot the war. The nights were a little nervy because the VC continually harassed them with sporadic mortar fire. The VC would wait until the camp had settled down for the night and then send a couple of rounds into it. When the men heard the popping sound coming from the jungle, they would start yelling, "Incoming!" as they jumped out of their tents and scrambled down to their bunkers on the perimeter. Once at their assigned bunkers, they would throw themselves down behind it and hope that no mortar rounds landed on or near them.

No one would go into the bunkers, not even during the worst attacks. When humans did not continually occupy a bunker, scorpions and snakes immediately claimed them. Since these were firing bunkers on the defensive perimeter and not large enough to live in, the jungle creatures resided there. Inside any one of them during the light of day was at least one snake hanging from the roof logs. No man was going to dive in there at night. Better to be blown to bits.

Despite this nighttime harassment, the men were relaxing. They were allowed to go to the village of Ben Cat a few times during their two weeks of rest. And Carson, Leary, Folger, and Branden had on a couple of occasions enjoyed drinking hot beer on the wooden patio of a beer hall in the village. They could never completely relax, not like at home, and they always had their rifles at the ready, never drinking enough to become lax. The few times they did drink a little too much, it was at base camp where they were the safest but, even then, they drank in shifts. They always had a designated nondrinking guard.

When their two weeks were up, so was their reprieve. Captain Haps was quick to volunteer the platoon for any mission or chore.

The two trucks carrying the Second Platoon entered the village of Ben Cat from the east on Highway One. Two blocks into town, the highway swung almost due north. The Lia Kae rubber plantation was seven miles farther up this paved highway. Carson was standing in the front of the truck bed on the driver's side facing forward. He had the second squad with him and what was left of the first squad. The other truck transported the lieutenant, the third squad, and the weapons squad with its two machine guns.

The second truck followed fifty meters behind the first. For safety's sake, a distance was always maintained between vehicles. If the first truck was blown up, hit a mine, or was hit with a RPG-7 antitank weapon, the second truck would be spared the attack and would have time to stop, unload, and fight. The same was true if the second truck was hit first. While this strategic distance was to be maintained at all times, at no time was either truck to lose sight of the other. Thus, if the road were full of short twists and turns in a jungle-thick area, the trucks would have to travel closer together than they would in an open area. Maintaining this distance was the responsibility of the drivers, and they were constantly analyzing and making corrections. In addition, all trucks that transported troops had sandbags lining the bottom of the bed and cab. The sandbags reduced death and wounding greatly, especially if a mine planted in the road blew up the truck from below.

Carson was pleased with his driver. He seemed to be experienced, and Carson knew that could make the difference between life and death. Carson was acting more and more as the platoon sergeant since Cambel's death. It was not strategically prudent to have the platoon leader and the platoon sergeant riding together in the same vehicle. What was left of the platoon could probably have fit into one truck, but there were two trucks available and, for safety reasons, they took them both.

Looking back at the rear truck, Carson could see Tooley at the front of his truck leaning on the railing, looking forward, watching, and ready. *We are professional soldiers*, he thought. *Less and less do the men need to be told what to do. We're starting to operate automatically.*

*We are becoming what we do. Like breathing. Yeah, we're now a
dangerous, well-trained, and tested force. I'd hate to have to do battle
with us. We're valuable over here, but what do we do if we get home?
What kind of training do they have to make us good civilians again?*
     In the rear truck, Tooley's mind was alive with thoughts, too.
*This village was friendly and unspoiled when we first got here a
few months ago. But things in the village have changed. The prices
have doubled and tripled. More importantly, though, there have been
killings on both sides, and some we've killed probably lived in Ben Cat.
Hell, they probably live and come to the village at night when we're
gone. Well, on the other hand, they could be standing in the streets
waving at us now. Without a Northern Army uniform or a gun, we'd
never know. The VC all dress just like the peasants. Of course, we've
changed toward them too. We've become hardened and less friendly.
After people who look a certain way have attacked you, it's hard to be
friendly to others who look the same way. Yeah, we've lost men too, and
it has affected our thinking about them. But look at them,* he thought
as the truck turned north and headed out of town, *standing in front
of their small shops and stores, all watching us, some of them waving.
Kids yelling at us to stop, running alongside the trucks begging for gum
and Salem cigarettes. All of them wanting our money but hating our
guts. Much like the merchants back home around the army posts. Well,
to hell with them,* Tooley decided, *I don't like them either. Lousy fence
riders. Hypocritical, two-faced storekeepers.*
     *Yeah, storekeepers are like that all over. They're eager to take our
money and beg us to defend their merchandise. We go to war for them
and then they call us down behind our backs. Damn all storekeepers,*
he though, as he remembered some of the treatment he'd received
in the military towns back home. *It's the same everywhere, except
they don't shoot us back home. But it's the storekeepers' fault we're
over here. If the lousy storekeepers of the world weren't so two-faced,
there wouldn't be any wars to fight.* He knew he was over-simplifying
things, but blaming everything on the storekeepers of the world gave
him a place to vent his anger, and that felt good. *Yes,* he fantasized,
*shoot them all. That would solve the world's problems. Look at them,
those liars standing in their shop doors pretending they like us. Like a
bunch of whores telling us they love only us. That were special, and
they're glad we're here. Dumb old us, we come over here to defend
their right to be free. They must think we're really stupid. Coming over
here and dying for a bunch of storekeepers who would cheat us in a
minute. We protect their democratic society, while all the time, behind*

our backs, behind their smiles, they're hiding the enemy, feeding the
enemy, and upping their prices on us.

As the truck passed the last shop, Tooley was relieved and
disappointed. Relieved that he hadn't blasted a few of the two-faced
storekeepers and disappointed for the very same reason. He felt
confused. *I would have liked to blast them, and then you'd see the
phony smiles come off their faces. You can't shoot civilians. Screw that
civilian crap. How in the hell can anyone tell? Shit, I'll bet they don't
even know from one minute to the next who's really on their side. The
wishy-washy bastards.*

He shook his head, trying to clear his mixed thinking and the
feelings they produced. The jungle began immediately after leaving
the village and thickened as they headed north along the east side of
the road. It was ideal terrain for an ambush. The noise of firing could
now be heard over the roar of the truck engines and the whine of
the tires.

Tooley strained his eyes trying to see. The distance between
their truck and the first truck had now narrowed to about thirty
meters. Tooley didn't know this driver and was reluctant to trust his
judgment. He leaned down and shouted, "Don't get too close." The
driver just raised his right hand off of the wheel and waved in a "no
shit" way. *Hell,* he chastised himself, *I should be in the first truck, not
Carson. I'm the platoon leader. What am I doing in the last truck?
Ranking man is supposed to ride in the front truck with the driver. Am
I losing control of my platoon? Am I becoming 'one of the men'? I need
to lead more. I need to control more. I'm the responsible one. Maybe the
colonel was right. Maybe I'm starting to think I'm one of them instead
of their leader. Where is my head? If Carson runs us into the ambush,
or even a new one, there'll be a lot of questions asked of me concerning
the loss of my men.*

Whoa, he told himself, *get hold of yourself. To hell with what those
jerks, your superiors, may think of you and your platoon's positioning in
these trucks. They don't know shit about you or your men. They don't
know the capabilities of men like Carson, Folger, and Leary, and how
they work together. So, whatever happens, don't let what they might
think have any influence on you. Not at all. They just can't count. This
is the best positioning of the men. Carson is a capable, experienced
leader of men. If he runs us into the fire then no one,* his mind repeated
it loudly and clearly, *no one could have done better, no one.*

*But by God, I am going to lead more. If I lose these men, I'll lose
them from the front, leading them. And I'm not going to do anything
that I couldn't live with back home if I survive. So no more thoughts*

of shooting storekeepers. Don't want to take that back home with me;
they're not worth it.

His thinking time was over now. The staccato firing was very
close. The first truck had stopped and the second truck was applying
its brakes. The men wasted no times unloading. The drivers retrieved
their M-14 rifles from the rack between the driver's seat and the
passenger seat and, with their flak jackets and helmets on, went to
the front of the forward truck. Flak jackets had been issued to all of
the men of that division before going to Vietnam. The vests were
heavy, and wearing them in the jungle took too much energy. Most
of the men in the Second Platoon didn't even know where their vests
were anymore. Unused equipment just seemed to disappear, like the
ropes and climbing equipment they had brought over.

The drivers were obviously nervous. The enemy was right
around the next bend in the road and who knew where else. As the
platoon formed up on each side of the road, Leary automatically took
the point on the right side. Folger positioned himself on the left side
of the road and back about ten meters. Carson aligned himself on
the right and twenty meters behind Leary, and so on. The formation
developed automatically; no words were spoken. In less than two
minutes from the time the truck had come to a complete stop, the
strategically arranged platoon was headed north down the road and
around the bend.

"What now?" The second truck driver asked the first, who was
the ranking man.

"Don't know. Wait, I guess."

"Wait! For what?" The second driver asked, a plea more than a
question.

"Look, I don't like standing here waiting any more than you do.
But we've been assigned to this platoon and we've got to take our
orders from them." He paused, and then said, "Shut up and stay alert.
We stay with our trucks and we wait. So take up a position and
cover the rear."

"Well, by God, I don't like it out here by ourselves."

"So what. You should be glad you don't have to go with them. So
get to the rear of your truck and stay awake."

"Well, what did the lieutenant say to you? Did he give you any
orders?"

"Yeah, he said to wait here. Now get to the rear."

"Okay, I'm going, but this is all screwed up. This is a strange
bunch. Scary bunch."

"Sure they're scary. They've been in the shit a lot. There were forty-four of them a few weeks ago and now what is there, maybe twenty-five. Thirty at most."

"I don't know, but couldn't be more than thirty of them."

"There's a bounty on them."

"Come on?"

"Yeah, Hanoi Hannah said she was gonna get 'em."

"You mean that North Vietnamese bitch on the radio?"

"That's the one. She announced just the other day that these men, the Sixteenth, were giving them a lot of trouble and that they'd become a priority for extermination. Something like that."

"Damn our luck, we're stuck here with them. I hate this army shit."

"Yeah, she named their unit, their base camp, and where they'd been. Spooky, huh?"

"Shit, more than spooky; we're screwed. I don't want any part of this bunch. If we ever get back to base camp alive, I'll quit complaining, no matter what happens, I swear. I'll be happy."

"Impossible to be happy over here, so just cover the damn rear."

As Leary came around the bend, it was easy to sum up the situation. The jungle receded on both sides of the road, and there were three empty trucks pulled off the west side of the road and parked in sloppy, hurried positions. Two of the trucks had their doors open. Twelve of the men from the trucks were all lying in a drainage ditch between the trucks and the road, and another three were across the road in the ditch on the other side. They all had rifles and were facing the thick jungle about fifty meters from the road. *They must have hit them as they came around the bend*, Leary thought. *None of them seem to be firing. No one seems to be wounded or dead.*

At that moment, the colonel's chopper came across the top of the east jungle, strafing it from north to south. His small, two-man chopper was equipped with a light electrically fired machine-gun mounted above each of its two skids. Compared to the big choppers, it looked like a toy and, when Leary glanced back at Folger, they both laughed. Then, Leary looked down at the men lying in the ditches. *Christ, there are enough of them to attack. At least not stay in these ditches. They're not even firing back and, judging by the lack of empty shell casings, haven't been. The firing we heard when driving up must have been from the colonel's chopper. Look at 'em, just waiting here to be saved, like a bunch of victims. And where is the enemy fire? Where is the danger? There doesn't seem to be any firing coming from the jungle.* Half disgusted, he led the platoon straight down the road right between the troops lying in the ditches. After passing the last man, he made a flanking movement to the right and began walking right towards the thick jungle wall. The platoon followed their point man.

As soon as the platoon started towards the jungle, about fifty meters from the road, artillery explosions started detonating in the jungle. *The colonel must have called it in,* Leary thought. The platoon, taking its lead from Leary, had turned and was now walking toward the jungle, too. They stepped over and around the men lying in the ditches without taking their eyes off the jungle. Shortly after Leary and Folger turned towards the jungle, a large sliver of metal from the artillery bombardment whizzed by and bounced on the ground between the two men. Leary glanced over at Folger, who just shrugged his shoulders. Leary laughed. *Crazy Folger, nothing fazes him.*

The smell of cordite sobered his thinking. *Hell, maybe they are lying there waiting to shoot us, and I've got us walking point-blank into the jungle. We'd better start them ducking,* Leary decided, as he started firing his rifle. When he fired, the platoon, though they hadn't seen any sign of the enemy either, opened up too. The artillery stopped shortly after seeing the platoon advance closer to the jungle. The colonel's chopper continued to fly overhead but had quit firing its machine guns as the line of men continued straight toward the jungle. All the men now fired their weapons from the hip. Step by step, they fired until their weapons were empty, then changed magazines and began shooting again.

Many hip-shooting rounds later, the platoon entered the thick foliage. They were all relieved that they were no longer in the open. Now they, too, could hide and shoot. Once they were about ten meters inside the jungle, Tooley halted them, and they automatically set up positions. There was no sign of the enemy, and they could no longer see the road. Tooley's face purpled with anger. *That damned Leary, he just turned and marched directly into this chaos, and everyone just followed him in. Then he started firing at who knows what, everyone else started firing, and I doubt that anyone has much ammo left. They just followed him, dumping magazine after magazine into this mess. That boy needs to be controlled more. I need to take a stronger leadership position.*

He took a couple of deep breaths as he fought down his anger. Then he asked in a hoarse, strained voice, already knowing the answer. "Any casualties?"

"No, sir, none," Carson calmly answered.

"Thank God for that," Tooley said. "Count ammo and report."

Tooley forced himself to take deep slow breaths as he waited for the ammo count to come in. When it came, it was as he feared. Everyone had only one magazine left, except Leary and Hart. The machine gunners were both almost out of ammo, with less than a half belt apiece. Hart, of course, had all of his one hundred and twenty rounds, and Leary had two magazines or forty rounds. Tooley angrily picked his way through the dense bamboo and thick brush to Leary's position. Once there, he signaled for Carson to join him. Leary sat calmly, facing away from the road, with his back leaning against a large tree. His helmet was off and lying on the ground next to his rifle butt. He looked infuriatingly relaxed.

Carson knelt by Tooley, who was almost on top of Leary because of the limited space. Tooley was close enough for Leary to smell his foul breath. He could plainly see that they were both angry with him, especially the lieutenant. But he didn't respond to their anger. He just sat there starring blankly.

In a low whisper, the kind one would use in church, Tooley said, "Damn you, Leary, what did you think you were doing?"

Leary still didn't respond. By now, everyone knew what was going on and the tension was thick enough to cut with a knife. Everyone watched and waited. "Why did you walk straight down the damn road, then God help us, turn and take us right into this jungle?" Leary still didn't move, not even a facial muscle. Tooley was so angry now that he screeched, "Have you gone completely mad? Are you trying to get us all killed?"

Finally, Leary looked Tooley straight in the eye for a moment before saying, "I honestly don't know, Lieutenant. It just seemed like the right thing to do. One step at a time. Or maybe I just felt like it. I really don't know."

The purple veins in Tooley's neck pulsated as he said, "You felt like it? Leary, you *felt* like it?! What kind of shit-for-brains reason is that? Since when do we do what we *feel* like? We do what makes sense, what we're trained to do, but we never do what we *feel* like!"

There was a ten-second pause before Leary responded, and his voice was strangely calm. "Well then, sir, maybe you've had the wrong man on point all this time. What, besides gut feelings, did you think I was going by?"

Tooley was shocked. He hadn't really thought about it before. Not in that way. "You mean all this time, you've been leading based on how you felt at the moment? I let you lead because you seemed to have a special talent for the point, but I figured it was some kind of super-analytical ability. Some great detective type of brain function. I had no idea that you were leading us around with your damn *feelings*."

With no note of apology, Leary answered, "Yes, Lieutenant Tooley, feelings, always feelings. No analysis at all. In fact, thinking of any nature seems to interfere with its functioning."

The shock of it all caused Tooley to start laughing, at first from frustration and then because of the irony of it. It was infectious, and soon the others burst out laughing, too. Even those who couldn't hear what had been said were caught up in the moment. After a minute, Tooley stood up and said loud enough for everyone to hear, "This life is sure a funny one." He paused to control his laughter. "It'll sure surprise you. All this time, I thought Leary was leading us by some super-sleuth thing, some great gifted power of observation and detection. Wrong. Now I find out he's been leading us with whims of feeling. He does what he feels like. Now that's scary."

"Lieutenant, sir," Carson said. "What difference does it make what Leary calls it, as long as it works? And it does work. There was no danger here. Not when we got here. Those were a bunch of rear-echelon people from the airborne. Cooks, supply people, not combat people. They probably had one shot fired at them. I sure didn't see any dead or wounded among them. I don't remember even seeing any bullet holes in the trucks or scars on the ground or pavement. Probably one shot drove them off the road and into the ditches where they called for help. Or, maybe the colonel saw them from his helicopter and called us and the artillery in. All of this could have been caused by one rifle shot. The sniper fired once and took off. Job done. They do it all the time."

The laughter had released the tension from Tooley's body, and he was more relaxed as he said, "You're right, Sergeant Carson. Guess I overreacted a little. Do it any way you have to, Leary; just don't call it feelings in front of me. Shit, I just can't deal with our lives being directed by a feeling. Anyway, what do we do now? We are out of ammo and the sniper is probably long gone and who knows in what direction."

Folger spoke without looking over at the three men. "I think we just sit here for a couple of hours. It's nice here, cool and quiet. I hear the airborne taking off now, and the colonel's chopper is gone. The game is over. Why take this thing any further? If we go back now, the captain might still have time to find something else for us to do. Let's just rest right here. Give it a couple of hours, then circle back to the trucks, and get back in time for supper."

"What'll I report when we get back?" Tooley asked

"The truth," Folger said. "Tell the truth. We came, broke up the ambush, went into the jungle but found no enemy dead or alive. Tell them we burnt up a lot of ammo, and we're back without any casualties or bodies. Just leave out the part about us napping before we came back."

And that is what they did. It was peaceful in the jungle and they felt safe there. They dozed off occasionally. There was no talking, no visiting, just the normal jungle noises. The longer they were there, the more the small, crawly creatures of the jungle accepted their presence, and it had a healing effect on them.

When they got back to the trucks around 1600 hours, the drivers were worn out with tension. No one in the platoon said anything as they loaded into the trucks and returned to base camp.

At base camp, the captain was pleased. Oh, he was a little disappointed that they hadn't killed any of the enemy. Disappointed that the thorn in his side, Leary, was still around, but his attitude remained clear. The Second Platoon was the point of his spear, and he would hurl it at the enemy whenever and wherever he could. Of course, from as far back as he could. Eventually, he knew, he would be rid of them. And fortunately, he thought, *I already have new plans for my spear point.*

22

THE CARSON FAMILY

The Carson residence was three houses down from the Patkins' home at Fort Riley, Kansas. It had the same floor plan as the other houses in the noncommissioned officers housing area. They were all red brick homes with the kitchen, dining room, and living room downstairs, plus two bedrooms and a bath upstairs. Jessica Carson was sitting on the couch mending her son Jerome's blue jeans. She was in her early forties with the figure of a much younger woman and strikingly beautiful skin. It was every bit as black as her husband's, but unlike his, it was blemish free. She was missing Alexander more than ever this evening.

Jerome, at twelve, was their oldest child, and he was very hard on his clothing. He was never much for books but was an accomplished athlete who never missed a chance to play sports. Not just any sport, though, preferably football or basketball. He liked his sports full of rough and fast physical action. His younger brother, ten-year-old Henry, was more the intellectual type and was even now diligently doing his homework.

Jerome is lighter-skinned than the rest of us, she thought. *Must have been a honky in the woodpile somewhere in our past.* She chuckled. *My Alexander would frown if he ever heard me say such a thing. He has no humor when it comes to racial remarks. Probably gets it from his father. But I think it's funny and I'm woman enough to keep it to myself. It's my man's strong principles that make him such a good husband. Well, that and the way he looks at me.*

The phone rang, its loud obnoxious noise making them jump.

"Hello," she said into the receiver.

"Hello, Jessica, how are you?"

"I'm fine, Dad Carson, how're you and Mom there in Atlanta?"

"Well, honey, we're just fine. How are the boys doing without their dad?"

"Oh, they seem to be handling it all right. I mean Jerome's grades are still poor, but his athletic participation is as strong as ever."

Abraham Carson laughed. "That Jerome is some athlete all right, a fine boy. You know his dad was the same way when he was growing up. Leastways until he got into high school, then he took more interest in academics. So I wouldn't worry much about it. What about little Henry, is he still an 'A' student?"

Now Jessica laughed. "Yes, indeed. He's a delight and is working on his homework at the kitchen table as we speak. How is the church doing, Dad?"

"Well we're barely keeping the roof on, as usual. I'm still giving them fire and brimstone on Sundays, but I believe I've become milder in my sermons the last couple of years. Either getting old or don't think scaring them half to death does any good anymore. Whatever, the attendance is higher than it's ever been and I'm pleased. Of course, I still work at the plant, too. The church has never brought in enough to pay me anything, much less support us. We are poor working people here and that's just the way it is. Though sometimes, especially on Monday morning as I'm heading to work, I think about finding another church to preach in, one that has a little more affluent congregation. Of course, you know I never will. I love these people and will preach for free as long as I can, or as long as they will have me."

"Well, we're all very proud of you here, and Alexander is extremely proud of you."

"How is my boy? His mother and I don't hear much from him. Seems like he writes less and less. We watch the news every night, hoping for good news. News like he's coming home soon or the war is over. But all we see is about troops being built up."

"To tell you the truth, Dad, I don't hear as much as I want to either. He doesn't write me often either. I know they're in the thick of it because several of the wives have already gotten telegrams. Poor Mrs. Cambel, her husband was their platoon sergeant. She got a telegram last week saying that her husband had been killed."

"Oh, I am so sorry to hear that. Scares me."

"Well, Dad, losing her husband is just part of it. She will also lose her home and most of her income."

"How's that?"

"Well, he's the one in the army. When he gets killed, she no longer qualifies for housing, and her income gets reduced to survivor benefits. I don't know how much that is but I doubt it's even half of what they get now, which is just enough to live on. And Mrs. Patkins, her husband is one of Alexander's sergeants, got a telegram at the same time saying that he had been wounded. The week before, they lost half of the first squad and, the week before that, they lost three men in an ambush." Jessica lowered her voice, realizing that Jerome could hear her. She need not have bothered, though, because the kids at school knew it all. "Dad, I'm scared to death. I mean his own platoon sergeant and his own sergeant both getting it. It's all around him, Dad, and I just don't know. I'm sick in my stomach most of the time. I just try and hold an optimistic but realistic attitude with the boys. I don't lie to them, but I don't talk about it much with them either."

"I know it's hard, honey, but we must keep the faith. We must believe in the rightness of God's direction. You know you can always talk to Mom and me. Of course, we are worried too, more now than ever."

"I'm sorry, Dad, I don't want to worry you two. Maybe nothing will happen to Alexander, I hope not."

Abraham Carson sounded solemn and reflective as he said, "It's God's will whatever happens. I'm not God and I have to continually remember that he has a better, smarter view than I do. I suppose in some ways it's my fault that he's over there. It's my fault that he's in the army. I named him Alexander, fully knowing that the name means 'defender of mankind.' And that's what the boy is doing; he's over there in Vietnam defending those people from the godless Communists. He is doing God's work and, if he's taken in the process, I'll hurt, and badly, but I must accept it."

"Dad, I can't even think like that. I can't think of life without that man as my husband. I just can't. It would cause me to break down completely. I'm so close to losing it now, we'd better talk about something else."

"You know what the boys' names mean?"

"No," she said, welcoming the diversion.

"Henry means 'ruler of an estate.'"

She managed a laugh. "Let's hope that name carries some power. I wouldn't mind if he grew up to rule an estate, give Alexander and me a place to go when we get old." They both laughed at that.

"And Jerome means 'holy name.' I think that fits him, too. He's a special, smart, and loving boy."

"Indeed, my baby is special."

"Do you know what your name means, Jessica?"

"No, Dad, I don't have any idea, but I hope it's a good one."

"It surely is. It is the best, it means 'grace of God,' and that you are."

"Thank you, Dad. I'll let you know, when I know something. Don't feel too bad about the shortage of letters from Alexander. They are busy."

"Yes dear, doing God's work can be very time-consuming."

"Yes . . . well, how's Mom?"

"She's fine and she wants to speak with you. Here she is now. You take care and keep us posted. We love you all."

"We love you too, Dad."

23

REST

The captain had accepted the lieutenant's report on the ambush yesterday without comment. *Maybe our luck is changing,* Tooley thought. *Maybe we can get some good duty for a change. It's good to be here. It isn't much, but it's home.* In truth, it was far from his home. But, compared to the jungle, it was definitely better. The base camp was a place where they had a change of clothes, some fresh spring water to bathe in, and a shelter, be it ever so humble, to sleep in. Now, hopefully, they could lie around for days, regroup, rest, and maybe even have some fun. Though they had received some mail along the way, judging by the amount waiting for them when they got back, a large amount of it had been held. Tooley sat on a cot in the platoon bunker that only he and Nash now occupied. Cambel's absence made the place lonely. Worse yet, they had to deal with his stuff. Pack it up and send it home. Neither Tooley nor Nash wanted to do it. It was so final and they had liked him so much. *The people deemed valuable live underground while the more expendable ones live above the ground in small two-man tents,* Tooley thought.

The command bunkers were huge in comparison to the fighting bunkers on the perimeter. They were back behind the lines, had no firing ports in them, and were for the protection of the men in charge only. Since they were lived in most of the time, the slithering and crawling critters weren't as eager to occupy them as they were the defensive bunkers. Still, upon their return, "Killer Nash" had to eliminate a small constrictor that had taken up residence behind the sandbags on the south wall.

But none of that bothered the lieutenant anymore. He had never had a great fear of bugs and snakes anyway. Like most boys, he had had his share of them as pets. He had even had a rattlesnake for a while. Well, he and his buddies did when they were all about twelve. Rattlesnakes were plentiful on the outer limits of Pueblo, Colorado, in the summertime. They had taken a long hike one hot summer day just to get one. The search had scared them several times before they finally trapped one in the shade of a large rock. They dug it out with their sticks, almost killing it, and scooted it into a sack they had brought with them. They had taken turns hiding it, and it had been exciting. Moving it from garage to garage. It was a big secret, a great and dangerous secret, one they didn't dare share with their parents. Just as the secret was on the verge of becoming parental knowledge, having been hinted at once too often, the snake was found dead one morning by Jimmy Loger, whose turn it was to keep the snake. They never did know what killed it. They had only had it for six days but, although they would not admit it, they were all relieved when it died.

Truth was, he smiled to himself, *we were all afraid of it, and having it around was starting to get on our nerves. It was easy to see that we were all scared of it. Being brave can wear a person out. Sure, it was easy to be brave at first, when it was a new adventure. When it was a thrill that produced all the adrenaline necessary to overcome fear, then it was easy. But later, as the days wore on, the adventure of it turned to dread. Dread not admitted, but clearly visible in each boy when it was his turn to look after the snake.*

How life can change us, he thought. *Now I sleep, walk among, and lie near, hopefully not on, snakes, bugs, and spiders all the time.* A smile appeared on his face. *Over here, we've come to judge a creature, big or small, by whether or not it considers us a member of its food chain. Now, leeches certainly want our blood and need to be burnt or scraped off. Mosquitoes see us as food too, but most of the rest of the crawly things over here don't and are just trying to make their way through life. Even the deadly cobra,* and Tooley had already seen two of them, *just wants to be left alone. Once they sense that we humans are too large to eat, they just want to get away from us. Of course, if surprised and cornered, one might strike at you, but only if it has no other choice. Yeah, I've made peace with the jungle and its occupants. To survive in this place one has to have respect for it and its residents—you've got to mind your own business. Sure, be respectful of another animals' space but, whenever possible, just let it live in peace. Violate any living being's space and you leave it no choice: it must fight you. If you stick your hand in a dark place, you could be violating the home of a scorpion. If so, it has no choice; it must sting you. It certainly doesn't hold a grudge; it can't think. It doesn't say, "I can't wait to bite*

*a human." Humans do that, though, yeah, they're always looking for
another of their kind to attack, put down and, in cases like Vietnam,
kill each other. So, with few exceptions, creatures are a peaceful bunch.
The exceptions,* he decided, *would have to be the bamboo viper and
fire ants. Well, not the ants, though they are mean. But still, you have
to bump their tree or bush before they'll drop on you.* He winced as he
remembered. *They turn their big ass straight up and bury their sizable
pincers into the flesh. God, it hurts. Feels like fire all over your arms,
neck, face, and any other exposed areas. Of course, the answer is don't
bump their trees or bushes. But that silly snake,* he mused, *it could be
the exception to the rule. It's a mean little bastard and, if you piss it
off, you've got to kill it. That's why they call it "two steps" because you
only have two steps worth of life left after it bites you. I don't know how
much of that I believe. I haven't known anybody who's been bitten by
one, but it is aggressive, I've seen that for myself. Hell, Leary says he
"feels" better when he sees an animal up ahead—if the animals are
visible, then he knows there are no humans there.*

He smiled, remembering. *We'd been sitting in a small group
talking, down the hill in the platoon area. It was a few days after
first arriving at the base campsite. The platoon had been working on
the bunkers and was taking a break in the shade. For the most part,
we were all lying back on an elbow or our backs and were smoking,
talking, and eating. Saying whatever might came into our minds. We
were pretty tight then as a group of men on a team, but we hadn't been
bloodied yet. No killing had been done on either side. It was during a
time when the conversations had died out that that little camouflaged
snake slithered out of the grass and into the clearing at the bottom of
the hill about twenty feet from where we were. Everyone saw it because
of how the red gravel contrasted with its natural colors.*

Soon after that, he mused, *Folger had picked up a couple of small
pebbles from a crumbling granite outcropping near his position and
pitched them at the bamboo viper. He clearly wasn't endangering the
snake with the size of pebbles he was using, when he missed. Having
missed, he picked up a couple more pebbles and tried again. Repetition
improved his accuracy, and everyone started laughing as one of his
shots landed close to the little snake's V-shaped head. It turned toward
us and, as if taking offense to the laughter as well as the attack, started
up the hill straight at us. Well, in a few seconds, the fun was over. We all
scrambled to our feet, and the ones closest to it peppered him with dirt
but that was no deterrent. Most critters would have changed direction,
but not this species—it just kept coming up the hill. Of course it couldn't
win and it finally lost the battle at the top of the hill with Folger's rifle*

butt. *Nonetheless, it kept attacking, right up to the very last, to that
final butt-stroke which smashed the brains out of its small poisonous
head. It fought Folger without the slightest hint of diminished purpose
until it could no longer move. When it was over, we all felt a little bad
about it. Even Folger.* Nothing much was said, Tooley remembered,
a few exclamations, like: *"Damn, that little shit was tough," "Christ,
he wouldn't quit coming,"* and *"He wouldn't stop for nothing."* But
*everyone knew, from that moment on, that that high –spirited little
snake was nothing to mess with and if you did one of you would have
to die.* He was pleased to find that he could feel affection towards
something again, even if it were just a snake. And he chuckled as he
mumbled to himself, "The snake just wouldn't be pushed around."
The radio operator heard the mumbling but didn't even look up.
These days, he was comfortable with people mumbling.

Well, Tooley decided, *I'd better read these letters. I haven't read
or written any since I burnt those letters—when was that,* he tried to
remember and finally he decided it was both a hundred years ago and
last month sometime. *Why can't I write? Maybe 'cause to write you
need to be a certain person, with certain interests that you like to talk
about. I'm not sure anymore that I'm anyone they would like to hear
from. I'm afraid to write about what I'm interested in now because the
people I love couldn't understand and would think less of me. I'll try
and remember who I was a month ago and maybe mimic that person so
I can get some of these letters answered. If I read the letters carefully,
maybe I can get back to the person they know and want to hear from.*
But, even after reading the letters, he couldn't get into writing home
and decided to take a walk through the platoon area, hoping he
would come across something or someone who might jar him out of
his mind-freeze.

"I'll be down in the platoon area," he told Nash as he left.

"Yes, sir."

As he climbed the ramp coming out of the bunker, he could
not shut his mind off. *We were once close,* he thought as weariness
overwhelmed him, *all of us, my family, my friends, my lover, but they
have remained the same or even grown in a loving direction. They have
probably become more loving. But me, I'm so alone now, I'm afraid
I don't have any loving feelings left inside me. I am empty of feeling
for them and the things that they do. How could I explain any of this
to them at home? It was only a short time ago that I held sacred the
same things they do. Now, anymore, what I value no one back home
could possibly understand. I've come to hold dear the spirit of a snake
willing to die fighting, no matter what the odds. The heavy feel of a*

powerful rifle in my hands, the feeling of power when I fire it. Even the smell of it is good, the smell when it fires and the burning oil when it gets hot from continual firing. God help me, I even get pleasure from such things as seeing an enemy soldier go down after shooting him with that same rifle, the taste of a good drink of water, a cool breeze to dry the continual sweat from my smelly body, a clean pair of socks. And the vicious anger that I'm capable of producing. Those are the things that I enjoy. How can I pretend, even long enough to write home, that I care anymore about them or the things in their lives? On some level, we are already dead to each other, they to me and me to them. Barely audibly, he mumbled to himself, "I cannot, and could never pretend to be something I'm not."

Tooley walked through the platoon area asking his men how they were doing and if they needed anything. He stopped and squatted down at the small tent Leary shared with Folger. From what Tooley had seen, most of his men appeared to be having the same trouble that he was. Those men who were writing letters seemed to be doing more pausing than writing. Soldiers in Vietnam didn't have to have real stationery on which to write home. There was no soap for the soldiers, but there was plenty of paper. A soldier could write on the back of a C-ration box and, if properly addressed, it would be delivered, as would all mail, free of charge. Leary looked up and said, "Hi, Lieutenant, I can't think of anything to say to Mary. I used to write pages about what we do over here. Now I can't think of anything to say. How could she understand? What can I say that doesn't make me sound like a crazy killer? I don't think the people back home could really understand that we're fighting for our lives over here. Killing is what we're here to do. She wouldn't want to hear the truth, like, 'Dear Mary, we haven't had to kill any gooks for a couple of weeks and we're enjoying the rest. We had an ideal chance to kill a bunch of them a couple a weeks ago, but the colonel wouldn't let us do it. Oh well, Mary, maybe next time.'"

It struck them both as funny, more from frustration over the problem than because it was humorous. Whatever the reason, it was a good release and they approached hysteria as they fought to control their laughter. Tooley sank to his knees, and Leary thought he might pass out when he saw stars before his eyes. Carson, Folger, and several other men of the Second Platoon came over to see what was so hilarious. Everyone needed a good laugh and, as soon as they had gathered around, Tooley, still fighting for control, explained, "Leary and I were talking about how hard it is to find anything to write home about, and Leary started pretending like he was writing the truth and," Tooley had to stop to control his mirth enough to continue, "hell, Leary finish your pretend letter."

"OK, I'll try," Leary, said, wiping the tears off his cheeks with the back of his hand. "Dear Mom and Dad, You know how you always taught me to wash after going to the bathroom. Well I don't wash over here at all. Not much anyway, we don't have any washing facilities, and soap is as scarce as hen's teeth. We all stink to high heaven, and I haven't had a bath with soap since I got here. I hate to tell you this, Mom, but you were wrong to make such a big thing out of washing all the time. The smart way is to not wash at all. It's just a matter of time before everyone gets accustomed to the smell. Once that happens, we've eliminated a burdensome chore. Oh, and Mom, about wearing clean underwear, you know, in case you go to the hospital, well, we've solved that problem too, we just don't wear any at all. Dad, remember when I was little and you caught me going to the toilet outside? You said that it was unsanitary and could cause disease. Well, my friends and I have been going outside, and not washing our hands either, for almost two months now and we can't seem to catch anything. Dad, it appears as if you have been misinformed by your parents, from their parents, and so on, and that you have been burdened with doing and passing on a lot of needless things." Everyone shrieked with laughter, more from the need to laugh and the ability to identify with the problem than the humor of the material. Leary paused for a breath and then continued, "I will admit that all of us, my friends here at camp as well as myself, do have cracked and bleeding feet, especially between the toes. I do think, though, that this condition is caused more from the wrong footwear than the lack of washing. It seems, Mom, that they want us to wear out the old clothes first. You would be very disappointed to know that it is very wet here and we don't have any rubbers, of any kind." Egged on by the laughter, Leary continued. "Oh, Mom, Dad, the funniest thing, I've just got to tell you about it, happened to one of the guys, a couple of days ago, while he was doing his daily business in the jungle. Yeah, you're going to love this. He was out there in the bushes with his pants down when the shooting started. Was that ever funny. Him trying to get his pants up, not wanting to die like that. I thought we would die laughing."

The laughter stopped abruptly. Everything became quiet. The men were serious again, Leary too, and he quit talking. The moment was lost and the men dispersed, making comments like, "Yeah, the folks would be interested in that, all right," "We haven't got shit to say to them," and "No wonder I can't think of anything to write about, and they wouldn't want to hear about our life, or lack of it, over here, it would depress them."

When he saw the captain's radio operator waving for him, Tooley said, "We're alone in this. They don't care back home. They can't know, no one can but us and what you don't know about you can't really care about. There is no way for us to tell them. You need to be here to know this world. It's unimaginable otherwise." With that, he walked up the hill to the company command post bunker where he learned that the captain had plans for Leary and his men that would bring Tooley to the brink of mutiny.

24

DEATH PATROL

Lieutenant Tooley lay on his cot in the platoon command post bunker. The briefing had been long, frustrating, and left him bursting with anger. He had broken protocol, interrupting the captain as he shouted, "What idiot dreamt this up? We're here to rest up, spend a few days, weeks maybe, doing nothing but taking care of ourselves. You know, sir, rest, as in not working, not doing what one normally does. But doing things like relaxing, writing letters home, drying out boots, and letting the warm sun heal cracked and bleeding feet."

The captain had held up his hand in an effort to halt Tooley's building rage. He was afraid that his lieutenant might question his right to command in front of his radio operator, in his own CP. This would be a terrible loss of face, dignity, and possible position in his climb up the career ladder. The captain of Charlie Company needed to shut his lieutenant up.

But Tooley would not be stopped, and the captain knew that if he tried to do any more than just hold out his hand, it would only pour fuel on Tooley's already raging fire. As Tooley ranted, his face turning ever darker, the captain thought, *Damn, what's wrong with these men over here? Can't any of them just take orders like they did in the States? Why is it that this place is full of insubordinate soldiers?* Tooley ranted, "We were told, and we told the men, that we would have at least three weeks to rest up. Now you tell me that we'll move out tomorrow and string out along Highway One."

"Yes, Lieutenant, the battalion will spend a couple of days getting familiar with the area so we can guard against an attack on the truck convoy that will be coming up from Saigon in four days. From now on, a convoy will be coming up to resupply this camp every month. So get used to it. This will be a monthly duty for us."

Now Tooley's face was turning back to its normal red color as he consciously took deep breaths, his anger subsiding with the effort. The captain continued. "Yes, Lieutenant Tooley, that's what Charlie Company has been ordered to do. This base camp, our base camp, needs fresh supplies at least once a month. It's the only home we have and a truck convoy is the only way of getting the necessary supplies up here." Then, in a firm West Point voice, he asked, "Do you have any problem with that, Lieutenant?"

Tooley, still struggling to get his rage under control, wanted to blurt out, "You bet your sweet ass, you toy soldier." But somehow he didn't. Instead he said, "Yes, sir, I do have a problem with those orders. So do the rest of my fellow officers, though they may not admit it. Supply this base camp with what? What do they need here, what does the camp exist for, what good is it if we cannot rest our men here?"

"Lieutenant," the captain said, thinking he'd finally found a way to put Tooley back in his place, "this base camp exists for us, in support of us. We come back here for hot meals, a few nights rest in a fairly secure area, a place to watch a movie on the outdoor theater built, I would add, while we were gone, to drink beer and to rest. In order to enjoy these things, Lieutenant Tooley, this base camp needs to be supplied on a monthly basis. And to make sure that the convoys get safely up here from Saigon, we all need to do our part in securing the road."

"Bull," Tooley exclaimed, "what do they need to be resupplied for? Let me see if I understand this, Captain. In the future, from tomorrow on, we will spend our free time, our rest time, going to ambushes for other battalions, seeing that these people here in base camp have enough candy bars, movies, beer, steaks, and potatoes to enjoy themselves with while we're out hunting in the jungle, eating C-rations, sleeping on the ground and dying. In short, when will we have time to enjoy these goodies? These luxury supplies that we need to see get up here? What do the men in this base camp really do for us? Here's the way my men will see it. They're gone for about twenty-five days, surviving, if they can, under the worst of conditions and then, when they get a few days off, a few days to regain their sanity, to try and save the part of themselves that is still human, they're sent out to guard a string of trucks bringing luxuries they will be too busy to enjoy. Now is that going to make any sense to them? Hell, no, it won't."

He flinched inside, remembering that he had shouted that part, stopping the captain, his company commander, from speaking. But he couldn't stop himself as he leaned his head down towards the captain, looked him directly in the eye, and asked, "Have you ever heard the term our men use to describe the people in the base camps, the safe areas, Saigon, et cetera?"

"Personally, Lieutenant, I don't give one damn what they think. I really can't afford to care what they think and neither can you. Hell, if you left it up to them, they wouldn't want to do a damn thing. And you know it."

Calmer now, almost resigned, Tooley said, "There is a balance that must be maintained. A fairness that must be consistent and visible if men in these conditions are to stay above a rabble."

"That's your job, Lieutenant, and mine. We must demand that they do what is expected of them. We must get the most out of them. All they have to give. It's our only job. Anything else is shit and you know it."

"Sir, you can't push men who have nothing to lose. They are at that place now, sir. We have nothing left to take away from them. They must be led from here on out. To lead them, fairness must be maintained."

"So what's the problem, Lieutenant? Lead them, push them, embarrass them, I don't care. Just make them do what we need to have done."

"I just don't know how they're going to like protecting the goodies for these REMFs, sir."

"Knock that shit off, Lieutenant. The rear-echelon motherfuckers are over here doing their jobs too—just like you and your fighting boys."

"Not the same at all, Captain. Not the same at all—and you know it"

Though in his heart the captain partly agreed, he could do nothing about it and was tired of the whole conversation. "That's enough. Damn it, Lieutenant, I didn't make these orders up. I'm just a company commander. These things are out of my control, and I'm sick of getting the heat for them."

Well, damn if you aren't the holy one, Tooley thought.

"Some decisions, of course, are mine to make. Humble as they might be. I do have the say about who does what in the company." Being extra careful now, choosing his words. "Of course, within the scope of our mission. Like," he paused for effect, doling out the words slowly, making Tooley wait for the punch line, "what person, or group of people, are best suited for a particular task or position. Speaking of which, we've been assigned a special mission, an important one, to be sure. One that must be preformed every month before the convoy comes up. At first, I didn't know who to give this responsibility to."

What a bunch of crap, Tooley thought, *he loves it.*

"Of course, the answer was there all the time. The colonel was right to give this special mission to our company; we have the right men for the job. Actually, you have the right men for the job. So, thank you, Lieutenant, and understand this, because I will only tell you once, though you may ask questions when I'm through. But do confine your questions to tactical matters and not command ones. In other words, stay in your place, Lieutenant. That is a formal order. And from this point on this is a formal briefing."

The captain pointed to a map folded on his field desk and said, "Here, Lieutenant Tooley, is what I want Sergeant Leary and the men of Carson's old squad to do."

It was strange, Leary thought. *Strange and yet logical based upon the way things are here in Vietnam. The lieutenant had admitted, after calling Sergeant Carson and me to the platoon CP, that it was highly irregular for a squad to be temporarily assigned to Leary, the youngest sergeant in it.* "The captain wants Leary and the Second Squad to go by truck to the South Vietnamese fort south of the village of Ben Cat. We've all seen it. It's been arranged with the commander of this fort for you and the men," he looked directly at Leary," to stay there at night. We think you will be safe there. They've never been attacked, even though they are on the edge of the Iron Triangle. You and your men are to run a daily patrol out of that fort." He directed their attention to a map on his field desk, to this rice paddy here at the edge of the Triangle. You'll make a daily reconnaissance sweep from the fort through the jungle area here." Using his pen, he pointed out a darker green area representing dense jungle west of the fort.

The symbols for a rice paddy were clearly marked by a light green area with many groups of three vertical slashes. He looked up again to make sure that he had their attention and to take a reading of their attitudes. He could see that both sergeants were affected by his words. Whether it was anger, irritation, or fear, he could not determine. They were both starting to fidget.

Tooley looked away immediately; he did not want questions, not yet anyway. He had to present this in the best possible way. He could not let these men, especially Leary, know how it was that he was selected to lead this patrol. Not that Tooley wasn't a man for truth, it was just that he believed that Leary would perform better not knowing the captain's attitude about him. In truth, the lieutenant was so angry with the captain that he had entertained the fantasy of blowing the captain's brains out with his forty-five. Be that what it may, he could tell that both men sensed what had happened and knew that the exclusion of a senior NCO's on a patrol of this nature was highly unusual. *Well*, Tooley told himself, *it was within the rights of any commander in war.* But he knew that this was an irregular and unbalancing situation.

As Tooley turned his attention back to the map, his manner disallowed the questions that he knew were coming. "Once you break out of the jungle here," he pointed to a large rice paddy area on the map, "you will swing south about four hundred meters. Stay on the east edge of the rice paddy until you come to this clearing here. As you can see, this clearing is grassy and has a small river, a creek really, which heads due east, about two miles. It runs under Highway One. This bridge on the highway, over the river, is also the responsibility of our company. According to headquarters, our company will from now on and until further notice guard this bridge during the several days it takes to get a resupply convoy up from Saigon. The convoy will come up once a month. Your job, Leary, will be to make this sweep every month. So get familiar with the area. Your mission, and only job, is to make sure that there is no large enemy force in the area that could surprise the battalion and threaten the destruction of the bridge." Anticipating the question, he said, "I know, what about the bridge during the rest of the month? Our engineers can install a culvert in a couple of days, should the bridge be knocked out when we're not there. Thus, the reason for being on the road two days before the convoy comes up from Saigon. Until we get there to guard the bridge, your only mission is to get familiar with the area. Without the bridge, there can be no resupply convoy. As you can see by the map, the jungle comes up close to the edge of the road here by the bridge, and you and your men are our only warning of an attack large enough to take the bridge from us and destroy it.

"So to recap, Sergeant Leary, your job is to conduct a patrol every day. You and your men will be trucked to the fort this afternoon. You can use today to get acquainted with your Vietnamese hosts and run your first patrol tomorrow. You will have two days, two patrols, before the company and the rest of the battalion string out along the road to guard for the convoy. The third day, your third patrol, will be the day that the trucks should start coming through from Saigon. It will probably take a couple of days for the convoy to get through. The trucks will not need guarding on the way back; our enemy is too smart to waste men and arms on empty trucks. Questions?"

"Yes, sir," Carson held Tooley's gaze as he spoke. "What's going on here, sir? Why, in all that is good, are Leary and the squad going out on this patrol and leaving me, their squad leader, here?"

"Fair question, Sergeant Carson. Sergeant Patkins is still in the hospital and, as of right now, you have been assigned to this company CP. You, Sergeant Carson, are our new platoon sergeant." There was a moment of silence. "That should be no surprise to you or to anyone else. Unofficially, you have been since Sergeant Cambel's death; now it's official. Congratulations, Sergeant Carson, you are the right man for the job. The captain," Tooley's tone made this word interchangeable with the word 'shit,' "feels, and rightly so, that the second squad, with Leary in charge, is the best we have for this job. The second squad has been bloodied the most and survived. It is the best point squad in the battalion. Let's face it, gentlemen, this is a lonely patrol in a lonely place, and the second squad of this platoon is the one best suited for the task."

"I appreciate you putting me in as platoon sergeant, sir," Carson said, "but I would just feel better if I were along on this one patrol, to back up Leary, sir."

"Sergeant, I know how you feel. You are one hell of a man, an ace of a soldier, and the best friend anyone could have. It's true that Leary and the boys of the second could use you out there. If I had two of you, I would risk letting one of you go." He didn't want to make matters worse by telling them that the captain had specified that Carson would not go. "I don't, however, and the rest of the men in this platoon need you, too. There are more of them and they are in more need of you than Leary. It's time to let the rest of the platoon have some of you. Sergeant Cambel was a good friend to me, a better platoon sergeant than anyone could ask for, but he's dead, and you are the one to fill his position." He could tell by the look on Carson's face that he was searching for some possible counter, some argument, that might change the situation so that he could go with

Leary. Finally, resignation shown on his face as he realized that there was no recourse. As reluctant acceptance became evident in Carson's eyes, Tooley said, "That is final, Sergeant Carson. There will be no changes in those orders. Any other questions?"

"Sir, will we have a radio?" Leary asked. "It seems like quite a distance to patrol with such a small force. If we get into trouble, we'll need to be able to call for help. And judging by what we know of the area, it's a territory which the enemy owns."

"No, Sergeant Leary, you won't have a radio. You are to patrol and familiarize only. You are to engage the enemy only when necessary to make good your escape." From the look on Leary's face, it was clear to Tooley that he wasn't buying the explanation for not having a radio, so Tooley made an attempt to explain further. "We just have so many radios, not that we couldn't get more, I suppose, but the amount of radio traffic in Vietnam is horrendous as it is. Our army, air force, navy, and marines are all operating in this small country and they all have radios. All are constantly talking on them. Then, on top of that, the South Vietnamese forces all have radios and then there are the other United Nations forces such as the Korean Army and so on. Not to leave out the enemy and what radios they might have. So the airwaves are crowded and besides, we have only one radio operator and he needs to stay with the company CP."

"Well, sir," Leary said, making one more attempt to get a radio, "I'm a trained and experienced radio operator. That was my job in Korea, and I'm qualified to calibrate and know radio procedures."

"Yes, I know that, Sergeant, and so does the captain. In truth, I did ask him for a radio, using the same arguments that you've used and the reply was still no."

Leary's voice was higher than normal when he said, "Sir, these patrols are going to take us at least a couple of miles away from the road. We're going into known hostile territory and for the first two patrols, tomorrow and the next day, neither you nor the battalion will be near. If we get ambushed, booby-trapped, snake bit, or whatever, what do we do? We won't have a litter to carry out our dead or wounded, no medic to bandage them, and no way to ask for help. If we have dead or wounded before the battalion gets there, who's going to come and help us?" He was truly angry now, and he paused to catch his breath and try to calm himself. "Who, sir? Tell me, will the Vietnamese at the fort listen for the sound of gunfire and come running? Did they say that they would and, even if they did, can they be counted on? Our experience with them so far says that they wouldn't be any help if they were right there with us. What if, sir," his anger was now clearly evident from his swollen face, thickened lips, and high shallow breathing, "we get hit, and I can't get help for my men? Sir, this is a bad thing. It's wrong. Just wrong. Besides, we can't just keep going in the same area each time. Why, they'll ambush and booby-trap us. It's against all common sense. "

Tooley looked Leary in the face, but not in the eye. He didn't want to challenge him in any way, but just to let him know that he understood. His voice was laced with sorrow, despair, and resignation as he said, "No one, Sergeant, no one will be there. You and your men will be completely on your own. On your own tomorrow and the next day. Three days from today, the rest of us will be there, but even then you will be left to your own devices, luck, whatever, to survive. No radio, no one assigned to back you up. As to taking the same trail twice, well, do the best you can with that. Try and find different trails in the jungle, that end up in the same place. Do the best you can."

Leary's anger filled the room as he whispered, "So, Lieutenant Tooley, sir, what do you suggest that I tell the men? Should I tell them that we're going to live with the South Vietnamese? People they have no respect for as soldiers? Say that we'll be doing highly dangerous, on-our-own patrols that serve no one? You know how we all feel about being captured by the enemy. That is not an option. No one is going to kneel me down and shoot me in the back of the head. No, sir. We'll have to fight to the death if we get hit. It's crap any way we look at it and you know it."

Tooley felt a stab of pain in his heart. *I hate this war, and I hate the captain. I have to say something.* "It is an important patrol, and I have my orders. Now you have yours." Tooley thought he detected a shift in Leary—an indefinable something that made him different than he had been only a moment before. Not a good thing—a look, a stance, an attitude. *My God*, he thought, *like the bamboo viper, deadly and unyielding.* It was scary and he looked hard into his eyes, trying to see some of the old Leary, but he saw none. He'd tried to soften things up with an appeal to Leary's sense of duty, responsibility, and sacrifice. But it didn't work and the lieutenant felt defeated as he listened to Leary's rebuttal.

"An important patrol, sure, sir, I'll explain it to them. I'll say, men we're going to pull a patrol, the seven of us, in search of the enemy. We're doing this so that a large enemy force cannot sneak up on the battalion camped along the road and possibly blow up the bridge. The bridge must be saved so that candy bars and such, which you will not be allowed to enjoy since you will be back in the jungle, can get through. Rest well, men. Yes, this is your rest period. Your job during your rest period will be to tell the battalion if we see any enemy. Now we won't have any radio to warn them, so let's hope that we don't see them until we are almost back from the patrol. If we do see them, we'll probably be eliminated. If there are shootings or explosions coming from the direction of our patrol, say we have to fight or something, no one will come to our aid. No one is even assigned to come and look for our dead bodies. So, if we get hit, we're on our own. The best we can hope for is to die like men, keep our dignity, and not get captured, save the last round for our buddy or ourselves. In a nutshell, Lieutenant Tooley, who would we tell if we are dying three miles from the damn road? Who will we tell the first two days, period? Huh, Lieutenant, who? Tell me so that I can explain this to my men—your men, sir."

"I don't know, Sergeant Leary, tell them what you want or think you have to."

"Well, sir, there is one option that occurs to me, something that has not been discussed here." Tooley lifted his head in a questioning gesture. "We can go a short way into the jungle and sit out the day. Do nothing, put up a defensive perimeter and wait until the proper time to come in."

Tooley's face started to show the dark purple of his coming rage. Then, just as suddenly as it began, it went away, and he relaxed visibly as he said, "No, Sergeant Leary, you cannot do that. The captain knows you cannot do that, and I know that you cannot do that. Someone else might, but you won't. We all know that you will finish each and every patrol, as long as you are physically able. You will, every time, every day, God help you, to the death of yourself and your men if need be. That much is for sure. So you see, Leary, perhaps the captain is right. You are the man for the job."

"Is that all, sir?" Leary said, leaving Tooley wondering if he had misjudged Leary, if Leary had changed, and if the new Leary would fake the patrol.

By 1500 hours of the same day, Leary was sitting on a table in a small room close to the entrance of the fort near Ben Cat. His pants were down and the fort's medic was massaging his right knee. The medic had volunteered to try to fix it after he had seen Leary limp through the fort entrance at the front of his squad. After the fort commander, Lieutenant Giap, who spoke excellent English, had introduced himself and the squad to the people living at his fort, he had told Leary that his medic would like to take a look at his injured knee. Leary, though reluctant and untrusting, felt he shouldn't refuse. He did, however, almost stop the medic from giving him a shot in his knee. After a moment's hesitation, he had decided, *what the hell, might as well go all the way.* Right after the pain of the shot had dissipated, the knee started feeling unbelievably better. As the small man worked on his knee, Leary recalled what had happened on the road earlier.

Maybe I'm going nuts, he thought. *I was almost blind with rage after getting this assignment. Felt like something snapped in my head, like a tearing in my brain. Why I tried to do that, I don't know. It's still hazy in spots. I need to remember it and figure out why I would do something like that. This is bad. Logically, morally, I know it was wrong, but damn if I feel any sorrow at trying to do it. Hell, if provoked, I would probably do it again. I just snapped and it felt good and justified, but I know it was a bad thing to do. What the hell led up to it? How could I have considered doing that?*

Maybe it was because I didn't really level with the squad about the patrol. I told them about it as optimistically as I could. I didn't lie, but I left most of the crap out. I'm getting as bad as the rest of these 'order-givers.' Maybe that's it. I feel bad about selling them out. Yeah, it could have been that that set me off. I could have been angry at myself. Anyway, it happened, and I need to face it. Let's see. I was leading the squad down that small dusty road from base camp to Highway One. Calling that cow trail a road is a stretch, but it's the main road from the base camp to the asphalt. Outside the perimeter wire were those three armored personnel carriers on tracks with those assholes in them. The tracks were all evenly spaced, pointing downhill, ready for action. They all had a fifty mounted on a swivel in the top hatch. I would guess their job is to cover the loading and unloading of choppers and vehicles in that grassy clearing outside the perimeter wire. Those tracks aren't much use in a war like this. They're limited by their size and configuration to the roads. Most of the real aggressive, hunting-type fighting is done in places that only a man can maneuver in. So, they probably sit there in the same spot for days, doing nothing really, glad that they have a steel home which protects them and keeps them out of the man-to-man jungle fighting. They're probably bored as hell, too.

Maybe that's why that dumb ass did what he did. Almost got himself killed. Hell, I almost killed him. Would have too, if it hadn't been for Folger. That dumb ass is one of our men, too. God help me, I must be going over the edge. That's one man who should've kept his mouth shut, though. A smile shone on Leary's face. *I bet he won't laugh at anyone again, ever.* The ARVN medic smiled back, thinking that Leary was smiling at him. Leary nodded his head and went on replaying the incident in his mind. What did bother him, a little, was that, before now, he could only remember deciding to blow up the track. Now that his anger had subsided, though, he was starting to recall what he had done after that.

He remembered it all now, how irritating and weary he had felt when walking down the road to get in the truck. *Then I heard the shit coming out of that skinny, ugly, white-faced, pink-lipped dummy's mouth. He was sitting on top of the last track, the one closest to the road and right next to the truck that was to take us to this fort. He wouldn't let up; he kept ragging on us. I remember trying to ignore him. The squad tried to ignore him too. None of us even acknowledged his jeering comments, "Dumb grunts are humping back out. Is this all that's left of the 'gook magnets'? I thought you dummies came in to rest. But don't let us stop you. We're almost out of beer, and word has it you all are going to see that more of it gets up here from Saigon, so-o-o we can drink it while you're gone." It was as much his laughing as what he said that set me off. Then, maybe I wouldn't have done it if the truck driver hadn't screwed up.*

Yeah, we were tired and loaded down with gear. Folger and I had just finished pushing the last man up and into the truck. Then I boosted Folger up, and he turned around and reached down to help me. That's when it happened. That's what triggered me off. Stupid driver, just when I was in the air, my left foot off the ground, the truck took off, dumping Folger and me in a heap on the ground. I remember it all now. I realized that I had twisted my knee and that I'd have to limp on it for days. The next thing I noticed was that ass laughing his guts out, as I was on my butt holding my knee. Yeah, me hurt, and him up on his safe, easy-duty machine laughing at me. That's when I lost it. Guess it was the combination of everything that happened before, topped off with my butt in the dirt, my knee starting to swell, and Mr. Pink Lips having a good laugh over it. Hell, he remembered, *the whole crew was laughing at us. They were all sticking their heads out of their little hatches, like prairie dogs looking out of their holes. All were laughing. Not for long, though.* He smiled again at the thought.

He couldn't remember getting up off the ground. The thing he could remember now was pulling up on the hatch of the track, with the laughing man inside but not laughing anymore as he tried desperately to hold it down long enough to activate the lock. *No, sir, he wasn't laughing anymore then. I wasn't bluffing either. I was trying to throw a grenade into the vehicle. Now that is scary, to think that I would kill three of my own men because they were making fun of us. They must have watched me in shock as I pulled the pin and made a hobbling run toward their track. Should have scared them all real good; I know it scares me now to think about it. He beat me by a second or two. If I hadn't been limping, they'd be history now, and I'd be on my way to jail or dead. I don't want to be known as the man who killed his own people for laughing at him. It would hurt my loved ones. I'd better get a grip. The captain would win, then, too. Don't want that.*

Early in the morning, sometime after midnight, Mary woke up feeling a great sense of loss. She had an overwhelming urge to cry and buried her face in a pillow so that she would not wake her mother. But their home was small and wasn't nearly soundproof enough to keep a mother's tuned ear from hearing her child's distress. She did her best to comfort Mary, mainly just holding her and letting her cry. When Mary could stop sobbing long enough to get out a few words, she said that it wasn't a nightmare. She didn't think Tim was dead or even wounded, but she knew that some change, some loss had taken place. Not physical loss, but something worse.

25

GIAP'S FORT

The peaceful atmosphere of the fort tugged Leary's heart back to a more loving side of him. *When was it?* he asked himself. *Was it a previous life, ten years ago, or only a few months? When did I last feel at peace? When was the last time I felt the warm glow of love in my heart? Damn sure wasn't this morning. No, this morning I almost crossed a line from which I could never return. I would have gladly done it, too, and without regret. Only a few months ago, I would never have dreamt of doing such a thing. Still, I'm not sorry for what I tried to do, even though a small, weak voice from somewhere deep in my head says that I should be. Surprisingly, it was Folger who kept me from doing it and I am not even mad at him. But still, I am not sorry for trying to do it.*

Leary was standing in the open area of the fort's center. The earth was a gray mixture of sand and clay, bare of any vegetation, and packed brick-hard from millions of footsteps. He had just left a small bunker, not much larger than their walk-in closet at home, where the fort's medic, a diminutive Vietnamese man with good teeth and a huge smile, had tended to his recently sprained knee.

Though Leary did not trust the medic or even like him, the man's genuine smile had finally won him over and he consented to the examination. Leary almost bolted when the still-smiling medic filled the syringe but then, after initially tensing, he relaxed again. Finally, trusting his instincts that it would be all right, he nodded and the medic stuck the needle into his freshly massaged joint. The pain began to leave soon after the shot and now, ten minutes later, he was standing, free of pain, in the middle of the fort, looking for his men.

Lieutenant Giap didn't waste any time in getting me to his medic after he saw me come limping through the gate. Where are my men?

195

*Oh, there they are in the shade of that awning where the chairs and
tables are. Can't believe that medic. Didn't trust him when he brought
out that needle. Glad I let him give me the shot, though, hurt like
hell going in, but not now. No pain at all now. Still don't trust these
people. Can't. The intelligence and warmth of the fort commander is
refreshing, but can he really be trusted? No, can't trust any of the little
bastards. My opinion of their soldiering hasn't changed. In fact, they're
worse soldiers than I thought. Still, I'm starting to like them, and it's
uncomfortable. Felt better when I could hate them.*

The people of Giap's fort were warm and gracious towards
Sergeant Leary and his men, even though it was obvious that the
American soldiers didn't like where they were or the people there.
Leary smelled the burning charcoal of cook fires and the sharp odor
of spices contrasting with the occasional stench from the latrine.
*People here seem nice enough. Still, they can't be trusted as soldiers,
and it's safer to hate them for their incompetence and lack of purpose
than to excuse them because you like them. What the hell does "like"
have to do with anything in this world, anyway?* He asked himself.
Nothing, not a damn thing, he easily answered.

*As soldiers, these people are a joke. Christ, they're just as lousy
at being soldiers as I thought they were. Hell, they have their families
living with them in these dirt bunkers. Kids are running around freely,
and there are booby-traps everywhere. Dumb-ass booby-traps, too, too
damn obvious. No one is stupid enough to fall for those traps, no one
except maybe the kids.*

The fort, like many other forts in South Vietnam, formed an
equilateral triangle constructed of dirt, logs, and sandbags. Most of
the South Vietnamese soldiers assigned to the fort had their families
living within its dirt walls. There were children running around,
playing games in the dirt, hanging onto their mothers, and looking
for things to satisfy their curiosity. The triangular fort was built high
enough above the water table to allow the bunkers to remain dry
even during the heavy rains of the monsoon season. Bunkers lined
all three sides of the triangle, except at the fort entrance and in the
narrow spaces between the bunkers. The pattern of bunkers was
broken up on the southeast third of the triangle by the small cafe. It
had a wooden patio table and chairs, and its entrance faced the center
of the triangle. It was also equipped with the only window in the
fort. All of the entrances had blankets hanging in their doorways, and
those not shut were pulled back and tied to a peg in the doorframe.
When entering any of the bunkers, except the patio bunker which
was at ground level, it was necessary to step down a log-constructed

staircase to the dirt floor, which was about four feet below the courtyard elevation. The interior walls of the bunkers were made of sandbags and had paper-covered logs supporting their ceilings. Above the bunkers was four feet of dirt which, on occasion, made its way through the paper and fell irritatingly into the space below, usually, but not always, as a soldier walked the parapet above. The edge of these walls was lined with two rows of sandbags about two feet high. Many of the sandbags were in various stages of rotting and could be seen spilling sand out onto the parapet. The parapet ran at the same level around the entire perimeter of the fort, except where the patio bunker was, and there it was higher.

The bunkers provided a cave-like feeling of safety and, except for the sporadic dirt showers, most were kept very clean. Like a medieval European castle, the fort was designed so that the fighting could be done from its walls, minus the moat and drawbridge. The bamboo gates were left open. They sagged and leaned and showed no sign of ever having been closed. Though the fort had a safe and peaceful feeling about it, Leary did not trust anything about it.

It's almost like the war doesn't belong in here. Oh, sure, there are signs of war. But the signs are from the past, unused relics like those old World War II machine guns, sort of there. Men just lie by them, sleeping in the sun. This place is weird; it's much too calm, too easy. Dying and tension everywhere else we've been, except here. Yeah, unbelievable and spooky, like an oasis in the desert. Nothing but burning, horribly dry, and sterile sand everywhere except in one small place. Places in the harsh desert where trees, grass, and water miraculously appear. That's what this place seems like. Why? I damn well better find out.

Leary shook his head to clear it. *These feelings aren't real. There is no peace in this land,* he told himself. *Don't believe it. Keep your head and don't be duped by this false impression. Hell, this whole fort might be one big booby-trap and its apparently peaceful existence the lure.*

On close observation, over a couple of days, he would see that the gun nests were occupied twenty-four hours a day, but to say that they were manned would be generous. Slept in twenty-four hours a day was more accurate. However, there were always men in them, and the ammo belts were always in the guns, and the guns gleamed of oil. The Vietnamese men all wore the U.S. Army's green fatigues, the same ones that Leary and his men wore. *Yeah, they have the shirts and pants of soldiers, but little else. Except Lieutenant Giap, he's in full uniform. But the rest of his men are a hodge-podge army.* He looked again to be sure, and what he saw were little brown-yellow men of all ages wearing various parts of uniforms, some mixed with articles of civilian clothing. The women and children wore the black pajama-like clothing of the farmer. Seldom did a soldier wear any kind of belt or hat. No steel helmets were in sight anywhere. Few wore boots; most wore sandals made out of woven bamboo strips or no footwear at all. To Leary, it seemed a strange way for a military outpost to be, especially in a war zone.

Civilians and partially uniformed soldiers engaged in every kind of activity, from washing themselves with a pan of water to napping in hammocks tied up outside their bunkers. Conspicuously absent were personal weapons—none were in sight. Leary caught a flicker of movement off to his right and saw Giap walking towards him with a slow and easy gate. His general physical appearance was one of a relaxed and emotionally balanced man. His stride was sure and unhurried.

After exchanging pleasantries in which Giap inquired after Leary's knee, Leary bade his men to follow. The lieutenant took them to an empty bunker that he said would be their quarters. Telling them to get comfortable, Giap asked Leary to join him for coffee at the small patio mess hall for the bachelors of the fort at his earliest convenience. Leary agreed and thanked the lieutenant.

Inside the bunker, it was reasonably cool, though slightly musty, and Leary watched as his men automatically divided the room into sevenths, unbuckled their gear and, with much groaning, settled into their portion of space. Leary's heart warmed toward these men. He rarely had to tell them anything anymore. Certainly not about readiness, formations, and the like. Even Hart did those things automatically. They were like a close family with each member automatically assuming his position and duty in it. Knowing them as he did, he could tell that they felt strange and insecure in the bunker. Though the room was large, very generous considering the covered and protected space available in the fort, he knew it was still confining to them.

Naturally, they're nervous. It's new and different in here. Up until now, those of us who have survived have done so by being in the open. Even in the confines of the jungle there is usually a place to go for protection. You can always dive off the trail. Not here, though. Here we're closed in this box, which is inside huge dirt walls. The men are feeling like animals whose den has no back door. That, along with our natural distrust of the Vietnamese, whom we now depend on to guard this place, makes it a little tense here. Still, there's something more wrong here than just that. It's a little too relaxed in this fort for my liking. I'll be interested to see what Folger thinks.

Leary sat down next to the stairs, his back against the wall, facing into the dim room. He looked from man to man, trying to see their eyes. Just from looking at their faces, he intuited their tension. He knew them. *They're like doomed men waiting to die. Maybe not today, or tomorrow, but soon. Or, maybe in the next second with a direct hit by an artillery round. Or maybe one of the soldiers in this fort is a VC or NVC and is right now getting ready to throw a grenade in here. Could be. Either way, by now they all know that whatever life they'd hoped to create for themselves back home is gone.*

He sat there like that, looking and thinking, for a full five minutes. Then he rose stiffly, dropped his pack, helmet, and web gear in a pile behind him, and said, "I'm going to visit with Lieutenant Giap. I'll be back when I'm through. You can all sleep, eat, whatever. If you have to take a shit, I saw what serves as a latrine off the east wall. In fact, when the wind is right you can smell it. It's just a big dirty slit trench, really. But we had better use it. Anyway, move around inside the fort all you want, but carry your rifle with you. I don't care if these people don't, we do. Furthermore, be polite. We are guests here and no matter what we think, we'd better act like it. I don't want to have to camp out there in the jungle by ourselves for the next three days. Especially not this close to the Iron Triangle, so don't get us thrown out of here." When he was half out of the bunker, partially blocking the sun, he turned and said, "Okay, then we know what we can and cannot do. Any questions?"

Marlin, on loan from the first squad, spoke first; the obnoxious attitude that they had observed in him was now gone. "Sarge, how long do you think we're gonna be here? These people seem nice enough but I feel a little hung out to dry here. They don't seem that, I don't know, well . . . hell, yes, I do; I don't think they're very alert around here. I mean, they have kids running all over the damn place. Soldiers in fatigues walking around without carrying weapons. My rifle has never left my reach since we landed in this place, and these guys don't seem to even have weapons, except for those old machine guns and, even then, men in those gun pits look more like they're sleeping and sunning themselves than guarding a position. And those booby-traps in the wire, at the front gate... ha, did ya see those? They're the biggest joke yet. You guys see it?" He looked around left and right, but didn't wait for acknowledgment before going on. "It's plain stupid. There's some old 30 06 ammo in an old weather-stained, sun-bleached, bandolier just sitting on top of one of our M-26A hand grenades. Damn pin is gone, man, and just the weight of the ammo keeps the grenade from going off. Shit, wouldn't fool anyone. Christ, can you imagine kids running around and some dumb-ass thing like that, jus' laying out there." No one spoke; there was hardly any movement at all. "I tell ya, Sarge, there's some weird-ass shit happenin' here, an' it ain't good."

Leary could see by their body language that the rest of them felt the same way. All except Folger, who just sat on the other side of the stairs, back against the wall, hands lovingly holding his automatic rifle, its butt on the ground between his bent knees and the barrel pointing at the ceiling. Folger, silent and ready, as always.

"I agree," Leary said. "I'm going to go talk to the lieutenant and see what I can find out . . . I'll damn sure find something out. Meanwhile, stay close together . . . stay in pairs when outside of this room, I don't want one of you wandering off somewhere. At least, not till I'm satisfied that it's safe in here. Keep your damn eyes open. Folger, would you follow me out?"

Folger didn't say a word. He just dumped his gear and, slinging his automatic rifle over his right shoulder, climbed the stairs, and went through the door into the bright sunlight behind Leary. In a low voice, Leary said, "I know I don't have to tell you this, but keep an eye on things. Stay here and watch me over there with the lieutenant. If anything happens, take out the machine guns first."

"Right, Sarge. I can get all three from here. I got some extra magazines in my shirt."

"OK, Folger, I'm off." Folger nodded and leaned against the sandbags, which made up the corner of the bunker.

"Sarge."

"Yeah," Leary said, turning around.

"You okay?"

"Sure. Why?"

Folger hesitated for just a second. "Well, you know, what you tried to do this morning at base camp."

"Oh, that. Sure, I'm all right. Son of a bitch deserved it. Okay, Folger?"

"Sure, Sarge, just be careful. I'll watch your back."

"I know you will, Folger. You're a good man. Don't forget to watch the men, mostly. And those machine gun pits. Those guns are old but they look in working order."

"No problem, Sarge, I got it all."

"Thanks, Folger. And about this morning, I'll be careful. I'm okay."

Christ, and I thought I was bad, Folger thought.

Leary stepped up on the patio platform where Giap waited for him. He tried to look trusting and nonaggressive, though clearly he felt the opposite. He knew he looked awkward and self-conscious about the rifle he carried in the crook of his left arm as he took the few steps to the table where Giap sat facing him. The bamboo tables and chairs looked comfortable. Leary stared expressionlessly down at the small lieutenant for a moment. *Wonder if I should salute him? No, no one salutes over here. Makes targets out of them. Besides, I haven't seen anyone in this fort salute him.*

"Please sit, Sergeant Leary," Giap said, smiling warmly but sadly and gesturing with his open right hand to the chair opposite his. "We are pleased to have you here, Sergeant, and hope that you find your quarters adequate though not too comfortable, I am sure. We don't have much in the way of creature comforts here."

He's a likable little bastard, Leary thought, smiling slightly as he sat down. "Lieutenant Giap, our quarters are more than adequate and, as to the creature comforts, we have long since forgotten what they're like and have lost our dependency on them." He paused for breath before continuing, wanting to get to the question but knowing that if he rushed it he might come off as confrontational—he did not want that to happen. He needed Giap's support. He and his men were clearly all alone in this. "We are grateful to you for allowing us to stay here, within the protection of your fort, especially at night." Giap just smiled. His hands were lightly clasped and lying on top of the table. "I presume, sir, you've been briefed on our reason for being here."

"Yes, Sergeant Leary, I was told of your mission by your captain. He talked to Saigon by radio and they connected him with me through our landline. We do have a phone here connecting us with ARVN Headquarters in Saigon. It is nothing more than a field phone, really, but does seem to work, at times. Generally, it seems to work especially well when they want something from us." He laughed lightly. "Anyway, your Captain Haps called and explained that you have a need to familiarize yourself with the area around my fort. He asked that you be afforded the protection of the fort at night as there are few of you and you have no radio." Leary nodded. "He also said that a convoy was due to come through this area next week and that you were to start pulling regular daily patrols tomorrow."

Damn, the captain lied to him. He told Giap the convoy was coming through here next week instead of the end of this week. Captain must not trust him. No doubt, he thinks that, if Giap knows, the Cong will know. Shit, the silence is getting awkward. I'll bet the truth is written all over my face. I never could lie. Screw it all, I'm sick of lies. This whole war is a lie. How can I stay here after lying to him? Hell, when he finds out, when that convoy shows up early, all trust between us will be gone. He'll probably throw us out of here. Couldn't blame him if he did either. Well, my instincts say tell him the truth and that's damn sure what I'm gonna do. Leary spoke slowly, sincerity apparent in his tone of his voice. "Well, sir, that is not the truth. The truth is that the convoy is due through here in three days." Now Leary stared hard and straight into Giap's coffee-brown eyes, aware of the welcome weight of his rifle still cradled in his left arm.

"Thank you, Leary, for trusting me. The truth is that I heard a week ago that the convoy was coming up at the end of this week."

"That's interesting Lieutenant, how'd you know that? Did your people tell you?"

"No, not my leaders in Saigon, surely not them. The information came from the VC."

Leary was so startled by the statement that his first impulse was to slam his rifle butt into the lieutenant's jaw. But he held his desire and let it play itself out. The unused energy caused some slight muscle twitches in his arms and legs. When the last quivering had dissipated, he asked in a calm but strained and barely audible voice: "I'm a little confused here . . . I thought we . . . you know, you and I, were enemies with the VC." His voice, though still calm, was clearly laced with sarcasm as he continued. "Aren't we dying over here to help you rid yourselves, your free democratic selves, of the Communist menace? The damn Communists are supposed to be our mutual enemy." Slower now, his voice lower, even more sarcastic, Leary said, "Your English is very good, Lieutenant Giap, but the word 'mutual' means both of us."

Giap felt the full force of Leary's building rage. *My God*, he thought, *this kid is over the edge and he's about to do me in.* In a clearly defensive display, Giap slowly turned his hands palms up and then pushed them out towards Leary. Seeing that Leary was barely restraining himself, with his hands still in the defensive position, Giap kept his eyes on Leary, as he spoke a few words loudly in Vietnamese over his shoulder toward the entrance to the mess kitchen. Even more alert now, Leary grabbed the trigger-guard of his rifle with his right hand, put his thumb on the safety, and prepared to push it off. His moves were swift and smooth, and the look emanating from his eyes had a finality about it that made Giap's body shiver, even in the ninety-five-degree heat.

Damn, Giap thought, *it was hard enough to stay alive before the Americans came. Now it's even worse.* "Hold it. Hold it. My friend, I have only ordered us some coffee. You are safe here. Please relax, and I will explain." Leary maintained his position but seemed to relax a little as he nodded his head, which Giap correctly interpreted as a signal to keep talking. *Whoa, this man-boy is touchy. I had better play it carefully with him.* "Since you trusted me and seem like an honorable man, I will trust you. Please let me explain how it is here. But, before I do, understand that it is not a good thing I am about to tell you. It will surely diminish your spirit, especially concerning the fighting of this war."

Leary relaxed a little as he saw the old bent-over cook hobble out through the blanketed door, carrying a tray with two tiny cups on it. The tray was held low in the knotted hands of an old man who had spent years planting rice, and Leary could see that the toy-sized cups were filled with a thick black liquid. But his hackles rose as he observed the old man's twisted fingers removing the small cups of French-style coffee from the wooden tray. He calmly placed them on the table and then silently turned and shuffled back into the kitchen-bunker.

Leary's anger defused as he removed his hand from the trigger-guard of his rifle. He said, "Well, Lieutenant, our spirit is already greatly diminished, and our sense of purpose has completely changed from the one we came over here with. I don't mean to offend your sense of purpose either, but we are now mostly fighting to stay alive. We fight for each other—little else. We don't believe in your freedom fight anymore, and we don't believe that you South Vietnamese have ever believed in it."

He paused for a moment and, using his free right hand, took a sip of the bitter coffee. He wasn't a coffee drinker and drank it only to be polite. Leary wanted to like the old man but, although he had an untouchable peacefulness about him that Leary found refreshing, his instincts made him uneasy. He continued, "In short, your army's dedication to winning this war is lousy, at best. Sorry if I have offended you, Lieutenant, but since we're being honest here, how can you be an honorable man and still be a part of this lie of a war?"

Giap winced at the sting of Leary's last words. *There is much truth in what he's saying,* Giap thought as he pulled off his hat to display a thick head of short, dark-black, slightly greasy hair. He pushed the hair on both sides of his head back in place with his other hand and then placed the dull green baseball cap back on his head.

He paused for breath before consciously focusing his kindly, almost
paternal, eyes on Leary, and said in a slow, clear voice, "Once again,
Sergeant Leary, thank you for your honesty. Things are as they seem.
We South Vietnamese do not have much faith in, nor willingness
to die, for the cause. I mean, what does this cause, the democratic
one, mean, or seem to mean to the people of South Vietnam? To
most of us, democracy means more of what we already have and
what we've had in the past. For some Vietnamese, like those of the
villages deep in the jungle, far away from schools, roads, and radios,
the very words 'North,' 'South,' 'Communism,' 'Democratic,' or even
'nation,' mean nothing. The only things that they know about are
how to plant rice, harvest rice, trade rice, and love and care for their
families and the village water buffalo. For those living in the more
'civilized' areas of South Vietnam, democracy means long years in
military service. A military dedicated to keeping the old regime
intact. A regime founded by the French, educated by the French,
bought and sold by the French. A regime that makes slaves out of
the Vietnamese people. Both sides, the French side, which is the
one you fight for, and the North Vietnamese Communist side, want
to control us for their own profit. All sides want to tell us how to
live and what is worth dying for. Even China and Russia have plans
for Vietnam and the Vietnamese people. It all amounts to the same
thing for us—slavery. Most of us, Sergeant Leary, just want to love
our families in peace. We are sick of fighting and death. But the
children, that is the worst. How much longer can we watch our
children die horrible and bloody deaths?" Leary did not move. He
did not even change the blank look in his normally expressive eyes.
But Giap could tell he was listening to every word. And also Giap
believed he could tell that the thoughts these words produced were
not new to Leary. Encouraged by this, he continued.

"Our poor country has been fighting for generations, and we are
numb with the sickness of it. Fighting, killing, and being killed are
so familiar to most of us that we have become unimpressed by it.
Except, as I said, for the children. With them it hurts freshly every
time. So, we do not really believe that our conditions will change, no
matter what side we support. Most of us just try and get along. We
do the bare minimum necessary to get by, to stay alive, no matter
what side we find ourselves on. Our hopes are not that the North
will win, or that the South will win but that we, as a people, will
win. We're not sure which side would best let us win. It's not clear,
they both seem bad."

He paused for a breath and took a sip of his thick, hickory-flavored coffee. After setting the cup gently back on its small saucer, he looked up and continued, "See, Sergeant Leary, we just want the right to live in peace. A peace without killing. A peace without a corrupt bunch of bureaucrats, no matter what their professed beliefs might be, telling us to shoot some of our fellow countrymen just so that they can be assured of their positions of power. Frankly, Sergeant Leary, I am sorry that you and your people are over here. I am extremely sorry for you. You are into something that is so thick with corruption that no light can possibly shine through. It is so crooked that it can only produce death and destruction. Truly, I believe that the South Vietnamese government is less democratic than even those of China or Russia. Our generals are so dishonest, so greedy for personal power, that they cannot even trust each other long enough to wage an effective campaign against their sworn enemy from the North. So your country can give them all the arms and supplies they need, as well as send fine soldiers like yourself, but they will still lose. Why? Because our leaders are like children in charge. They are too busy thinking about their individual wants to see the larger picture. Like children, our leaders seem to believe that the rest of the people in the world exist only to serve them.

"Yes, I am sorry that fine men such as yourself, men willing to go and fight for someone else, people that you don't even know, will be frivolously used up for such a corrupt cause like this one. I am also sorry for us, for myself and my countrymen. If America hadn't entered this war, the South would have lost several years ago, and, one way or the other, the killing would be over now."

Leary felt mixed emotions—relief and anger. Relief that his suspicions were true. Relief in being right that this was a worthless cause. But, the relief was short-lived compared to the anger that he, his friends, and fellow soldiers were sent over here to die for. *God almighty, how could our own people send us into such a terrible situation? What can they possibly hope to gain back home by our fighting and dying over here? These damn people don't even want us here. Not the real people. And, if what we've seen of the North is an example of the big Communist threat that we've had shoved down our throats the last twenty years, that's a lie, too. What in the hell are we going to do now? How can we fight and risk dying without a cause? Worse yet, how can we fight for a cause in which winning has worse consequences overall than losing? Damn, makes me sick to my stomach. Or maybe it's the crappy coffee, or both. Wonder what's showing on my face?* With shocked realization dawning on his face, an obviously fatigued

Leary asked, "I need to know, Giap, where do you stand? Should I get my men out of this fort tonight? Are you our enemy?"

Without hesitation, expecting the question, Giap spoke in a voice of assurance and confidence. "No, I am not your enemy, Leary." His brown head bobbing affirmatively, he continued, "You and your men are, at least for now, safer here than most places in Vietnam, including your own bases. If, however, what I have just told you were reported to the wrong people, then I would soon be a dead man. Tomorrow or next week maybe, but sometime, somehow, they would do away with me. I doubt I would live a month after the South Vietnamese Army heard what I have just told you. So you see, Sergeant Leary, I have entrusted you with my life. Don't ask me why, I don't really know. Instinct perhaps, or maybe I have just become weary of not having anyone to trust with the truth. Well, you have told me the truth, and now I have told you the truth." He took another sip of his coffee; Leary noticed that his hands had a slight tremor.

"The VC do not attack this fort, or haven't yet, because I and my men are no threat to them. We go to the village of Ben Cat, as I am sure you have observed, without weapons. We do not patrol the area around this fort. In truth, we simply live here, all of us. 'We make no waves,' I believe you Americans say."

"Close enough," Leary said.

"We just wait to see what will happen. We wait to see if we will be around when it is all over. We live life moment by moment, day to day; we just live to exist. Or perhaps we exist so that we may someday live. Whatever, we dare not hope too much. We dare not think too much. We just hope and live for some future day when we can feel secure and freely love our wives and children." He stopped for another sip of coffee from his almost empty toy cup. Leary said nothing. He knew there was more. "As for me, I live from one third weekend a month to the next third weekend a month. That is the weekend when I am permitted to go to Saigon and see my wife and boy child. Every month that I am alive to do that, I am a grateful man. Sooner or later, one side or the other will win. My men and I work hard to stay alive. We spend all of our energies staying in the middle."

Leary felt awful. He had hoped to be backed up by these people. The captain had hung them out to dry. He had sent them out alone, without hope of backup, and now, even though he hadn't believed that the Vietnamese would be much help, he never figured that they would not even try to help should he and his men get in trouble while on patrol. *Christ, no backup at all. What a sad state of affairs.* "Well," Leary spoke slowly, strongly, with hot anger showing in his piercing blue eyes, "Isn't it more difficult to stay in the middle like you do, being a fence-rider, than to wholeheartedly get on one side or the other? Don't you and your people ever feel like committing to one side or the other and then fighting it out to death or a victory? Don't you want to bring this shit to a conclusion? One way or another?"

"No, Sergeant Leary, we don't," Giap shook his head. "It's just not that clear. If the South wins, doubtful as that seems, my people and I lose. Then the French will be right back here running their plantations again. They have just pulled offshore to let you and us clear a path for them and, if we do, it will be back to the same old thing. For us, it will be a future of more slavery to foreign powers that own and milk our plantations. We will live like servants again, while they live like kings. Of course, on the other hand, if the Communists win, they will probably start out acting like the common farmer and merchant is going to be better off. Then, of course, they will kill unimaginable thousands of South Vietnamese in what they will call 'purging.' After this killing, which they deem to be a threat to their power, they will then, no doubt, attempt to make good their promise of reform and equality for everyone. At first, conditions will take on an air of improvement. But, unfortunately, that will be short-lived and their corrupt leaders will surface and, in time, one way or another, the common man will be right back in the same shape he is in now. In the end, the only thing that will be different is the color of the uniforms that the soldiers wear as they carry out their orders. Orders that are always meant to make slaves out of the general population. It is always the same, history dictates it, and history is always repeated. The peasant will be on the bottom again. So I live to see my family and to not make waves between visits."

Once again the anger left Leary's face, to be replaced by puzzlement. Giap shrugged his shoulders and continued, "Hard to understand? How can I get away with it? Well, I believe it seems to them at headquarters like I am doing a good job here. Not that I'm sure any of them really care, not the little guys for sure, they are like me. They are the report takers; they aren't any better off than I am. I look good on paper, Sergeant Leary. I hardly ever have a casualty. I never call for ammunition or more men, nor do I complain about conditions. Things are quiet at this fort. The conclusion they seem to draw from that is that everything must be all right then. I must be doing a good job. Of course, that I don't do much is overlooked or lost in the fact that the area I am responsible for is quiet. Or, at least, it was quiet until you and yours came here." Seeing that the last statement irritated Leary anew, Giap said hastily, "Understand me, Leary. I am not blaming you. I am just trying to tell you how I believe things to be."

Leary nodded his assent. His expression was stern and unreadable. "I suppose we have and will change the whole balance of things here. But you understand that we are an old army here in your country—we have a reputation of winning. Furthermore, almost all of the sergeants in my company are career army men. They have a lot of experience and are professional soldiers. Well, bottom line here, Lieutenant Giap, is that we came over here to fight. Even if there isn't anything to win over here, we will still fight. It's expected of us. We expect it of ourselves. So brace yourself and hang on to that fence you're riding because the shit's gonna happen." With that, Leary drained the last of the bitter coffee from the tiny cup.

"Yes, I fear that you are right. Already it is harder. The enemy of the North is already angry as a result of the killing. Your people, your artillery, or your aircraft have killed quite a few of them and their tempers are short. The war has already begun to escalate, and it is tougher to stay out of it. Word has already reached me that they have given up on your going home without causing any trouble and that they must fight you. I fear that we are all headed down a bloody path from which there is no escape."

As Giap's words sank in, Leary's anger rose, once again, to an almost uncontrollable point. The urge to release it was unbearable. It was as powerful as that exerted in the morning when he'd attacked his own people. *Get hold of yourself, damn it. You can't afford to lose it like that again. Folger is already worried and he doesn't worry. So quit it. Respond, don't react.* Still, the rage was clearly visible and trying to free itself as he rose slightly in his chair and asked, "What the hell do you mean 'word has already reached me'? Just how damn tight are you with the boys at the Triangle? You have coffee with them, too?"

Giap moved nervously on his chair, attempting to remain calm but finding it impossible while Leary was so close to igniting. Desperately rushing his words, he said, "No, I don't really know any of them. I get the information from some of my men. Truth is, sometimes, some of my men drink an occasional beer with North Vietnamese and Vietcong soldiers in the village. In some cases, they have known each other all of their lives. Most of them were forced into the war by the side they're on. None of them, that I know, want to kill or even be soldiers. No more than I do. Of course, that will all

change now. They will get angry with you for those of their friends
you kill, and they will try harder to kill your people, and on it will
go. Once again, believe me when I say that I am truly sorry that you
and yours have to be a part of this. Please accept my apology as a
Vietnamese man, for what may happen to you in our country."

Leary, still fighting back rage, said, "Well, it hasn't happened yet,
Lieutenant Giap. So don't write me off yet."

"Please, Sergeant Leary, I am truly sorry for the mess you have
become a part of."

"Let me make sure I have this right, Lieutenant Giap. Forgive
me if I need to reaffirm what you already told me, but I need to ask
it again."

Giap acquiesced, "Please."

"First off, we are safe here?" Leary asked, and Giap nodded.
"And that is so because you have an unwritten, unsaid, pact with
the enemy, a let-it-be deal." The lieutenant once again nodded. "Am
I also correct in understanding that my men and I are safe in here as
long as this balance of mutual coexistence is not broken? And that if
my men and I find, stumble onto, or into, any enemy while pulling
our patrols and kill or wound any of them, we could jeopardize this
balance? Furthermore, that if this balance is disturbed, then our
safety and the safety of this fort might be compromised?" For the
third time, Giap nodded. "Well, if that should happen, Lieutenant,
I repeat, will you and/or your men turn on us? Will we, Lieutenant
Giap, be attacked or otherwise blamed by your people?"

Leary's face was red-blue with the blood pumping in his head as
he fought for self-control. Behind him, Folger rose from his squatting
position and prepared to act. Not knowing what was bothering his
sergeant, but seeing even from behind that something clearly was.

Leary's muscles tensed, begging for release, and his voice cracked
under the strain, but he spoke slowly and distinctly. "In short,
Lieutenant, if we should disturb this delicate balance, if you and/or
your men should fall from the fence, which side will you land on?"

Without hesitation, Giap eagerly replied, "If forced off of the
fence I will not, cannot, do not dare, for reasons I will tell you about
at another time, land on the Communist side. As for my men, I
cannot honestly vouch for them. I will, however, give you my word
that I will do my best to see that my men do not harm you or your
men in any way. I cannot absolutely guarantee it, of course, but most
of my people are peaceful and loving, just trying to get by." Now,
Leary's face returned to its normal sunburned brown as his anger

turned to contempt. He was pleased to see that Giap could correctly read the look on his face. He did not care.

Giap felt his own anger as he thought, *You asshole. I can take your anger but don't disgrace me with your foul contempt. Not that, no.* His voice quavered. "I may seem complacent to you, Sergeant, but I am in charge here and I am a man of honor. No matter what you and the enemy do or do not do to each other, I will, for as long as you are my guest, protect you with my life."

Leary's rage suddenly dissipated. He was tired of it and the energy it took, and Giap had gotten to him. *Christ, I must have misjudged the man; I believe he will defend us with his life.* "Okay, Lieutenant. Peace between us?" Leary said as he offered Giap his hand. As Leary's energy drained, it showed in his limp body and weak hand. *I'm tired of it all. I'm tired of being angry and tired of being tired. I'm even starting to like Giap. God, what a mess. I may, probably will, die over here, but if I do survive I got a place to go. He's already home and yet has no future. Poor bastard,* Leary thought, as Giap reached for and shook his hand. Behind Leary, Folger squatted back down and lit a cigarette.

"Lieutenant Giap, can you, through your pass-the-word connections with the enemy, find out if they have any intention of attacking the convoy, especially in our area of responsibility?"

The hurt gone now, Giap answered, "No, I do not think they would tell us and, more importantly, it would not be wise to believe it. They might get a new leader, a new attitude, and new orders from the North at any time. Any change in their situation could cause a plan, or an attitude, to change without notice. My best advice to you, Leary, is to do what you have to do."

Yeah, guess it's really all any of us can do, Leary thought, as he said, "I appreciate all that you've told me, Lieutenant Giap. I'll pull the patrols like they expect me to. Not because I believe in any cause, not any longer but, if I don't do the patrols and do them right, I could be responsible for the loss of the only lives I give a damn about. I couldn't live with myself if I didn't do the patrols. It's just who I am. Must be nice to have a fort like yours, a place in which to sit this war out. Got to be comforting to have a mutual agreement with the enemy to live and let live." He sighed with fatigue. "But I don't have one of those agreements, Lieutenant Giap, I've got to go out and see if the enemy is there." He paused to catch his breath, not that he was breathing hard, but he was tired of spirit and even drawing breath seemed to be an effort. "If they are out there, in my area of patrol, I have to do my best to get them. If it happens, if we fight and you and your men have to get down off the fence, well, that's too bad. But nobody can ride a damn fence forever. I'll do what I gotta do and I fully understand that you'll do what you gotta do. So, whatever happens, from here on out, I do appreciate this talk. I'll keep what we've discussed to myself. You have my word on that. I, too, am an honorable man." He made an attempt to lighten up his spirit as he said, "Hell, I wouldn't know what to tell them anyway. No use all of us knowing what a worthless cause we fight for."

"You're right, Sergeant, there isn't much men like you and I can share with others, especially our men. I, of course, never mention the things I've told you, not to anyone. This situation at this fort just evolved to the hands-off place that it is. None of us speak of it; we dare not even say it out loud. Even the information that I spoke of, which comes to me from the enemy's meeting with some of my men in the village, even that is not admitted to, nor spoken verbally. It is told to me as rumors like 'I have heard that it is said in the village' and so on. Much of it comes to me through Vo Nguyen, the old man who served our coffee. He claims that he hears information from some other of my soldiers. Thus, exactly who of my men are friendly with the enemy soldiers, I don't really know. I have suspicions, of course, but do not know for sure, nor in all honesty do I want to know. If my superiors should become aware of this communication with the enemy, then I would just as soon be able to honestly swear that I did not know who did the communicating."

Giap paused a moment to make sure that Leary was still with him. Leary nodded, then Giap continued, "I cannot help you with much, Sergeant, I cannot protect you outside of this fort, not in the usual sense, but let me give you some information that could prove to be invaluable. Let me explain how the VC and North Vietnamese mark the trails to indicate that they have been booby-trapped. Let me try and help you survive this war."

26

FIRST PATROL

At 0800 hours the next morning, on their first patrol, Sergeant Leary and the Second Squad of the Second Platoon of Charlie Company left Giap's fort in a spread formation. The men were twenty meters apart with Leary on the point, Folger backing him up, Sanchez on drag, and Branden, Hart, and Marlin proportionately between them. The more open the space, the more exposed the group was, and the greater the distance needed between the men. The men kept a twenty-meter distance between each other because they would have a three-hundred-meter open distance to cover from the fort to the jungle. When they got to the jungle southwest of the fort, they tightened the formation to allow for the limited visibility. No matter what formation was used, it was always dangerous to walk from a clearing into the dense jungle.

With every step, they feared that the enemy was waiting unseen to annihilate them. Leary's intuition was on maximum power as they neared the jungle's edge. *This must be the trail Lieutenant Giap told me about,* he thought, as he cautiously stepped on sand-packed trail.

According to Giap, the trail took off through the jungle almost due west for about fifty meters. Then there was a fork that allowed for travel southwest before heading due south. Eventually, both trails broke out of the jungle into an active, and productive, rice paddy. The distance from the trail's beginning to the rice paddy, which Giap said was the outer perimeter of the Iron Triangle, via the south trail, and the shortest route was through approximately eight hundred meters of nearly impenetrable jungle. The only passages through this jungle were these two trails.

"The paddies," Giap had said, "belonged to the enemy, and the peasants working the paddies were VC and North Vietnamese soldiers who also serve as an early warning system for the Iron Triangle. The Triangle's perimeter begins just across the paddies. Beware," he warned, "the jungle between the fort and the paddies is full of possible ambush sites and will surely be booby-trapped. However," Giap said apologetically, "neither I nor my men have been down that trail in the last five years. The booby-traps are intended as another early warning for the Triangle as well, of course, as a means of harming their enemy. Be very careful. They will be there. They are very professional and they are well armed, and they will try to kill you." He had shrugged and then said, "It is their territory and they will not take your intrusion lightly. The first day, your main threat will probably come from previously planted booby-traps which are a serious danger by themselves. Your enemy will probably not know you are there until the second day. I will keep my people in the fort tonight to lessen the possibility of one of them warning them about you. But after the first day, look out. It will be increasingly dangerous for you and your men. Don't ever take the same trail two days in a row. Of course, you are limited in your choices, and they know that."

Giap had made his points painfully clear. "Avoid being predictable. There are only the two trails and you have at least three days of patrols. So, vary your course and time of travel whenever possible. Maybe even reverse your direction and go to the bridge first on one of those days." After a pause, with both hands held in front of him, he continued, "Of course, always stay quiet, do not talk, stop to listen often, and above all, remember the signs I have taught you for booby-raps. Do not develop a predictable or discernible pattern. If they can predict your movements, they will kill you.

"Once through the jungle, do not cross the rice paddy. If you do, they will most certainly wipe you and your men out. Make your patrols, take your looks as quietly as possible, and then get back. Protect yourself, but try and avoid contact with them. They will probably try to bloody you but, if you bloody them, they will surely come after you with everything they have. Good luck. You will need it."

Giap seemed genuinely concerned about our safety last night, Leary thought, as he stepped cautiously down the trail. *I must be aware of any unusual terrain features. Giap said that anything out of place is a marker for booby-traps.* "The marker will be a nature sign," he told Leary. "Many of the Vietnamese people cannot read. In addition, it would be a mammoth job to map the jungles of South Vietnam. In short, they have no maps telling them where the booby-traps are. Not like your mapping of mine fields and such. To counter this, to keep their own people from falling victim to the traps, they have devised a system of marking the location of booby-traps. This is done on each side of the approach to a booby-trap and, if one is alert and trained, he can read the sign and avoid the trap. It can be difficult because the signs are not all the same. A universal sign—but one that's not always used—is a cut branch on the trail." Leary remembered how intently he had listened to these words. He knew that he needed to make them a part of his permanent thinking instantly and that his very existence would depend upon his knowing and understanding these things.

"The cut branch, usually along one side of the trail, will be hit once with a machete or knife causing it to fall over, symbolically blocking the path. This is the most universal way. It is the most obvious way to tell if a trail has explosive devices, but it is not the only way. The rule is, that if there is anything unusual on or near the trail, then the trail is booby-trapped." When Leary looked puzzled, Giap nodded his head and said, "For example, if you are walking down a trail, jungle or otherwise, and you see anything out of place, anything that does not naturally fit, then you must be wary. A clump of grass tied into a small bunch with a strand of grass, a broken branch, a tied branch, any disturbance to the natural features of the area. Especially be careful when you see something done by man to the natural setting. These are always markings for booby- traps."

Leary indicated that he understood and Giap said, "That, unfortunately, is only half of it—the easy half. In addition to the signs made by men, there are the signs made by nature. A man of the jungle will recognize these natural signs as something unusual. These nature-made signs might be as simple as a place where the trail comes to the river and then turns back abruptly or an unusual vine crossing the trail. It could even be as subtle as a strange-looking tree or plant. Something, or anything, that nature has made that denotes a difference, an eye-catcher, a noticeable thing to the trained jungle observer. These, too, can be markings for booby-traps."

Giap paused to allow his pupil to assimilate the information and then continued. "Sergeant Leary, looking for the triggering device of a booby-trap or the trap itself is not enough. They can be well camouflaged. You must train your mind to look for the signs, natural or man-made, which say: 'There are booby-traps here.' Rarely will you see battery-operated devices, except close to their base. Batteries are undependable in this wet climate and need constant replacement.

So the manual, pull-wire devices are more common. If you do find a battery-operated device, you are close to their lair."

As they neared the jungle wall, Leary wished that he had had more time to explain the booby-trap identification procedure to Folger. It had been 2200 hours when he had returned to the bunker and all were asleep except Hart and Branden. Folger was sleeping and, according to Branden, one of Patkins' riflemen, Folger had assigned each man a one-hour guard-duty at the door. Hart had been left out of the guard completely. *It is a good opportunity for all of them to get more sleep than usual.* The sleep they usually got was so little that, though he wanted very much to talk to Folger, he didn't wake him up.

Branden had told Leary that his guard was from 0600 hours to 0700 hours. Even though Folger had been awake for the last half-hour of his guard, Leary knew he had not been able to fully explain what Giap had told him. Folger was tired and reluctant to fully awaken. Consequently, in the end, Folger ended up with more of a puzzled look on his face than one of understanding or revelation. Furthermore, Leary wasn't sure that he had had time to fully incorporate the new learning into his own awareness. Leary felt alone and incompetent as he eased his way into the jungle.

Last night was the first time he had heard of this identification method for booby- traps. It angered him to think that no one in his army had bothered to find out and to tell them. Now he knew and if he didn't get it right, the information might die with him. His anger increased as he asked himself, *Why didn't our people know this? After all, they've been over here for years. Didn't anyone like the Special Forces or CIA ever get this information before? More than likely, they just dropped the ball somewhere along the way. How they, the brass, could let something like this slip through the cracks is beyond me. This information is so important, it could've already saved countless American lives, and I hear about it for the first time last night, from a neutral fort commander.* In his mind he cursed them all for their lack of concern. He felt betrayed and knew that the anger rising in him was sinister. Anger would warp his intuition. Back in Korea, his karate instructor had taught him that. Now, he cleared his mind of all disturbing thoughts. The need to survive helped. *I need to become an undisturbed receiver.* As his mind cleared, he stopped thinking and began only receiving. Walking and looking for the signs he knew he would have to recognize.

Forty cautious steps later, it was there in plain sight. Thanks to Giap, he now knew what plain sight looked like. He was twenty meters past the trail junction and had chosen the due west trail when he spotted it. One branch, very insignificant really, on the side of the trail, not even that visible. But there it was, an enemy booby-trap marker. *Clear as a bell,* he thought, as he held his clenched left fist up, the signal to halt. He did not have to look back or even think about whether or not they were watching him; he knew that they would be. Folger saw the signal and passed it on to the man behind him. Each man's responsibility was to keep track of the men in front of and behind him. Even Hart did this procedure well. The only man exempt from this rule was the point man. The point man's only worry was the trail ahead.

The small tree, new vegetation competing for sunlight, moisture, and soil, had been struggling to grow. It would not have to struggle any longer because some enemy soldier had cut it almost in two, letting its dying leafy top fall to the ground. Only a thin bit of young uncut bark attached the freshly cut two halves of the young tree, Leary noticed.

Having seen the marker, now he must find the booby-trap. *According to Giap, it would be near, usually within feet. Sometimes inches. Damn, I'm looking hard but just can't see any type of triggering device.* To kill time and teach Folger, who was watching him, Leary squatted in the center of the trail and pointed without looking at the small, cut tree to his left. *Judging by the amount of green left in the tree, it must have been cut late last night or early this morning. Like they knew we were coming and wanted to make sure that we got the message.* These thoughts coursed through his mind without emotion as he slowly moved his eyes from left to right, sweeping the trail and its surroundings. Trying, with this exercise, to let his side vision see things that his forward vision was unable to. Part of him, from another area in his brain, could almost see the two-man team that had planted the booby-trap. With effort, he pulled himself back from this intuitive mode and looked for the triggering device. Hunting for the man killer that he knew was there, somewhere.

What was that? His brain recognized something in his last sweep. Like the instant replay of a modern sporting event, he replayed what his peripheral vision had seen. His adrenaline pumped and he felt the familiar rush of fear that one has when nearly stepping on a snake or picking up a board to see something scurry away. Now he recognized it for what it was, and it was less than a meter in front of him. So close that he wasn't expecting it there. It was so fine a wire that only the dew that hit the thick foliage, making the slightest of splashes, could have brought it to his attention. The last drops of dew running off a large leaf had saved their lives.

After a few seconds in which he calmed himself, Leary examined the hard-packed sandy trail immediately in front of his position. He was looking for any discoloration or other signs of excavation or disturbance. Once he had determined that the ground to his immediate front was safe, he got down on his hands and knees. Then he carefully removed his heavy ammo belt, web gear, and rifle, laying them on the trail behind him. With his equipment secure, he slowly crawled the three feet to the place where the moisture had disclosed the trip wire.

Creeping forward, his anxiety dissipated and he welcomed the calm, thinking, *I hope there isn't another trigger. Maybe the wire is just a decoy for the real one. Could be I'm placing my hand on the real trigger now. Well, screw it, if I die, I die. They can kill me, but they're through scaring me.* Now, he was close enough to the wire to carefully look down it in both directions. To the right, he could see where it had been tied off, dead-ended, and anchored at the base of another small tree. Slowly, he turned his head to the left, following the wire under the leaf where it was attached to the end of a good old U.S. of A. C-ration can. The can was slipped over the end of an M-26A hand grenade. The C-ration cans that the men discarded daily were just the perfect size to fit over a hand grenade. When placed over the grenade it held the detonation lever in place, thus providing the enemy with a good, simple trigger. It was easy to tie the can to the base of a tree or large plant, then tie the other end to the hand grenade, slip the butt of the hand grenade into the can. And tie the other end of the C-ration can to a branch or string it across a trail or stream. Then one only had to pull the safety-pin from the grenade and the booby-trap was armed and ready for its victim. Pull or step on the wire and, four seconds later, it was over.

Leary knew what he must do. Trying to stay in the exact same tracks he had made on his move forward, he crawled backwards to Folger. Still not trusting his vision or his emotions, dreading the pop of the grenade and the horrible concussion it would bring, he eased back to his equipment. *God, don't let my life end screaming and soiling myself. I'm not really afraid anymore; I just don't want to go out that way, seeing pieces of my body torn off and lying around or hanging in the trees. That's the worst part, waiting to die in a body with pieces missing.* He stopped and shook his head violently, trying to clear the gruesome images from his mind. *I'd better get a grip.* Folger didn't respond to Leary's head shaking. He was getting used to seeing men do strange things. Leary did not take his eyes off the trip-wire as he retrieved his equipment and whispered to Folger, "Do you see the wire?"

"I just spotted it."

"Right. Well, Lieutenant Giap was sure as hell right about how to read trail sign. That's how I picked up on it. I'd have missed it otherwise. Yesterday, I'd have gotten us killed."

"What do we do about it?"

"Get the commo wire I saw last night. Some of the men in the squad have some, I can't remember who just now, but some of them have it. I can see it in my mind." Commo wire was the plentiful and tough telephone wire that could be tied in a knot. It was used for everything, from tying up tents to fastening their packs high up on their web gear. Many of the men carried it for shoelaces and other emergency repairs.

Without a word, Folger went to the next man back and passed the word for everyone to pass all commo wire up to the front. Within a few minutes several bunches of black wire were passed forward. Leary and Folger tied them all together, ending up with about thirty meters.

Silently, Leary removed his equipment again and crawled carefully forward. When he got to the trip-wire, he signaled for Folger to back the squad out. *If I screw this up, it'll save the squad.* Leary thought, *but it feels damn lonely. Oh well, on with it.* He waited for Folger's whistle, signaling that the wire was unrolled and that they were all back and lying down. Then Leary carefully attached the commo wire to the trip-wire. He made a large loop in the commo wire, carefully keeping it from touching the trip-wire with sticks he picked off the jungle floor. *It's a good thing I was good at playing pick-up sticks as a kid.*

After securing the commo wire to the trip-wire, Leary crawled back and picked up his rifle, gear, and helmet. Being careful not to disturb the black commo wire strung out along the trail, he joined the squad. Folger had backed them into the pre-jungle area and had set up a defensive perimeter. On the way out, Leary consciously checked every knot to see if it was tied adequately. They were all good, tight, square knots. *Good man, that Folger*, Leary thought as he lay down on the ground next to his automatic rifleman. He took one glance back over the squad perimeter to see that they were all down and shouted, "Fire in the hole!" A few seconds later, Folger, his helmeted head between his outstretched arms, visor in the dirt, began pulling the wire—pulling and waiting, pulling and waiting.

When he had pulled it farther than he believed he should have had to, he stopped and they waited. Four seconds can be a long time. When the blast came, in spite of expecting it, they were all shocked. It was far more violent than expected. Finally, after it had passed, they all waited a few horrifying seconds for their bodies to tell them that they weren't seriously wounded or dying. It just didn't seem possible that something that powerfully destructive could pass over them without harming them.

And then they all began to relax. The time between the first and second explosion was less than a second. They were expecting only one hand-grenade explosion from a certain place, so they were shocked at the two large explosions—and at their source. The pieces of leaves, branches, and ants that rained down on them left them looking like they had been lying in front of the discharge chute of a tree-mulcher. Some large branches flew through the air too, and one of them smacked the ground next to Hart. Though startled and stunned, no one was hurt. Reluctantly, they stood shaking their heads, trying to stop the ringing in their ears. They tried to brush the dust from their sweaty clothes and equipment.

"Damn," Folger said, "look at that. The jungle is gone where the explosion was. Both trails blew up . . . That was sure as hell more than one or two grenades could do. God, the foliage is stripped bare at the trail junction and beyond."

"Yeah, it's all over us," Leary said, trying to brush the dirt off. "I only saw the one grenade. Must have been another trip-wire that I didn't see. Something, going to another couple of grenades, or maybe an artillery round or two. Whatever it was, it was one hell of a bomb."

"Could've been a large explosive buried under the grenade," Folger said. "Whatever, we'll never know. Guess it doesn't matter, really. We're alive now and that's all we need to deal with."

"Yeah, that was one of our grenades, the one we tied on to. It pisses me off. They sure don't have any trouble getting our food and equipment."

"I hear you, Sarge," Folger said, echoing Leary's anger. "I'm going to kill as many of these little bastards as I can. All the odds are against us here, but I'm gonna take as many of 'em with me as I can before I go. And we're all going to go here, that's for sure. It's a good thing we are gonna die here too, because the longer I'm here, the more I hate those bastards back home."

Puzzled, Leary asked, "Who back home?"

"You know, the stinking government jerks who are letting this happen over here. Letting this corruption crap go on. They must be getting rich supplying both sides. They sure as hell don't want to win this thing. It's the stupidest, most perverse thing I've ever seen. They'd better hope to hell I don't get back. 'Cause if I do, I swear I'll kill 'em all."

Leary replied clearly, "And I hear you, Folger. If you get back, you can kill all of them you want, no argument here, but now let's see who we can kill here." Last night's compassion for the plight of the Vietnamese people and the squeeze they were in was all gone. Gone with the explosion, blown out of his consciousness. The mood was set, the day was young, and Leary knew that any Vietnamese Folger might meet up with on this patrol were in trouble. *He helped me yesterday when I almost killed our own men; now I've got to try and help him. Still, it's not easy. What he says seems so right.*

Profoundly numb, the men drifted back into the jungle. Slowly, step by step, stage by stage, they were evolving into people who, for the most part, would be unrecognizable by those who had known them in the past. Everyone was, to one degree or another, a new man, a man whose previous belief system had been destroyed. They had transformed into men who were thickly calloused toward all physical exhaustion, terror, pain, and death, their own as well as that of their enemies. The harsh conditions were changing them from loving men to insensitive killing soldiers.

The development of new beliefs would aid their survival. All of them now accepted the new beliefs, at first subconsciously, but more and more consciously. They would not be prisoners nor would they take prisoners. They would go down shooting. They would fight for their lives because dying was the easy way out. They would not leave any of their people anywhere, dead or alive. They would go anywhere they damn well pleased.

Necessity dictated this new creed. Rarely verbalized, it was not written anywhere but, to one degree or another, it was now their value system. It was a pact, an agreement between them about how they would conduct themselves and what they would value. All of the men in the squad accepted the new creed, all except Hart, who had no creed and valued only himself.

Leary expected no response from the fort or the base camp, and he wasn't disappointed. As he looked back at the fort, he clearly saw a group of uniformed men watching them from the west wall, but no one waved or left the fort to see if they were all right. *No one will come from the base camp, either, and they must have heard the explosion. It was a big one. Well, screw them all. I guess I'm a little disappointed. I could never have imagined this happening a few months ago. Back home, people care about their own and back them up, even when they're mad at them. Well, screw the captain, the South Vietnamese Army, and all those worthless bastards back at base camp. We may die out here today, but we'll die like men. I'll never forget this, though. Never.*

⌘

Tooley and Carson were sitting on the company CP bunker looking over the platoon area when they heard the explosions. Some of the men in the platoon were still sleeping; others were cleaning their weapons. A few wrote letters; the rest were smoking and talking quietly. It was a full twenty seconds after the explosion before Tooley broke the silence by saying, "That sounded like it came from their area. God, I hate this. It's like abandoning your kids."

"Yeah," Carson said, his voice full of helpless guilt, "it surely did, sir. Definitely came from the southwest, had to be near where they are about now." He glanced down at his watch as he made the statement. "About the time I would be headed west, if I'd been there. Wish we'd been able to go, sir—know we couldn't, but still feel bad about it."

"Me too, Platoon Sergeant, me too. Maybe the Vietnamese are looking out for them."

"We can only hope . . . I doubt it though."

"I doubt it too, Sergeant Carson, I doubt it too."

Neither man spoke again for fifteen minutes. Both made a mental note to snoop around the company CP and see if there was any information or rumors floating about. Rumors possibly gotten from radio conversations heard through the battalion radio. Anything at all, air sightings, ARVN reports—anything. Sergeant Carson would inquire through the first sergeant and Tooley through the company executive officer.

Later, neither man was surprised to see the other at the company CP. Carson grinned knowingly and Tooley said, "See you later at the platoon CP?"

"About fifteen, twenty minutes, I'd expect, sir."

When they were both back at the platoon CP, Tooley asked, "Find out anything, Sergeant?"

"No, sir, not a damn thing. You?"

"No, no word, no whisper, no opinion, no interest. I finally came right out and asked the captain. He said, 'Haven't heard anything, Lieutenant, didn't even ask, really. I expect if they don't come back we'll hear about it, or if they or some of them come back wounded, we'll be informed. Nothing any of us can do until then. Nothing we can do then, either.' He didn't seem bothered about it, either. The look on my face must have been shock, anger, or something because I didn't say anything, just looked at him and then finally he said, 'It should be fine, Lieutenant; after all, we have Sergeant Leary and his hell squad on the job. What could be better, what could be worse for the enemy? Lieutenant, just knowing that they're between us and the Triangle makes me sleep better.' He had a mocking tone that left me dumbfounded."

"Those were his words?"

"Yep, Sergeant, they were. The anger must have really shown on my face because he got a kind of panicked look, and his voice was squeaky as he said, 'Dismissed, Lieutenant' three times before I moved. I don't remember exactly what my thoughts were, but they weren't healthy toward him."

Sergeant Carson, who was becoming more and more worried about his young platoon leader's propensity towards violence, especially at the captain, replied almost pleadingly, "Wouldn't help them, sir. Even if you killed him, you'd go to jail and who'd look after the platoon then?"

"Just don't feel like I'm doing a very good job of looking after them lately. The captain plays the role of a god with a personal vengeance, Leary keeps pointing out the error of such thinking to the captain, the captain in turn keeps trying to get Leary and whoever else happens to be with him killed, and I can do nothing about it."

"Yes, sir, it might have helped if Leary hadn't stuck it in the captain's face a couple of times. I hasten to say, though, that by all that's holy I believe Leary was right."

"Yeah, my problem too. I think the captain is wrong, but he has the power. That's why, at times, it seems that the solution would be to shoot the captain. The urge is so strong, sometimes, that I'm not always sure I can control it."

"I understand, sir, but," he paused, "you've just got to control it, sir. You cannot, under any circumstances, shoot the company commander. If you live through this, you could not go back home knowing that, sir. When the Nam wore off, when you were sitting by the fireplace, maybe years down the road, it would come back on you. Some things, Tooley, a man just cannot do because he cannot live with them afterwards. So, please, sir, for your sake, for the sake of all of us, don't ever mention shooting the captain again. Don't even think about it, sir."

Annoyed at the reprimand, Tooley said formally, "Thank you for your concern, Sergeant Carson, I'll take it under advisement."

Carson, aware of the mood swing, said, "Yes, sir," and started to leave. When his back was turned, Tooley's voice stopped him, causing him to look back over his shoulder.

"Thanks, Carson, you are right and I appreciate it."

Carson, still a little miffed, "No problem, sir." They parted company then, under the guise of duties to perform.

Giap watched the seven Americans coming towards his fort. The south machine gunner had announced that they were coming after he had seen them climb the embankment two miles down the road, at the other side of the bridge. Giap climbed the ladder to the pit and watched them through a pair of U.S. Army binoculars. He could see that, though tired, none of them appeared to be wounded. They had the look and hurried walk that one gets when getting close to home after a long day's march.

The last two miles seemed like forever to the squad, and it took them an hour and a half to make it to the fort entrance. Both Giap and Leary were surprised to see how many Vietnamese seemed happy at their return. Most of Giap's soldiers and their families were at the entrance to greet them. As the men straggled through the entrance, Leary and his men tried their best to return the grins from the Vietnamese welcoming committee. They all felt twinges of the old welcome home they had once received from their parents and families. It was a good feeling and it settled deep inside some of those hardened hearts. However, the knowledge…dampened the happiness. The knowledge that Giap and his people hadn't cared enough to come and see if they had needed help.

Giap walked up to Leary, shook his hand, and then noticed the bullet-torn sleeve on his left forearm and said, "You are wounded."

"No," Leary, his rifle in his right hand, held up the left forearm so that Giap could see it better and said, "Missed me, hit the sleeve. Burnt me a little, but no blood. Guess I was lucky."

"What of the enemy?"

"He was lucky too," Leary managed a grin, "because I missed him too."

Giap's face showed immediate relief and Leary became irritated, thinking it was because he hadn't drawn blood, hadn't changed their delicate neutral balance. *At least not for one more night,* he thought.

"I would very much like to share some coffee tonight, again at your convenience, Sergeant Leary. One question, though, did you find my information useful?"

"Life saving, Lieutenant Giap," he paused for effect, "life saving."

"Good. Until later then, after you have rested and eaten?"

"Yes, Lieutenant, I look forward to it, but one question. A request, really."

"Surely, Leary, anything within my power."

"I was noticing that you have a carpenter shop. Some tools, some material."

"Yes, we also have a couple of soldiers who are good with the tools. May we be of service? You need something fixed?" He asked with a puzzled look. For clearly it would be hard to imagine what a carpenter shop could do for these men, whose only possessions were of cloth and metal. Oh, there were the rifle stocks, made of wood, but none of them were broken.

"No, sir, we need to make a grappling hook."

"One of those hooks seen in the movies for climbing walls and such?"

"Yes, something like that, but in this case for throwing down over a discovered, or suspected, booby-trap, then backing off and pulling it to set it off."

"I see. Of course, anything we have is at your disposal. Keep in mind that we have no welding facilities and no electricity, but whatever we have is yours. I will take you to the shop and introduce you to our best carpenter when you are ready."

"Good, sir. Folger here," Leary nodded in Folger's direction, "has some ideas and will handle the making of it. Explain what you'll need to the lieutenant, Folger."

"Well, Lieutenant, we won't need much in the way of materials. A piece of a tree trunk, about four inches long, and about four inches thick for the base. Some heavy wire to use as hooks, some electrical tape, or other material to attach the hooks to the wood base and about fifty meters of commo wire to use as rope."

"No problem, gentlemen, we have all of those things. Folger, go over to the carpenter shop when you are ready; they will be expecting

you. Now I would imagine your men wish to rest, Sergeant Leary."
Giap bowed slightly. "At your convenience, coffee, please."

"In about an hour, Lieutenant, thank you."

With that, everyone dispersed. Giap and a couple of men went
to the carpenter shop. Leary, Folger, and the rest of the squad went
to their bunker to drop the heavy gear, get their boots off of their
cracked and bleeding feet, and drink water. Leary felt a twinge of
embarrassment at their condition. He knew they all smelled rank,
but there was nothing they could do about it. The fort had no well.
The residents carried their water from the nearest creek and used
it mainly for cooking. Again, today Leary's group had soaked their
already dirty shirts and pants with sweat. He turned his face to clear
his nose with a new smell and then turned it back to the squad to see
if he could smell them. He certainly could. They stank of stale old
sweat, mixed with the smell of fear. *The Vietnamese always manage
to look clean and sweat-free*, he thought. *I wish I could bathe and put
on clean clothes before having coffee with Giap.* But, in despair, he
realized that was not possible. *I will just have to stink, and poor Giap,
too polite to ever mention it, will have to bear it. Perhaps I could try and
sit downwind*, he thought, *Ha, what wind?*

The sun was going down two hours later when Leary joined
the lieutenant at one of the small cafe tables. Giap was already
enjoying a cup of coffee. The sun was bright red-orange and so large
it covered most of the horizon. *The only good things in life are free*,
Leary thought, as he stopped for a full minute to admire its beauty.
Feeling a little self-conscious at having been distracted on his way
to the cafe, Leary had a sheepish grin on his face as he said, "Good
evening, Lieutenant."

"The sunset tonight is truly magnificent, is it not, Sergeant
Leary?"

"Yes, it is. It never ceases to impress me, especially when it's
like it is today. Back home in Montana, we also have some beautiful
sunsets, but nothing like this." Leary found that, when he spoke with
Giap, he was better understood if he spoke more formally.

"Then perhaps, not all in Vietnam is bad?"

"No, Lieutenant, not all here is bad. I have seen many beautiful
things in your country. Unfortunately, few of them were human.
The human things I have seen here, on both sides, are not good. And
for us, it isn't over yet."

"No, it is not over yet. I will most probably die at this fort, and
for you, unfortunately, your last breath will probably be Vietnamese
air. In fact, I thought at first, that your last breath had been taken

this morning. I watched your patrol go into the jungle, and then I came down to make my rounds of the fort. I was about halfway through when the explosions shook the fort. They were so powerful that many of our bunker-homes needed to have dirt shoveled out of them afterwards. I ran up to the south gun pit and watch with disbelief as the cloud cleared, and then I saw you and your men, unbelievably, get up and go back into the jungle. Then, about a half-hour later, when I had come down to finish my examination of the fort, the gunfire. First, the chatter of an AK-47 and then the equally pounding fire of one of your M-14 rifles, evidently yours?" He had a slightly amused but questioning look on his face.

All of a sudden, the whole business seemed so stupid that he broke out in laughter. Good, releasing, gut-laughter.

Giap started laughing too, but not hysterically, not uncontrollably like Leary. Evidently, Leary could see something that he couldn't. Giap wanted to laugh unfettered too; he needed to laugh. People were poking their heads out of their holes, stopping their chores to look, and all attention was on Leary's unabashed laughter. In an effort to join him, Giap asked, "What is so funny, Leary? I too wish to laugh."

"Well, damn, Giap," he exclaimed, "It all just strikes me as funny. How could one not see it as funny and still remain sane? For that matter," he said, exercising effort to control his laughter enough to speak clearly, "who the hell wants to be sane? It's insane to be sane." With that revelation, he broke down in laughter again. Tears streamed down his face. What Leary had said didn't cause Giap to laugh, but the infectious nature of his laughter soon had both of them on the wooden patio floor of the cafe. Both were doubled up. This letting-go was so out of character for Giap that some of his people started towards him thinking that something must be wrong, that their commander and friend must be in trouble. The old cook just stood in the door and watched, no expression on his wrinkled old face.

They were partially right. Both the lieutenant and Leary were having an emotional breakdown. Fortunately, they took their release with laughter instead of bullets. Finally, Giap righted his chair, still holding his stomach. Once back in the chair, he held his hand up to the approaching people, letting them know that he was all right. Leary stayed on the floor for another minute or two before reseating himself at the table.

Finally, they were able to calm down enough to talk and sip the thick, bitter coffee from the small cups. Cups that the old, black-

toothed and stooped Vietnamese cook periodically replenished.
Though people surrounded them, they felt isolated, alone. The
Vietnamese people were very polite and, even when they passed
within hearing distance, it did not seem as if they heard anything.

At last, all laughed out, they spoke seriously.

"You say the instructions I gave you last night helped today?"

"Yes, we hadn't gone thirty meters into the jungle, just past the
left fork, when I spotted a small tree cut, the top allowed to drop. It
was not cut all the way through, just as you described. It was after
seeing the sign that I spotted the wire. Even then, I still might not
have seen it if the dew off a leaf had not splashed onto the wire.
Ten minutes more heat from the sun, another couple of steps, and
I would've been dead and my men with me. From the size of the
explosion, I don't see how any of us would have survived."

"From the sound of it and the damage to the foliage, I would
say the same thing. It was a tremendous explosion. What did you
see? Was it a huge bomb, bundles of dynamite, plastic explosives,
what?"

"One damn American-made hand grenade, with a bursting
radius of fifteen meters in the open. In that jungle, it would have
only been a muffled bang. Obviously, I only found part of the bomb.
I'm grateful for that, though. Damn lucky."

"The word I heard today, through the Ben Cat grapevine, was
that they were out to stop you and your people. It seems that you
have had quite a bit of blood-letting over in War Zone C. The North
Vietnamese command is very angry with your outfit and has sworn
vengeance."

"That is true. It was an exchange, though—they got some of
ours and we got some of theirs. I do believe that they are more upset
about the food we took back from them. We had a pretty damn
good battle over it. They killed our platoon sergeant; he was a good
man."

"Unfortunately, there are many good men in this war, on both
sides, killing each other. The bad men are, as usual, not doing any
fighting. It seems the worse a man is at leading, the higher rank he
has."

"Well, we did what we had to, or thought we had to. They did
what they had to and will do what they think they have to now.
What kind of place is this Iron Triangle? What is the scoop on it?"

"The Iron Triangle is a large area, a complete town really, mostly
underground. It is a complete war-making place. Hospitals, arms
repair, ammo loading, training camps, everything right there. It all

belongs to the North Vietnamese, and everyone knows it and allows it."

"You say everyone knows that this place exists. That they know this, our government too, and they allow it to happen?"

"I'm sorry to inform you that it is true, Leary. Everyone knows about—even you and your people here at the fort."

"Well, Lieutenant Giap, we know that there is such a place. It irritates me that it's allowed to exist here. It seems stupid at best, and smelly with corruption at the worst. But, yeah, we all do know about it. We also know that it is no small matter. That it is no small outpost and should be a first priority. That it should be wiped out—now."

"See, Leary, you too know about it. It is a fully equipped fortress. A place which the enemy feels so confident about that they exude a cocky arrogance concerning its existence. They act as if they are immune. Oh, they are careful. They have the best of everything there. The best demolition experts, the best booby-trap men, the best scouts, the very best are assigned to the Iron Triangle."

"Reminds me of the bootleggers during Prohibition who could move their product openly because they had the cops on their payroll."

"I don't know what a bootlegger is, nor Prohibition, but I do understand having the police on their payroll. It is similar to that. Only subtler, more like we are here at this fort. 'Fence-sitting,' I believe you called it."

"Damn, this war stinks. They probably all did, but I'm in this one and it smells really bad."

"What happened with the shooting? You were shot at and nearly injured?"

"Well, not too long after we went back into the jungle, after triggering the booby-traps, I came around a curve in the trail. The jungle was so thick that I couldn't see through the bend so I had the slack out of the trigger when I saw him. He must have heard us creeping along; we were being very quiet. We just got a glimpse of each other and both fired at the same time. He was quick, as quick as I was, and we both missed. At least, I don't think I hit him. It didn't seem like I did and there wasn't any blood or anything. I held up for a while, maybe five minutes, and then dove around the bend and he was gone. He was a good man, I could tell. Very clean, pressed almost, good-fitting clothes, more tan than black. I saw his face quickly but clearly. Only got a glimpse at him, but I can still see him clearly in my mind."

"He was probably a scout. From the North, or at least trained in the North. They have many skilled men at the Triangle. He probably came to see what happened with the booby-trap. Most likely, they heard the explosions and sent him to see how many of you the booby-traps had gotten. Then you and he shot at each other. You and your men survived a very good booby-trap; they now know that you, too, are good. Hard to say what they will do. They may either let you go on your future patrols as long as you do not threaten them, or they may decide to get you and/or the convoy at all costs. If it is the latter, then I am afraid that we are all in for it, especially you and your men. What they decide to do will be up to their commander."

"Well, my position cannot change, Lieutenant Giap. I'll pull my patrols as ordered. I'll do my best to survive and see that my men survive. I'll not, should I happen to live beyond my tour of duty in your country, live any of my future life feeling ashamed of myself for not doing what is expected of me now."

"I respect your sense of honor and duty, Sergeant Leary. I hope you don't judge me too harshly for my attitude about the fighting of this war. You may live through this assignment here and go back to your home. A place where, I understand, it is reasonably safe, except maybe in Chicago where the gangsters are," He laughed, indicating that it was common knowledge that gangsters were in Chicago. Leary smiled in his best attempt at amusement. Not sincere, not really amused, but polite. Serious again, Giap said, "My point, I believe, is that you do have some home to go back to. Some country where there isn't any war and has not been for some time. I am home. I have a wife in Saigon and one small child. I have nowhere to go. I am an educated man. I have a master's degree in English from the University of Saigon. I have studied your language and country for the last ten years."

He paused. Leary could tell that he had more to say, but also that he wanted a response, something to encourage him to go on. " 'Professor Giap' has a nice sound to it. Why aren't you somewhere back in Saigon teaching English, Professor Giap?"

Pleased that Leary was genuinely interested in him as an individual apart from his position, Giap continued. "Originally, I thought that my dedication to English would assure me of a position with the university. It was understood that when I finished getting my degree, I would have five years of army service to do. I figured it would be in Saigon working with the American army or something like that. I did not feel that they could afford to waste a man who had developed the skills with the English language that I have. Well,

I was guilty of being too honest, of saying what I believed to be the truth of everything. Not just about politics, although there is little else that affects our lives here in Vietnam, but about anything and everything. I overestimated my worth and earned a reputation for speaking out, so they ignored my language skills and assigned me here. Just last month, my time in the army was extended when the government arbitrarily added another three years to my military obligation. You see, they will never let a loose cannon like me out. I am doomed to be in the army until the South loses—or I die. Because of the lack of benefit to the South Vietnamese to win against the North and because of our government's corruption, I hold no hopes of the South winning."

Leary said, "Why not move your wife and kid up here, into this fort? Many of your other soldiers have done it. At least then you would be able to have them with you as you wait for your future to get here."

"That would be pleasant, yes, to have her and my child with me. Enjoy them on a daily basis, but that cannot be. Unfortunately, my orders specifically say that my wife and child are to remain in Saigon. She must report daily, with my son, to a government office. Seven days a week. That is the only leverage they have over me. They are afraid that, if my family should join me for even a day here at this fort, then we would be quickly on our way north. In short, they do not trust me. They feel the need to hold my family hostage, a way to keep their lieutenant in line."

"Are they right, Lieutenant Giap?"

"More so every day, Sergeant Leary. Not at first, but more so with each passing day."

"Why don't you take them and run on your next visit? You said you visit them."

"Yes, I get to visit them one weekend per month and then only in a guarded compound. They have a place just for that. They call it a secured resort, a place where we can safely visit, but it is a jail."

"Do what you have to do, Lieutenant Giap. We all do what we must do. North or South. Don't sell us out and I will always honor our friendship."

In an effort to lighten the conversation, Giap laughed as he said, "Not while you are here, Leary, no North while you are in my fort. What happens after that only the future will tell. Perhaps another time, a better time, a better place for both of us."

27

SECOND PATROL

Folger pulled guard until sunup, an hour longer than he was supposed to. He didn't feel like sleeping; it was Leary's hour of guard and he figured that he would just let the sergeant sleep. Leary awoke when it was his time for guard, though. *As usual*, Folger thought, *he never misses.* But he did go right back to sleep when Folger waved him off, letting him know that he was handling it.

For the last thirty minutes of his guard duty, Folger delighted in watching the sun's first light creep across the fort's yard, enter through the bunker door, cross the floor and, finally, stop right at Hart's closed eyes. *Christ, he's already dead,* Folger was amused to think, *even with the intense light in his eyes he keeps sleeping. He keeps more to himself every day. Doesn't talk at all anymore. Not that he ever had anything worth saying. He's sort of in a walking coma, for damn sure. Thank God we only have one Hart. Anyone else in the squad would have awakened, changed positions, something, but not good old Hart. Yes*, he thought, *every day he gets deader.*

In fact, Hart was awake. Not alert, but awake. He was in total depression. He had been so scared for so long that the only way he could breathe properly was not to think of where he was. If he allowed himself to realize that he was in Vietnam, fear made his anxiety rise to the point of panic. The more anxiety he experienced, the more breathing problems he had. He often went from hyperventilation to having his throat close down, making breathing extremely difficult. Sometimes, he felt as if he would never be able to get another breath of air into his lungs. His solution to this was simple; he would not be in Vietnam. He would be home, where his family was. Where he was loved and cared for, a place where no harm could come to him. So, more and more he had developed the ability to not really be here.

Everything in Vietnam was not what it seemed to be. As far as Hart
was concerned, he was now lying in his bed, and soon his mother
would call him for breakfast.

Folger was still watching Hart and saw a smile cross his face
when Hart fantasized that his mother had come in to wake him.
Folger mumbled to himself, "That Hart is smiling as if he had good
sense." Embarrassed and not wanting his mumbling to wake the
others, Folger turned back to silent thinking. *Christ, now I'm starting
to mumble like Leary and the rest of them. But Hart's getting wackier
every day. He doesn't even acknowledge our existence anymore. On
patrols and such, he sort of mechanically follows the man in front of
him. Seems to do whatever he has to, so we won't get on him, but
no more. Bottom line,* Folger decided, *Hart isn't here anymore. Don't
know where he is. He doesn't talk anymore, not that I ever listened to
him in the past. Still, he definitely is not here. Not in Vietnam. Man,
how strange. What the hell,* he laughed to himself, *he seems to like
it, wherever he is. And his not being here is not hurting our cause; we
have no cause. We're only marking time till we die. Just like old Hart.
Maybe he's better off, doing it his way. No, not my style.*

The patrol was a little late leaving the fort that morning. Everyone
dragged their feet and Leary had no motivation to push them. They
were tired, dirty, hungry for something beside old C-rations, and
starved for love and affection. But because they had a duty, empty
as it seemed, they straggled out at about 0900 hours. Leary led them
down the road across the bridge—a reverse pattern from the day
before. He did this for two reasons: one, he wanted to get them
warmed up to the situation before they hit the potentially dangerous
jungle; and two, more importantly, he knew that it wasn't safe to
follow the same route twice. Giap had reminded him of what Leary
had learned in jungle warfare class—that it was fatal to set up a
predictable pattern. Predictability meant begging for an ambush. The
less expected one was, the better chance he had of survival.

Leary set a slow and easy pace, letting the hot sun and the walking
ease the soreness out of their muscles. The fresh sweat mixing with
old dried sweat caused a noticeable odor until the mind identified it
and the will tuned it out. They all felt a little better knowing that, by
the time they came back this evening, the battalion should be strung

out along the road. They were sure that they would feel safer and be happier to see the rest of their platoon.

Giap watched helplessly as the patrol turned west after crossing the bridge and started up the valley on the south side of the river. *Leary is reversing his patrol direction. Don't know if that will fool the men of the Triangle. Surely, they have someone watching him. Of course, Leary knows they will be waiting for him today. They lost face yesterday by not getting Leary and his men. Only time will tell.* Then he climbed down the ladder from the south gun pit and went about making his daily inspection of the fort. As usual, it was more of a "good morning" to everyone than an inspection.

While he was negotiating the steep embankment from the road down to the grass on the south side of the creek, Leary made up his mind that, if they did nothing else today, they would get a bath. *Maybe we don't have any soap, perhaps it's dangerous and there really isn't time for it, but by the God above we will get a bath today. That is the real goal for today,* he thought, *to take an hour off, have a bath, and let everyone swim or soak himself in this cool, clear water. What the hell, if we're going to die, we might as well die clean.*

Forty minutes later, he decided he had found the best place for it. He remembered this place from yesterday's return patrol. There was a sufficiently high bank on the south where one man could see far enough on all sides to keep watch while the rest of the squad bathed. It was such a refreshing event that Leary let them stay longer than good judgment would justify. Leary had taken the first watch with Folger's automatic rifle on the hill. It was a strain to maintain a 360-degree watch, but he did it. He had Folger and Branden pull the second watch. That way, they could sit back to back and cover 180 degrees each without continually turning their bodies. The water was slightly warm and felt so good that the spirits of the men were noticeably and immediately lifted. After almost two hours, reasonably clean and totally refreshed, they headed due north to the jungle.

Leary hoped to find a trail that would let them cut the patrol in half. *We'll still have made a sweep,* he assured his slightly guilty conscience, *just a shorter one.* He had seen what looked like a very faint animal trail coming out of the jungle yesterday when they made their way down the valley toward the road. Giap had not mentioned anything about a trail being there, but Leary thought Giap had little firsthand knowledge of the jungle around his fort. *Since he never goes out into it.*

Leary led them through the tall grass. *This damn grass is hateful stuff, and it's difficult to see through and is always trying to cut you. Fortunately,* he thought, *the closer we get to the jungle, the shorter and less thick the grass becomes.* It finally petered out close to the jungle's edge.

On reaching the wall of the jungle, Leary led the patrol west, staying close to its edge. When they had walked west about fifty meters, Leary found the trail he had noticed yesterday. It was barely wide enough for a man and, even then, they had to stoop, push branches out of the way, and generally inch their way through. *Dangerous,* Leary thought, *any time a man has to move, bump, or otherwise make contact with the foliage along a trail—it's dangerous.* Giap had said that booby traps were often tied to branches, vines, and the like. *Well, I have no desire to make the full swing. I'll just be extra careful and hope that the trail does not dead-end in this jungle and force us to go back out the way we came.* Before picking his way in, he consciously cleared his mind from the pleasures of the refreshing water and tuned it to awareness of a hostile environment. He forced his eyes to look closely at the kind of foliage, the things common to this area, so that he might be able to spot anything out of place. He needed to see any signs left by the enemy, any markings that might denote the location of booby-traps. No one said anything about his stopping and contemplating; they just accepted anything that he did. In a few minutes he was ready and, unrushed, he signaled with his hand and slowly started sneaking his way into the jungle.

Two hours later, Leary was worried. After maneuvering their way along the narrow winding trail, he suddenly lost all sense of direction. If the trail quit now, they would lose many hours and might not get back to the fort until after dark. He did not want to approach the fort, or any military establishment in Vietnam, after dark. If that should happen, he decided, they would hide in the jungle and wait until morning. Just as he sensed danger and thought that coming this way was a major mistake, he heard the voices.

They were Vietnamese, and they were close but muffled. His fist shot up immediately, signaling halt. The signal wasn't necessary; most of the squad, having also heard, was already frozen in place. Then he made a downward pumping motion with his fist, indicating that everyone should squat or kneel down and form a perimeter. The urgency and strength put into the signals also said make no noise. *Fortunately*, he thought as they squatted, *we filled our canteens at the stream and they don't make that slopping, half-empty sound.* They were supposed to drink one canteen until it was dry to avoid the noise caused by half-empty canteens, but that never seemed to work. More importantly, it wasn't necessary because they had all learned to walk silently, in spite of the many pieces of equipment that they carried.

After they were all down, Leary signaled to Folger that he was going to crawl forward. Folger, he knew, would keep him in sight. A hard and fast rule of survival was that no man disappeared from the sight of the man behind him. Leary slipped his web gear and helmet off, setting them gently on the trail behind him. He reached back into one of his ammo pouches and secured an additional magazine and slipped it into the rear pocket of his sweat-soaked fatigue pants. Then he pulled a grenade from his belt and, holding it in his left hand next to the hand guard of his rifle, he crept forward in a crouching duck-walk. Folger eased the safety off his automatic rifle without making a sound—a hard thing to do, but he and Leary had practiced it to perfection. The rest of the squad dared not take their safety catches off. It was so distinctive a sound and traveled so far that it would have been an immediate giveaway. As they had learned in training at Fort Riley, Kansas, the safety snapping off of an M-14 rifle can be heard for a half-mile. Even though Folger and Leary were good at taking their safeties off quietly, it was a very risky thing to do. Without consultation, they decided to take that chance because having the safety off would provide a fraction of a second they might need.

Leary was surprised to find out how close he was to the southwest branch of the main trail. He would have been relieved too, if it hadn't been for the Vietnamese voices. As he waddled forward, he slipped down into a crawl on his stomach. *It has become quiet, too quiet. I hope they haven't heard us,* he worried, as he fearfully poked his head out onto the larger trail. He scooted out quietly like a turtle with its head coming out of the shell. He left his body where it was as he stretched out his neck, looking up the trail as far as the foliage would allow. *To really look, one must see what is not meant to be seen. One must study the foliage for something out of place, something that might indicate a camouflaged man, a hidden danger not visible at first glance.* He recited this drill to himself as he strained to interpret the secrets of the jungle. He forced himself to stare up the southwest trail for what seemed like a torturous amount of time. He concentrated, making sure that they were not there, before he dared slowly turn his head in the other direction, down trail. All the time, while looking up the trail, he fought the fear that they were down the trail and about to shoot him. Finally, he decided there was nothing to see in that direction, resisted the urge to turn his head quickly, knowing that sharp movements are easily detected, and slowly turned his head in the other direction. *I feel like a child sticking its head out of a doggie door,* he thought, as he concentrated on focusing his eyes on the jungle trail to his right. He was afraid to blink for fear that even that miniscule movement might attract attention to his presence.

Damn, there they are, how silly, he thought, *no, stupid. The one on the left is facing this way but has his head turned toward his buddy who is facing the other way.* They were whispering something to each other. *Hell, there's a bunch of them. Sitting in a small clearing.* Once in a while, he would catch a sound or piece of whispered verbal communication. *One of them must be briefing the others,* he thought. *Wonder what they are doing here? Then he knew: Shit, they're waiting for us. It's late; we went the other way, stopped to take a bath. They've gotten lax—thinking that we weren't coming. I've got a surprise for you gooks. We're here.* Keeping his eyes on them, he pushed his body back, pulling his head into the foliage, hoping against hope that he would make no noise while retracting his body.

He carefully backed to where his gear and Folger were. When he turned behind him and looked Folger in the face, he knew that Folger could tell what he had seen. Folger gave his famous "whatever" shrug. *Well, we have no choice. We have to go out this way,* he affirmed in his mind. *If we try and back out, not make contact, then we won't make it back to safety tonight and, if they hear us, we lose the edge. No,* he decided, *that's the way out for two reasons. First, I don't believe we can get out of here without making noise. If those men hear us, they will come after us. They're here to get us and it's only a circumstance of fate that we have ended up where we are and they are where they are. The second reason is that, even now, another group of them could have seen us and are crawling up on our rear or waiting to ambush us if we do back out. Hell,* he assured himself, his adrenaline flowing, *Stupid to assume all trails aren't blocked. Old number three is the most important reason why we'll go out through these suckers. We go any goddamn place we please.*

He knew then what he had to do. He put his finger to his lips. After he knew everyone had received the signal, he indicated the number of NVA on the trail with the fingers of that same hand. First five, then two—seven enemy. Then he shook his open hand back and forth to indicate that it was only a guess, that there may be more. Pointing in the direction of the enemy, he signaled that they should fire blindly through the jungle foliage at about a foot above ground level, hoping that some of the bullets would find human targets through the thick brush. Then he, with Folger right behind him, would jump out on the trail with a hand grenade in each hand and throw them at the clearing where he had seen the enemy. He would then jump up-trail, allowing Folger to fall on the trail behind him, firing his automatic weapon. After loading a fresh magazine, Folger would jump up and attack the soldiers with his automatic rifle—who would by then hopefully be dead or at least stunned. Hart and Branden, after firing a few rounds, would follow them out on the trail, leaving Sanchez to cover the rear. Leary would then move west up the trail to protect them from any enemy from that direction.

The likelihood of a man being on guard up-trail is almost a certainty. It will be tight and very dangerous. Hate having Hart in the third position, wish it were Sanchez. But Branden will cover Folger, and I'll take care of the west trail. Need Sanchez to guard our rear, anyway. The grenades could get any or all of us. It's all a risk, but what isn't over here? So to hell with it, no more thinking; let's just do it.

One final look at the men, they all nodded their heads that they understood, but we won't know who really understood what until it's all over. With that, he held the grenades up to Folger, who pulled the pins as quietly as possible before handing them back to Leary, one at a time, making sure he had a firm grip on the lever. Folger helped Leary sling his rifle over his left shoulder and, without further hesitation, Leary leapt through the foliage and out on to the main trail reminding himself, as he leapt, *take time to throw the grenades correctly.*

Five hours later, Leary was sitting with Giap at the cafe drinking their coffee. He was sweat-stained again, the effects of his earlier bath long since gone. He was not only sticky and unclean; he also had blood caked on his web gear and on the front and rear of his shirt-smeared clear down and onto his belt. This was the only shirt he had until he could get back to base camp, where he had one more in his duffel bag. He thought about the huge bloodstains on his shirt. He was even slightly embarrassed about them, but then disgust about the blood flooded through him for a moment until he decided those feelings were only affordable in another life, another place. *I just don't care anymore. It just doesn't mean a damn thing.*

After their greetings and Leary's coffee had been delivered, there was an uncomfortable silence, as if they were strangers again, and as if they hadn't spent hours getting to know one another.

Finally, Giap broke the uncomfortable silence. "Bad day, Leary?"

"Yes, one of the worst. I suppose you saw us come by the fort on the way to the battalion at the bridge." Giap nodded. "You heard the shooting too, I imagine. Thankfully, we were close; only about fifty meters from the split in the trail and about a hundred meters from the clearing." Once again, Giap nodded. "Damn it, Giap, none of my people came to look for us. They heard the shooting, too. That cuts it, by God, to hell with all of 'em."

"What about us, Leary? We did not come either."

"Well, damn you, too." An expression of sad acceptance crossed Giap's face. "No, Giap," Leary heaved a defeated sigh. "You told me why you wouldn't come, and your coming would not have saved Hart." His voice was filled with despair as he said, "Nothing could have saved Hart, really, not one damn thing. Hell, I didn't even think I liked him. Didn't think I would care when he died. I was wrong."

"You had another man wounded?"

"Yeah, Branden got it through the upper arm. His shooting arm, too. Good for him. He'll get a rest now. Not much of one, though, since it was only a light flesh wound."

"He will come back?"

"Question is, will they send him back? The answer is yes."

"What determines if a man comes back after being wounded?"

"From what I hear, if he is permanently disabled he doesn't come back, if he gets three Purple Hearts he doesn't come back, and if he's dead he doesn't come back."

"Then if they can repair the arm, if it heals, he will come back to finish his time here?"

Giap stared at Leary—as if he had more to say.

In response to the look, Leary said, "I never thought I'd wish a man a permanent disability, or even death." He paused for a minute, noticed how cool the sweat dripping down his back was, and then continued, "I did wish Hart's death, many times. At first, I felt like killing him myself, but that was before I had killed. Then later, I could feel no ill will toward him. Oh, he frustrated me plenty in our time together. He was such a lousy soldier, but I learned over time that he had a kindness to him. I didn't wish his death for those reasons, but because that man suffered from fear every minute he was over here. The fear built and built until he was almost a zombie." Giap raised his faint eyebrows at the word "zombie." "Oh, 'zombie,' walking dead man." Giap understood and Leary continued. "He hardly ever spoke and might not have gotten shot in the chest like that if he'd been more responsive to the situation." He shrugged, "Hell, who can say, really? It was his time to go. He'd suffered all a man can and still be a part of this stinking world."

Giap wanted to hear more, and he had a look of kindness on his face as he said, "You and all of your men have blood all over the front of your shirts. Did you all carry him and did he take a long time to die?"

"Yeah, we thought he was dead, but he must not have been because usually they stop bleeding after they die and he bled all over us." His face was sorrowful as he recalled. "We tried to bandage him, I used his bandage first, on his front, and then mine on his back. We tied his belt tight around his chest so that the bandages would stay tight against the holes. That hole in the back was so big that I stuffed the bandage right into it. The bullet went in below his left nipple and I think it got him in the heart." He laughed, a crazy man's laugh, as he said, "Hart in the heart." Embarrassed, he sobered and went on. "Well, anyway, I couldn't tell if it had gotten a lung. There wasn't any blood coming out of the mouth and no bubbles when he was breathing. Which wasn't long. We did try to seal the wounds off just in case. We used the foil out of a couple of packs of cigarettes, but in truth, it wasn't sealed tight enough. I think, and thought then, that he was a goner. He never came to, not that I saw, and never made a sound or a move. He was sure heavy, though, and I was so tired."

"You carried him first?"

"No, at first Folger put him over his shoulder and I took the point. It was still dangerous. We didn't have a clue if there were any more of them around or where they might be. It was the one up the trail, out of sight and around the bend—he shot Hart and Branden."

"What was he a rear guard?"

"I guess so. It was such a mess. I jumped out on to the trail after we found them and threw the grenades and dove up the trail facing west. Folger flopped out onto the east trail right behind me and started shooting at them. They'd all heard, and probably seen, the grenades and tried to get away from them. They stumbled over each other trying to get up and down the trail, anywhere but the clearing where I'd pitched the smoking grenades. God, it was a mess. I'm only just now able to start putting together what happened."

Giap gestured with his hands for more. Leary looked up to the left, as if viewing a screen in his head, and then began putting the chain of events together. "Well, like I said, I sort of hopped out on the trail. The trail junction was such that they didn't really meet, you kind of had to bust through the brush of the main trail to get on it. Must have been a small animal trail, certainly wasn't much of a man-made trail. Anyway, I had a grenade in each hand and my rifle slung backwards over my shoulder. Folger had pulled the pins on the grenades, and according to the plan, was ready to push out behind me and start spraying them after I threw the grenades. I was hoping, conditions being what they were with the foliage and all, that I could throw the grenades into the clearing. It wasn't that large of a clearing. They were all crammed into it. I was also worried that with Folger and me on the ground and with their bodies being between the grenades and us, the shrapnel might hit us. It was a lot of big 'ifs,' but I didn't see any other way to do it. As it turned out, fortunately, I was right." Leary paused again, relaxed in thought, and then went on. "Good old Folger. He just followed the plan in his usual brave manner. I didn't dare risk letting him take a look, too.

"Like I said, I pushed my way out onto the trail as fast as I could, let the grenades cook off for one second—seemed like an hour—then with them all staring at me, eyes big and scared, I pitched, first one, then the other, right up and to the far side of their little group. I turned my back to them and dove on the ground trying like hell to get my rifle off my shoulder and under me. It was hung up on my front ammo pouch, or canteen, or some damn thing. But Folger pushed out on the trail right after me and dove down facing east, and started pouring bullets into them. The grenades went off and out of the dust, two of them—the two closest to us—came running right at Folger. Folger said his first burst stopped the front one in mid-stride. Christ, he must have taken five rounds, or the grenades got him, too. It's unclear, it was so violent and confusing, but his chest disintegrated. Well, as Folger tells it, the second man must have gotten some of the bullets that went through the first man, but he was so frantic that he just pushed the first man right on toward Folger's gun. They both ended up lying on top of Folger. He was still firing his weapon and frantically tried to get them off. The barrel of his automatic rifle was so hot that the blood from the first man cooked on the barrel. His rifle smelled like cooked meat."

"Anyway, right on cue, Branden pushed Hart out on to the trail.
They stumbled and fell on Folger and the two dying NVA soldiers,
and then there was a heap of screaming, shouting, and dying men.
The grenades had hit five of them, killed three outright, left one
dying, and one, though wounded seriously, began firing at the pile
that I was now part of. He was either out of his head or he just
figured that his two men lying on the heap were dead, because he
kept screaming and shooting. Meanwhile, Branden and Hart were
trying to get out of his line of fire and were scrambling over me—
they climbed right over me and headed up-trail. Hart just left his
rifle where it had fallen and crawled right over me. Once past me and
on his feet, Hart started running east right up the trail. Branden, right
behind him, was at least trying to drag his weapon with him. His rifle
butt put a bump on my head as he dragged it over me. For a second,
I was afraid he'd knocked me out. They were desperate. I don't blame
them—that wounded man was pouring it on us. He kept firing even
though he had wounds all over him."

Leary paused reflectively and Giap asked, "Then the wounded
North Vietnamese soldier shot Branden and Hart?"

"No, thankfully he shot his own people, the ones lying between
us and him. He didn't even hit Folger, but it must have been close.
We were sort of low and on the ground. Still, it was a miracle because
Folger said he was shaking and pointing at the pile and just kept
pulling the trigger. Might have been nuts by then." Once again, Giap
looked puzzled at the word. "Oh, 'nuts,' insane, crazy from the terror
and the wounds," Leary explained. "According to Folger, when his
magazine went dry, he just sat there looking at us, his eyes glazing
over as he died. By the time Folger had gotten the gooks—sorry—off
his rifle, he reloaded, stood up, and fired a three-round burst blowing
the whole top of the man's head off."

"If he didn't shoot your men, who did?"

"The man up the trail. The very one I was supposed to be
guarding against. And I'd have gotten him too, right away but, like
I said, they climbed right over me trying to get out of there, and it
cost them. I can see it clearly, Hart first, with Branden right behind
him, dragging his weapon by the barrel. By this time, I'd gotten my
rifle out in front of me and was trying to bring it into a position to
cover the trail. But they were both in my way, blocking my vision
and line of sight. Then an NVA soldier, their up-trail guard, came
running around the bend in the trail, stuck his AK-47 in Hart's chest
and pulled the trigger. The whole thing probably didn't take more
than fifteen seconds, four for the grenades to go off and eleven for

the rest to happen. Seemed like an hour, though. So poor old Hart ran right into that guy's rifle, and he pulled the trigger, blowing Hart right into the air. He must have been on semiautomatic because he had to pull the trigger again after moving it to Branden, who was frantic. In his desperation, he didn't have much time to aim, he just pulled the trigger again getting Branden, who was now only a couple of feet from him. He hit Branden in his right bicep. The impact spun Branden to his left, causing him to fall backwards into the jungle. He was sort of planted there, held up by the foliage, just waiting for the next shot to finish him. Fortunately for Branden, the enemy soldier was more worried about me than Branden, and he turned, trying to line his rifle up on me. He got off two shots but they were high and wild. I think he pulled the trigger out of pure frustration because I had him and he knew it. I hammered a couple of them into his chest, throwing him back and killing him quickly. Well, at least a few moments later when I looked him over, he was dead."

Fatigued from reliving it, Leary summed up with, "We made sure they were all dead, but quickly, since we figured there were probably more of them around. We bandaged Hart and Branden the best we could and took off carrying Hart and leading Branden. Hart was so heavy we all had to take a turn at him. Actually, we all had a couple of turns at carrying him. Dead people are really heavy; at least, Hart was."

"Yes, an old saying but true," Giap, replied.

"First, I tried carrying him with his front on my front, that's why the blood here," Leary indicated his stained and caked shirtfront. "Then, when that proved to be too awkward, I turned him around holding his legs down over my shoulder with my left arm. No matter how we did it, it was too much. In the end, and we got more than a few bad looks from the platoon's soldiers because of it, we dragged him by his web gear letting his heels, legs, and butt drag in the dirt. You could see, looking back, the drag marks in the dirt. We felt badly, but we just couldn't do it any better. No one could carry him for long. We all tried. First I took a turn, then Folger, and so on. We tried to be more respectful, but we were just too tired and he was too heavy. We took both of them to the road and turned them over to the platoon medic. Then, after explaining what had happened to the captain, the platoon leader, and Sergeant Carson, we walked off and came here."

"Why didn't you just leave him? He was dead. His spirit had left his body."

"We couldn't. We have a pact among us that we won't leave anyone, anywhere, dead or alive. After seeing what the enemy does to prisoners, all of us in the platoon made the agreement. One can never be sure that a man is dead, not for sure, unless he's in small pieces, but even then we agreed that we'd bring back what we could. It's one of the few things that we still believe in. There aren't many things in this war that we can depend on. So we must depend upon each other. We made new rules for ourselves, rules that apply to us here, and we must live up to them. If not, we'll surely go insane." He paused for a second and then continued. "We may go insane anyway."

At dusk, the captain came to the gate of the fort with his radio operator and asked Giap if he could spend the night in the protection of the fort. By this time, the men of the second squad were so used to their captain that they never expected him to spend the night out on the road with his men, not if there was any way out of it. So, seeing him come through the gate with his radio operator carrying his sleeping bag was no surprise. Giap obviously did not care much for the captain but he reluctantly gave him permission to sleep in his fort. He told him that he had no extra room but that the captain could find a corner in the yard if he wished.

The captain chose the wood patio of the small cafe to roll out his sleeping bag. Things would have been all right if the captain had remembered who was in charge of the fort, but he didn't and Giap gave him one more reason to hate Leary. It was late and Leary and Giap were still talking, paying no attention to the captain who lay close by. They were mostly off the war and enjoying telling each other about their friends and families. It was about 2200 hours when the captain spoke up.

Rising up in his sleeping bag, as Leary and the lieutenant both were wondering how anyone could sleep in something that hot and clumsy, the captain said with authority, "You men go on to bed now. I'm trying to get some sleep and your chatter is keeping me awake." Looking at him in the dim light that came from the cafe windows, Leary chuckled with the amusement one reserves for a boastful child. But Giap's face registered first shock and then anger as he said, "Captain, out there with your men," he pointed east through the cafe, "you are in charge. In here," he bent his finger straight down in a ninety-degree angle, "I am in charge. I will talk as long or as late as I wish to. Leary is also in my fort, as a guest, and you could learn much from him about politeness. So, Captain, you may sleep where you are, you may get up and find another, quieter, place to sleep, or you can leave the protection of my fort, but you cannot," he stared hard at him through the dark, with a look of reprimand for a mouthy child, "tell me what and when to do anything in this fort."

With that, he and Leary ignored the captain, who lay back down and never spoke another word.

The next morning, however, he was waiting for Leary and his now three-man patrol at the fort entrance. Leary started to walk on by the captain with only a nod of his head. He was not in a good mood, and neither were Folger or Sanchez. "Hold up a minute, Sergeant Leary," the captain replied, a little too sweetly, "tonight you and your men will sleep along the road with your platoon. It isn't fair to the other men in your platoon for you to sleep in here while they have to guard the bridge. Beside, they might need you out there tonight." In an attempt to solicit some stateside military response, the captain sternly asked, "Do I make myself clear?" He paused a moment for effect, then added, "Sergeant?"

Leary didn't respond at all to the captain but turned his attention to Giap, who was standing back a few steps from the captain. "Thank you for your time, friendship, and information, Lieutenant Giap. Since we won't be coming back here, I will see you at another time, in a better place."

"It has been my pleasure, Leary, good luck to you in this life."

Then, Leary turned slowly and headed out through the gate, Folger and Sanchez following ten meters apart. When they entered the clearing outside the fort, they automatically increased their interval to twenty meters. None of them, not a man, not even with a look, acknowledged their captain as they went by. He was angry. *Punk, I'll get him. Maybe today, Leary. I'll win in the end.*

Feeling nothing, wanting nothing, expecting nothing, not even to live, the remaining men of the second squad ambled out across the clearing and turned west, toward the Triangle, toward the dangerous and blood-soaked jungle, toward another patrol.

28

WAR ZONE C

The third and final patrol was completed without loss of life or limb on either side. The enemy did not attack the patrol or the convoy. Leary and his men made a complete sweep of the area and returned in time to catch the last truck of the convoy, which transported them back to their base camp above the village of Ben Cat. Leary had taken the patrol on the south fork of the trail, through the killing ground of the day before. Evidence of the battle still existed. There was blood, the smell of rotting flesh, some pieces of bloody clothing, and a huge accumulation of flies, but nothing else. Not even one piece of expended ammo brass was left. Leary and his remaining four men were void of emotion as they passed through the site; they were numb and without fear.

The men of the battalion were exhausted, all of them, even those who had spent the days sitting alongside the road. Mostly, they suffered from the weariness of living on the edge of death twenty-four hours a day, seven days a week. Just before dark, they had heard through the enlisted man's rumor mill that the battalion would be going back to the most dangerous part of War Zone C tomorrow. Their battalion would be part of a larger operation whose mission was to seize, sweep and block, and search and destroy any and all enemy in the zone.

Last time, they had been almost through the southern half when they were sent to find the lost South Vietnamese company. Now, several battalions would hunt through the entire northern half of the zone. A month ago, this would have been fearful and depressing information to the men; there would have been grousing and other displays of anger and fear. But now they took the information with a certain pronounced resignation. Like rowers on a slave galley who

247

had finally accepted their fate to row until they die, the men of the Sixteenth Infantry accepted their orders without comment. After the formal briefing, the men went to their places in the base camp and bedded down. There was little conversation. Most had just run out of anything to say.

The next morning, with little fanfare and less conversation or laughter, the men received their rations and ammo. They boarded the choppers, took their flight, and unloaded without incident in a cool LZ. By 1300 hours, the whole battalion was headed north down a two-lane dirt road under the canopy of the jungle. The jungle canopy was high there, leaving only sparse vegetation on the jungle floor. Still, it was at least a hundred degrees Fahrenheit, with humidity high enough to make breathing difficult and an overwhelming smell of rotten vegetation.

Their first mission was a sweep and block. The Sixteenth was to move north at the best possible speed, covering as wide an area as possible and, hopefully, sweep the enemy into the waiting Twenty-second Infantry Battalion. The Twenty-second, whose base camp was seven miles north of Ben Cat at Lia Kae, had been flown farther north to set up the blocking ambush and were now waiting for the Sixteenth to push the enemy into their trap.

Charlie Company was on point for the battalion, and the Second Platoon was on the point for the company. Aside from the captain's desire to get rid of Leary, he and Folger now had a reputation as survivors and everyone, including the captain, felt better with them in front. The colonel was where he felt the safest, in his helicopter above the battalion, watching his men move north like a long line of green ants. The jungle was so dense that even from the air he couldn't ever see all of them at once, but he could always see some of them as they appeared and disappeared, picking their way north. He had to return to Lia Kae for fuel several times during the day, but he didn't mind. He no longer felt safe down in the jungle with his men and had made up his mind to spend as little time as possible there.

Leary's awareness increased every day. His internal radar was operating on full power, and it was so easy to use. It was intuition, instinct, or maybe clairvoyance or second sight. He was finding out that he just knew things. Only strong emotions seemed to interfere with its function. Anger was the worst; it completely scattered his mind. As he become more aware of this, Leary made great efforts to keep his mind calm and clear. Learning to accept things for what they were and not what he wanted them to be, he knew, was a must. *Back home they'd think I'm crazy, "elevator doesn't go all the way to*

the top," "round the bend," etc., but by God, there's something to it. I
can feel it out there. I can tell where it is and what kind of danger it is
too. I can tell if it's human danger or something left behind by humans.
I'll never admit this to anyone, though, sounds too wacky.

Yes, he told himself, *my old radar has definitely increased in range
and detail-detecting ability. Sometimes I feel like I get impressions from
life clear out there. Like now, I know they're all around us. Not real
close but out there. I can feel them. I can see pictures of them in my
mind. It's a knowing, really, about men and women working at supply
dumps above and below ground. Of people laughing, loving, eating,
and dying in their underground dwellings everywhere. Sometimes it's
overwhelming.*

Leary had started to see his enemy differently than he wished to.
He saw them as men and women trying to live through another day
and see their loved ones again. *Damn, I'm seeing people, not enemies.
People—men, women, and children in their own homeland. And the
children, the orphan population growing every day, right or wrong. Our
being here is killing the regular people. Oh, I have no illusions about
the serious threat these people are to my life. The rules haven't really
changed for us. For them, it's winning at any price. Individual lives
aren't as important to them as winning. If they think terror and brutality
will serve their purpose, they use it. In that, they aren't much different
from the South Vietnamese government. Look at the position they have
Giap in. They use Giap like a rug and will throw him away when
it suits them. The thing the North has to offer that the South doesn't
is that they are fighting to let the Vietnamese own Vietnam. In that
respect, they have a definite philosophical advantage. Their enemy is
clearly defined as all foreigners and those who support foreign presence
in Vietnam. So they can be just as brutal as they want to towards those
who aren't on their side and still not violate any rules. Still be right. It's
simple,* he thought, *anyone who doesn't support the North's war efforts
is either a traitor or a draft-dodger. And, as such, they can be killed or
brutalized. It's probably always been like that in every war throughout
history and it probably always will be. It's the nature of things. Still, I
would feel better if I could see them in the old way. Well, we are their
enemy,* he reminded himself, *and I need to keep that in mind. I damn
sure can't afford to forget whose side I'm on. The rules don't change for
me. Can't change just because if I were on their side I might do things
the same way that they do. Damn Giap,* he thought, *it was easier to
hate these people before I met him. It was sure a damn sight easier when
I could just write them off as gooks. When I didn't see them as humans,
but as some demon bent on destroying my home, it was better.* Then

he laughed to himself at the thought of them island-hopping all the
way to the United States. *That domino theory is a stupid bill of goods.
Even as dedicated as the North Vietnamese government is to taking the
South, I certainly can't see them, ever, being a threat to America. Once
they leave the confines of their country, they lose the "Free Our Home"
motto and end up in the same boat we're in, and our boat is one of just
fighting to stay alive long enough to get back home.*

He heard the wooden thump and looked back at Folger, who
had his closed fist in the air, signaling a halt. It was a signal made by
lightly smacking the wood of one's rifle stock with a couple of fingers,
a nonmetallic sound that the men knew wouldn't travel far. Not like
a voice or a metal against metal sound which could, depending upon
the wind, foliage, and such, be heard for miles.

Someone was halting the column from the rear. It was the
battalion executive officer, whom the men rarely saw and didn't
know. At first, their colonel had been a very visible leader. He had
always been around, but lately all noticed his lack of presence. Today,
he had left his executive officer in charge on the ground.

Leary knelt in the sand of the truck trail they had been following.
Fear rushed through him like an incoming tide. Not fear of something
outside of himself, but from within. He had been locked in his
own thoughts, bopping along like a child, distracted by the mental
discourse in his own head. *How could you do that?* he chastised
himself. *You've fallen into complacency and were not even looking for
the signs that Giap told you about. Damn you, you got caught up in
some stupid thinking in your own head and weren't even here. You need
to be here. You have to make yourself be here or you'll walk the platoon,
maybe even the company or battalion, right into something. There is
more at stake here than just yourself. These men depend upon you. If
you can't do it, give up the slot.* Realizing that the critical voice in his
mind was just as distracting as the daydreaming one, he cleared his
mind of all such nagging and declared himself back.

At the same time, Tooley was waiting and thinking, too. *Platoon
Sergeant Carson is positioned several men back from the front of the
formation. That's as close to the front as I can tolerate him being. I do
not want to lose my platoon sergeant. I not only like Sergeant Carson
but, by the God above, I depend upon him. We need him; we would
be hard put to replace his wisdom. Sure, he still has an emotional tie
to Leary and the men of the second squad. He hangs around them a
little more than I'd like. Not that Sergeant Carson neglects the rest of
the platoon,* Tooley corrected himself, *but it'll be better when he sees*

himself completely as our platoon sergeant and not as their old squad leader.

Tooley looked up and down the trail at his men. Everyone was down on one knee, many continuously wiping the sweat off of their heads and faces. Some carried green towels tied to their web gear just for that purpose. A few, he noticed, had just learned to ignore the sweat, letting it tickle to wherever gravity dictated. Everyone was facing out, toward his individual area of responsibility. *Good*, he thought, *they don't have to be told anymore. They have adjusted, a point of trust, really. Trust that, while one man is guarding a particular direction, he knows his back is covered. This way, everyone's back is always covered. Not much consolation, but some. Keeps a man from going completely crazy trying to cover his front, back, and sides at the same time. Yeah,* he decided, *it isn't dying or being shot that's our real fear. No, it's more the shock from the surprise of it that we're afraid of. It's that instant of unexpected destruction which comes fast and without warning. The startling violence that tears a man apart without letting him fight back. That's our terror, that's our nightmare. A man just feels better if he knows he can go down shooting. Surprise deprives a man of that last bit of dignity.*

While they rested, Leary, back on track, analyzed his surroundings. *The road we're following north is just two ruts in the jungle floor and, judging from the fresh tire tracks, has been used recently.* He looked up at the jungle canopy. *Can't be seen from the air. Where the hell do they put the trucks during the day?* He asked himself. *Well, that's silly,* he corrected, *they could've parked them almost anywhere because, though it's light enough to see down here, the canopy is still tight enough to hide even trucks from being spotted from above. They do most of their moving at night and probably have a fully equipped motor pool around here somewhere. Could be up the road a ways or just around the next bend. They're definitely careful, though. In some places where the protective canopy peters out, they've moved the road along the jungle's edge, keeping it in the jungle's shadow. The thicker the canopy,* he observed, *the less light and the sparser the grass and other vegetation is on the jungle floor. The largest trees wipe out all the vegetation under them. It looks kind of like the big cathedral in Helena with only the sunlight filtering through the stained-glass windows, typical of nature everywhere, really. Stronger always pushing out the weak. Stronger life always consumes weaker life. Large trees snuff all the life out of the grass beneath. They take all of the sunlight and hog all the rain; life at all levels is only a struggle to survive.*

Damn, if my mind hasn't tried to drift on me again, he thought. *I went from analyzing the terrain to philosophy of life. Well, just screw it all. I'm going to do and think about what I want to. I know that the information Giap gave me is valuable, but so is my instinct. It got us this far, before we ever heard about marking the trail. Hell, I know what trail markings are; I just have to trust that I know it. I understand it and I've used it before but I can't let myself be so consumed with it that I push out my real ace—my intuition, or whatever that instinct thing is. I believe in me and that'll have to be good enough. If I fail and people get killed, that's tough shit. If they want to put someone else on point, suits me. I'm just not worrying about it anymore. It's out of my hands. Let nature take its course just like it does in this jungle all around me. We die when we die, and that's all there is to it.*

No sooner had Leary noted the peace from his new attitude than the muffled sounds of rifle fire and explosions could be heard east of them. Everyone who wasn't already peering in that direction did so now. Not that they believed they would be able to see anything, but turning their head toward of the noise allowed both ears to zero in on the commotion.

Moments later, word spread to change course and move back down the trail. Because the middle of the battalion had headed on an easterly trail, toward the battle noise, C Company merged in behind A Company, which had now assumed the point, leaving B Company behind the battalion, on drag. The Second Platoon was now in the middle of the formation. As they began moving east, the sounds of battle changed from heavy rapid fire to sporadic rifle fire, and then, finally, to silence. By 1600 hours, they were set up in a defensive perimeter around the battle site.

The whole battalion set up on an elevated area of jungle and grass with great trees for shade. There were active, water-filled rice paddies halfway around the high ground. The other half of the perimeter had a well-used dirt road that went from the north end of the battalion encampment to the south end. The southern half of the road came out of the thick jungle across a grassy elevated meadow, slicing through C Company's area of responsibility and then on southeast across a well-constructed log bridge and disappearing into a village of about thirty domestic dwellings made of mud mixed with straw and thatched roofs—hooches. A Company tied in with the troops of C Company's southern position and with B Company to their north. B Company then connected with A Company in the north and C Company to their south, forming a protective perimeter around a large clump of dense jungle that, at about three hundred meters in diameter, was an area the brass was determined to hang on to.

B Company and C Company had the easiest area to defend because, for most of their areas, they had the wide open spaces of rice paddies in front of them, and C Company even had an open grassy area in part of its perimeter. A Company, on the other hand, had only the width of the small road between them and the jungle wall. The Second Platoon had a fortunate spot in the perimeter. Leary's platoon's area was between the First and Third Platoons. The First Platoon tied in with B Company on their right, and the Third Platoon had the grassy area and tied in with A Company to the north. Leary, Folger, and the other men of the Second Platoon had about forty meters of water-filled rice paddy to defend. The distance across the paddy to their front was a hundred meters, and the water was about two feet deep. Though the platoon curved away to form the perimeter, the paddy continued on southeast for about another hundred meters before funneling down and running under the bridge. After the creek ran under the bridge, it turned southwest and continued below the village.

The jungle began again after the bridge and followed the east side of the creek past the village where it then continued west, curving around the village and out of sight. If the battalion had not turned east and then north on their way here, they would have crossed this creek, which eventually flowed into the river separating Cambodia from South Vietnam. The varied hues of lush green vegetation, clear water, and blue sky presented an appearance, deceptively, of tranquil beauty.

Down on one knee, Folger poked at the fire with a stick. Carson and Leary watched him, mesmerized by the flames. They were back about twenty meters from the paddy water. Leary sat in the grass, leaning against one of two sizeable trees that grew out of the grassy hill. Carson sat on the grass too, hugging his knees tightly against his chest with his arms. Each man's web gear, helmet, and weapon lay within easy reach. They were all tired, dirty, and sweat stained. In the heat and humidity the smells of fire, sweat, and gun oil were heavy in their nostrils.

"Damn," Leary said, as he gazed at the unruffled creek flowing by the deserted village, "I don't know why we bother to make a fire.

It's so damned hot here the water is already boiling when we pour it out of our canteens. I can't remember what cold water tastes like and certainly not ice. Still, it looks too peaceful here. Hard to believe that anything like war and killing could happen here."

Carson and Folger both followed Leary's line of sight toward the valley. After a few seconds, Carson said, "Yeah, that's the spooky part about this whole country. Especially back here in these jungle communities. Everything is so quiet, so full of life, so natural, and then—bang!—it's all over. It gets you so fast and hard that you're dead before you know it."

"What is this place, Sergeant Carson?" Folger asked, as he resumed burning the end of his stick in the fire.

"The word is that back in the middle of that clump of jungle," he pointed with his right index finger while not completely releasing his grip on his folded knees, "under that ground, there is a complete bunker complex system. It's elaborate enough to have a hospital, gun repair shop, ammo reloading facilities, and so on."

"Doesn't look high enough to me," Folger said.

"It is, though," Carson said. "If you get down on the ground and look up to where the jungle starts, you'll see there's a lot of hill there. It doesn't look like it at first glance, but there is and that's what makes it so hidden." Folger lowered himself down to the level of the grass and sighted uphill past the platoon and company's CP which, because of the limited space available, were all in the same area.

"Damn, sure as hell. Big rise," Folger said, pushing himself back up on his knees. They both looked over at Leary, who hadn't moved.

Leary broke into a grin, with his forearms resting on his pulled-up knees, he looked in their general direction and said, "Men, men, I don't need to look. Our platoon sergeant told us it was so and I accept it as the truth." In a mock-chastising voice he continued, "What's the use of having a quality man like Carson as our platoon sergeant if you're going to doubt him, Folger? You know, double-check everything he tells you."

All three laughed and Carson said, "Hear, hear, a man who knows what he's talking about."

"Still," Folger said, "it isn't that obvious. At least I know, Leary; I looked. You don't really know. Sergeant Carson and I might both be shitting you."

"Well, Folger, that could be true. But I don't care. If you two went to all of that trouble to fool me, then so be it, I am fooled."

"So now what, Sergeant Carson? Not that it makes much difference to me. I mean, I got lots of time. How much more? Ten

months, nine, I really don't even know what day it is. And that doesn't
matter anymore either. Sunday, Friday, or Wednesday, they're all the
same. But since we have nothing else to be curious about, what more
do you know, Sergeant Carson?"

Carson grinned, displaying his perfect white teeth as he said,
"Okay, here's the scoop. Such as I heard, from a conversation between
the captain and Lieutenant Tooley." He paused a minute to let his
black eyes roll up into his head, remembering. "The flankers from A
Company walked out into this clearing on the same trail we all came
here on. They'd been trying to stay parallel with us, but seems as if
we were a little slow, Mr. Leary."

Leary laughed. "Heavy on the mister, but slow, indeed I was a
little slow this morning. The new me can see no reason to get in a
hurry over here. I am beginning to believe in the old tortoise and
hare story. The tortoise, though slower, always seemed to win the
race. No strain, no pain. That's the new me."

Still smiling broadly, Carson continued. "Well, the rabbits were
definitely a little ahead of us on our journey north but, thankfully, not
that far. Anyway, seems their point man spotted them without them
seeing him and he pulled back into the jungle. Their platoon leader
came up to take a look and there were three of them sitting on three
bicycles, AKs slung on their backs, just chewing the fat and smoking.
The platoon leader told his radio operator to call it in to the colonel,
which he did. They waited and watched and then while the colonel
was trying to get a fix on their position from above, his chopper came
buzzing right over the jungle top and over the heads of the Charley
Congs. Well, all hell broke loose then, as they hurriedly let their
bikes drop and started shooting at the colonel's chopper. The colonel
and his pilot must have been startled too, because the chopper didn't
just whiz on by, no, it pulled into a steep climb, almost stalling. Then
I guess it got dicey. The colonel's chopper evidently just floated in
the air like they were daring them to shoot at 'em." Carson paused
to let everyone get the picture. "Which, indeed, they did, shoot at
the chopper. Well, the men of Company A couldn't allow that to
happen and they started blasting away at the VC. According to the
A Company platoon leader, once they started shooting, more of his
men moved up and began to blast away, which sounds like what we
heard. Grenade launchers, machine guns—well, we heard them."

Leary raised his eyebrows and asked. "They get all three of
'em?"

"No," Carson said, "Nobody got nobody. They did get the bikes,
though. Did you see them over there? They're cheap to start with,

not a Schwinn in the bunch, but those M-79 grenades sure made a mess out of 'em. Spokes, pipe, and wheels everywhere."

"How in the hell could they, with all of those men, not hit any of them?" Leary asked, "Hell, it's only about a hundred meters from the jungle to the place where the bike pieces are."

"Well, they couldn't all get to the front to shoot at once, and the enemy rabbited right out of there. Once they saw all those GIs, they forgot about the colonel's chopper and their bikes and headed straight into this clump of jungle we now own. This prize we're now guarding."

"So the flanker platoon followed them into the jungle and found the underground facility?" Folger asked.

"No, they didn't," Carson replied calmly, "they waited for us to catch up with them, and then their whole company made a sweep through it and found it. It was the right thing to do, even though it gave Charlie a chance to clear out. I guess they left in a hurry, though, because they left a lot of stuff behind. Guns, food, and medical stuff."

"So now what?" Folger asked.

"Now we keep it. Show it off. Bring in people from Saigon to examine the place, take pictures, and generally brag about it through the press," Carson replied, with a tired Southern drawl.

"Well, if they asked me," Leary said, "I think we should blow the damn thing and get the hell out of here. They might have made a hasty retreat but they're still out there. I don't think that they're going to let us just hang around and make sport of our catch."

"Is this another of those feelings that the lieutenant is so glad you have?" Carson asked.

"As a matter of fact, it is, Sergeant. And the new me doesn't care if the lieutenant likes it or not. I think we're in for a hard time of it here. Seems out of place, too, in this quiet valley. That apparently empty village down there has probably been feeding these people for generations."

"Well, Leary, feelings aside," they all smiled at Folger's attempt at humor, "maybe they'll let it go like they did when we found that warehouse full of food."

"Shit," Leary said, "they didn't let that go at all. I don't know how we got out of there with our lives. If they'd known how isolated and out of ammo we were, they'd have wiped us out. We did get a bunch of them, though."

"Yeah," Folger said, "we were in deep trouble. They just didn't know it."

"Time will tell. We'll all do what we do. They'll do what they do and whoever is left on either side will do something else after that," Leary replied. "What about the battalion blocking for us?"

"Guess they've been told to wait, or something. I don't know, really," Carson said.

"The coals are ready for heating C-rations, and the water is hot," Folger said, spreading out the coals with what was left of his burnt stick.

Carson laughed and said, "I hate cooking for myself. Especially when I got the dreaded ham and lima beans for supper."

There was very little conversation as the men cooked and ate their meals. The other men from the squad and some from other squads came up in pairs from their positions and heated their C-ration cans of food. It was now an expected thing, getting the coals ready every night for the men in the Second Platoon to take turns heating and eating their food by the fire.

By 1800 hours, everyone was in his assigned position waiting for the night to come. They made places for themselves in the grass to sleep. Most found logs to lie behind for protection. They did not dig foxholes because the water table was too high, causing the holes to fill with water soon after they were dug. As a result, most of them had quit carrying their entrenching tools and had left them at base camp. Like their air mattresses, flak jackets, and other unused gear, most of them didn't even know where their entrenching tools were anymore. There were very few conversations and little noise of any kind around the perimeter. These days, the men could generally speak all the words in a few minutes. They had learned to become quiet communicators because, in their new world, talking was dangerous.

At sunset, the huge, brilliant orange sun dipped out of sight as Tooley and Carson made their rounds. Working their way down the line, talking to their squad leaders and the men. Quietly, they moved from position to position, checking everything before darkness fell.

When they came to Leary and Folger's position, three men from B Company on their right entered the jungle after wading across the rice paddy directly in front of their company's position. Leary and Folger lay next to each other behind two large logs that they had found earlier and dragged down to the water's edge.

Leary was on his back, his head on his pack, facing the inner circle of the perimeter. Folger lay on his stomach, behind the log and facing across the rice paddy. His rifle perched over the logs, ready for use. Leary's rifle barrel was propped up out of the dirt on the log beside him. There were four grenades on the ground between them at the base of the logs. All were within easy reach, placed where they could be found quickly in the dark.

"Evening, Lieutenant, Sergeant Carson. Pleasant night," Leary said with a tongue-in-cheek formality. Folger turned fully around, nodded recognition, and then turned back to watch the men of B Company disappear into the jungle.

"How is everything, Sergeant Leary? Got everything you and your men need?" Tooley asked.

Leary resisted the urge to give him a smart-ass answer about what his men needed but instead voiced his concern. "Yes, we've got everything we need, but what in the hell are those men from B Company doing going across the paddy unrolling wire and carrying a phone?"

Carson never moved, didn't even twitch, just looked straight ahead, his rifle cradled in his arms, and waited for Tooley to answer. The lieutenant was nervous, his voice squeaky, and he had trouble deciding what to do with his hands. First he hooked his thumbs on his pistol belt, then in the suspenders of his web gear, and finally he placed them behind his back, tightly gripping each other. When he spoke, he reverted back to the safety of his training. Almost as if reading a military order, he began. "They are setting up a listening post for the night. One sergeant and two men from each company will go to the nearest cover, but not less than fifty meters from the company area. They will go just before dark. They will bring a field phone with them, unrolling the wire as they go, and call in a report every hour."

"Whose idea was that, sir? Why, it's fucking suicide. If it wasn't so tragic, it would be the funniest thing I ever heard of." The lieutenant hated it too and made no attempt to defend it. "And call in every hour, why, what better way to tell them where you are. Whose harebrained idea was that?"

"The colonel's," Tooley said flatly. "Guess they used them against the Japs in the Second World War, or something like that."

"Well, then, who's going out from our company tonight?"

"They already have. It was a squad from the Third Platoon. They have dry area out in front of them so their post was set up just into the jungle, about fifty meters from the perimeter."

"Well, that surprises me," Leary said, anger creeping into his voice. "I am surprised that the captain didn't pick me for the job."

"Look, Leary, we know it's a shitty job. We know that the colonel wants to hold this place and drag a lot of recognition out of it. It will look good on his record. Hell, he might get a star out of it somewhere down the road, especially if it makes a big enough news splash. But no one selected anyone. We put all the sergeant E-5s names in a helmet and drew them out. The sergeant from the Third Platoon's name came out first so he went out tonight."

"Whose name came out second?"

"Yours, Leary. Tomorrow night you, Folger, and whoever else from your squad you choose will go out across this paddy and set up a listening post. Just like you saw them do from B Company."

"Sir, this is wrong. There are angry Vietnamese out there right where those soldiers went. Why not shoot us here and now? Save us the wade across the water and the waiting."

"How do you know that, Leary? Is this one of your feelings? Well, if it is, I don't buy that crap. I go by sight, sound, and real evidence. And I saw no sign or evidence to indicate that there are any enemy soldiers around here. Hell, Leary, even the village is deserted."

"That should be evidence enough, sir. Where are they? They all have to eat, sleep, and drink somewhere. I think then, sir, that they are across that rice paddy, in that jungle, and that they have a lot of men and weapons over there and they're just waiting for us to attack them. When they hear us blow this place, they expect us to attack them. They don't believe we would be stupid enough to just sit on this place and stop long enough for people to come in and take pictures. They fully expect us to get on with our search and destroy mission. I guess this is a real war for them, and they can't imagine how any people could fuck around, play with, stop and take pictures of something as serious as a war. Have they got a lot to learn about us, and I pity us combat troops when they do learn what we are about."

The lieutenant had heard enough. He would hear no more, and, as he turned to go, he said, "Tomorrow, Leary. Tomorrow night you go. Patkins should be back tomorrow and the next night he goes. His was the third name out of the pot. That's the way it is and nothing can change it. The colonel ordered it."

About midnight, the phone rang for the last time. The shaky whisper from the B Company sergeant reported all quiet and then hung up. Ten minutes later, B Company received fire from two American M-14 rifles and one grenade launcher. No one was hit or wounded by the forty rounds of rifle fire or from the two poorly aimed M-79 grenades. The three men of B Company did not come in the next morning, and a patrol from B Company went to look for them. They found nothing except the black commo wire for the phone. Tonight, it would be Leary, Folger, and Sanchez.

29

LISTENING POST

By 0900 hours of the second day at the underground warehouse, everyone knew what had happened to B Company's listening post. Well, they knew the men were missing and, hopefully, dead. Nothing else of significance had happened the previous night, but Leary wished on several occasions throughout the night that he had gotten his turn over with the night before. He told Sanchez over the breakfast fire that they had to go on the listening post that night. There was no getting out of it, not unless something happened to change the plans. But that something would have to be big. An overrunning attack from the enemy or something else bad enough to make the colonel forget the publicity he was seeking here, destroy the complex, and move them out.

He and Folger sat in their position, leaning against their logs, their boots and socks off in an attempt to heal their cracked and bloody feet in the sun.

"So how'd Sanchez like the idea of going tonight?" Folger asked.

"Well, he wasn't too happy, but he didn't say much. Just mumbled something about not being taken like those guys were last night. Said if they show up to get us they'll hear the noise he makes over here. Sanchez is a good man. I'm glad he'll be with us."

"Well, I don't mean to speak poorly about one of our war buddies, but having to go with Patkins tomorrow night would scare the crap out of me."

Leary laughed. "Folger, you haven't been scared of a damn thing since you got here and maybe not before . . . but I didn't know you then."

"Well, if scared is an increase in heart rate or shaky knees, then I've had my share of it back home and over here too."

"You damn sure don't show it."

"If I thought showing it would help any, I damn sure would."
Then, as if remembering who he was, his voice became determined.
"But I'm not about to lose my human dignity over being scared of
death or any other damn thing in this life."

Still chuckling, Leary said, "You're a man after my own heart,
Folger."

Folger changed the subject. "It's going to be bright again tonight.
Probably no rain and, if the moon is anything like last night, you'll be
able to read by it."

"Yeah, the rain has died down a lot since we first got here. I
thought it was never going to quit the first few weeks. We must have
gotten here in the last of the monsoon season and now it's all over."

"That suits me just fine. I don't mind dying so much, but I don't
like to be wet all the time."

"Wasn't that something, the way they fired those guys' weapons
back at B Company?"

Folger grunted. "I wonder what goes through their little slant-
eyed minds? What makes them do shit like that?"

"They probably wanted to let us know that they had our men,
sort of a terror tactic. They rule this country with terror. It's in their
minds to do the same thing to us. Probably figure it works with their
own people, and they have no reason to believe it won't work with
us. Those men just being gone, not a sign, it's like something out of a
horror movie. Meant to spook us."

"Well, I don't know if I'm afraid of it, but I know I won't tolerate
it, tonight or any night."

Folger paused and Leary, thinking he might have gotten tired
of talking and had quit without finishing his thought, asked, "What
won't you tolerate?"

Until now they'd been talking while looking straight ahead, but
now Folger turned his face toward Leary. In a no-nonsense, end-of-
discussion voice, he said, "I will not be captured by these people.
Never. I carry an extra round in my pocket for myself, and I will
blow my own head off before I ever turn myself over to them."

"We all feel that way. Look what happened to that South
Vietnamese platoon—shot 'em in the back of the head after they'd
surrendered."

"Yeah, they must have liked them. I've heard stories about how
they treat American prisoners, and it isn't a quick execution. They
keep 'em alive forever, just so they can torture 'em."

"I've heard those stories too and, from what we've seen so far, I wouldn't put it past 'em. I agree, if you run out of ammo, put that pocket round through your own brain. I just don't know if I can do it. I hope it never comes to that."

"Well, I can, but if something happens tonight or anytime for that matter, and I'm wounded, out cold or something, and you figure we're going to be captured, give me your word, Leary, that you'll kill me." Leary looked into Folger's eyes, which squinted with concentration. "I have to know you'll kill me if need be, Leary. I can't let those little bastards take me alive."

Leary said solemnly, "I promise you, Folger, that if you're in danger of capture tonight, or any time, I'll kill you."

Obviously relieved, Folger said, "Thanks, Leary, I feel much better now. I'll do the same for you."

Leary broke into a smile as he said, "Just use good judgment about my situation, will you, Folger?" And they both started laughing.

After they quieted, Leary said, "Don't worry about tonight. I'm working out a plan to increase our odds."

"Good, I'm with you, whatever you decide."

At dusk, the crimson sun dipped below the horizon. But the bright moon meant that it would not be a dark night. The moon and the stars had a brilliance all their own. Under other circumstances, it would have been a good night for admiring the beauty of creation. But in the angst of the evening, the beauty went unnoticed. Leary, Folger, and Sanchez received a final briefing from Tooley and Carson. The captain was drinking a cup of coffee nearby—listening.

"Well, Leary, you know what you have to do," Tooley said. Leary nodded. "You have the phone and the wire." Sanchez had a roll of wire on a spool in one hand and a phone in the other. His rifle was slung on his shoulder and he held up the wire and the phone to indicate the obvious. "Good," Tooley said. "You need to go across the paddy directly in front of your position and into the jungle about fifty meters." Leary nodded as the lieutenant continued. "Roll the wire out as you go. Once inside the jungle, find your position as quickly as possible. It should be one that will afford you cover while still allowing a reasonable amount of visibility. Though this is supposed to be a listening post, the moon is bright, so take advantage of it." He waited for Leary's nod. "Once you've set up in your position, check in with us by phone. The phone will be monitored all night. You are to call in every hour. Let us know everything is all right. Keep it short, just say everything is okay. Of course, if you see or hear anything, call it in and then get back here as fast as you can. Any questions?"

"Well, sir, I think I understand everything all right, but I'm a little skittish about coming back across that rice paddy before daylight. The men are pretty jumpy and, if we see or hear the enemy—after we call in, of course—aren't we likely to get shot by our own people? Especially if we've had to do any shooting ourselves."

Before the lieutenant could answer, the captain, who had been waiting for a chance to blast Leary, spoke as he stepped over to join the group. "What's wrong with you, Sergeant Leary? Don't you even trust your own people?" He shook his head with disgust as he spoke. "Do your job, soldier. Quit being such a wimp."

Carson saw the rage building in Leary's tightened lips and narrowed eyes and jumped in front of him, thrusting two claymore mines at him. "Easy, son, easy. I got you a couple of claymore mines to put out in front of your position. If you see or hear them, pull these triggers and a thousand steel balls will mow them down. Then come back running and shouting. I'll hear you. I'll be down there, and I'll keep them from firing on you."

Leary, knowing that he would have to go through Carson to get at the captain, calmed himself, and lowered his rifle. He was not aware that he had snapped the safety off as he raised his rifle to a firing position. It was a loud and harsh noise with an unmistakable meaning. Leary had come a hair's-breadth away from killing the captain, and the certainty of it ran cold sweat from the pores of the captain's body as he tried to make a last statement. It was to have been a statement denying Leary the claymore mines. He'd fully intended to say it, but he was just too frightened.

As they prepared to go into the paddy, Leary paused to tell all the men who could hear him, "We're going out now, straight out from here, across the paddies and into the jungle on the other side. I ask you all to get behind your guns and sight at the jungle on the other side. We may need cover on the way over." He pointed with his rifle. "At any time during the night, we might come running back across that paddy. Do not shoot at us. You have plenty of light and plenty of time to shoot if Charlie should come running out behind us. We will not be able to run fast in the water and may need cover on our way back. So, be ready. If you hear two claymore mines go off, be looking for us. Hopefully, we will be right behind them. We are going to cross now. Remember, tomorrow night, or some other night, you'll be going."

Everyone got down behind his weapon. The machine gunners and their ammo-bearers, the riflemen and the grenadiers—everyone who could cover them, did, including Tooley and Carson.

A moment later, the three of them sloshed across the paddy. Leary and Folger, followed by Sanchez unrolling the wire. Leary and Folger moved as speedily as they could through the knee-deep water, so they could cover the slower Sanchez. It was hard going and rough at the bottom because of the ridges and old clumps of rice.

They all made it without incident, except Leary and Sanchez had each fallen once and were wet and muddy from the waist down and up one arm. The other arm was dry because of the necessity of keeping their weapons dry. The jungle was a conglomeration of bushes, with small clearings under thick trees and vines. The variety of vegetation cast eerie shadows as they stopped to rest. They were nervous, squinting, trying desperately to force their eyes to take advantage of the sparse light. Hoping to see into the dark shadowy areas.

As soon as they caught their breath and felt reasonably secure, Folger whispered, without taking his eyes off of the area in front of them, "Nice speech. I hope that wasn't your plan."

"No way, that was just a smokescreen. Here's what we do." Leary paused briefly, inhaling deeply, and then continued. "Connect only one wire to the phone." He pointed at Sanchez, indicating that he should do it now.

"But it won't work then," Sanchez said.

"Right, it won't work, but we can swear we connected it. We damn sure won't be calling them at all tonight, or anytime on that damn phone, and we sure as hell don't want them calling us. Shit, you would hear that ring for miles."

"You really think," Sanchez asked, "they would call us? Ring the phone out here, give us away?"

"Bet on it," Folger said, "especially when they don't hear from us, I'll bet that the captain will be trying all night."

"Right," Leary said, nodding approval at Sanchez's freshly connected wire. "Good, now just put it down. When we leave here, we won't talk at all for the rest of the night. We'll move in the direction of the road for at least fifty meters, way the hell away from here. Then we'll find a place to hide and set up the claymore mines. If we see them and we're sure they won't see us, we let them go by. If we have to fight, we blow the claymore mines and head to the road. Cross it and spend the rest of the night under the bridge." He looked at each of them until he saw affirmative nods. "Got it? Let's go, silence from here on. Not even a whisper until we are out of here in the morning."

They moved south until Leary found them some bushes that he hoped were free of ants and snakes. Taking care to disguise them as much as possible without ruining their effectiveness, they placed the claymore mines. Then, pulling the claymore wires in after them, they crawled into the roomy hiding area that consisted of several bushes close together, giving the impression of one large bush. There was room in its center for them to lie down and see out under the leaves—close to the ground. Like children who have found safety in a hiding place, they felt good. They did not move, but slept on and off throughout the night. They heard occasional firing that they thought came from their own people, but they saw and heard nothing else except the crickets, animal, and other creatures of the night.

Just before sunrise the next morning, they moved back to the unmolested phone and wire spool. They disconnected the wire they had connected the night before and started rolling up the wire. Before they broke through the cover of the jungle into the rice paddy, Leary yelled, "Sergeant Carson, hey, Sergeant Carson."

In less than thirty seconds, Carson yelled back, "I hear you, Leary, wait until I tell you to come out."

They could hear Carson and others yelling up and down the perimeter, "Hold your fire, our listening post is coming out. Hold your fire, no firing."

After the shouting died down, Carson yelled, "Okay, Leary, come on out. We're ready. We'll cover you, but make it fast."

When they climbed out into the paddy, Sanchez was first, quickly rolling up the wire. Leary and Folger came out twenty meters behind him and twenty meters apart. They both backed across the paddy, providing protection for Sanchez. Carson, Tooley, and the captain were waiting for them under the trees by the morning's fire.

The captain had just started to speak when Leary said in what he hoped was a disappointed voice, "Is your phone working? We hooked ours up but didn't get anyone on it all night."

"Bullshit. Our phone was hooked up and someone was listening for your call all night. We even tried to call you a couple of times, but you wouldn't answer," the captain said angrily, his voice dry and crackly. "Sergeant Carson, check their phone out, and it had better not work."

"Yes, sir, I'll do that. But it could be that it got wet when Sanchez fell in the water on the way over. If it's dried out, sir, it might work now. Could start working any time sir, I've seen it happen before." Seeing the defeated anger on the captain's face, Carson hastened to tell him, "I'll check it sir, but we'll never really know. Will we, sir? Not really."

"Yes, we already damn well know. You did not hook up that phone, did you, Leary?"

"Sure did, Captain, hooked it right to the wire in that spool," Leary pointed as he spoke.

"I have half a notion to send you back out again tonight. Do it until you get it right. All of you."

"Well, Captain, it's certainly within the power of your position to send me back out. No use sending these guys, though, I was the man in charge. I don't mind, really, but it would tend to make the rest of the people in your command think you were showing favoritism towards me. It would also make them doubt the validity of drawing the name out of a hat. Make it seem like you were cheating, in my favor, on a game of chance. I appreciate the offer, but I wouldn't want the men to lose faith in your leadership."

As the captain's rage and frustration peaked, he was on the brink of tears—a situation to be avoided at all cost. Cursing under his breath, he turned and stalked stiffly up the hill to his CP.

When he was safely out of hearing, Carson was the first to open the conversation. "Damn, we're glad to see you. Lieutenant Tooley and I waited up all night checking the phone every hour, watching the jungle in between. One of us watched the jungle for you all night. We didn't try to call you, though. That was the captain." His words quickened as he spoke, "Hell, none of us in this platoon slept for worrying about you. We all wondered all night, minute by minute, if the same was happening to you that happened to the men from B Company. Of course, if the North Vietnamese knew what a pain in the ass you are to the captain, they probably would have given you back. " Everyone smiled at the humor, too tired to laugh.

Later in the morning, Leary and Folger were sunning their feet with their boots and socks off, sunning their feet, when the choppers started arriving. Several men with cameras and other dignitaries, including Vietnamese Army officers, came and went all day. They had all come to see and take pictures of the bunker complex. None of the men on the perimeter paid much attention to them, and by 1800 hours the visitors had all gone back to their clean sheets and whiskey.

Chewing through some stale C-ration gum, Folger asked Leary, "Did you tell anyone what we did last night?"

"No, was afraid it might get back to the captain and then we'd be back out there every night. You?"

"No, same reasons. Spoke to Sanchez too, and he's not telling anyone either. Afraid to, which is a good thing—keeps him quiet."

"Everyone ask you, too?"

"Everyone, including Carson and the lieutenant. I just said that what you said is what happened."

"Carson and the lieutenant didn't come right out and ask me, but they hinted and fished, trying to get me to volunteer. Finally, I just said, 'You don't want to know,' and they both nodded and quit talking about it. Patkins came in on one of those choppers and I wanted to tell him but decided against it. He seems different."

"Yeah, nice scar on his forehead, and that nose is crooked as a dog's hind leg," Folger said.

"His face is a mess, all right."

"Yeah, it looks good on him. Gives him a rough look. Takes away that baby face of his."

"That's true, but it's something more. He's different. Doesn't seem scared anymore. Seems kind of mean."

"There is something different about him all right, now that you've mentioned it."

"You suppose that whack on the head changed him?"

"I hope to hell so. He sure was a wimp. He was only slightly better than Hart."

"Yeah, well, I think I'll tell him. Hell, I got to tell him, we can't let him go out there like that. Better to tell him just before he goes out."

"Yeah, he and the rest of them need to be scared enough not to tell anyone. Of course, it might not work again," Folger said.

"True, the captain already knows what we did. Hell, they all do, they just aren't sure of the details. Let them figure on it all they want. But if we're here long enough to have to go out there again, we're going to do it exactly the same way. It's a bunch of crap. An illogical, needless risk of our lives, and I just won't play that stupid game anymore. From now on, now that we know what our leaders' commitment to this war is, I'm going to play the game differently."

"How's that?"

"I don't know if I can explain my new attitude. I certainly won't let our people down. The platoon mainly, but I don't believe the brass, from the captain up, have any real determination to win this thing. I think they all know it's a lost cause but are using it to better their military careers. And I didn't come into this war to be a rung on their ladder."

"It's a mess, all right. I'm with you, like I've always been. You do it and I'll back you."

"I know that, Folger, and it honors me."

They quit talking then. It was getting a little too emotional for them. They both knew that either one of them, or both of them, could be gone, dead, or wounded at any time and it was foolish to care any more than they already did. It might warp their judgment, slow their reactions, or worse, cause unbearable pain when one of them got it.

It was just as well that they pulled back into their defensive shells, because the worst night was yet to come.

30

PATKINS' TURN

It was 1700 hours, and the third night at the underground bunker complex was approaching. With Hart's death and Branden's wounding, fire team leader Patkins was given Marlin and Jackson from the weapons squad. They were not happy. Marlin was to be Patkins' automatic rifleman, and Jackson would carry the M-79 grenade launcher. It was a light and valuable weapon, and they took turns carrying it along with their own. With the promotion of Carson to platoon sergeant, and then Hart and Branden, the squad was down to two fire teams of three men each. A full-strength rifle squad would consist of ten men: a squad leader, two fire team leaders, two automatic riflemen, two grenadiers, and three riflemen. The second squad had been short one man to start with, and now it was down to a total of six men. The A Fire Team leader was normally the ranking man over the B Fire Team leader, and this placed Patkins in charge. Technically, he was now the new squad leader.

Anyone who had known Patkins before his injury could immediately tell that he was different. It wasn't just his weight loss, scarred forehead, or crooked nose—it was his attitude. No one would have called the old Patkins mean. Now it wasn't that he was mean, but he gave the impression that he could be. Where he had been scared of battles before, he now seemed to embrace fighting. He had taken the order to go out on the listening post tonight as routine; no big deal. He was obviously glad to be back and, for the men of the Second Platoon, that seemed crazy, especially for the Patkins they'd known.

Patkins leaned back in Jackson and Marlin's position and cleaned his rifle. He hadn't eaten much that day; just a little fruit cocktail earlier that morning. He liked how it felt to be hungry. It was a wide-awake feeling. It was an alive and ready feeling. However, as he got thinner, he was noticing a slight shaking in his hands. *Nothing serious,* he told himself, *probably a result of the weight loss and my recent heavy smoking. It's good to be back in the jungle, though. I just wish night would get here so we can get across the paddy and screw up some of those gooks. That was some shit Leary pulled. He wants to talk to me before I go out. I suppose he wants to tell me how he did it. Well, I'll listen and then make up my own mind about what we're going to do. Leary's a good man, but I wouldn't want to miss a chance to shoot some of those bastards. Damn, these hands sure do have a slight quiver in them. Guess they're itching for some action. Since I killed my old man, I haven't had much action. Sure, the doctors say it was a dream, that he's alive at home, but they'll say anything to keep me here killing gooks.*

He didn't want to admit it, but the shaking and the weight loss had gotten worse every day since the sniper shot him. It was natural to lose weight in a coma and in the hospital so the doctors weren't worried about it, but they did make note of it in his records. His pants were bunched up at the waist and looked like they belonged to someone else. His formerly handsome face now looked like the face of a concentration camp victim from World War II. His cheeks were starting to hollow, and his eyes were beginning to bulge out of sunken sockets. The skeletal structure stretched the skin on his cheeks. The break in his nose from the warehouse incident left his nose crooked and witch-like, and his forehead had a jagged scar right in the middle. *The scar of Cain,* he'd told himself, when first seeing it at the hospital. *The scar that God marked Cain with for killing his brother, Abel. Well, I guess I got mine from killing the old man, mean old son of a bitch that he was. It's okay, well worth the scar; I'd kill him again if I could.*

In the next position north, Leary and Folger relaxed. Both were reloading and oiling their magazines. They took each of the twenty rounds out, wiped them down with an oily rag, cleaned and oiled the magazine, and then carefully replaced each one in its pouch on their web gear. This was done every day, no matter what. Folger had just reloaded a magazine and had tapped it on his rifle butt to make sure the spring-loaded bullets were flush against the back of the magazine. They all knew this lessened their chance of jamming. Leary spoke while polishing a round with a small oily cloth.

"About Patkins, tonight."

"Yeah," Folger said while continuing to lightly tap the magazine. "The time is getting near."

"I think I'd better tell him now, give him time to digest it."

"Do what you like."

"No, it's your ass, too, if word gets back to the captain. And, of course, Sanchez's. You both might be affected by it."

"No, not really. You were in charge, and," Folger added, grinning a little, "it's you the captain hates."

"Too true, too true, he and I'll never be fishing buddies, but still, I don't want to risk getting either of you in trouble."

"Well, don't let that stop you. What are they going to do to us, send us to Vietnam? They can't do any more to us than they've already tried to do. Let's be real about this. There just isn't anything worse within the captain's power that he can do to us. Death is the end of our suffering for a lousy cause. So screw the captain, the president, and the U.S. Army. Let 'em give it their best shot. If it bothers you, I'll go to the captain now and tell him what we did and then shoot him. I don't give a damn anymore. I'm sick of that son of a bitch screwing with us. Weak-kneed jerk, he's starting to make my old man back home look good, and I never thought that would happen. No, my dad is just weak; this prick is weak and corrupt, twice as bad. I say, tell Patkins. If he or those other two blab it, so what? Who gives a good goddamn? I sure don't." His voice cracked with anger. "I wouldn't worry about Sanchez either. If you want to tell Patkins, go ahead. Hell, Sanchez can't have anything worse done to him, either. I mean, who gives a shit? We're still trying to play this game like it had rules or something. There are no rules we have to obey, except those we agree to among ourselves. So screw all those chickenshit rules made up by weak-ass dummies somewhere else. We're here and we will make the rules. If the captain finds out and sends us back out to punish us, we'll go back out and do exactly what we did before. Only difference between what we did then and what I'll do on the next listening post will be what I do during the night." Leary looked at him, puzzled. "'Cause I promise you, I'll be looking back across that rice paddy all night, trying to get a shot at the captain. I can promise you that." He looked up then to see Patkins walking the short distance towards them, his well-oiled rifle glinting in the sunlight.

"Damn, he's losing a lot of weight," Folger mumbled.

"Leary, Folger." He stopped between and in front of the two men and, with hands trembling slightly, he squatted on his skinny haunches. They were both slightly fascinated watching his jerky hands push the fire from a C-ration match to the cigarette dangling in his mouth.

"Christ, Sergeant Patkins, get a grip on yourself. You sick? You're shaking like an old man and skinny as a rail. Have you been eating at all, or are you hoping that if you get skinny enough they'll ship you out of here?"

"Screw you, Folger. I didn't have to come back at all. It was my choice. The doctors said I had such a major head injury that they wanted to keep me longer. Coming back was my idea. I'd have come sooner if they'd've let me."

"You're right, Patkins, screw me. But who the hell are you? You're not the old Patkins we used to know. What the hell happened to you? Can you even remember who you used to be?"

"Sure, I can. Everything just changed when I realized that I'd killed my old man."

Leary and Folger were hard to shock these days, but both of their faces registered surprise at Patkins' words. "What the hell you talking about?" Leary asked. "You didn't kill your dad or anyone before you were sent over here. They never would have let you come if you had."

"No, they haven't found the body yet."

"Well, this I know for sure. I'd stake my life on it. The old Patkins could not kill his father or anyone else. Now you, whoever the hell you are, I don't know about. I don't think you know who you are either but, if you want to know what we did on that listening post last night, say so."

"Sure, I want to know, Leary. I'm not taking any shit while I'm over here, but I'll use anything I can that'll help us kill as many of them as we can. I don't care about dying. I don't want to be wounded again. I don't want to go back to that hospital. I belong out here killing these gooks and anything that'll help me do that I'll listen to. So, say what you got to say, and then I'll decide if we're going to use your method or devise another."

"Well, you're definitely not the Patkins we sent to the hospital, but welcome, whoever the hell you are." Patkins nodded; then Leary continued. "It's simple. Listen to it, don't think about it and don't tell Marlin or Jackson until you get to the other side. Then just tell them what you have to. At the briefing, agree with everything they tell you to do. No questions. No comments. Then," he paused for a breath, "tell everyone you're going over. No, leave that part up to me. I'll give 'em a speech similar to the one I made last night. You go over where we did, like we did. Two of you spread out and go ahead of the man with the phone and wire. You know, to cover him. No, better yet, you carry the phone and stumble, fall into the water keeping your rifle out of the water but letting the phone get wet. You can't forget to dunk the phone, that's part of what makes the story workable." When Patkins nodded, Leary laughed. "Falling is no problem. You probably won't have to fake that. We sure didn't—well, Folger didn't fall, but Sanchez and I did. Anyway, once you fall, make it close to the jungle so they don't have time to call you back, hold the phone in the air and shake it so we can all see, back here, that it has gotten wet. Then don't listen to anyone from here. If someone shouts for you to come back, ignore him and get out of sight into the jungle as quickly as possible. Make sense so far?"

"Yeah, I'm with you. What then, once we're in the jungle on the other side?"

"You connect only one wire to phone, not both of them, but only one."

"It won't work then?"

"Exactly. It won't work, but you can say later that you connected it. Just be careful, if you don't want to lie, although I don't know why you shouldn't. Anyway, when I was asked, I pointed to the spool of wire and said 'I connected the wire to the phone.' I did not say 'wires.' I said 'wire.' The captain didn't catch it and, for some perverse reason, I felt like I hadn't lied. Remember, we'll all see you dunk the phone anyway and, if you're fast enough, no one will be able to call you back for a dry one. If they do try and call you back, ignore 'em. Then you'll all have to lie, and tell 'em you didn't hear. But whatever you tell 'em, stick with it."

"No problem, dunk the phone, connect only one wire, and pay attention to no one as we scramble into the jungle. What next?"

"Once inside the jungle, where it's especially thick along the paddy edge but thins out with bushes and big trees farther in, move south. The visibility should be good. Go south towards the road, about fifty meters. It's probably about a hundred meters to the bridge. So move halfway. Find a large bush or group of bushes; there are quite a few of 'em there. Once there, set the claymores up in front of the bushes and all three of you crawl into the bushes. The noise you make should scare any critters out of the bushes. Okay so far?"

"Okay, what if they come at us?"

And so it went, Leary explaining in detail what to do, how to do it, including hiding under the bridge, and even how they should not try and come back in until the following morning.

Patkins was smoking his third cigarette by the time Leary finished. "That's it. What do you think?"

"Sounds good," Patkins replied. "I'll decide by tonight if I'm going to use it. I guess I would rather fight them if they come."

"You heard what happened to B Company?"

Folger jumped into the conversation. "I don't know who you are anymore, Sergeant Patkins, but you have two men going out there besides yourself. You may want to go down in a blaze of glory or risk getting captured, but they don't. So get real and quit smoking so many cigarettes or everyone will hear you coughing all night."

"Don't worry about me coughing, Folger, I never do. And as for the men, I'm their sergeant and I'll decide what we do tonight. Me and no one else, but thanks for the tip." And with that, he got up and walked up the hill towards the CP, ambling to all appearances without purpose or worry.

"Holy Christ, that boy is short a few cards. I'll bet he has fruitcake stamped all over his file," Folger said.

"Yeah, he's screwy, even by our standards. And that's really bad."

They both laughed and then quieted again. Sleeping, eating, and watching.

Patkins led his men out that night and his decision was clear as he carried the phone and unrolled the wire himself. There were loud cheers as he pulled the phone out of the water and shook it in an exaggerated manner. Everyone laughed, even Tooley and Carson. The captain did not laugh. He couldn't see any humor in it at all. He had been watching from the crest of the grassy hill and, when they entered the jungle, he turned and stomped up the hill towards his new CP.

Leary watched Carson speak to Tooley. They stood by what was left of the platoon fire. They exchanged a few words and, as Tooley walked back up towards the CP, Carson came down to Leary and Folger's position. They were sitting down behind their logs, their ammo and grenades out, ready for action. Both were still grinning as he approached and knelt down on one knee.

"Too bad," Carson said, "about getting the phone wet. I doubt that they'll be able to get any calls through on that phone tonight. Too late to send a patrol over with a new phone."

Folger's body language said, "I'll listen but I've done my share of talking for the day." It was a quality about Folger that everyone had come to accept. They all knew that, when he closed down, it was futile to try and get anything out of him. So Carson looked at Leary and spoke to him as if Folger wasn't there.

"Yes," Leary said, "I doubt that phone will work tonight."

"Maybe not ever, if you men keep dunking it in the water." Then Carson became more serious, as he said, "I guess it's just as well. I'm going to brief the others along the perimeter line and thought I would start with you." Leary nodded, and Folger did not respond. "All indicators say that it's going to be a rough night. Masses of troops in NVA uniforms were spotted late this afternoon by choppers west of us. They're supposed to be close and could attack at any time. They'll probably hit us sometime before morning. Of course nothing's for sure. It's just a guess, really. It's hard to imagine 'em coming across those rice paddies, through all that water and open fields of fire. If they do, we should cut them to pieces. But we need to be ready. If they try and come at us, we should have plenty of time to get 'em. Make your shots count. I don't have to tell you two that, but I'm telling everyone. Use your grenade launcher the minute you see them come out of the jungle. Then the hand grenades, and then shoot them carefully and accurately. As you know, we don't have an unlimited supply of ammo." After a pause he went on. "They tried a few probing actions last night, up the road in A Company and at our Third Platoon over on the trail we came in on."

"Yeah, we heard the firing and grenades last night."

"Well, their probes failed. I think they'll try to get at us down the road across the bridge or across our rice paddy."

"That makes Patkins' position look even worse."

"I know. I hope that whatever you told him to do will work for 'em." Leary gave a "who knows" shrug." There's more. We have some heavy artillery coming over soon. It should be far enough west of Patkins' post." After a quiet pause, "At least, I hope so. They moved the company CP out of the grassy area and back into the jungle area around the bunker complex for safety. Our platoon CP will be moved down by the fire, behind those trees." They both looked up, Folger too, to see Nash and Tooley dragging some dead logs down the hill to make a protective barrier. Carson turned back to Leary and continued, "already happening, in fact. Well, that's about it. Do what you feel you have to do when you see it. You know, tell your men single shots, make them count, we won't get any more ammo till daylight. Or any help, other than the artillery I told you about."

"You mean in a place as volatile as this, we didn't have any extra ammo brought in this morning with those news people?"

"No, both the lieutenant and I requested it, but they didn't bring any. When we asked about it, the colonel said he didn't think we'd need it and we'd just have to get a chopper to fly it back out in the morning."

Folger spoke up finally. "I wonder what he thinks now?"

"Don't know. He is back at Lia Kae." And then Carson got up and went to the next position.

⌘

At 2200 hours, the first freight train came over their heads. That was what it sounded like. The heavy projectiles came from a long way off. Initially, three of them roared in the air above the men's heads before exploding out in front of B Company's area. The first volley tore up the trees, earth, and jungle, very close to where the listening post had been two nights previously before it went missing.

The concussions were horrendous, making the water jump in the paddy and shaking the earth throughout the platoon's positions. Trees, foliage, dirt, and metal scattered and splashed across the rice paddy, varying in size and degrees. The splashing continued for what seemed like an eternity after the last explosions. A single large sliver of metal whizzed over Leary and Folger, thumping to the ground just north of the new CP. When they could hear again, someone from B Company yelled, "Add a hundred meters to those bitches and fire for effect."

As if it were a command, twenty seconds later the airborne freight trains started coming again, volley after volley, ripping huge fiery holes in the jungle. The thundering, unrestrained violence of that heavy artillery attack violated every nerve in their bodies. Each man buried his helmeted head into the ground, hoping that he could live through it while wondering how. Fortunately, the second barrage started about fifty meters farther away than the first and, gratefully, moved west, explosion after explosion. No one dared look as whole trees flew through the air high above the jungle canopy. The huge bursts changed from a brilliant yellow-orange to white-hot as they pulverized everything in their path. This devastation lasted for ten unrelenting minutes. By 2211 hours it was over.

Folger said, "I bet old Patkins has some messy drawers."

"I don't think he eats enough to mess his drawers," Leary said. "I do hope he found a mighty thick bush, though."

"Yeah, Christ, it was bad enough over here. Over there, they must have thought the world ended."

"If NVA are over there, they've got to be hurting."

"Probably all stirred up like a bunch of pissed-off wasps," Folger chuckled. *Good for them*, he thought.

"I think it's over now, Folger. Why don't you try and get some sleep? Old Charlie has to be too shook up to attack for a while."

"Why not? I hope there're lots of little gooks dripping from the trees out there."

Leary joked, "You're having trouble finding people to like over here, Folger."

Also joking, but with a strain of truth in his voice, Folger said, "I don't have many people anywhere I like."

Then there was complete silence for fifteen minutes. The quiet was both welcome and frightening.

Two hours later, "Damn, there they are," Leary said. Then he rose up on both knees and yelled as loudly as he could. "Patkins, get your ass in here. Goddamn it, run." But they kept walking, reluctantly, as if they didn't know if they should come in. Leary was just about to yell for everyone to hold his fire when he heard the easily distinguishable pop of a hand grenade lever flying off. Patkins, Marlin, and Jackson had heard it too and they froze. *All three of them are bunched up, close together, like they don't have good sense,* Leary thought.

Then he realized why they were moving so slowly. They had come out of the jungle and into the water about twenty-five meters from the damming effects of the bridge and road. The water here was at its deepest. It was waist high, and moving through it was slow and hard. Leary watched in horror as the smoking hand grenade dropped into the water not five meters from the men. Two seconds had gone by since they'd first heard the pop. Patkins and his men froze as they realized that they only had two more seconds to live.

Folger had raised himself up and was in a firing position over the log as the grenade splashed into the water.

The explosion hid the men from view for what seemed like forever. Though only seconds in reality, it was enough time for Leary to say, "Shit, they're dead."

But as the funnel of water found its way back to the paddy and the visibility increased, all three of them were still standing. Leary, Folger, and by now all of the men on the line waited with baited breath for the three men to topple over, dead or seriously wounded.

Then, miraculously, they started moving again. As they got closer to the perimeter, it was plain to see that they were only soaking wet and covered with mud.

Elated, Leary realized what had happened. In anger, he yelled, "Those are our men. Goddamn you, the next man that throws a grenade or fires at them, I'll kill." Patkins and his men had started trying to run, falling, getting up, and then falling again. Jackson had forgotten to fasten his chinstrap and lost his helmet, which sank immediately. Finally, exhausted, wet, and scared, they made it to Leary and Folger's position. There was a shocked silence. No one believed what had happened or how these men could have survived it.

Once on shore, all three men gasping for breath, Patkins demanded, "Who did it? Who threw that grenade at us?"

Without hesitation, Leary answered, "The first man you come to in B Company." Still gasping for air and without further hesitation, the furious men took off running toward B Company.

Carson had been at the platoon's easternmost part of the perimeter. Now, he ran to Leary's position as fast as caution would allow.

He was out of breath when he came sliding to a halt on the wet grass at Leary and Folger's position. "What's going on here, Leary?" Just then, cursing and yelling, as well as cries begging for mercy, could be heard coming from B Company.

Leary didn't even bother to look in B Company's direction as he stated calmly, "Oh, some guy in B Company threw a grenade at Patkins and the boys when they were trying to come back in. So, they're killing him."

Momentarily stunned, Carson headed toward B Company and said, "I thought you were more responsible than that, Leary. Why didn't you stop them?"

Leary yelled after Carson, "I am responsible. Killing him is the responsible thing to do."

He looked back at Folger and said, "Be good for Patkins to kill someone. Especially that asshole."

"Yeah. You know, Leary, I'm starting to like Patkins."

By the time Carson had gotten to the B Company man, Patkins, Jackson, and Marlin had all taken a couple of turns at whacking him with their rifle butts, and the man who had mistakenly thrown the grenade was bloody and unconscious. Carson stopped the attack and sent the enraged Patkins and his men back to the platoon area. Carson, as depressed as he had ever been, helped the B Company medic take the wounded man to their company CP. Without explanation to anyone at B Company, he silently returned to the platoon CP. Part of him wondered if there would be repercussions, possibly war between the companies. *Christ*, he thought as he made his way back to C Company, *we've sunk to killing each other.*

As Carson went by Leary and Folger, no words were spoken. They didn't even look at each other. Patkins, Marlin, and Jackson returned to their positions in the perimeter. No one mentioned it that night, neither among themselves nor among the brass. Later, the general consensus, including the men of B Company, was that the man who had thrown the grenade deserved the beating. He had been asleep on guard when he heard the voices. He had awakened in a panic, pulled the pin, and thrown the grenade without thinking. Had he let the grenade burn for two seconds, like he should have, Patkins and the boys would have probably been killed. As it turned out, the grenade sank in the water and mud before it went off, negating its effectiveness. Beating him wasn't a nice thing to do. It wasn't Christian, but Christ wasn't fighting in this war.

The men settled down again; some slept, some watched. It was truly a beautiful, stunning night. The moon was so bright that one could read a letter by it. It stayed a beautiful and peaceful night until 0200 hours. Then they came—like the nest of angry wasps Folger had described.

31

WARRIORS NOW

It was 0800, and the tropical sun had pushed the shadows back and put its first heat of the day on the men. It hadn't really been cold before, but the first heat from the sun was always welcome. It dried out any wet clothing and warmed and added a healing quality to their bodies' many scratches, gouges, and rashes. Then later when the sun's heat became punishing, these same men would curse it for its unbearable heat. With the heat of the sun came foul moods, so the men were meanest at midday.

Patkins and Marlin were at their position cleaning their weapons and talking. Patkins felt good and at peace for the first time since coming to Vietnam.

"You know, Sarge, you were something else last night," Marlin said. "Especially after we came in and thumped that guy from B Company. Yeah, back home in New York, where I come from, you'd've been called a 'bad ass.' You'd've had respect in the neighborhood."

Patkins laughed in a way that only a man who was fearless, insane, or both could. He laughed for the pure pleasure of it and not from tension or as a substitute for crying. "Well, Marlin, you were slightly out of character yourself."

Marlin looked up at his sergeant, using his palm to push his hair back. His well-oiled, jet-black hair was just getting long enough so that he could comb it back, if he had had a comb. Instead, he smoothed it back with his hand, causing his hair to lie flat and exaggerating his newly receding hairline. Patkins looked at him, thinking, *Marlin looks ten years older than he did a couple of months ago.*

Marlin's beard was black and heavy, as it had been since ninth grade. His parents had wanted him to finish high school, but he had quit going soon after starting his sophomore year. *Hell*, he had thought, *it just wasn't any fun and the streets were so exciting.* He had his pals, gang members, and they had taken care of each other. *It was a miracle*, he now realized, *that they hadn't all gone to jail. Some of them had, but the judge gave him a choice.* Since he was a lesser offender in the auto theft and drunkenness charges of which he and some of his buddies were convicted, the judge had said, "Go in the army or go to jail." He had enlisted for three years and had regretted it until early this morning. He was now what and where he had always wanted to be. By his neighborhood standards, a real man was someone to be respected and feared. He would be the envy of all of his neighborhood buddies, had they been there to see him. His dark brown eyes showed some humor in them as he said, "We kicked some butt last night, didn't we, Sarge? We showed 'em all what it means if they screw with us. I'm not sorry about it, not one little bit."

Patkins needed a shave now, too. His beard was not nearly as heavy as Marlin's and was more brown than black, but the few days' growth and a certain look on his face gave him a rakish look. "Okay, Mr. Hombre, since you started it, how in the hell did an Italian-American get a name like Marlin?"

"A question I've been asked many times. And because I've been asked many times, I find it easy to give the appropriate answer. Not the truthful answer, but the appropriate one." Patkins raised his eyebrows to show Marlin that he was interested, and Marlin slowly said, "You see, Sarge, the answer depends upon who's asking. I'll give you a couple of examples. If one of the boys from the neighborhood asks me, I tell him it's an old royal name that originally came from Spain. Now, Sarge, he may not quite believe it, but he doesn't know it ain't true, neither. Say it enough and, sooner or later, he accepts it; he starts telling others about it. Begins to believe it himself. This eventually led me to be called 'Mr. Royal.' That's my gang name. Now if someone else asks me, a teacher, an employer, or a person with some authority, you know, not from my neighborhood, I tell 'em it's a name my grandfather took on when he came to the U.S. of A. sometime after the turn of the century."

Patkins chuckled low and heartily and asked, "What do you tell me, Marlin? Which one for me?"

Marlin paused as if thinking and then, with a more serious look on his face than he felt, said, "For you, Sergeant Patkins, I tell the truth. And from now on, I'll tell the truth. I haven't a clue and even my father doesn't know. He said that he's always been a Marlin and that's all there is to it. He says that 'one need not explain his name,' that 'one only needs to be proud of it.' Yeah," he laughed, "If the old man had ever heard me making up stories about our name or ever apologizing for it, he'd have beat me till his fists hurt. But still, now, I wish I could see him again. Maybe never will. In the total of everything, he was good to me."

"Your dad beat you a lot?"

"No, not really. He was a kind, strong man. Oh, he could lay some belt leather on my butt, but I never thought of him as mean, not to me or anyone. But he had such pride about who he was. He worked so hard just to feed us. Delivered coal in an old truck till everyone all got on natural gas. By then, he already had a severe lung problem from the coal dust. Then, after a couple of months starving and barely making the rent, Mom working as a dishwasher, he got a job as the oil changer at a Buick garage. That's why I believe if he ever heard me joke about our name, he'd have used his fists on me." It got quiet for a minute, both men digging the burnt carbon out of the receivers of their rifles.

Then Patkins asked, "Did your old man put you down?"

"No, he always wanted me to take advantage of the opportunities his father moved to our country for. He was more than a little disappointed when I dropped out of school. He believed that I was taking lightly what they had struggled so hard to bring me. I guess he was right. If I ever get out of this place alive, I'll make them both proud of me. It's the least I can do. It was hard for them and still is. Sometimes I'm ashamed that I didn't realize it and do better with it. What about you, Sarge? How was your old man to you?"

Patkins looked down before replying, an old reflex from a previous battering. Though it didn't hurt much to remember them anymore, some of his physical reaction was still programmed in. "He never hit me much. I would have preferred that. His words were cutting, though, and he never got tired of saying them. I don't remember the bastard ever hugging me or anything like that. Yeah, he slapped me a few times but mostly he just used words on me. He called me no good, worthless, a sissy, and stupid. From my first memories of him, he put me down with his foul mouth right up until the day before we left to come over here. Can you believe it? I called that old bastard the day before we left. You know, I called just to say goodbye to Mom and him. My mistake was in hoping against hope that he might say one damn word of encouragement to me. One 'I'm proud of you son' or 'Take care of yourself, and come back safe.' But no, you know what the son of a bitch said?"

Marlin looked at him, shaking his head no.

"That dirty, no good, rotten, filthy excuse for a father said, 'Try and not wimp out over there. They won't put up with your chickening out of everything, so don't disgrace your mother and me.' "

"What did you say back at him?"

"I don't know how I got home. I must have flown home or something. I only remember killing him, and it felt good."

Marlin thought, *Holy shit, they're right. He's off his rocker.*

He saw the look on Marlin's face. "I know, sounds unreal, and in a way it seems unreal to me, too. The doctors said I was wrong and that I wouldn't be over here if it were true. Still, I can clearly see myself doing it. I believe it happened and they know about it. They just don't believe I'm going to make it over here and figure it's no use sending me back. At least over here, I can do some good."

"You really believe that, Sergeant?"

"Damn right I do. I mean, my father is no father. He was a mean-mouthed evil man, and it makes sense that I would have killed him. I did everyone a favor back home, especially my mother. It makes a hell of a lot more sense to kill him than it does killing these people. I don't know what they'll do to me if I get back, you know, for killing him. But by all that's holy, as God is my judge, it makes more sense to kill him than it does to kill these people. I just can't believe they would have me kill these people over here, who have done nothing to me, and not allow me to kill a man like him who's done so much to me."

It was quiet for a while and finally Marlin said, "Sarge. You're probably right. It only makes sense." But he was thinking: *He's far gone. Poor bastard. No way he's done that. He's not even the same man he was before that sniper hit him. His father was right about that; he was a wimp. Well, at least he's happy with the illusion.*

Leary and Folger were almost to their position, and Tooley and Carson were on their way down the hill from the platoon CP. It was a newfound respect, *and well deserved,* Patkins thought, that these four men wanted to talk with him and were willing to come to his position to do so. *By now they all know about my father and that I am a warrior.*

They greeted each other and found places to sit or kneel on the ground. Carson and Tooley were each on one knee, indicating that they would not stay as long as Folger and Leary, who had settled themselves comfortably. Leary sat with his back towards the rice paddy, his feet flat on the ground, his knees bent. Folger promptly flopped onto his back. He laid his head on his pack with his helmet resting on his head and down over his eyes, shading them from the burning sun. Folger's fingers were interlocked behind his head, and he looked like he might doze off at any time.

"What happened here last night, Sergeant Patkins?" Tooley asked.

"What do you mean, Lieutenant? Marlin, Jackson, and I were just doing our jobs."

"What the hell are you talking about? You don't attack one of our own men, ever, Sergeant Patkins. Do you hear me?"

"I didn't initiate that attack, Lieutenant. He did. I just reacted to an attack. If he's on our side, he shouldn't attack me or my men."

"It was a mistake, Sergeant Patkins. It happens in war."

"Well, sir, he'd better be careful about who he makes mistakes with. He'll be a lot more careful in the future."

"If he has a future. You and your men severely injured that man. He's out of this war. He has a damaged kidney, a concussion, and his spleen will have to be removed."

"Lucky him."

"You listen, Sergeant Patkins, this is serious shit. You're lucky charges haven't been brought against you. The only reason they haven't is because he was sleeping on guard and it's generally felt that he was wrong, and you and your men were delirious. But I don't want any more of this kind of thing. It could spread like wildfire, and we could be fighting amongst ourselves. Do you understand?"

"Sure, sir, I understand. They'd better understand, too. That if they, any of them, do anything so irresponsible again, then they'll have to suffer the penalty for it."

"You've been an excellent soldier and a good NCO. I'm willing to overlook certain things, but you'd better get with the program."

"I think I am with the program, sir. We're here to kill any and everything that threatens us, and that is just what I'm doing. Nothing more, but nothing less, either."

"You men are going nuts, all of you." Tooley looked at Leary and Folger. "All of you. You think I don't know what you tried to do to that track, Leary? Well, I damn sure do. I want you men to settle down. This isn't a free-for-all here."

Leary didn't respond and Tooley's anger was obvious as he said, "You all heard me," then rose and stomped off. Carson rose too, paused a minute, looked at the men in a fatherly way, and then followed the lieutenant up the hill.

It was quiet for a minute. Then Folger said, "War is hell." No one laughed. They all liked the lieutenant, and Carson was like a father or older brother to them, and, inside, they knew they were getting out of hand. They also knew that, to survive, the structure needed to be intact.

Leary finally spoke. "I think he's partially right. I was totally in agreement with you last night, Patkins. And I agree with you today. We've got to stay loose and aggressive, but on the other hand we have to stay civilized. I just don't know where the line is anymore."

"Well, I do," Patkins said. "This is an uncivilized place and we must adjust to its way of doing things. I'm a warrior. I didn't want to be, but now I am and everything that threatens me, everything that steps into my killing area, is going to get it. I'll die with my rifle barrel smoking. That's it and I've nothing more to think or say on the matter."

"How could it be anything else?" Leary asked as he and Folger got up and went back to their positions.

The next morning, after a long and eventful third night at the underground complex, Tooley and Carson were again back at Patkins and Marlin's position. Because of what had happened the night before, Tooley was again upset with the actions of these two men. "Don't you think I should be the one to say when we attack and when we stay holding our positions?"

"Best defense is a good offense, sir."

"Don't give me that bull, Patkins. You and Marlin were out of character and out of line last night. We need to discuss it. What I don't need," his face was red with growing rage, "is a smart-assed answer from you. I just don't deserve that from you, Patkins, and you know it."

"Well, that's the way you see it, sir. Now let me tell you the way I see it. Yeah, you've been square with us. I'll give you that. You've been a good officer. But that don't change the facts."

"What facts?" He was still angry but curiosity won out.

"That we are warriors, old Marlin and I. We weren't a month ago but we are today. Now you're a good man, Lieutenant, you want the best you can get for us, your men, over here. But the truth is this whole business stinks, and you're just a victim of it like the rest of us.

I learned a few things at the hospital. For instance, the captain only has to do six months here, then he goes to a rear and safe command. You, being a lieutenant, have to do the whole thirteen months in the jungle with us. Your chances of survival are no better than ours."

Trying to maintain his dissipating anger, Tooley asked, "What is this 'victim' crap?"

"Well, we're all up in the front of this war. It's stupid to call it a war. This isn't a war; it's some kind of game. The only trouble with this game is it's a death game. Death is the measure of who wins or who loses. You know, body count and so forth. We're the ones who have to do the dying and the killing. There's no winning here; it isn't being fought to win. It's being fought for the pure sport of killing. It's like a movie I saw once of some rich white Englishmen hunting the feared tiger of India. They were riding in basket-like platforms on the backs of huge elephants. They had their rifles and were completely safe. They were excited about and enjoying the hunt. On the ground were fifty or sixty unarmed natives, all in an on-line formation, just like the ones we use. They were walking through the jungle making noise and trying to drive a tiger out so that these sporting men could shoot it. Well, we may not be noisy but we are all beaters, including you, Lieutenant, and we're doing it for the sport of it and, if not sport, then certainly not to win. So I, for one, Lieutenant, being a beater and all, am not going to wait around for the old tiger to jump up out of the bush and kill me. If they ever send me on another listening post, I'll go out there all right, but I won't sit in fear all night waiting for them to decide when and where they want to jump me. No, I'll go hunting them and kill 'em. When morning comes, I'll have engaged any and all that I could find. I'll either return or be dead out there. I will not be a beater any longer."

"You can't just do whatever you want whenever you want to," Carson said. "You're not in charge here, Patkins. We must follow orders as they are passed down. We cannot personalize this war, and it is a war. We don't always see the big picture here at our level."

"What level is that, Sergeant?" Marlin asked, not wanting nor waiting for an answer. "Is that the expendable level?" He looked at them both, not waiting for a response, and went on, "Sure, it is. Well, everyone at the 'other levels' seems to forget that we, down here on this level, don't have much to lose except our dignity as human beings. I'm a Marlin and I'll never again sit in the jungle waiting for someone to sneak up and kill me just so I can warn others who're sleeping. I'll no longer be a beater, like Patkins says, warning those on the elephants that the tiger is coming." He looked at Patkins, ignoring the two men in authority and said, "Count me in, Sarge. I hope they send us back out tonight, and we'll kill all the damn gooks we can find out there."

Defeated, out of words, and out of belief, Tooley signaled with body language to Carson that it was time to go. As they were getting up, he said, "There will be no more listening posts. B Company refuses to go. We've only one phone left. The colonel only flew in one setup per platoon, and B Company has ignored the captain's offer to loan them ours. They're not happy with you beating up their man and our not sharing our ammo with them last night." He looked directly at Patkins and Marlin, who gestured, "So what?" Without another word, the two leaders headed south to the next position on their morning rounds.

As they left, Marlin said loudly, "B Company, what a bunch of dumb shits. If they can't shoot any better than what we saw last night, they shouldn't be given ammo at all." Tooley and Carson didn't turn around, but just kept walking.

"One thing's for sure, they didn't hit much for the shooting they did. Just those two who are still lying in the water out there," said Leary, who was still resting with Folger north of Patkins and Marlin. Leary glanced over his shoulder at two bodies, one face down and the other face up, in the paddy directly in front of B Company's position. "I suppose they're proud of themselves for those two, but they must've missed a hundred of 'em."

"Yeah, they only got those and managed to get a perfectly good chopper and crew wasted. And they're mad at us. Well, good, with friends like them, we don't need any enemies," Folger mumbled without moving.

"That was a good crew to come in like that, in the dark and right after that ridiculous charge made by the NVA, but they're all dead now. They came blowing out of that chopper like pieces of the explosion itself. That pilot and copilot looked like they came right through the windshields of that thing. They're probably scattered all over B Company and the jungle. The door gunners didn't seem to go that far, but they sure burned. Must have been fuel on them or something," Leary said matter-of-factly.

"I saw 'em looking for pieces of the crew this morning. Looked like they were hunting for litter, looking around and then putting pieces in those plastic bags. Christ," Folger said.

Leary turned his head towards Patkins and Marlin and said loudly enough so that he was sure they could hear, "Speaking of things in the night, what was that screaming and hollering coming from you guys last night?" Leary asked.

"We were just pissed off," Patkins said resignedly. "You know, those gooks charging across the paddy like that and B Company shooting all of their ammo at 'em, and then the dumb shits only put two in the water. God, that water sure churned up from all of the bullets they shot into it. I hear that no one in B Company was hit by the NVA, so it looks like they can't shoot worth a damn either."

"Well, they could damn sure shoot when that chopper landed," Folger said. "That was a heavy gun, must have been their equivalent of a fifty. Whoever was using it was damn good, too. Those tracers went right in the front of the chopper. They'd almost made it. The door gunners had just kicked the last ammo out, and she was lifting off when she started taking fire. I can still see the four crew members in the light from their engine, just before they scattered in all directions. I guess I'll always be able to see that."

"You two," Leary exclaimed, disbelievingly, "you both stood up, first you, Patkins, then you, Marlin. Both of you were standing, shaking your rifles in the air, and swearing at them. Daring them to show themselves." Folger chuckled quietly to himself as Leary described the incident. "Then you both ran down into the damn water and fired off a couple from the hip into the jungle where that machine gun fire had come from. Both of you were swearing and daring 'em to do something. You're both lucky; if that sharpshooter with the heavy gun had still been there, he'd've cut you both to pieces." He paused a minute. "I agree with the lieutenant on one thing. You two are something else. Sure as hell not what you used to be." Then, almost as an afterthought, "I guess, if we'd agreed to share our ammo with B Company after they used all of theirs, that chopper wouldn't have had to come in and get blown up."

"Screw B Company, Leary, that would've been like throwing good ammo after bad," Folger said. "Too bad about the chopper crew, but that's what they get paid for. But you two, Patkins, you and Marlin, well, you two are men after my own heart." Folger rose up on his elbows. "Like my old daddy used to say about the bull standing on the railroad track waiting for the train, 'There's glory in your spunk, but your judgment's not too good.' Anyway, what I don't get is, why didn't they try and pound us with a few more of those machine gun rounds? It's the only thing anyone on either side could hit anything with. Why not chew us up a little? They're as stupid as we are."

"I'd say they pulled out right after they nailed the chopper. Maybe they pulled out because they didn't want to get caught by any of those big-ass artillery shells," Patkins said. "What do you think, Leary?"

"That's probably true. And well, they did haul ass too, because those shells did come a-pounding. I can still hear and see those damn things now. Hell, look at what they did to the jungle. Maybe we shouldn't even be here. You know, let the navy just shell the place twenty-four hours a day. Hell, in a year or two, they could clear all the jungle out of Vietnam. They wouldn't have any place to hide then. I don't blame 'em, though; I sure as hell wouldn't wait around for any of that big artillery either. I'll bet it's why their charge across the rice paddy was so half-assed. They probably didn't want to linger and have that artillery catch 'em. Could have been a probing action, too. Once they found out B Company had a lot of shooters, even poor ones, they hauled their butts out of there."

"I think we should've started the artillery then. You know, way behind 'em and walked it this way into 'em. Nice and tight, walked it right up to the paddy edge and pushed 'em across at us, so we could finish the little bastards. Then, at first light, jets strike the whole area, including the village. Burn it to the ground. After that, send us in to finish off anyone left. Now, that's a war," Folger said. "Something that if a man got killed doing, he wouldn't feel so bad about. Wouldn't feel like he was being wasted."

Everyone agreed. "Yeah." "Hell, yes." "Damn right."

"I'm beginning to become very fond of you two," Folger said, "and I used to think you were both worthless."

"Well, we were. Or at least I was, I can't speak for Marlin, but I was afraid of death before I killed my dad. Now, I don't seem to have any fear of it at all. I know, deep inside, I'll never fear it again. It's such a relief to not worry about something that has haunted me since I can remember. The whole world looks different to me now and I feel for those who still live with such fears." He stood up then and said, "I'm Patkins and I am a warrior. I can't think of ever wanting to be anything else. If I die over here, so be it. I'll die without fear. I will die as a warrior."

"Me too," Marlin said, "me too."

It was a good step in the right psychological direction because, after tomorrow, conditions wouldn't allow for being anything less than a warrior.

32

COST INCREASE

Cautiously and rhythmically, Tooley moved ahead with the rest of his platoon, his pace a slow, strange dance. With each step, he glanced down to make sure he wasn't stepping on something lethal. First surveying the ground in his immediate direction of travel and then scanning everywhere: left and right, forward and to the rear, before moving on. While maintaining this dancer-like control over his own body, he continually monitored and evaluated his platoon, too.

He walked a mental tightrope, and he could not allow himself to be distracted by anything that had nothing to do with where they were or what they were doing. Each new sensory input set off an alarm in his body. It could be the faint aroma of Vietnamese cooking in the air. Or it might not even be an identifiable smell—just something that alerted his nose to warn his brain of danger. It could come from his eyes, waiting, watching for the slightest movement or difference in coloring from the jungle ahead or to his side. He knew that even one of his men acting strangely could mean something. Then there were the senses of hearing and touch. He acknowledged and evaluated any strange sound or the slightest movement of earth under his feet.

Yes, Tooley told himself, *these are my men, or what is left of them.* He hated to think of the numbers that were gone. He only wanted to keep track of the number he still had, not the number he had lost. *Too bad*, he thought, as they worked their way northeast of A Company's position. They were on point for the battalion, traveling the road that headed through A Company and northward. It was almost 1100 hours and they had moved just far enough north before stopping to allow the rest of the battalion to string out on the road behind them.

293

C Company was on point with A Company in the middle and B Company on drag. The plan was that, once everyone had cleared the bunker complex, B Company would blow it. Engineers choppered in yesterday had planted the explosives.

Tooley was worried that they wouldn't have any flanker patrols. The jungle was too dense in this area, and they hadn't found any trails for the flankers to travel on. "A jungle too thick for us is too thick for the enemy, too," the colonel had said. *Well, maybe the jungle is too thick for the flankers,* Tooley thought, *but we should've at least tried it. Maybe the enemy doesn't think it's too thick. There might be a trail or clearing in that thick overgrown jungle. A trail that they know about and have already used to set traps for us.* He had no doubt that the enemy was out there. He had seen them and they were sharply uniformed and well armed.

The vibrations from the explosions could be felt from the ground up through their feet. The sound came shortly after ground vibrations and was muffled by the earth and heavy vegetation. Tooley counted six separate explosions, less than a second apart. As he waited for the word from battalion telling them to move out, he heard the colonel's helicopter buzz overhead.

Leary was on point followed by Folger, Sanchez, Tooley, Patkins, Marlin, Carson, and finally Jackson. Sergeant Carson was in the latter half of the platoon, which wasn't that far back since their loss of men but, still, Tooley was happy to have him away from the point. *Oh God,* he thought, *how things change over here. Carson is now a full platoon sergeant and not half a squad leader. He has expanded his areas of concern from squad leader to platoon sergeant. Damn,* he wondered, *was that last night or the night before,* and then thought, *Who cares? It happened after Patkins, Marlin, and Jackson beat that man from B Company nearly to death, with Leary pointing the way. A month ago, hell no, two weeks ago Leary would have tried to talk Patkins out of it. Would have told him that it was an accident, a mistake. That killing one's own man, no matter how careless or irresponsible it might be, was never justified. But then we've all changed, and who am I to talk,* he decided. Guiltily, he remembered, *I even contemplated blowing the captain's head off with my forty-five. So we've all changed. Can't help it, I guess. This place changes a man into something he would never have dreamed he could be. Hell, look at Patkins, he's changed the most drastically. He used to be a scared rabbit and now he's some kind of charmed killer. Twice a sniper has tried to kill him, and this last time he missed altogether. Nutty Patkins was doing some kind of skinny spastic dance and turned just as the shot was fired. Just like before, he*

*does something at precisely the right moment to render a sniper's bullet
ineffective. No one who wasn't here would believe it could've happened
twice.* Amused, he wondered, *What if it was the same sniper both
times. Wouldn't he be pissed off?*

*Then the new Patkins didn't even hit the dirt, just shook his fist
at the jungle and yelled, "You dumb gook—you need glasses." If Leary
hadn't pulled him down, he might have been hit by a second shot.
There was no second shot, though, since the machine gunner opened
up right away. Knowing we'd soon fill the jungle with lead, he must
have fired and then split. Yes, Sergeant Patkins has changed from a
man plagued by fear to one who doesn't even have enough fear left to
keep him cautious. Of course, to some degree, we're all like that now.
Give up the desire to live and lose the fear. Hart was the only holdout,
the only man who refused to change. Well, refused to or was unable to,
we'll never know which. Guess wherever he is, Hart knows now.*

*Patkins isn't the only one who's gone crazy, but that crap about
killing his father takes the big trophy. The remaining few are here
completely now. We've adapted ourselves to our environment. Like
survival has always demanded men do—change or die. So far, those
of us who are left have changed our attitudes about life. Except maybe
Carson, he seems the same. But maybe he has changed relative to the
rest of us, and we just can't see it. If he gets home, his wife will be able
to tell at a glance. Poor Sally, she probably won't even know me. May
not want me. Hell, I don't even want me. I hope we can change back if
we do get home. Too bad we don't have something more worthwhile to
believe in than this cause. Patkins is right about that. This isn't a war;
it's some kind of a game, a game without a clear purpose.* The radio
operator's signal that the battalion was to move out interrupted his
thoughts.

When the signal came, Leary responded automatically. If he had
any thoughts now about what he was doing in the jungles of South
Vietnam in War Zone C, it was that things were easier. Sometime
in the last couple of days, he had quit worrying. Sure, he cared,
but he just couldn't worry anymore. He had accepted his fate, his
conditions, and the costs. So he was light in both mind and body
as he moved out. The heavily loaded pack, water, and ammo were
no longer a burden, only things that he needed. They were his tools
for being what he was, for doing what he did. In fact, the weight
of it made him feel secure and natural. He too, was a warrior now,
completely. He no longer had worries about death, or purpose, or
Hart. *I see what Patkins was raving about; there's freedom in being
a warrior. It's something I've never really experienced to this degree*

before. Living minute by minute right on the edge of death isn't bad at all. In fact, it has a freedom. It creates a high that I never knew existed. Yes, it's not being afraid I might die at any minute but a joy in being alive every minute.

It's a simple, pure life. We don't have to worry about what we're going to wear. We all have the same clothes, and damn few of those. We don't have to worry about the approval of other people. The number of people we deal with is limited and we all accept each other as we are. The captain is the exception to the rule. No, on further thought, I accept the captain for what he is: a rank-grabbing, butt-kissing chicken. He smiled with pleasure at making derogatory statements about the captain, if only in his mind. *Bottom line, though, there's a tremendous euphoria from accepting your death as a natural condition of your life. Once you accept your death, all other worries pale by comparison and then take their rightful place as having little or no effect on your happiness. Once everything is taken away and you're left with just yourself and the possibility of a next breath, strangely, it leaves you feeling pretty damn good. It's probably not explainable back home, but I've never felt better.*

Folger's mind was running on a little different track than Tooley's and Leary's. He noticed that the grappling hook Gaip's people had made him was gouging his back, and he scooted his shoulders a little to move it. *That damn colonel is a weak shit,* he told himself as the colonel's chopper buzzed overhead. *We shouldn't be going down this poor-ass excuse for a road. Why go look for gooks somewhere else when we know where they are? I just can't believe the decisions that are made in "this man's army." We should've hit those little shits right after another artillery barrage, right at first light this morning. We damn sure shouldn't have left until we either destroyed them or they destroyed us. And if they ran, we should've chased 'em clear into hell if we had to. But, no, our chickenshit colonel has decided to look somewhere else for them. Guess these gooks weren't good enough for him. Maybe he wants to find some taller ones.* He chuckled at the absurdity of the thought.

Some of the guys make excuses for the colonel. They say that he's old, that he's fought his wars, and that he shouldn't be blamed for where we go or what we do. They say he doesn't have a free hand, he's only following orders, etc. Well, that's just so much weak-kneed garbage. The son of a bitch signed on as our colonel and he should act like one, even if it costs him his life or his job. He's leading men now in a killing and dying situation, and he should step up and be the man in charge. I give him no excuses; he can see what's going on here, the damn lack of commitment on the part of our leaders and the South

*Vietnamese. He's got no right to worry about anything else than doing
what we came over here to do. We came over here to kill the North
Vietnamese at every opportunity, to hell with what those REMFs think
or say, to hell with Saigon's orders or his damn career. When you ask
men to kill or be killed, your only loyalty should be to them. Because
of what you're asking them to do, you owe only to them. He asks us to
be his men, to fight and die for the freedom of South Vietnam. Once he
makes that type of commitment, solicits that kind of commitment from
his men, his only loyalty from that point on should be to winning the
war. We've already killed and been killed over this cause, and the rules
should be clear. The game is on, and anything less than an all-out hunt
and kill is dishonoring our dead and us. Hell, the colonel has deserted
his mission in the face of the enemy and should be shot. Just like any
other deserter in thousands of wars past. Our country was founded to
protect the weak, not put the bastards in charge. The weak are clearly
in charge of directing this war but they won't fight in it. I'll bet none
of them have their kids fighting over here either. Screw 'em all. They'd
better hope I don't live. If I get home, I'll deal with the bastards.*

They stayed on the road for almost four hours. Leary was on point
and, eventually, when the jungle density thinned out, the captain
put the First and Third Platoons out on the flanks. They had had no
contact with the enemy, but signs were everywhere. The road snaked
east and then west on its way north. Sometimes it went around
thick jungle areas and sometimes straight through them. Twice, they
crossed the same slow-moving, winding, deep, and muddy stream.
At first, Leary couldn't see how the enemy had crossed the stream.
Then Folger, with the butt of his automatic rifle, discovered a bridge
built a foot under the water. They had built bridges that could not
be detected from the air. The water barely created a ripple as it
passed over the sunken wooden structure. *Clever little bastards,*
Leary thought.

Before sunset that night, they camped in a large grassy area only
a few miles northeast of the now-destroyed bunker complex. During
the day's travel, Leary took his time, moving like a man with no
particular place to go. Just walking cautiously. No one seemed to
mind, and no one offered to take point or even passed the word for
him to hurry. He stopped the forward movement of the battalion

several times during the day. Most of the stops were done just because he felt like it. *What's the hurry?* He asked himself before each halt. *There's really no reason to hurry anymore. We've got about ten more months to walk around this country, time to slow the game down. Hell, even if I make it out of this place, I may never hurry anywhere again.*

The camping spot for the night was cramped but adequate, with some grassy areas in the perimeter for sleeping. Four of them—Leary, Folger, Patkins, and Marlin—were heating their C-rations on Patkins' fire and talking when they felt like it. Jackson and Sanchez were in another position about ten feet away. Lately, these two had paired up. Sometimes nothing was said for fifteen or twenty minutes, then maybe one of them would make a statement or comment. Sometimes no one responded verbally, or maybe there was just a nod or grunt. Their need for communication, for idle chatting, was diminishing as the days in Vietnam passed. More and more, they were communicating with grunts, hand signals, or other physical gestures. Their need to be quiet on the trail during the day was becoming a practice at night, too.

"What now?" Marlin asked. Everyone knew he wanted to know what his mission was now. Or at least what the brass said it was.

"Still sweep into the Twenty-second," Leary answered.

"Still there?" Folger asked.

"Been waiting, I guess," Patkins mumbled, barely audibly, as he poked at the fire.

"Stupid shits," Marlin remembered.

"Yeah," Folger piped up, "been too long in one place. Gonna get it."

"I heard their colonel is a dumb shit anyway," Marlin said.

Leary and Patkins said they had heard the same thing and Folger spoke up, "Dumb as ours?"

"At least. Worse, maybe," Marlin said.

"I sure don't see how. He's pretending to be a colonel and keepin' us from gettin' a good one."

Patkins looked up from the fire, more in reflection than to make eye contact and said, "Wouldn't make any difference who we got. Nothing is going to change for us. We are here, it's the way it is, and that's that."

Leary didn't respond; just stared out over the short, dark green grass to his front. Though his eyes were open, he saw nothing. He had developed the thousand-yard stare.

Morning came and went while Leary followed the road with the
battalion strung out behind him. The flanker platoons were once
again out, trying to stay parallel. There was no effort or even
discussion about changing the positions of point, drag, or flanker
platoons. The formation was set up exactly the way it had been
yesterday. They hadn't had any trouble yesterday, so nothing was
changed today. They were becoming complacent in their thinking.
Complacency led to predictability and predictability was the best
way to get killed in a jungle war. No one seemed to care.

Everything changed at 1020 hours as Leary followed the road
right up to the entrance of a North Vietnamese fort. The road was in
a slight valley and, when he rounded a curve, there it was on his left.
He halted the column, called up the lieutenant and Carson, and they
observed and reported. It was definitely an operational fort. They just
couldn't see anyone. It had a very nice trench coming down a small,
jungle-covered hill about halfway and then followed the ridgeline
north and out of sight. There were triple rolls of concertina wire and
a gate, clearly marked and open. Many bunkers were in clear sight
of the road, and the entrance to a large single bunker was visible at
the top of the hill.

Tooley and Carson pulled back to report and discuss the
situation by radio with the colonel. Leary and Folger were left up
front to observe the fort. They continually scanned it for movement.
Within a few minutes, the signal came up to move ahead. As Leary
looked back at Tooley, he signaled that Leary should go uphill and
into the fort. Without so much as a shrug, Leary, with Folger at his
back and to his left, cautiously entered the fort and started following
the trench around to the north. *Shit, this is spooky. It reminds me of
the stories about finding ghost ships on the ocean. Hell, there's food,
ammo, canteens, clothes, and bedding everywhere. What the hell is
going on around here? This is bad. How could they just leave all this
stuff here like this?* He was halfway through the fort when they heard
the sounds of battle.

Just before dark, they were once again set up in a defensive perimeter for the night. The perimeter was two miles north and five miles east of the North Vietnamese fort they had discovered that morning. Leary, Folger, Patkins, Marlin, and Carson were around the dying fire. All of them had eaten, the defensive positions for the night had been assigned, and so far it was quiet. It had been a full, hard day, and they needed to put the pieces together. Taking the scattered bits that they might have known or seen individually, they tried to assemble them into some kind of order.

"Seemed like it took you forever to get us through that fort this morning, Leary," Patkins said in a questioning but nonaccusatory way as he sat cross-legged while moving the coals around the fire with a long stick.

"Yeah, it did, and then I felt like I was rushing it," Leary replied. "If we hadn't heard those fifties going off, I'd have been slower. That place was just too dangerous. Christ, it was spooky. Their stuff was lying all over the place. I couldn't believe they weren't there. That rice and God knows what concoction was still warm in that pot at the first bunker."

Carson spoke quietly, almost sadly. "I don't think we could've made any difference if we'd run through that fort. Hell, most of the men in that battalion were dead within fifteen minutes from when we first heard the noise from the ambush." Everyone turned to look at him, some in disbelief. "I timed it. I don't know why, but I did. The shooting and explosions only lasted that long. We never could've made it to them in time. Nothing we could've done. The colonel realized that and sent us to cut off their retreat. They were probably trying to get back to the fort."

"I don't understand how they could've lost so many men. It pisses me off to think they could be dumb enough to get caught that way. I heard there's only enough left of them to make up one platoon. Only one lousy platoon left out of that whole damn battalion." Marlin shook his head, and then continued. "I heard their sixty-gunners and bearers were all pretty much spaced out along the road at the edge of the jungle. All dead."

Carson's dark head nodded. He was tired mentally and physically and, for the first time in his life, was willing to consider the fact that he might be getting old. Might be old at thirty-eight. He wriggled his body as if to fit it into a more comfortable spot in the grass. His feet were flat on the ground, his knees were bent, and his arms held his rifle pointing up toward the sky, with the butt plate on the grass between his cracked and bleached-out boots. He had no desire to tell what he knew, but he would. They needed to know. *Better they get the straight scoop from me than from fabricated rumors and wrong assumptions. God knows the straight truth is horrible enough.* In the weary voice that tired parents often use on their inquisitive children at the end of a long day, he said, "As you know, the Twenty-second Battalion, was to set up the block for our sweep. We were originally to push the enemy into their ambush. Then our flankers found the bunker complex and we were delayed for a few days, during which time the Twenty-second sat on their asses in the same spot for the days it took for us to get out of there. They should've known that by this morning when we left the bunker complex, every Vietnamese in the whole country knew where the Twenty-second was. Of course, they knew where we were, too. They had tried several times to get us so no surprise there. The powers-that-be decided that the Twenty-second should move farther east and set up an ambush across the road, the same road we were traveling on. The brass believed, and rightly so, that there was at least a battalion of North Vietnamese regulars between us and the Twenty-second." He paused for a breath and then continued. "The brass was right, too, because that was their empty fort that we were in this morning."

"About time they got something right," an angry Marlin growled. He was lying on his side chewing on a straw, with his weapon and web gear on the grass between him and the fire. No one even looked in his direction as Carson continued.

"Well, as it turns out, the NVA anticipated their movement and set up an ambush just east of them. They knew that, with us pushing down the road, the Twenty-second would have to move east to catch them coming out of the jungle, hopefully in a great hurry and carrying everything they could grab." He paused again, and this time everyone's eyes riveted toward him. "Well, as you all know, the Twenty-second Battalion was trying to set an ambush for the North Vietnamese who occupied the deserted fort we went through. However, the NVA ambushed the Twenty-second and then ran. We chased them and our planes roasted them with napalm." He stopped, the tone of his voice indicating that he was through. They all knew that now he would only answer specific questions. He was tired and he needed rest.

"What I don't understand," Folger said, "is how those damn machine gunners got caught and slaughtered in the open like that, all of them. I just can't fathom that. Hell, I knew the gooks had fifties, and that big heavy slug they fire can go through a small tree and still kill a man on the other side. I don't argue with that, but I just don't understand how all of those damn gunners, the battalion's major source of firepower, could all be caught in the open and together like they were." He looked up at Carson.

"That's exactly what happened. Seems the gunners were complaining about having to carry their sixties in the brush, so their colonel let 'em walk in a line following the clearing at the jungle's edge. Lined up like a bunch of walking ducks, one after the other. Naturally, they were the first to die. Once they were down, and I guess they and their ammo bearers were pretty much all dead, the rest was easy. The fifties cut through the jungle about a foot above the ground and slaughtered all but about forty of them."

"I don't doubt it," Leary said as he shifted his body in an effort to get comfortable on the knobby grass. "What I can't believe is how they had those fifties in the first place. I mean, where did they get them and the ammo? Also, I can't believe that their colonel or any officer or NCO would let all his firepower get caught in the open like that. It's against all the rules of war. Our colonel would punish any man who even made the request. And I know the lieutenant or even the captain wouldn't allow such crap. Hell, I'm only a lowly sergeant and I wouldn't allow it."

"Could be from the French," Patkins said. Everyone looked at him in disbelief.

Patkins grinned, "You know the fifties. Hell, they've been around for a long time. We could have supplied them to the French, and the Vietnamese could have gotten 'em from them when they threw them out of here."

"Yeah, well." Shaking his head disgustedly, Leary said, "Screw the fifties, what kind of an officer would let his sixties walk in the open like that?"

"A dead one." Carson paused before going on. "We'll never know for sure because their colonel and most of his brass were dead on the ground with their men. It was a textbook ambush, made even better by human error. Slaughtered them all, or most of them."

"Human error. More like big time stupidity," Folger added. Everyone nodded in agreement.

"Sort of makes Custer's last stand not that big a deal," Leary said.

"Custer is remembered as a hero for his stupidity," Marlin declared with a bitter voice. "I doubt that this'll get a single line in Time magazine. No one will give a shit about those who died today, except maybe their families. And then only till they find someone to replace 'em."

"Hell," Folger mumbled as he lay flat on his back, "their families have probably already replaced 'em. Wives and girlfriends have found new lovers, mothers and fathers have put them out of their minds, and brothers or sisters have probably already moved into their rooms. For most of the people back home, we and those guys of the Twenty-second are already dead and replaced. Has to be that way."

"Damn, Folger," Marlin said, "you could depress anyone."

"Not trying to depress anyone. Just trying to live in life as it really is. When we came over here, our friends and relatives knew that we might get it. Might not come back. They naturally started planning on how they'd live without us. We filled a need in their lives, a need that won't just go away because we're gone. No, the need is still there, and they'll fill it with someone else. Fact is, if they didn't have a need, they wouldn't have needed us in the first place, just common sense. No blame."

Everyone was quiet. No one wanted to pursue that line of conversation. Marlin, outwardly the most disturbed by Folger's statements, made an effort to change the subject.

"Well, those gooks might have gotten the entire Twenty-second but our jets sure cooked them."

"Cooked is right," Patkins said. "I doubt if I'll ever get the picture of those charred bodies out of my mind."

"It's the smell I can't seem to clear out of my head," Marlin said. "The smell of roasted humans is something that'll change my eating habits forever. Maybe it's in my clothes." He raised his right shirtsleeve—smelling it. "At least, I hope it is. Then maybe I can wash it out. Get it out of me." He moved his sleeve away from his noise and sniffed different air, trying to determine if the smell was in his clothes. With a look of despair on his face, he said, "I don't think it's in my clothes. I think it's inside my body, and I'll never get it cleared out. It's kind of burned into my brain, welded forever into me."

"A good washing will make a world of difference," Folger said. "Anyway, they got their just desserts. Saved us a lot of ammo. Some of them, even though they were dead, weren't that badly burnt."

"Oxygen sucked out of them from the fire," Carson said. "The jets probably didn't get all of 'em, but they did catch a bunch of 'em in the open. Caught 'em just like they caught our boys, and then put the heat on them."

"We going to go back to their fort tomorrow and clean up what's left of 'em, Sarge?" Marlin asked.

"No, word is they are flying us out tomorrow. They won't say why or where, just that if all goes well tonight, be ready to load choppers by 0900 hours."

"Ain't that the way?" Folger said. They all looked at him. "We don't finish anything over here. Not one thing. We leave what's left of them, and their home, intact and pull out to some other place. Damn them, they never let us finish anything, not one thing. I don't mind dying. I just hate dying with such a bunch of weak ding-a-lings leading us."

If Folger had cursed them, it probably wouldn't have been funny, but the expression "ding-a-lings" broke the tension and they all started laughing. They laughed hard for a full five minutes and then stopped as suddenly as they had begun.

The costs of the war were too high for either side to pay any more that night. By 1000 hours the next morning, the helicopters had arrived. They were an hour late, but no one cared. Time had lost its power over them and meant nothing. Still, not knowing what was ahead of them, and with no briefing, they boarded the choppers believing that, wherever they were going, it would not be good.

33

MOVING BASE CAMP

The battalion flew to their base camp above Ben Cat without incident. They rested, bathed, washed clothes, slept, talked, and some wrote letters home. Most of the letters didn't say much. They were just a few lines of scratchy writing. A few empty answers and responses to the news from loved ones at home. There just wasn't that much they could tell their people back home. Nothing was said that could depress or scare them. Most of the soldiers couldn't think of anything to say. Their fate seemed sealed, and nothing they knew of would change that. Why worry their families, they were dead men anyway.

On the second day at base camp, the brass informed them that they would move their base camp to Lia Kae. The Twenty-second had been based there and, now that most of them were gone, there was more room. Furthermore, they were told, Lia Kae would be a better base camp. The river ran right by it and there was fresh processed water available. The camp was in a large rubber tree plantation, where their senior officers were housed. Lia Kae had a field hospital, a landing area for choppers inside the wire, and even a swimming pool. In addition to these obvious comforts, a landing strip was under construction that would eventually allow C-130 cargo planes to land, making the need for monthly convoys a rare occurrence. In all aspects, it was presented as a better place to be, and this boosted the spirits of the men, at least temporarily.

In reality, it was worse. Someone in command determined that the perimeter should be enlarged to accommodate the new battalion. This was done by cutting a slice out of the jungle south of Lia Kae towards the village of Ben Cat. For twenty-five days, the men cut the jungle back and built bunkers and dwellings. They trucked over, camped in the jungle, and worked like slave labor to clear a semicircular path through the foliage and set up defensive fields of fire. Barbed wire was strung and brush was burned. The jungle was thick there and, with the monsoons over, it was hot, dry, and dusty. The animal life was reluctant to give up their habitat, so snakes, scorpions, and all other forms of life had to be dealt with. For the first few days, they had a bulldozer but the majority of the work was done by hand. At the end of the twenty-five days, they were finished and A, B, and C Companies had a large open area with individual tents and sandbag shelters along the inner jungle line of their hand-carved clearing.

Fifty meters south of the newly delineated jungle line were the new bunkers—already occupied by wildlife and therefore uninhabitable. One hundred meters in front of the bunkers were two rows of concertina wire. Each row had two rolls of wire on the bottom and one roll on the top, forming two triangular barriers about three meters high and six meters apart. They had tied C-ration cans filled with rocks to the wire at various locations so it would rattle if moved. The flesh-tearing wire provided a sense of comfort to their front, but to their rear was a mile-deep belt of jungle. Through this belt, they had cut a small trail going back to the coolly shaded rubber tree area where the company CP was located. No one would travel the trail at night because of the large cobra and bamboo viper population in that dense strip of jungle. It was a no-man's-land separating them from their cooks, supply people, medical facilities, and, gratefully, the captain. During the clearing of the defensive perimeter, a large population of snakes had been driven into and then trapped in this no-man's-land. Though most of the men were not at peace with the creatures of the jungle, they still had a natural fear of snakes and were constantly on the lookout for them.

Compared to this new base camp, Ben Cat seemed like a resort. The new camp was high, hot, dusty, dry, and infested with every kind of insect and reptile in the country. The men had been lied to, and every day they were there, they became more and more disheartened with those who commanded them. Their officers had promised better facilities but had given the men worse. Gone were the pools for bathing. Whatever they wanted or needed at their new homemade living quarters had to be carried down a mile of snake-infested jungle trail.

Trying to make the best of a bad situation, Leary and Folger had built a large tent area. They had cut down trees and skinned off the branches, making logs. They then dug holes in the sandy ground, put one end of the logs in the hole, and packed the dirt back in around them. After creating six upright poles, they cross-braced them and made sloping roof supports. The result was a large frame, resembling a small pole barn. On the sides of this frame, they tied their tent halves, as well as pieces of plastic that they had scrounged, stolen, or bought in the village. For the roof, they bought sheets of corrugated metal from Ben Cat and nailed them on the pitched frame. When it was finished, they had a completely enclosed roof area covered with corrugated tin from the village, and canvas, plastic, and bamboo drop curtains covering the sides. Around the bottom, they placed four feet of protective sandbags. Hard-packed sand had raised the floor by twelve inches, and there was a large round area in the front, almost a separate room, which was also protected by sandbag walls. The bamboo curtains kept the sun out during the day and the lantern-light in at night.

This structure became a sanctuary for the men. They met there often, usually during the early afternoon and in the evening. It was as close to a clubhouse as they had. The men of the platoon used it to play cards, drink the beer which now seemed to be frequently available, and talk. Their furniture consisted of a table and chairs that they had constructed from jungle trees. Card games often went on well into the night. Guard was always maintained, but only one shift per night. Things were getting better. They left once during the month to guard for a convoy. Again, Leary, Patkins, and the squad pulled their patrol every day for three days, but there was no fighting, and they did not see Giap during this time. It had taken almost a month for the move to be completed. It could have been done more quickly, but they were no longer in a hurry.

At 1300 hours, on December 24, 1965, Leary, Folger, Patkins, and Marlin were in the "big tent," as Leary and Folger's place had come to be called, playing cards. Opened care packages from home were scattered all around the floor. All of them contained cookies, cakes, and candy in different stages of consumption and freshness. They occasionally played other card games, but canasta had come to be their favorite. Winning or losing the game wasn't as important to them as having something to do with their hands. They needed movement to talk. Talking was no longer an end in itself, and they found it easier to talk while playing cards. Lately, however, they were starting to reaccustom themselves to communicating verbally. The last thirty days had been relatively safe for them, or at least safer than what they had been doing. No one had been wounded or killed, and it was a bonus time for them.

"How you coming on the well?" Leary asked Marlin and Patkins as he dealt the first hand. The two had decided to dig a well so everyone could have water for bathing. After putting up their tent with a sandbag wall around it for protection, they started digging. They built a ladder out of trees and scrounged an ammo box and rope to use for hauling the dirt out of the hole. As the hole grew deeper, they tied more rope to the box. One man would dig, usually the still-skinny Patkins, and fill the box, which Marlin lowered into the hole. Once the box was as full as the straining Marlin could manage, he pulled it up and dumped it.

At the beginning, Patkins filled the box too full for Marlin to pull out by himself, and they asked for help. Patkins said it would be much faster if they had two men on the box. Leary and Folger tried ignoring him and stayed busy working on the big tent. After a few of these annoying requests, Leary finally told them to either get someone else from the platoon or keep the loads light. At first, Patkins and Marlin were angry with Leary and Folger's lack of enthusiasm for the well, but soon they got over it and resigned themselves to digging the well alone. Still, they couldn't understand why no one else was interested in helping do something that would mean so much to all of them.

Patkins, hoping Leary's comment meant he was interested in helping with the well, said, "We're doing good. We must be down about twenty feet." He paused, and Leary grunted in admiration. "We could get to water a lot faster, though, if we had another man on the dirt box." He looked up from his cards at Leary and Folger. "Either of you guys interested? Now that the big tent is finished?"

Folger didn't even look up from his cards. Leary, sorry that he had brought it up, looked up from his hand and said, "No, not really. I don't mean to dampen your project, Patkins, and I'll be the first one to congratulate you if you do hit water, but I don't think you will."

"Dig deep enough, we have to. I mean there's a river not more than a mile or so from us. Has to be water down there."

"Yeah, but have you seen where that river is?" He paused, threw his hand in, and said, "Damn, Patkins, I hate to tell you this, but that river is way lower than we are. We're on a plateau here, a high, sandy, clay plateau. I just don't see how you could hit water in less than a couple of hundred feet."

"Well, if that's what it takes, that's what we'll do. I can't live another nine months here without having water to wash up. I got to at least try."

Marlin was obviously shocked. "Two hundred feet. Shit, that's a mining project."

"Look, Patkins," Leary said, "we won't ever stay here long enough to worry about a bath. The only reason we've been here this long is because they needed us to cut all this jungle down. It's better here for the officers, but it sure as hell isn't for us. Just because we haven't had it bad doesn't mean it's over for us. If tomorrow wasn't Christmas, we'd be out there somewhere now." He gestured toward the jungle with the new cards he'd picked up off the table. "Out in the jungle hunting our little slant-eyed buddies."

"Hell, Christmas isn't the reason we're not out there," Marlin blurted out. "It's the damn New Year's truce. That's the reason we got this time off. The gooks and us have a truce till after the New Year, and that's the only reason. What our people think and give a damn about us hasn't changed. They just made a deal."

"Yeah," Folger said as he threw a card on the pile, "it's typical of this damn war. Made a truce with the enemy to call off the hunting till after the New Year. I never heard of such crap in my life. It no doubt gives the little Charlies time to get more supplies and troops down here. Time to repair the damage we did to them. I can't believe how stupid this all is. Every time I think I've heard it all, our stupid leaders surprise me. I've got to quit being surprised."

"Careful with that kind of talk," Patkins said. He was joking, but Folger didn't take it that way.

"Huh, careful? No sense in worrying about that. I don't give one damn about who hears me, but even if I did, none of those REMFs would come out here to get me. Hell, when was the last time any of you saw the captain out here?"

"He came out a couple of times when we were building the bunkers," Marlin said.

"Right," Folger continued, "that's the last time you'll ever see him out here again, too, I guar-an-damn-tee. In fact, with the exception of the lieutenant, who stays out here even though he could be back at headquarters in their big tents, you don't, you won't, see any of those rear-type people come out here. They don't want to take that snake-walk down our little trail."

"Either that, or they are afraid of us," Marlin said.

"Well, I know damn well they are, Marlin," Folger added. Leary and Patkins didn't say a thing, just kept playing cards. "They should be, too. The longer they stay way back behind us, the softer and more afraid they get. And so they make rules to try and diminish their fears. Now they got paths that everyone is supposed to walk on. Why that company area is starting to look like a stateside camp. Every time I go to chow, it seems like they've added some new nicety. They've even painted those tubes that mortar rounds come in and placed the silly things in front of the tent flaps to designate walkways. It's getting more stupid every day."

"That's not all. One of the cook jerk-offs told me at lunch that after Christmas no one would be served hot meals if they haven't shaved that day. He said from now on, when we get back from the field, we have half a day to get shaved or no hot meal. I asked him where he thought we were going to get the water. He said carry it to our position, he guessed. I explained to that ass that it was a mile carrying forty-five pounds just to get five gallons down here and that I'll be damned if I'm going to shave with it once I get it here. He said it wasn't his rule but the mess sergeant's rule and that he had to enforce it." The more Marlin talked, the angrier he became. His blood was hot and killing-mad when he said, "I ought to walk up the snake trail now and shoot that fat son-of-a-bitchin' mess sergeant right now."

"Hold, it Marlin. That fat shit isn't worth the bullet. Besides I need you, hell, you and Jackson are the only men I have left," Patkins interjected.

"Okay, Sarge, I hear you," he said, obviously making an effort to calm himself while still looking Patkins in the eye. "I won't kill the son of a bitch, not yet, not unless I tell you first. But I got to say this, Sarge, if he don't feed me because I haven't shaved, well then, I'm gonna do something. Enough is enough."

Leary and Folger remained quiet and still. They knew that, more and more lately, Marlin went into a killing rage and, when he was like that, the only one he would listen to was Patkins.

If something happens to Patkins, who'll stop Marlin? Leary thought. *Will he shoot the cook or some other rear-echelon man?* To change the subject, Leary said, "One thing good about this truce," he paused to lay down a card, "is that we didn't have any problems when guarding the convoy last time. I guess, if old Charlie is using this truce to bring up supplies, so are we."

"Yeah, that was a relief," Marlin acknowledged. "I did hear through the rumor mill that we're gonna be going on a big operation into the highlands when this truce crap is over."

"I heard it too, from the armory sergeant," Patkins said, "something about a big sweep into the highlands to clear an area for a new division coming from Hawaii."

"Any of you guys want some brownies?" Leary asked, holding up a box wrapped in brown paper that he'd picked up from its place on the floor. All three of them groaned. "Don't blame you. I can't eat any more of this stuff either. Seems too sweet after the diet we've been on, and then half of it's stale." After affirmative grunts from the other three, Leary said, "I guess we'd better bury all of it pretty soon; the ants have already found it." He looked down at two trails of small ants, one line coming in picking up sugar from a box of fudge left on the floor, and another line heading out on their way back to their nest carrying pinhead-sized pieces of fudge.

Folger chuckled, "Hell, let the ants clean it all out of here. They don't bother us, and they won't leave anything but the paper."

Leary laughed too as he played his cards. They would play hand after hand, game after game, automatically. No one remembered who had won the last one, no one cared, and they just kept playing. They did not compete with each other; they were friends in the truest sense, and they accepted each other for who they were and for what they might become. It did not occur to them to profit, in any way, at the expense of one of their comrades. "Speaking of letting critters go, Folger, I do appreciate the new 'animal-lover' you've become. I mean it's a nice quality you have, but don't you think letting that bamboo viper live is carrying it a little too far?"

"Leary, my Sergeant, I know that it bothers you some, though not to the degree that you protest. We've disrupted the snake's home. He was one of those babies we saw hatching when we were clearing and burning this place. He was small when he first set up housekeeping under the sandbags of our east wall. True, he is larger now, a fine specimen of a snake. After all, his entrance is on the outside, and he never invades our space by coming in here."

"You puzzle me, Folger," Marlin said, shaking his head, "the human killingest machine that I know, lets an ill-tempered and very dangerous snake live right under his own dwelling?"

"Marlin, I don't consider myself a killing machine. It's true that I've no real love for our little gook friends, but they're out to get me and all of us here. The snake has shown no such desire. I mean, it's rare that we ever see him, and when we do, hell, he just goes quietly on his way, no hissing, striking, or such. It's true, of course, that one should be careful not to walk around that side of the big tent at night, but only so as not to step on him or invade his space. It isn't that much of a problem to go the other way. It's the least we can do."

Laughing, Patkins threw a card down and said, "He probably thinks you're his mother, Folger. After all, he was just hatching when we found him. He's never seen his mother. So, naturally, he thinks it's you."

"Well, maybe so. He could be a girl, but I've no way of checking and besides, a mother would love it either way."

"Yeah, well," Leary laughed, "I hope your healthy baby boy or girl doesn't bite its mother or any of its mother's friends."

They continued the idle conversations until night. Slightly buzzed with beer, they set up the guard and retired at dark.

⌘

The platoon CP, which was a tent shared by Tooley and Carson, was farther back, closer to the snake trail. Tooley and Carson were sitting in a couple of cheap lawn chairs that they'd bought in Ben Cat. The area around their tent had been cleared of brush. A couple of large trees had been left for shade. It wasn't as visible from the jungle to the south, beyond the wire, as the big tent and the other platoon member's dwellings were. Though it was shady and cooler, it was closer to the snakes than the other tents, and most of the men preferred to be in the sun and away from the infested jungle. Directly to their front, just out of the tree line, was a platoon machine gun nest complete with sandbags and the gunner's two-man tent. About twenty-five meters in front of the machine gun nest was another bunker, the one they had built for the gun. Like everyone else, the gunners had no desire to occupy their bunker. The men just wouldn't go in them, and the officers and noncommissioned officers had long since quit trying to force them.

"Do you want some of this cake, Sergeant Carson?" Tooley asked.

"No, thank you, sir, I got plenty of goodies from my wife, mother, and aunts. More than I can eat. You're welcome to any of it you want. Just help yourself."

"I appreciate it. I've wanted sweets many times over the past few months." Tooley paused a second. "Now that we have 'em, they make me sick."

"I know what you mean. We must've been off of the sweets for so long that our bodies can't stand them anymore."

"You know, Sergeant, this new camp isn't so bad now that we are settled."

"No sir, not too bad. I do miss the springs, though, and snakes are not my favorite creatures. We sure have plenty of them around here."

"Mine, either. I hope that stuff you poured between our area and the jungle works. What exactly was that anyway?"

"Some mixture of diesel fuel and bug spray that the supply sergeant gave me. I hope it's a line that the snakes won't want to cross. I didn't tell the men, of course, but I saw one big black cobra crossing the trail going back to the company CP this morning. It must have been seven foot long."

"God, that's big. Let's hope the stuff works to keep it and its buddies from coming into our area. I hope we left enough rodents for them to eat in the jungle. Enough so they don't feel the need to come out here looking."

"Me too, but it isn't the snakes as much as the scorpions that worry me," Carson said. "Did you hear about the first sergeant getting it the other day?"

"Yeah, day before yesterday. Guess he was sleeping and one of them was crawling on his bare chest. He slapped it and it stung him. He's back now, though, guess they had to take him to the hospital at the plantation."

"I spoke to him this morning. He's still having a little trouble breathing. He said he thought he was going to die when it hit. It was like a fire burning on his chest. The doctor told him that, if he wasn't such a big man, it might have killed him."

They called him "Top," an affectionate term used for a first sergeant who looked out for the enlisted men. Their "Top" was coal black and a good man by every definition of the word. He was the type of man who seemed indestructible.

"Well, at least we know a scorpion can't kill him," Carson said. They both laughed.

"I am enjoying this time off, Sergeant. I do wish we had a place to take a bath but, outside of that, it seems downright pleasant for a change."

"Hell, sir, you could go to the plantation and get a bath with the rest of the officers. No one would blame you."

"No, I can't do that. My men can't go there to bathe and I won't. They might not blame me, but I would."

"Sir, has anyone mentioned to you when, or if, we can somehow get some sort of bathing facilities for these men?"

"It's been discussed, cussed, asked for, and debated. They can smell us, and the medics are worried about the health problems that come from not bathing regularly. Which, surprisingly, don't seem to be affecting any of the men, especially after they quit wearing underwear. Right now, the plantation is the only place that has bathing facilities, and then it's only a couple of small ones. The high-ranking officers have one of them and the captains and lieutenants have been assigned the other one. I guess, I've never really seen it; it's just a single showerhead in a work shed. There's supposed to be a large bathing area and whirlpool in what is now the hospital. The high-ranking officers' bathing facility consists of a tub in the main plantation area. The problem is that the hospital needs their area, the captains' and lieutenants' single shower is usually occupied, and the big brass are not about to let anyone in their quarters."

"Well, we both know the men were better off back at Ben Cat. Fewer snakes, less jungle, and fresh springs to bathe in."

"No argument from me there," Tooley said. "No doubt someday they'll figure out a way to get showers for the men, but for now there just isn't the water. The water purification plant is barely able to provide drinking water, and it's a long way from here to the river to pump water. So here we are—high, dry, and smelly. Top say anything to you about the operation we're going on after this truce is over?"

"He said it was going to be a major search and destroy, somewhere in the highlands. Northeast of War Zone C. Said a new division was coming in from Hawaii, and we are to clean out the enemy in that area. Give the new division a safe place to set up camp. His final words were, 'Enjoy the truce because it's going to be big and bad afterward.' You hear anything from your end?"

"Damn, once again you get better information from the NCO pipeline than I do from my officer buddies. I heard where we're going, but little else."

The time passed peacefully and, with the exception of no baths, the men started showing signs of becoming human again. Marlin refused to shave and the cooks refused to feed him. He punched one of them and walked back to his home in the jungle. No one came after him, nor did they send for him. Nothing was said except, no shave, no hot chow. Marlin ate C-rations the whole time and never did shave. If asked about it, he would reply, "It's worth it. I don't like them either, and their food tastes like shit."

As January 1966 neared its end, the monthly convoy came up unguarded and unmolested. Across South Vietnam with few exceptions, the truce was honored on both sides. The truce ended and, days before the "big and bad" operation was due to launch, preparations and tensions intensified. Fights broke out between the men on the line and those in the rear. The men on the line knew that soon they would hunt and be hunted in the jungles and, as the time to go drew near, they prepared themselves by fighting with the men who wouldn't have to go. Though they told themselves that they were the survivors, the ones who had been there and made it back, the question replayed in their minds, "Is this the one that'll get me?" Even Leary seemed to be affected. He had the knowing, the feeling, whatever it was, that he was going to get it on this one.

34

THE BIG AND THE BAD

The battalion was at the nearly finished landing strip for chopper loading at 0900 hours on the morning of February 1. At 0800 hours, Carson came to the big tent to tell Leary, Patkins, and their men to be at the platoon CP in thirty minutes. From there, they walked up the snake trail to the company CP, where they loaded on trucks and were driven to the airstrip. It had been almost forty-five days since they had seen combat. There had been some sniper fire since the truce ended, but mainly it had been a quiet time. Still no showers, no real change in anything, except the killing. The well was now forty feet deep, with four ladders working their way down toward the bottom, but still no damp ground, much less water. Carson had something else on his mind besides the briefing, though, and he pulled Leary aside to talk with him.

"Leary, you know we lost our platoon medic to malaria last month."

Leary shrugged and said, "Didn't think much of him anyway. We've done okay taking care of our own wounded."

"Well, we have one now, and he's going with us," Carson said. Leary nodded. "He's new and green. I need you to look after him." He saw the look of resistance on Leary's face and was quick to say, "As a personal favor."

Leary reluctantly, said, "No problem, Sergeant, but in what way?"

"Well, you know, keep him with you," he hesitated again, seeing the irritation on Leary's face, "till he gets used to the combat and the jungle."

"I take it then that he's never been out."

"Worse than that."

"Oh, shit, Sergeant, what could be worse than that? Isn't he trained?"

"Oh, he's had his medical training all right."

"Then what's the problem? Just tell him to stay with us, do what we do, remember his training, and he'll adjust."

"Look, I've met him, he's at the company CP right now, and if I'm any judge of human character, he is less than qualified as a combat medic." Leary gave Carson a puzzled look. "Well, we had to get him from the hospital. He's only been in-country a few weeks, and they no doubt gave us the man they were the least concerned about losing."

"Oh no, not another Hart. Christ, let someone else babysit him. I just don't know if I have it in me to take care of one more Hart."

"I don't think he's that bad, but he isn't good either. He's practically shaking in his brand-new boots as we speak. He's a small black man and looks like he is about fourteen." Leary inhaled deeply and then expelled his breath in disgust.

"Hell, Leary, what else am I to do?" Carson said. "You tell me. Should I give him to someone else? Who? If this boy has any chance of living, it's got to be with you. No smoke-blowing, just can't think of any other way to do it. If you can, you tell me!"

"Shit, all right, shit, shit, shit!" Resigned now, Leary said, "I'll do what I can for him. But, by God, when are they going to get real about who we are and what we have to do out here? Why don't they just shoot a poor kid like that themselves and save him and the rest of us the worrying?"

"I wish I could answer that for you, Leary. I appreciate what you're doing, and I feel badly about asking you. I'd do it myself if I could."

"I know you would, Sarge," Leary said, feeling a little better now that he had accepted the situation for what it was. "You got all you need to do being platoon sergeant. I'll do it the best I can."

"I know you will, Leary." Sadness was in his voice as he continued, "I tell you this as a friend. The boy hit me hard inside. I know he's at least eighteen but he looks so young. He seems so naive. He reminds me of my younger son, who's eleven today. I'm sorry. It's personal for me and I just can't help feeling like he's my own."

"It's okay, Sergeant Carson. That being the case, don't give it another thought. I'll do my damn best to keep him alive. But keep in mind that if I fail and he gets it, he's not your boy. Your boy is at home. I can only do so much. Some things are in the hands of God."

"You're right, Leary. Thanks, I owe you."

"No you don't, Sergeant Carson. Friends never owe friends."

Carson smiled, a weary but warm smile, and reached up to lightly touch Leary on the shoulder. Then he turned and walked back to the CP.

By 1000 hours, they were well on their way. The formation flew northwest, climbing for altitude to discourage ground fire and because of the increased elevation of the highlands. Though the loading was uneventful, the takeoff was almost disastrous. When the chopper that Leary and the new medic, Private First Class Jenkins, were riding in first lifted off the ground, it narrowly averted a collision with the tail rotor of the chopper in front of them.

The two parallel formations of choppers cleared the high plateau with about five hundred feet to spare. The cliff looked high and sandy as they approached it. Like the largest layer of a wedding cake, it had a pronounced and obvious increase in elevation. The terrain below the chopper looked much like that of Ben Cat with areas of jungle, valleys, and streams, as well as sporadic groupings of rubber trees. Once over the highlands, they headed northwest, coming directly over a valley with a small village and rice paddy below. It looked deceptively peaceful. Leary had sat Jenkins next to him in the left-hand side door. The seat was tight for the two of them, especially with all of their gear and, as usual, there were no seat belts or any other devices to hold them in. The ledge on which their feet rested was just wide enough for their feet, leaving the toes of their boots sticking out over the edge of the open doorway.

Carson's assessment of Jenkins was right on the money. I'd better be easy on him. Don't want to scare him any more than he is. A relaxed attitude might have worked in another time and place with two other men, but it didn't work here. These two were completely different types of men with dissimilar experiences. Furthermore, Leary wasn't aware of how far he had come from normal fears since being in Vietnam. He was unaware that he no longer paid attention to situations that might scare a new man to death. *Jenkins obviously has never been an athlete or participated in any physical or competitive training, except in boot camp and, even then, he could have slipped through the cracks.* Six months ago, Leary might have thought of Jenkins as a wimp or sissy, but now his thoughts were on how to keep him alive. *It's going to be tougher than I imagined. I hate to let Sergeant Carson down but, if this operation is half as hot as it's said to be, this guy doesn't stand a chance. Christ, I can feel him shaking. I'll try and not look at him. Might scare him more.*

Leary looked down at the village just as it started.

Tracer bullets from a fifty-caliber machine gun streaked between the two formations of choppers. The chopper noise was ear-splitting and, to communicate, one had to get very close and shout, use hand signals, or lip-read. Leary tried to lighten the situation as he leaned in to Jenkins and shouted in his ear, "Look at those dumb shits down there. They're stupid. If they'd just turn that gun one way or another, they'd get one of us." Looking into Jenkins' soft black face, Leary was shocked to see his eyes roll back into his head, revealing only the whites of his eyes. Realizing that Jenkins was passing out, he quickly took his left hand off the rifle barrel between his legs and stuck it out, pinning Jenkins back in the canvas seat like one would do to a child in a car. He reached through, grabbed the side of the chopper tightly with his hand, and bent his elbow, pushing it painfully into Jenkins' chest. The pain brought Jenkins back and Leary shouted, "Are you okay?" Jenkins nodded and Leary screamed, "Don't do that again." Jenkins nodded again, and Leary gave him another jab of pain, mostly from anger, before slowly releasing him.

Flushed with anger now, Leary sprayed Jenkins' face with spit as he screamed, "Don't you pass out on me, you little shit. Get it together. I can't hold you in, goddamn you." Leary nodded his helmeted head towards the green below, took a breath, and continued, "If you don't want to fall down there, right on top of those gooks, you'd better get your sorry shit together. Damn you, stay with me." Jenkins nodded an exaggerated up-and-down motion.

God almighty, Leary thought, *taking care of this kid is going to be worse than Carson or I could've imagined. At least Hart never passed out. Well, not on the ride in, anyway. At least I don't think he did.*

The formation swung west just past the village, maneuvering like a giant fishhook and coming in to dump the troops on the hot landing zone which was about ten miles from the village that had fired on them. The formation came in, barely clearing the trees of an old rubber plantation, and continued north over a good-sized rice paddy. The old plantation buildings were gone. All boards and metal were gone. Nothing was left of the once-large plantation except a few old concrete foundations and the rubber trees. The trees were plentiful and healthy in rows so straight that, if a man stood directly behind one tree, he would not be able to see the others in that row. All of the trees were planted with the same precision and accuracy with which the Vietnamese had tended their rice plants for centuries.

After traveling two hundred meters over the paddies, north of the rubber trees, the formation turned 180 degrees, pointing the choppers south, back toward the rubber trees. Once headed south, all but one hastened to set down as close to the water as they dared and then, on orders from the pilot, the copilot and door gunners frantically hurried the troops out of the choppers and into the paddies below.

As the first choppers lowered themselves into a position that would allow their nervous soldiers to disembark, the enemy opened up. From the edge of the rubber trees, the enemy machine guns and automatic rifles peppered the LZ at an overwhelming rate of fire, about two feet above the water.

No pilot wanted to set his chopper down into the murderous fire. They knew that it was much easier to hit a target that was straight across from the gun than one at an angle. To set the choppers within the two-foot range would have meant certain death. The soldiers knew they needed to lie flat in the water or mud, if they survived the fall through the grazing fire. But the pilot of Leary's chopper was extra cautious. He was reluctant to lower the chopper at all. Leary looked down, waiting for the chopper to get lower, but it didn't. It hung in the air at least twelve feet above the water. Leary emphatically pointed down with his index finger. *Damn green pilot, he almost wrecked on takeoff, and now he wants us to jump out twelve feet in the air.*

The copilot turned around in his seat to look at Leary, giving him the signal to jump. The other six men in the chopper—Patkins, Marlin, Folger, Sanchez, Jackson, and Jenkins—were all looking at Leary. They also knew they were too high. Each of them was heavily loaded with ammo, water, three days' supply of food, and weapons. They knew that jumping from that height would be devastating.

Now angry at the pilot's refusal to lower the machine, Leary glared at the copilot, who was in headset communication with the pilot, and shook his head no. With the hand that held up his magazine, he pointed down again. (When the men flew in choppers, it was one of the only times they did not keep their weapons loaded. If a weapon should be accidentally discharged in the chopper, the bullets could go up though the roof and bring the chopper down. Consequently, when the men jumped out of the chopper they loaded their weapons just before clearing the machine.) The copilot, who received another no from the pilot, shook his head while adamantly pointing to the big side door and mouthing the word "out." This exchange continued two more times, with each side getting angrier. The door gunner on Leary's side was busy burning up rounds at the enemy guns, while the other gunner nervously watched his side for possible enemy activity. Though they could both hear what was going on through their headsets, they paid no attention.

Finally, knowing that the delay increased the danger for them all and that the other choppers had already unloaded and were starting to move out, Leary jammed his magazine into his rifle, pulled the bolt back, putting a loaded and cocked round in the chamber. Shock flashed across the copilot's face at this threatening breach of safety. A second later, the copilot's fears were compounded as the rest of the squad, following Leary's lead, loaded their weapons too. Time stood still until Sanchez took the M-79 grenade launcher from his shoulder and loaded it.

Finally, Leary saw that the copilot was screaming into his headset, and the chopper began lowering.

Clumsily, they dropped several feet. They were still too high but Leary didn't believe that the scared pilot would go any lower, so he turned, grabbed Jenkins by his web gear, and threw him out of the chopper with such angry force that Jenkins landed on his back in the water below. Then Leary bailed out right behind him, nearly landing on his startled face, as the rest of the squad bailed out, too.

It was only while Leary was struggling to get himself and Jenkins out of the paddy and behind the dike that he realized that the pilot had been right. *Well, half-right anyway, because twelve feet is just too far to jump with that much weight. Hell, I'm stuck in the mud now. That jump was still at least six feet. Still, I don't think he'd have gotten any lower. Well, in his defense, he did get us over this lower rice paddy, behind a dike. It worked out, if I can get out of this mud, but still, with the differences in levels of the paddies, I did force him to come within a couple of feet of the grazing fire. Oh well, that's life.*

He looked over at the terrified Jenkins. *Muddy, wet, and scared, but still alive. There's Folger, Patkins, and the rest of the squad a little farther down the dike. Good, they all look okay. There, Patkins is giving me the sign. Time to find and join the rest of the platoon.*

As he tried to catch his breath, Leary regretted having to move so soon. *But there he is, Lieutenant Tooley, waving for us to come to his position a couple of paddies south of here.* Leary looked around to make sure everyone was going to follow and then headed out, clawing his way up on the dike, out of the sticky mud and water. Bending almost completely over, he ran down the dike past Patkins and the other men, who quickly followed. *Good, Jenkins is following, but he's right on my ass. Jesus, doesn't he know anything?* The position, the load, and the urgency made his body scream with pain. To his dread, when he started getting close to Tooley and Carson, they began moving too. *Shit, I could use a breather. But the lieutenant is right—we need to get out of the paddies and into the trees. The whole company seems to be following A Company, which is trying to get into the tree line at the south end of these paddies. Good, there are a couple of gun ships starting to pound the tree line.*

B Company had been in the choppers behind C Company and was unloading and heading south as the first platoons from A Company got to the trees. C Company was strung out between A Company and B Company, as all of the men, laden as they were with their equipment, sprinted for the trees. Just south and east of them, on a higher elevation, where the fire had been coming from, another gun ship made its run up the tree line. Its rockets exploded so close to A Company that they all dove into the water, desperately seeking cover. Though they could feel the concussions and see the black and white explosions off to their left, the men of C Company didn't seek cover but openly ran for the tree line.

Within a few minutes, the explosions ceased, leaving an eerie, tense quietness. The only sounds heard were heavy breathing and the sloshing of the water-filled boots as the men of C Company climbed the embankment to the dry land of the rubber trees.

Once inside the tree line, they stopped to rest and count heads. A few knocked leeches off of their mud-soaked pants. Moments later, a tired and soaked B Company sloshed up, following the tree line to their position. Then C Company, with Second Platoon in the lead, moved east through and past A Company, setting up a defensive line as they went. They strung out, lying down, facing into the rubber trees. The Second Platoon now occupied the area where the enemy gunners had been. There were no bodies, blood, or anything to indicate they had been there.

Thirty minutes after they landed, the LZ seemed reasonably secure. They now owned the edge of the rubber trees. Any further shooting from the enemy would have to come from the jungle two hundred meters east of the Second Platoon's position at a point where the rubber trees ended and the rice paddies funneled into a small river that flowed east out of the jungle and filled the rice paddies in which they had landed. It was the same river that flowed through the village that had fired on them on their flight to the LZ.

We can probably rest here, Leary thought, *at least until all the people coming in for this operation have landed.* The choppers behind him in the lower paddy landed continuously, unloading men and supplies, and then left, but they seemed a long way off. As Leary looked down between the rows of rubber trees, he saw clearly what was fifty meters in front of them. *Hell, yes, it's a damn trench. A nice trench, too. It clearly cuts a path between the rubber trees and goes as far in both directions as I can see. The dirt, nicely piled, is on our side; that means it's facing us. Man, it's enough trench for thousands of men. There must be a bunch of them out there. They either guessed where we'd land, or knew.*

That dirt is fresh, and that means they had plenty of time to get ready for us. Maybe we get our orders only after they've approved of 'em. Where are they? Why dig this elaborate ditch if they aren't going to defend it? Hell, maybe it's occupied. Just because I can't see anyone doesn't mean they aren't there. He sighted down his rifle as he realized that, any second, hundreds of heads could pop up and start firing at him. Seeing that his rifle was in the right position, he looked over at Folger, who was behind the next rubber tree to his left.

Folger looked over at him and, taking his hand off the pistol grip of his automatic rifle, pointed at the trench works with his right hand. He nodded and shrugged, "Whatever." Next, Leary turned to Patkins, who was two rubber trees to Leary's right in a position on the other side of Sanchez'. Patkins indicated that he had seen the trench too. By this time, Tooley, Carson, Nash, and Jenkins had set up a CP. They were directly behind Leary, lying on one of the old concrete floors from the old plantation buildings. *I wonder if they've seen it,* Leary thought. *Sooner or later, we have to find out who, if anyone, is in that trench. Maybe later is better if we wait, gives us more time to get troops on the ground.*

No sooner had he completed those thoughts than the explosions started—at least a hundred meters behind the trench and systematically moving toward Leary and Folger. *One of our gun ships has spotted the enemy in the trench ahead of us,* Leary decided. With more reaction than conscious thought, he got to his feet and signaled for Folger to do the same. He stood behind his rubber tree for a moment and watched the explosions coming toward the trench.

Then Leary made a mistake.

Floating in his movements, he stepped away from his rubber tree and started forward in a crouched position. Snapping the safety off his rifle, he cautiously moved forward. Folger followed Leary's lead. They were about thirty meters from the trench when Leary realized, *Holy shit, he's shooting at us. We're his targets.* Rockets streamed by them, leaving a vapor trail as they went. They were both in the open with only small rubber trees for protection. In desperation, they tried jumping the vapor trails, but, of course, by then it was too late. The rockets had already gone by.

Then Leary felt like a mule had kicked him as he flew into the air. *You're right*, he thought. *It's your time.*

35

MED-EVAC

It was 2000 hours and almost dark. The gun ship had just departed with Leary; Jenkins' dead body would have to wait until morning. They all wished his body could have gone, too. It would be ripe by morning, and they didn't have a body bag for him. Of course, Leary was a priority, because he was alive and one of them. Soon after Leary was wounded, the company moved out on a trail heading almost due east. The jungle was thick, and it was the end of the day before they found a small clearing several miles east of the morning's LZ. It wasn't much of a clearing, and they had to chop down several trees before they could get the chopper in for Leary. Thankfully, a couple of men from A Company still carried their machetes.

They were all grateful to the brave pilots who agreed to take the risky mission to pick up Leary. C Company set up in the clearing, and A Company and B Company had to do the best that they could on the trail east and west of the clearing. The lack of space made distance between the positions almost nonexistent. The danger of the close proximity was that one grenade or a mortar round could kill many people. It was claustrophobic.

C Company was point for the battalion, and few knew how many battalions and companies were strung out behind them, camping on the trails and clearings. Maybe the captain knew, but none of the rest of the company did, and few of them cared. There was no time and it was too dangerous for a fire this evening. They had traveled late, hoping to find a better place to camp. It was already dark, and they would have to eat their C- rations cold. It was food that most found distasteful even when heated. The Second Platoon was crammed together at their place in the company's perimeter, and they were experiencing a new level of discomfort.

The platoon, especially Carson and the second squad, were out of sorts with Leary's absence. Leary was an important part of their security and new family. They no longer believed that they would ever see their biological families again, and Leary had always been there with them.

"I sure feel bad about that Jenkins," Carson said. "Nothing anyone could do about it, though."

"Yeah," Folger said, "I figured he was a goner when he passed out trying to bandage Leary. Leary says, 'Jenkins, bandage this,' Leary's standing on that concrete, mad as hell, talking about shooting down the chopper himself, and the next thing I heard was a clunk, and there was medic Jenkins passed-ass out on the concrete."

"Well, hell, he just stood there and let that gook shoot him. Clear as that. Bang, a shot streaks by and we all duck except Jenkins. He just stood there." Marlin was gesturing with his hands as he spoke. "Leary was screaming for him to get down when the next shot flips Jenkins backwards like a rag doll. Bullet went right in his eye and out the back. Sort of jerked his head and, not more than a second later, his body followed it. I swear if the bullet hadn't messed up his brain, the impact would have broken his neck. Big mess out the back too. Can't be no open coffin at that guy's funeral."

"He was just a boy," Carson said regretfully.

"He was heavy for a little guy," Folger said. "But no one was as heavy as Hart. Christ, I'll never forget trying to get him back. I hope to God I never have to work that hard again. We finally had to drag old Hart. I felt like dragging Jenkins, too, after about ten steps. At least we had more guys to carry him than we did with Hart."

Patkins nodded from his position on the ground. His feet pointed toward the inner circle, his left armpit was propped up on his pack, and he nodded his head toward the dried blood on his fatigue shirt as he spoke. "You can tell who carried him by who has the blood and other sticky crap on 'em."

"True," Folger said, pointing to the stains all over the front of his shirt, "but you can also tell who got him when he was fresh, by the amount of junk on them."

Carson knew that these men didn't mean any disrespect for Jenkins; this was a harsh place, and they hadn't formed any attachment to him. But hate it as he did, he had formed strong feelings for the young man because of his likeness to his own son. He decided to change the subject. "I'm going to miss old Leary, though. Of course, he'll be back, right, Lieutenant?"

"Yeah, sure, if he doesn't get a court-martial," Tooley answered. "That doctor was pretty mad. Nash and I heard most of the conversation over the radio, between our captain and the doctor." Everyone looked puzzled.

"Okay," he chuckled slightly, "here's the scoop on Sergeant Leary. The chopper pilot thought Leary and Folger here," he nodded towards Folger, "were Charlies, so he came through and fired those rockets at them. Why they weren't killed, I'll never know. Anyway, Leary gets hit, and he and Folger come back to the CP. Jenkins passes out, and Carson and I examine the wound. We see that Leary has a hole below his left butt cheek about the size of a quarter. It's deep, and it's his ticket out on a chopper right away. I tell him, 'Leary you're out of here. Follow the tree line down, get on an incoming chopper, and get the hell out of here.' Well, he says, 'Lieutenant, I need to finish the day. If I can stay with the men until we get through the day, then they'll all be used to the jungle again, and they'll have a better chance of making it.' Of course, I tell him no. But he insists, you all know how he can be, and finally we agree that, if the doctor okays it, he can stay.

"I can see by the look on your faces, you're wondering what a doctor is doing out here, especially coming in on a hot LZ. Well, this is a large multibattalion operation, and the brass figured that, if a doctor was present, close to the battles, a lot of lives could be saved. From now on, they say, the doctors, especially the new and young ones, have to take turns coming out on large operations like this one. So this doctor drew the short straw and he wasn't too happy about it. And neither, so the rumor mill says, are any of the rest of the eligible doctors. Well, this scared and pissed-off doctor meets a wounded Leary. Not a pretty sight for anyone. You all saw what a mood he was in.

"He didn't even take the safe route that I'd told him to but walked across that rice paddy. I'd found out where the doctor was, using the radio. I also told him the longer but safer way to go. But did he do that? No, he took off, walking high and dry on the dike, straight across the paddy. Not even running, but walking, right in the open like he was suicidal or something. You men got to admit, he's getting kind of goofy. Well, he was about halfway across the paddy when the sniper started firing at him. Steady bang, bang, and bang. You all no doubt saw and heard that. What did Leary do then? Did he duck, throw himself into the paddy behind the dike? No, he actually stopped and defiantly flipped off the jungle where the firing was coming from. Then, he shouted obscenities in the sniper's direction and finally started walking again. Christ, I thought he'd be a goner at any time. But he wasn't even hit. So this is the mood he was in when he got to the doctor. A doctor who believed he was just a little too valuable a human to be out here with us.

"I know most of you saw all of that," Tooley went on, "and I only repeat it to paint a picture of Leary's mood for what he did next. Once he got to where the doctor was hiding below the lower rice paddy, the one we dropped into when we came here this morning, did Leary go down behind the dike where it was safe to talk to the doctor? Of course not. In fact, he stayed right on top of the bank, right in plain sight of the sniper. Evidently, he asked the doctor to look at his wound and give him permission to stay with us. The doctor, it seems, was reluctant to stick his head up over the dike and look at Leary's wound. So Leary, being short-tempered, reached down grabbed the doctor by his web gear, pulled him up, and shoved his face into his bleeding rear end." Everyone laughed, allowing the tensions of the day to roll out.

When they had quieted down, Tooley continued, "That's not all. While shoving the doctor's head in his ass, Leary said, 'You rear-echelon motherfucker, get your head up here where you can see something. Damn, you rear people are a bunch of yellow-bellies.' Well, that's what the doctor complained to the captain about. He evidently told our captain that something should be done about Leary. And I've got to hand it to the captain, I know he isn't too popular, but he told the doctor, 'Well, you had your opportunity, why didn't you do something?' "

"So old Leary isn't in trouble with the captain?" Folger asked.

"No, I do believe that the captain has resigned himself to, if not like Leary, at least tolerate him. In fact, the captain scrambled and begged to get that chopper in to pick Leary up tonight."

Patkins said, "Evidently then, the doctor did let Leary stay out here, because he did stay. Not that anyone could make him go. I mean the way he's acting, I'm surprised he even asked the doctor."

"'Cause the lieutenant told him to," Folger said. "It's clear to me. He belongs to this platoon, but doesn't believe in the rest of the army. Feel the same myself. But you shouldn't talk about how anyone is acting. Christ, Sergeant Patkins, you're the worst."

"This place is driving us all nuts," Tooley said. "But Folger's got it right. And Leary did listen to the doctor, though, for whatever reason. Anyway, the doctor said okay, probably scared not to, but he did give his consent on the condition that Leary would get out, and to a hospital, by tonight. The doctor said that Leary has a large piece of metal deep in his hip muscles. Sort of went up the bottom of the left cheek. He said it has to be surgically removed, and that Leary needed to go to a large hospital to get it done. I think the only reason he let him stay was because he was pissed at him and, maybe, afraid to tell him no."

"Why did two choppers come in?" Marlin asked.

"That's another story. It was because of that civilian shaking in his expensive boots, you know the guy with the camera, the freelance reporter. You all know they can go damn near anywhere they want. Well, evidently, when he decided to come with us, he didn't know that we wouldn't be able to chopper him out tonight. Hell, we didn't know where we'd be tonight. I know he kept whining to the captain when we were waiting for Leary's chopper, 'I can't stay the night. I have to get out tonight. I never stay the night.' Sickening bastard."

"Yeah, but he sure as hell did get out, and before Leary," Marlin added.

"True enough," Tooley continued, "but only because he could outrun Leary. By the time you men chopped the trees down so the chopper could land, it was almost dark. As you know, it's hot out there for choppers, and none of them wanted to chance it coming in for Leary. Like I said before, the captain used every trick in the book to get a chopper in—guilt, praise, anything he could think of. At last a chopper, a gun ship, said he was up and would come in. He said that he'd be looking for smoke and skimming the trees, but to have Leary ready because, the second his skids touched the ground, he'd be pulling back up again. Well, the reporter beat Leary to the chopper, dove in the door, and off it went. They were no sooner in the air than they started cussing us on the radio. Wanted to know why we said we had a wounded man when this guy was just a damn reporter. Well, the captain was smoking. He told them that man wasn't supposed to go out tonight, but that he'd beat Leary to the chopper. The captain told them to throw him back." Everyone laughed. "Anyway, a second gun ship was covering the first one and, after a minute, he said he'd try it. The first gun ship, the one with the reporter in it, took up a covering position behind and the other one, which dove in and picked up Leary. Goddamn brave, and a great piece of flying."

"Sounds fine to me," Marlin said, "What's to worry about Leary? Nice butt wound, a few weeks of drinking beer, a shower even, and he'll be back."

"That's not what's worrying me," Carson said. "What's worrying me is that, more and more lately, our boy Leary has developed a decided trend towards not only disrespecting authority but physically attacking it. He's fine with us but anyone outside this platoon is subject to his wrath, and rank be damned. That kind of attitude is tolerated out here, even encouraged as an asset, but back where he's going it could spell disaster for him. "

"What's new? We all feel that way, Sergeant. Marlin punches out the cooks. Those people are full of bullshit, and we're getting tired of it," Folger said.

"Yeah, we know about Marlin," Tooley said, looking directly at him. "So he punched someone in the nose, so what? It's not good, but it's nothing really bad, either. Although it wouldn't be tolerated in other safer places, what we're worried about, and have been for some time," Tooley looked at Carson, who nodded his agreement, "is Leary's willingness to do violence to our own people."

Patkins and Marlin groaned in disbelief, and Folger exclaimed, "Bullshit."

"Think about it, men. Sergeant Carson and I know that Leary tried to blow up an American track with a hand grenade. We didn't say anything, but we knew. Hell, we all know. No one pushed it." He paused. "Hell, I don't know why none of us mentioned it or did anything about it. It could have been serious. I mean, we thought about it. We talked about it, but what the hell do we do about it? We can't come up with anything. Maybe that's because we're all a little like him now, too. Or, maybe he's just the point man on everything we all do. I hope not. But, that's where the danger lies. He's landing at a hospital somewhere as we speak, a place where they may mistreat him. Mistreat him, hell, cross him, or just do or say something he doesn't agree with—he might blow them away."

"Maybe the captain should call ahead and tell them to treat him gently," Marlin blurted out. Then they all laughed at the ridiculousness of the thought.

As they were having this conversation, Leary's chopper set down in an almost dark ARVN fort. Leary's wounded left leg was very painful and had started to stiffen up. He had had trouble sitting in the chopper, but toughed it out. The chopper was a gun ship and did not carry stretchers. The powerful turbine engine wound down as he thanked the crew for coming in after him. He could see the other chopper in front of him winding down too. Leary squinted angrily at the reporter in the dim light as he got out of the first chopper, dragging his camera equipment with him. He had a sudden impulse to attack the reporter.

The door gunner standing next to him sensed it. He gently put his hand on Leary's shoulder and said, "You're welcome, Sergeant. The hospital, such as it is, is that way." He pointed to a tent barely visible in the fading sunlight about fifty meters east, just off the landing pad. "Let him go, Sarge. That reporter, someday, somewhere, he'll get his."

Damn guy can read my mind, Leary thought as he hobbled towards the medical tent. He dragged his leg, rather than walking on it. His web gear was still on, his belt was open, his helmet was on his head, and his rifle was in his left hand as he opened the tent flap and entered the medical tent. When his eyes adjusted to the bright light, he could see two men. One had captain's bars on his collar; the other was a specialist fourth class. *A doctor and a medic*, he concluded. They were talking and, as he got closer, the doctor didn't acknowledge his presence. He stopped a polite distance away from the two men, waiting to be recognized. The doctor was complaining to the medic about the new policy of having a doctor go out on all future large missions. *Don't let it bother you*, Leary told himself. *You're only here to have the metal taken out, get sewn up, and get back—nothing else.*

He stood there for an unbearable thirty seconds, his rage building. The doctor still did not look at him but kept turned toward the medic. *Complaining away. At least the medic is getting embarrassed at this doctor's rudeness.* The medic nodded repeatedly toward Leary, but the doctor kept going on about how stupid it was to go to all that schooling "just to be wasted in some damn fool battle somewhere."

Cool, Leary told himself, *be cool. It don't mean nothin' to me. He'll get to me. He thinks his life is worth more than that of my friends and mine, but I don't care.* He believed he was going to be able to handle it, too, when the doctor lit his short fuse.

Finally, the doctor turned toward Leary and, in a surly manner, asked, "What's your problem, soldier?"

Leary turned his left buttock toward the doctor and said in his best voice, "Here, sir." He pointed to the wound with his left hand.

Derisively, the doctor asked, "And which way were you going when you got hit?"

That does it. For him to insinuate that I was running away from the fight, this chicken-livered REMF. He lost all awareness. The next thing he could remember was the medic behind him trying to pull him off the doctor. He had a choke-hold on the doctor and, when he let go, there were red finger marks on the man's thin white neck.

Easily shrugging the medic off, Leary said calmly, "I'm okay now. I don't think I'm going to hurt him now." He stepped back a pace. It scared him a little, not because he had attacked the doctor, but because he still felt justified in doing it. He had used his right hand on the doctor's neck and was now holding his rifle in his left hand. *Christ, if I'd been farther away, I might have shot him.*

"Did you see that? He tried to choke me. He tried to kill me. I want him up on charges. You're my witness."

"No, sir, I didn't see him choke you. I was behind him. I don't believe he was trying to kill you either, sir, because he did not shoot you. I think he might have stumbled, what with his bad leg and all. He must have grabbed you trying to stay on his feet."

Leary hadn't moved. His eyes were open, but the doctor realized that he wasn't seeing. He had a blank look in his eyes. *Hell,* the doctor chastised himself, *who am I to say such things to this man? This man is my patient. I am a doctor and I've forgotten everything I spent years and thousands of dollars learning. It's the war. I've only been here a few months, and it's already changed me for the worse.* As he continued to look into Leary's blank eyes, he thought, *And look what it's done to this kid. He's almost shell-shocked. He has the thousand-yard stare.*

So the doctor relaxed and looked carefully, professionally, and compassionately at Leary's wound. "The metal must be removed. It's a touchy place where the shrapnel is, a lot of nerves in that area. Without proper equipment and staff, the operation could be a disaster for you. You need to go to a hospital with an operating room." Then he cleaned it, packed it, and had the medic take Leary to the chopper pilot's tent to sleep.

The tent was about thirty feet long and twenty feet wide and smelled of army canvas. Ten folding cots with mosquito netting were set up in two neat and evenly spaced rows. The medic told him to pick an empty cot as he held the flap open and allowed Leary to limp through. The doctor had asked if he wanted something for the pain, but he had refused, not wanting to cloud his senses or judgment. As he passed down the row between the cots, he saw one pilot lying on the second cot and two other pilots sitting on the first cot, facing the prone pilot. They were talking quietly, and they looked up and nodded a greeting as Leary passed them. He went to the fifth cot in the opposite corner, put his gear on the floor, and painfully eased himself onto the empty cot, leaving his clothes and boots on. As he lay down on the cot, he brought his rifle with him. He felt them silently watching him but did not look at them. When at last settled, he was on his back and had his rifle next to him on his right side, pointing toward the center of the tent. He figured he could best cover the tent opening from this position. He could not have had his head in the center of the tent. He felt them staring, but he ignored them.

He closed his eyes and tried to deal with the pain that now continuously burned and throbbed in his left hip and thigh. After a few minutes, the pilots resumed their quiet conversation. Leary tried not to listen. He told himself that he didn't care and couldn't think of anything they might have to talk about that would interest him. The throbbing became acute. He found he could keep time with it, each throb a second, sixty seconds a minute, and so on. He tried counting them, realizing that they were in time with his pulse, that his heart was beating sixty times a minute. *Handy*, he told himself, *don't need my trusty Timex. Just need to keep count.* He counted for a long time.

It continued relentlessly, ten minutes, thirty minutes; the pain was always there, steady and countable. Finally, he quit counting and thought he was asleep but was fully conscious when he heard someone approaching the tent. Leary turned his head, opening his eyes just as his first sergeant came in through the flaps. Top greeted the pilots while he adjusted his vision to the dim glow from the single low-wattage light bulb tied to one of the wooden posts that supported the tent. Somewhere off in the distance, the hum of a diesel generator could be heard. Since the dim light was tied on the second post of four, closest to the front, Leary's end of the tent was the darkest. He could see Top searching, straining his eyes to look for him.

One of the chopper pilots helped him out and said, "He's lying in the back, Top Sergeant."

Then Leary heard Top's powerful but quiet voice say, "Leary?"

"Over here, Top." The gravel and strangeness in Leary's own voice shocked him. Top walked steadily and unhurriedly between the cots toward Leary. When he got to the cot next to Leary's, he pushed up the mosquito netting, folding it back on itself, and sat down. He bent forward, letting his huge sleeved arms rest on his tree-trunk-sized thighs, and clasped his hands in an almost prayerful manner.

"Top, what are you doing here?" Leary paused a second. "Wherever 'here' is."

Top chuckled, "I came to see you. I heard you were coming in. I've been here all day. Flew in this morning. You okay?"

"Yeah, Top, I'm fine. Light wound. Helicopter got me."

Top nodded. "Too bad about that new boy. Jenkins, wasn't it?"

"Yeah, Jenkins, poor kid, didn't have a chance. I tried to keep him alive, Top. Just couldn't get it done."

"I know; heard how you stayed the day when you could've gotten out. Also, heard about the reporter and the doctor in the field."

"Heard anything about the doctor here, Top?"

Top smiled. "No, I asked him about you, but he didn't say anything. Well, not much anyway, except that you were pretty touchy. Said that he'd have felt better if you'd taken some painkiller. Did you manhandle him too?"

"Some, Top, but not too bad. I don't remember who I was before, but I know that who I am now is a little scary. I can go off on anyone who isn't one of us. I don't consider these support people as any of us anymore, even though they wear the same uniform. I just don't seem to be able to do anything but react with violence."

"Son, you are doing what survival calls for you to do. You react immediately, without thinking. What you've been through calls for it." Leary didn't move. He knew there was more. "I've seen it before. I've been there. What we have to do, Leary, is try and give you some frame of mind that can get you out of the jungle, long enough to survive the hospital you're going to." He paused again to let his words sink in. "You are going to see incompetence, rudeness, and lack of concern from people you no longer respect. On the other hand, you'll see a great organization, one that in spite of its faults will take care of you and help you. There are some great men and women over here, doing nothing but taking care of hundreds of wounded and dying American men. I would like you to remember that. Try and dig back into yourself for the old Leary. The bright young man I promoted to sergeant. Find that kind and patient young man who understood the way humans are and worked with them. Find that man who hadn't killed. Remember him. Be him for the time it takes to heal."

"I hear you, Top, and I'll try, but that fellow seems to be a long way off. I can sort of remember who he was, but I feel so old now. And there's a fog in my mind between who I am and who I used to be. My brain barely acknowledges that another me once existed. I can't find the desire to be him anymore. It's like I don't dare believe in the things he believed in. I can't get it out of my mind that these support people are, at some level, our enemies too."

"Look, son, I know who you are, what kind of a soldier you are, and I'm proud of you, all of you. But every time you men come back, I see the change in you. You're all harder, tougher, more prone to violence. I do my best to keep our support people doing their jobs, while leaving you 'jungle-pumpers' alone. I give them talks on it. I tell them to treat you all with the utmost gentleness." They both laughed a little, but not much. "But it gets worse and worse. Marlin's punching the cook and willing to eat C-rations. True, the hot chow isn't the best, but it's got to be better than the rations. Here's the thing. I have been a first sergeant for six years. My job is to see that you men in the field are taken care of. See that you get mail. See that you get resupplied, dusted off to the hospital, checked on at the hospital, and such. That's why I flew into this South Vietnamese camp. Usually, I can handle everything from base camp, but on this operation all supplies, choppers, and such are coming out of here. What doesn't come out of here comes directly from Saigon, but I direct it from here. This is the best place to take care of you men, so here I am. I just want you to know that we—no, I—will keep track of you. I'll see that you get what you need. Not always what you want, but always what you need. You're a tough man, Leary, too tough, too young, but I'm a tough old man and I'm backing you up. Help me when you can, son. Do not kill anyone on your trip to the hospital. Remember, they may not be what you think they should be, but they are not the enemy."

"I'll do my best, Top, but God help me I'm having trouble lately deciding just who the enemy is."

"Keep it simple. The enemy is not the man or woman wearing an American uniform."

They both laughed. "I got it, Top. Thanks." Then the first sergeant told him that a chopper pilot would come get him in the morning and take him to the hospital. When Top left, Leary felt a pain of loneliness far worse than that of his wounds.

When morning came, Leary was in a foul mood. All of Top's good advice had been used up during the night. The tent eventually filled up, and several of the pilots spent the night pouring down booze and trying to encourage a scared new pilot who did not want to fly anymore. Leary had all he could do, as the night progressed, not to get up and beat on the man. When morning finally came, a lieutenant-colonel came to get him. He told Leary he was his ride to the hospital at Lia Kae.

At the chopper, they argued about Leary taking his ammo and grenades with him. The lieutenant colonel argued that they were getting shot at coming in and out of the large fort and that hostile ground fire might set off his ammo and grenades. Leary flatly refused to get rid of his rifle and ammo but at last, after much arguing on both sides, he threw his two fragmentation grenades on the ground by the chopper. After a few more protests by the lieutenant-colonel and refusals on Leary's part, the lieutenant-colonel agreed to let him keep his weapon and ammo. The two men then flew to Lia Kae without incident and without another word or look exchanged between them. The other men of the chopper crew, including the copilot, ignored the confrontation between Leary and their lieutenant-colonel. From all they had been through, it seemed normal.

36

THE NINETY-THIRD EVACUATION HOSPITAL

L eary lay on his stomach in the stretcher as the helicopter strained to grab air. The lieutenant-colonel wanted to gain as much height and distance from the ARVN fort as quickly as he could. The chopper vibrated violently as he pulled all the lift he could out of it. Leary looked down over the end of his stretcher and noticed how similar the fort was to Gaip's fort; size was the only real difference. He continued watching as the rich emerald jungle around the fort and the road that passed by it diminished in size. Even though fields of fire had been cleared around the fort and massive amounts of wire had been strung, a chopper couldn't get in or out of the fort without being vulnerable to enemy fire from the jungle surrounding it. *Still,* he thought, *it's one huge fort. Large enough to have ten choppers on the ground as well as huge stacks of other cargo. Gaip could put ten of his forts in that one. From its size, it must be a full-bird colonel's fort.*

When they landed at the newly constructed runway at Lia Kae, a jeep with two men and a rack for hauling stretchers took Leary to the hospital. He felt a little foolish riding like that because, except for the pain, which was always there, he felt fine. But still, foolish or not, he was grateful for the prone position; sitting down was a real problem. The muscles in his hip were painfully stiff and he dreaded his daily bowel movement.

The jeep pulled in front of a large metal warehouse, now the hospital. It had evidently once been a large tractor or vehicle repair and parking garage but was now scrubbed clean. There were forty folding cots evenly spaced in the hospital, and ten of them had lightly wounded soldiers in them.

When the jeep stopped, the driver and stretcher-bearer tried to make Leary stay on the stretcher, but he would have no part of it.

As they protested, he got off the stretcher and hobbled through the stifling hot hospital ward, following them through the ward and into an adjoining building.

The building was about fifty feet by thirty feet and might have been a laboratory at one time. It had six cubicles down the center of the big room, and each had a table in it. At the other end were two large utility sinks and some shelving full of medical supplies.

The floor and walls were covered with white tile, and the wooden tables were painted white. The partitions separating the cubicles were also white and constructed from cotton cloth stretched over frames made from three-quarter-inch water pipe. Two doctor-nurse pairs worked busily on two wounded soldiers. Both soldiers were receiving blood through intravenous bottles hanging next to them. The place smelled of disinfectant and blood. The man closest to the door had an upper body wound—the tattered remains of his shirt lay in a bloody heap on the floor beside his table. The other man suffered from multiple leg wounds and was naked from the waist down. Blood liberally stained the doctors' and nurses' gowns.

Leary stood there for a minute taking it all in with his rifle in one hand, his web gear on but unbuckled, and his helmet hanging by its strap from the handle of his bayonet. After he stood there for sixty seconds, looking and smelling bad and feeling irritable, a nurse came out of the first cubicle, the one that held the man with the leg wounds. She was covered with blood and automatically removed her bloody gloves as she approached him. *She looks to be about twenty-five, with nice brown hair sticking out of each side of that silly-looking, sweat-soaked, green shower cap.* He found himself shocked back in time to another place, another world. *Mary's hair was like that,* he thought.

The nurse asked, "Where are you hit?"

But Leary's mind held him in another world, a world he had forgotten existed. Her soul-weary but stunning green eyes left him speechless, and he was embarrassed to be nonplussed like that. *Christ,* he thought, *I haven't been this woman-struck since I was in junior high.*

Recognizing his condition and not having time for it, she took action that she knew would bring him into reality, back to Vietnam. Harshly, she commanded, "Come on soldier, get with it. What the hell is your problem?"

It worked and he was back in Vietnam, her beauty disappearing as he retorted, "Hit in the butt by a chopper rocket."

"Okay, careful with that weapon, put it on the floor, drop your pants, and lie face down on that table." She nodded towards the table in the first empty cubicle to her right.

Shit, he thought, *she's treating me like some low-life she can order around. Easy, boy, remember what Top said, and remember she's a woman.*

He carefully laid his rifle on the table and started to drop his web gear and helmet behind him.

"Don't put that damn rifle on the table, put the goddamn thing on the floor where it belongs."

Screw her. I'm not about to lay my rifle on this floor. He slowly and defiantly unbuckled his pants, leaving his web gear on, hoping to get it over with as soon as possible. *Christ, this is embarrassing.* She didn't say a word but just stared at him, ignoring his nakedness as he undid his pants, letting them drop around his ankles. She kept staring at him. *All right, you bitch, I'll take the web gear off, but the rifle stays.* He took his web gear off, letting it fall noisily to the floor, slid himself up onto the table, next to his rifle. The cool tile felt good against his naked legs.

When he was settled, she came to the table and picked up his rifle, struggling a little with the weight of it. She then handed it to a medic whom Leary hadn't noticed before and said, "Hold his piece."

Leary started laughing. She managed a much-needed grin too at the double entendre. Then, serious and professional again, she moved around the table, stepped over his equipment and helmet, and began to examine his wound. She pulled the bandage off, pried the packing out, pushed the wound around a few times causing it to open up, and said, "I better have the doctor look at this. Why did they send you here?"

"I don't know, ma'am. This will be my third doctor. I just go where they take me."

"Yeah, I'll bet you go where they take you," she replied, her sarcastic protective barrier firmly back in place.

Just then the doctor with whom she had been working came into the cubicle. He stood next to her, frowning as he stepped over Leary's equipment on the floor. He put on a new pair of rubber gloves and bent over to get a better look at the wound. He didn't touch Leary, though. The nurse knew exactly what to show him, and did the poking and pinching while the doctor watched. They worked closely together, and no communication between them was necessary. After what seemed like an inordinate amount of time, the doctor asked, "How old is this wound?"

"Yesterday morning, sir."

"What in the hell took you so long to get here? Did you walk?"

That struck Leary as funny, but he decided the doctor wasn't in the mood, so he answered soberly. "No, sir, it just took that long to get here. Each of the other two doctors sent me further back. Both said the shrapnel needed to come out and they didn't have the people or equipment to do it."

'Well, they were right. I can't do it, either. You need to go to the Ninety-third Evacuation Hospital. You need to be operated on. That metal needs to come out. It probably has every bug in the world on it." He looked again, closer. "I can't believe it isn't more infected than it is."

Without further conversation, the nurse disinfected, repacked, and rebandaged the wound. When she was finished, she spoke to the medic and told him to get Leary on a chopper to the Ninety-third Evacuation Hospital as soon as possible. After she left, the driver told Leary to get dressed and meet him out by the jeep in a few minutes. He said he would tell the radio operator to have the first available chopper come and pick Leary up.

On the way to the airstrip, the jeep driver told Leary that a chopper was coming by with one dead and another seriously wounded man aboard and that they needed to be ready. The chopper was on its way from up north to the Ninety-third, and they were in a hurry.

The chopper landed as they sped onto the runway. Leary thought he was going to slide off the jeep stretcher. When the jeep skidded to a stop, he moved as quickly as possible to get off the jeep stretcher and onto the middle stretcher in the chopper. Dirt and rocks blew up as usual, but everyone ignored it. The door gunner helped him in, and he was barely face down on the middle stretcher when the machine started climbing. He could see that the man in the lower stretcher was dead. He had multiple face and chest wounds, and his bandages had been futile attempts to stop the bleeding. The man above him had a chest wound too, and fluid dripped into his veins from a clear plastic bag. His body twitched, and he was bleeding so much that blood ran off the end of the stretcher every time the chopper banked for a turn. Some of the blood splattered, blown up in Leary's face, but his attempts to scoot back on the stretcher were wasted. Within twenty minutes from their takeoff at Lia Kae, they set their chopper skids on the huge red cross that marked the landing pad of the Ninety-third Evacuation Hospital, thirty-five miles northeast of Saigon.

Before the chopper even set its skids on the asphalt, six stretcher-bearers were there. The chopper kept its blades turning; it was going to take off for another load as soon as these men were unloaded. Leary disembarked quickly and limped a short distance away from the idling machine. He watched the first pair of stretcher-bearers work in a practiced manner. They approached the chopper from the rear, one on each side. The bearer on Leary's side, the left, carried a folded-up stretcher to replace the occupied one they would take, and he immediately threw it toward the front of the chopper's interior, out of the way. The other man boarded the chopper, and they both grabbed their handles at the same time, pulling the stretcher with the wounded man off its shelf and out the door toward Leary. They only hesitated for a moment when the stretcher-bearer on the far side had to jump out of the helicopter onto the ground. The door gunners assisted a little, as needed. As soon as the first team had cleared the chopper and started running towards the emergency entrance, the second team unloaded the stretcher with the dead body the same way, although Leary couldn't see any need to hurry with him.

As soon as they had all cleared the machine, the pilot increased power and the machine began to lift off. When the chopper was clear and moving off, Leary began limping toward the swinging doors of the hospital. The hospital was a series of connected Quonset huts. It looked like a bunch of large tin cans cut in half down their length and then laid on the ground and fastened together. They had all been painted a light green, and air conditioning units could be seen sticking out of many of the windows. The heat on the asphalt was severe, but Leary wasn't bothered by it. He had only managed ten steps before the last team of stretcher-bearers ran out of the building and blocked his path.

"Sir," a pudgy stretcher-bearer said as he stepped in front of Leary.

Leary stopped less than two feet away from the man and asked roughly, "What?" Feeling that old irritation again. "And don't call me 'sir.'"

He could see that the other bearer, off to the side, was unfolding the stretcher they had brought with them.

"I'm sorry. No one wears rank in the bush, and we never know what rank a man is. So I just call everyone 'sir' till I find out."

Damn, these two guys are sickly white, soft looking, and overweight. Then he paused and reminded himself of Top's warning. "Okay, what do you want? That is the hospital door, right?" The bearer nodded. "Then get the hell out of my way so I can go through it."

By now, the other one had the stretcher unfolded and waited by his end of it, gripping the handles. The one in front of Leary said, "We just can't let you walk in there. You have to get on the stretcher and let us carry you in. We'll catch hell now because we let you walk this far."

Cooperate. These guys can get a worse job. They can be sent out where you're going, so don't get them in trouble. Top warned you and you said you'd do your best. So just go along with whatever they say. "Okay, I give. You got me." Without further communication, Leary wearily lay face down on the stretcher and let them, panting and puffing, carry him into the hospital. *This seems silly*, he thought, as he moved onto his good side, propping his head up on his right hand and elbow. *These people in the rear, their shit never ends.*

The reception area crowded with patients, doctors, medics, a couple of nonmedical officers, and several nonuniformed men with cameras, whom he correctly surmised must be reporters.

One of the reporters, seeing that Leary was awake, rushed over to him. When the reporter squatted down by Leary, he asked urgently, "What happened to you, soldier?"

"No big deal. One of our helicopters got me with a rocket yesterday."

At that moment a nonmedical officer—Leary could tell by the absence of the medical symbol on his collar—who had quickly followed the reporter over squatted down next to Leary too and said to the reporter, "Jim, you got to give me a minute with this soldier. Remember, we need to talk to them first, or you'll have to get out of here." The man frowned, looked disgustedly at the officer, and said, as he stood and backed up a few steps, "Good luck to you, son."

The officer, a captain with a collar insignia which Leary didn't recognize, whispered, almost too low for Leary to hear, "Look, soldier, don't tell these guys anything."

Angry again, Leary responded. "What the hell, captain? It happened, no big deal. I don't hold it against those guys."

"Don't you want a Purple Heart?"

Leary was still trying to be reasonable when he said. "Captain, I don't fight for a Purple Heart. I don't give a damn about all the medals in the whole army." *I'm getting better; I haven't once said "fuck."*

The captain nodded his head to Leary, stood up, and yelled over his shoulder, "Stretcher-bearers, take this man into the side room." The two men who had brought Leary into the emergency room picked him up without saying a word and carried him through the emergency room, down a short hall through two swinging doors, and into the connecting hut. From there, they took him into one of several small rooms in the building. Once inside the room, the man who had convinced Leary to get on the stretcher at the landing pad said as they were leaving the room, "Someone will be with you soon. Good luck."

They must be going to get me ready for surgery here. Guess one does all the talking for the other, he thought as they walked out, closing the door behind them. The place wasn't exactly soundproof and, though he could hear activity and voices coming through the walls from time to time, he felt isolated and irritated. The pain was intense. Though he sometimes forgot it for a while, especially when he was distracted, it always returned.

Ten minutes later, he was about to get up and walk out when a medic came in. He was a young specialist fourth class, very white and not a warrior type. *Probably good at what he does,* Leary assured himself, *whatever that is.*

He had a tray in his left hand covered with a large green cloth. Under the tray was a metal folding clipboard, Leary's soon-to-be medical chart. "Hi, Sergeant. I'm here to find out who you are and to sew you up."

He couldn't believe he'd heard correctly. "You're going to sew me what?"

"I was told to sew you up. You have a flesh wound, right?"

Now he struggled mightily to keep his anger under control. *Just a screwup. Top said there would be some. It can be straightened out.* "No, specialist. I came through three doctors and two hospitals over the last couple of days, just to get the metal taken out of my butt. Each doctor along the way told me that it had to be done but that he didn't have the equipment or personnel to do it. They were all three very clear that it had to come out. Any one of them could have sewn me up, but they didn't. Why? Because the damn nose-cone of that rocket is jammed up my ass, and it must come out. Surgery, they said." Narrow-eyed with focused rage, he glowered menacingly at the specialist and saw him shaking.

It was very quiet for a moment as Leary stared a hole through the man "Now, you tell me you are told to sew it up. Was it the fourth doctor who made that decision? Was it the one who glanced at me when they brought me in? The one who said, 'This man can wait a few minutes.' Is he the one who told you to just sew me up?"

"I'm sorry, it wasn't all the doctor's fault. You must have pissed off the public relations officer, and he got the doctor to go along with him. What do you want me to do?"

Leary's face was now so red with suppressed anger that it glowed brightly through his deep tan. Mesmerized, the medic watched as his lips swelled and his breathing became shallow and high up in his chest. As he struggled to focus his dark blue eyes, he said slowly, "Sew it up. I knew that you people were a bunch of squirrels—sew it up and be damn quick about it."

As the medic, his hands shaking slightly, pulled the green cloth off his tray, exposing needles, antiseptic, and bandage, he said, "I'm sorry, I really am."

He tried to keep his emotions numb, restraining the impulse toward violence, as he the medic sewed him up, took his rifle and clothes, gave him some blue cotton pajamas, and led him down the hall to a bunk. It was a hard folding army cot in a ward for the lightly wounded. He was weary and sick at heart, let down by everything he had previously valued in life and trapped by a system he had come to hate. He lay dormant in his bunk feeling totally betrayed. He didn't eat, he didn't sleep; he just lay there all afternoon and all that night. He couldn't take a shower, because the medic told him not to get the wound wet for a couple of days. He knew he was in shock and finally felt nothing but the throbbing in his hip.

When the morning sunlight shone across the ward through what was left of the windows above the air-conditioning units, using all the will he could muster, he decided he should try and eat.

He was grateful for the hospital slippers, which he could put on without having to bend over. Once he had his slippers on, he shuffled the thirty feet to the nurse's station. A tired but pleasant blonde nurse directed him to the Quonset hut containing the mess hall. Slow-moving, grubby, and foul-smelling, he kept his mind blank.

When he entered the mess hall, he noticed that a clock on the wall read seven-thirty. The lights were offensively bright in the mess area, a harsh contrast to the darker wards. There was a short line of pajama-clad patients ahead of him waiting to get their trays and food, but he was in no hurry. He had nowhere to go and didn't care any longer where he was. As he got to the table where the trays and silverware were kept, the medic who had sewn him up the previous afternoon spoke to him.

"Sergeant Leary, how are you?"

Leary turned and looked at the medic just as the moving line demanded that he step to the first server in the line. "Okay, Specialist. Not good, but okay. Why ask?"

"Well, when I treated your wound yesterday, I'd never done anything like that before."

Irritation flooded back into Leary's empty mind. *The audacity of these people. My people. They not only failed to take the shrapnel out, but also sent an inexperienced man to sew me up.* As he automatically held his tray up for the first server to put food on it, he asked again, "Why?"

"Well, I hit a bleeder when I was sewing you up, and wasn't sure I'd tied it off right."

At that moment, the server slapped scrambled eggs onto Leary's tray. He watched the water run away from the eggs and assumed they were powdered eggs. *They don't even care enough about their wounded to feed them real eggs. They send an inexperienced man in to sew me up. I should have had an operation. It's not the specialist's fault, though. He at least cared enough to find me and check on me. But the people running this place are corrupt.*

Then still watching the water run out from under the eggs, he said, almost unconsciously, "I don't want any powdered eggs."

He might have made it through the line but then the irritable cook replied, "Motherfucker, there ain't no powdered eggs in my kitchen."

Leary lost it.

If he hadn't had to run clear around the end of the serving line, if he hadn't been stiff and in slippers, which he soon lost, he might have caught the cook. The cook ran and Leary chased him back into the kitchen, around some tables, and then out a side door into the bright sunlight. He didn't know how long all of that took, but it was long enough for someone to get the military police. Outside now and pausing long enough to get his bearings and allow his sun-blinded eyes to direct him toward the fleeing cook again, he heard the familiar metallic noise an army forty-five caliber automatic makes when the slide is pulled back, chambering a round.

"Hold it, soldier. Move, and you're dead." Nothing more needed to be said.

Ten minutes later, standing in front of the colonel's desk with the two MPs standing guard behind him, he told the colonel the whole story.

"Well, Sergeant, I can appreciate your anger. Really, I can. However, I cannot let you run amuck in my hospital. We get men

like you every so often, and I'll make you the same offer I make
them. Stay and behave yourself, or go back to the jungle. The choice
is yours."

Leary didn't even have to think; the answer was clear to him.
"Give me back my rifle, serial number 926293, the rest of my gear, a
new pair of pants, and I'm gone."

And so they did. The pair of pants they gave him wasn't new
and it irritated him that they had "Lt. Linda Anderson" sewn in the
fly, but he didn't complain. He just wanted out of there. Before they
let him board a truck to the First Division staging area, they gave
him a bag of Epsom salts. Told him to find a pan somewhere, heat
some water, pour the salt in it, and soak his butt three times a day.
As he left the pharmacy, he dropped the bag of Epsom salts in a trash
barrel in the waiting area.

The man behind the pharmacy window saw him throw the bag
away and said, "Hey, what the hell are you doing?"

In answer, Leary yelled on his way out, "You want it, you dig
it out. Otherwise, all of you can go to hell. You're all a bunch of
motherfuckers, and you know it."

He stood up in the front of the truck all the way to the tent city
north of Saigon. It was a place that had a tent for everything. The
truck stopped in front of a gate with a small guard tent. The driver
told him to check in at the gate, where they would assign him a cot
and arrange transportation for him back to his unit. Behind the guard
gate was a huge fenced-in area with rows and rows of empty tents.
The place hadn't been there when their battalion had camped there
five months ago.

Leary stood in the road for a minute, just looking at the place.
*Looks like a prisoner of war camp, a compound. We're really doing well
over here; we have to put ourselves in compounds to be safe. Yeah, this
war is working. Feels good, though, to have my rifle in my hands again.
I guess I'm either going to have to die here or not get wounded again. I
damn sure can't stay in that hospital.*

A guard at the gate spoke up and told Leary that they would
take care of him in the tent just inside the gate. The sergeant first
class sitting inside the tent was polite as he took Leary's name and
unit and then said, "It might take a couple of days to get you a ride
back. But, in the meantime, take any cot you like. We got a hundred
empty ones. But choose the one you want, Sergeant, because we'll
be getting at least seventy-five fresh soldiers from the States this
afternoon. If you want a shower, there's one in the tent back of the
sleeping area, next to the latrines."

Leary found a corner cot in one of the huge middle tents and lay
down on his side for a much-needed nap. His leg was feeling better
all the time. The wound was draining a little, spotting his pants, but
he figured it was well on its way to recovery. *Chasing cooks must've
been good for it*, he thought as he rested carefully in the bunk, his rifle
at his right side. In a few minutes, he was asleep.

The trucks pulling up woke him, but he only moved enough to
look at his watch. It was 1300 hours and he hadn't eaten since day
before yesterday, but he still had a can of beans and franks in his
pack. They hadn't touched his equipment. Beans and franks were a
cherished food item on the C-ration menu. *I'll eat it in a minute*, he
thought, as he dozed back off. Fifteen minutes later, he looked up
to see troops coming into the tent carrying their duffel bags, their
clothes all clean and new. They were of all ages, all enlisted ranks
up to staff sergeant, and damn if they all didn't have jungle fatigues
and jungle boots. He silently cursed the army for not issuing his
unit jungle clothes as he forced himself into a one-cheeked sitting
position on his cot. Once upright, he started fishing in his pack for
the can of beans and franks. *Damn*, he thought, *sitting isn't good, but
it's not bad either*.

After finding the can, he blew the dust off the top and pulled his
dog tags out of his shirt. Fastened to the dog tags through a hole in
the chain was his P-38 can-opener. One came with every box of C-
rations. As he unfolded the can-opener and started to open the can,
a couple of pale white sergeants came down the aisle to claim their
cots. A sergeant, the same rank as Leary but about thirty years old,
threw his equipment on the cot next to Leary's, and a staff sergeant,
a couple of years older, took the cot directly across the aisle from
him.

Leary was still opening his beans and franks when the two
sergeants came over and introduced themselves. "Hi, Sergeant, I'm
Johnson," said the one who was the same rank as Leary, as he stuck
his hand out for Leary to shake. Leary stopped opening the can and
set it down on the floor, methodically, but friendly.

"Hello, Sergeant, good to meet you," Leary said as they shook
hands.

Then he turned to the other sergeant. The sergeant grabbed
Leary's hand firmly and said, "Hi, I'm Sergeant Cambel."

Leary said, "Cambel, huh? A good name. I knew a good platoon
sergeant by that name."

"Probably not related, there are a lot of us Cambels out there. No relation to the soup people either. Different spelling, too," he laughed.

"We heard from the sergeant at the check-in tent that you've been over here awhile. He said you were coming back from being wounded and are going back out as soon as they can get you a ride to your base camp," Johnson said.

"Yeah, no big deal. It's a way of life over here. You men have any idea where you're going to be assigned?"

"The Twenty-second," Johnson said. "Guess they need a lot of replacements. The sergeant at the tent said they were nearly wiped out?" It was more of a question than a statement.

"From a battalion down to a platoon in a short half-hour."

"No shit," Johnson said. "I hope it isn't a bad-luck outfit. I had plans on getting back home when our thirteen months are over."

"I'm sure you will." *No use scaring them with my real thoughts.* "What kind of an outfit it will be is up to you."

"I, we, would like to know what it's all about over here, really about. I suggest we divide up details, get them done, and then go over to the NCO tent, drink some beer and, hopefully, have you tell us."

"Sure, Sergeant Johnson, with a minor change. I'm going over to the NCO tent as soon as I eat. As to the details, you men do what you want with those. I don't mean to be a shithead, but I'm not taking charge of, or doing, any details. I'm going to drink beer every day until they get me a ride up to my base camp. Then, just as soon as I can, I'm going to get a ride back to my unit in the jungle. That's what I'm doing. You men will no doubt be here awhile to give you time to get used to the climate. So, if you want, you can join me when your chores are done, because that's where I'll be." They were a little taken aback by Leary's attitude, but he just marked it down to having a stateside mentality. He knew that in a month, if they were still alive and well, they would have adopted his attitude.

Drink beer was exactly what Leary did every day for the three days it took him to get a ride. Even though he was never able to get into the tent shower, he did enjoy washing up at the sink. Every day at 1100 hours, he went to the NCO tent. Around 1300 hours, the two sergeants joined him. By then he was already slightly lit with alcohol, and the three of them drank until it closed at 2200 hours. It was hot in the tent, no air- conditioning, but Leary loved it. The beer wasn't very cold but they drank it enthusiastically, without complaint. Leary told them everything he knew and believed about Vietnam. The two sergeants listened eagerly.

Two days later, he arrived at base camp. He was pleased to find that the cooks and other REMFs were truly glad to see him. He didn't know why, but he was glad to see them, too. *Strange*, he thought, as he flew out in a gun ship to rejoin the unit. The battalions had finished their sweep, had set up a huge perimeter, and were holding it. They were to hold the area until the new division, which was presently unloading in Saigon, came to take it over. It would be their new home. Soon after touching down in the center of the perimeter, Leary was happily back with his platoon. Everyone was still alive and unwounded. They talked for hours and, once Leary had the complete picture about the situation there in the highlands, he thought, *Poor bastards coming to this place, they think we've made it safe for them. They're in for a horrible surprise.*

37

OPERATION JOKE

An hour after rejoining his company in the field, Leary sat with Folger at their assigned places in the perimeter. This was their division's final objective. They had finished their mission, sweeping the jungle from west to east and ending up in this large natural clearing, the one chosen for the new Hawaii division's base camp.

The clearing was covered with sparse grass and sand. The entire circle was surrounded by jungle except for a three-hundred-meter opening northwest of the perimeter. The opening went down across a small river and into a huge rice paddy that was at least an additional three hundred meters wide. The water in the paddy ran from east to west, fed by the same small river that supplied the rice paddy they had landed in when they began this operation. The paddy maintained its width as it ran west for nearly a mile before being funneled by the jungle down into a small river again. The village, which a paddy of this size normally supported, was not there. Only one dilapidated hooch remained, and it was close to the paddy, just outside their perimeter.

Leary and Folger had a lot of catching up to do and, apparently, at least a couple of days to do it, so they talked nonstop. The division, which would make this place their base camp, would arrive the day after tomorrow.

Leary told Folger what had happened since the night he had been med-evaced out. Folger, in turn, explained that they had encountered booby-traps and occasional sniper fire, had destroyed many freshly deserted enemy dwellings and equipment, and had been strafed by their own choppers two more times since Leary had left them. Luckily, skillfully, or for whatever reasons, they had survived it all without any more losses to the company. Unfortunately, other companies had suffered casualties of varying degrees and for various reasons almost every day during the mission. Folger idly poked his bayonet in the remains of a fire built that morning. It was 1100 hours.

"So, this is the place those Hawaii boys are going to make their home?"

"Yeah, it won't be bad, for a tent-pitching. This area is flat and a little higher than the creek and paddies down in the opening." Folger nodded in the direction about which he was talking. His automatic rifle was resting on its bipod pointing toward the jungle a hundred and fifty meters to their front.

"Nice running water, green valley to look over, some large trees in the jungle on the other side of the paddy. Looks like about a thousand meters from here."

"One hell of a rifle shot, for sure. Especially with what they have." Folger thought for a minute, and then gestured toward his automatic rifle on the ground. "Us, too. I mean I wouldn't trade any of our weapons for any of theirs, except maybe their Russian RPG-7—that is one hell of a bazooka. Fortunately, they don't seem to have many of them, though, just like we can't seem to get any of our new bazookas, those new LAW rocket launchers. But their rifles, shit, what a bunch of junk. The AK isn't bad, but some of that other junk they have isn't good enough to shoot chickens with."

" 'Chickens,' Folger, where in the hell did that come from? You must need fresh food. But you're right, the AK is the best thing they've got and, as far as those Chicom bolt-action rifles and the old American carbines some of them carry, well, they just aren't the same quality as our 14s. Of course, give them time. The Russians and Chinese will have the NVA well supplied within the next couple of years."

"Them and the South Vietnamese Army." They both broke out in laughter at the sad truth of it.

"You think this place is safe for these new guys? I mean, they came over as a complete unit. They got that going for them. Having trained together in the past means not having to get used to working together and staying alive at the same time. Better off than those poor guys I met in Saigon. They're being sent out to refill the Twenty-second, a bad-luck unit to start with, and they don't even know each other. So these Hawaii guys have the together thing going for them. That and you guys running the gooks off for a while. Maybe, just maybe, they'll get some time to get used to this place before it starts."

Folger laughed again. "Shit, Leary, I thought I made it clear. They're all around us." He made a sweeping motion with his bayonet. "This morning, before you got here, I was getting fire from the damn jungle right in front of us. In fact, they quit just before you came. True, they aren't hitting much. Sort of quickly fire off a carbine round and then split."

"What've you guys been doing about it?"

"At first we fired back, but then gave it up as a waste of good ammo. No one has been hit yet, and they won't let us leave this perimeter to hunt them, so we just sit and wait." Folger paused to dig around in the ashes. "As far as the sweep goes, it was worthless. The gooks aren't in much worse shape now than if we hadn't come through at all. We did damn little damage to them. They just harassed us, killed a few, and we got a few of them, but mainly they spread out in front of us and probably came back in right behind us. If they didn't, they sure could have. We just kind of passed through. They knew they didn't have to bother with us. Just get out of our way and come back when we're gone. As usual, we never spent any time looking for their forts. We just walked through, dealt with what was in our way, and then kept on going—till we got here. This whole sweep thing is just a word, no real substance to it, another empty and meaningless word. What did we sweep? Sweeping to me has always meant cleaning up, pushing something in front of the broom. Pushing it into a pile and then getting rid of it. That didn't happen here."

"So, those poor green fools will be trucking up here, thinking that we've cleaned the area out for them," Leary paused for breath, "and it's not true."

"I don't see how it could be—we never had a major engagement. We killed very few of them. I don't know how many, but damn few. And there are lots of them here. That's for sure. I tell you, Leary, in just the area we walked through to get here, I saw facilities that would hold thousands of men. Deserted, of course. But fresh stuff, like that trench you got wounded checking out. They refused to engage us or let us engage them."

"Makes sense. Their information is better than ours, at least yours and mine. They no doubt know that we're seasoned troops and that the new men coming in aren't. Why fight us? We'll soon be gone, and they can have a field day with the new guys. Hell, their snipers are probably only trainees." They laughed uproariously at the thought.

"Yeah, that must be it. Probably letting the young and inexperienced get used to shooting at live targets. Give them the old rifles and let them practice sneaking up and taking potshots at us, don't care if they hit anyone. Waiting for easier game."

"I did hear back at base camp where they listen to the radio all day that Hanoi Hannah, the Tokyo Rose of the North Vietnamese, has been talking about us on the radio. This is the second time she's mentioned our unit by name, said that we'd done a lot of harm to them. She vowed to get us."

"Well, the blow-hard bitch had better get with it. She sure missed a good chance the last couple weeks. But as far as this operation goes, Leary, the 'Big and the Bad' should be renamed 'Operation Joke.' Have those new guys got a surprise waiting for them."

Folger had just finished speaking when a bullet whizzed over their heads, followed by the distant sound of a thirty-caliber carbine. Leary dove from sitting to flat on the ground facing the jungle ahead. Folger had moved to the prone position just before the sound reached them. He already lay on his side, propping his head up with his bent left arm and resting his left cheek in the palm of his hand. He did not move. "See what I mean, Leary? Guy's a lousy shot. He just likes to screw with us. He hasn't hit one damn thing all morning. Trainee or no trainee, that's some pretty poor shooting and they should replace him."

Leary still faced the jungle and was irritated at getting dust on his newly washed fatigue shirt and ladies' trousers as he said, "Hell, he probably needs glasses. Come to think of it, I haven't seen one pair of glasses on any of these gooks, nor have we ever found any glasses on the dead ones. Can't tell me some of these boys aren't a little nearsighted. What if they lost the war just because they didn't have glasses? Can't see, damn sure can't hit anything."

"Damn, if you aren't on to something." Folger's voice was mixed with serious revelation and humorous irony, as he said, "That explains a lot of their poor shooting. I mean, I know some of our boys are bad shots, but about half of our platoon has glasses. Dark glasses for the day and clear for night, but all of them are prescription. All of them brought to 20/20 for good seeing and shootin.' "

"Hell, I'm a little nearsighted at times myself, or have been in the past."

"No shit, you, Leary? We've had you on point all this time and you need glasses. Where in the hell are they?"

Leary chuckled. "Hold on a minute, Folger, I said 'a little' and 'used to be.' "

"What is a little? Some miracle cured you?"

"A little is that I never needed them to pass my driver's test, and the cure is I don't need 'em anymore."

"I don't remember you ever wearing glasses."

"You know those sunglasses I lost a couple months ago? You and Hart were holding me upside down in that well? Remember, they fired at us and Hart dropped one of my legs? I was filling canteens, if you recall, and the well was small and too deep to reach the water without going down into it. We needed the water, and you two were holding my feet so that I wouldn't fall head first into it."

"I do remember now. That's the only time you ever threatened me. I'm still a little pissed about that."

"Sorry about that. It was a reflex. I was afraid that if you dropped the other leg, I'd drown upside down in the well. It wasn't a large enough hole for me to turn over in. Well, that's when the glasses came off and sank in the well. At first after losing them, I was a little scared. I was afraid I wouldn't be able to see well enough without them." The look on Folger's face was doubtful. "Rest easy. They were just a crutch and I can see better now than I ever could."

"I guess so. We've made it this far and I didn't notice. You've made some damn good long shots. But, still, well, what about your clear glasses? Didn't you have a pair of them too? Army gives a man two pair."

"Yeah, I had a clear pair, but to tell the truth, I lost them on the boat over here. Just couldn't find them one day. Don't know what happened to 'em, but not to worry, my friend. I do see fine and I am sorry about scaring you like that."

"Shit, I'm not scared about it, if you can't see 'em, I damn sure can. I just can't believe I didn't notice it. That's all."

Then they heard the planes, and both maneuvered their bodies so that they could look for them. They soon spotted them shining in the sun coming out of the east. Folger couldn't resist asking, "You do see those three planes, don't you, Leary?"

"You damn right I do, Folger. Prop jobs coming right at us."

"Good, I feel better now. Wonder what they're up to?"

They were Sky Raider ground support fighters, and their first pass over the clearing was so low that the men could clearly see the faces of the three pilots. The pilot in the center, lead plane was an American, and the other two pilots, slightly behind and one on each wing, were clearly Vietnamese.

They made their first run from east to west. The noise was horrendous, and they flew so low that they looked like they would fly right into the jungle. The first pass was a strafing run and the men watched as twenty-millimeter cannons exploded into the ground, starting a short fifty meters in front of the western part of their perimeter and on into the jungle.

The men in the perimeter cheered and yelled as they watched the planes pull up and make a long sweeping turn southeast, coming around for another pass. The three planes stayed in formation as they completed the circle around the perimeter and lined themselves up for another run.

About a half-mile south of Leary and Folger's position, where the road came into the circle, there were three armored personnel carriers, or tracks. As the planes came over for their second run, a bombing run this time, the southernmost plane dropped its bombs short, which landed on and among the tracks on the south end of the perimeter. The other two planes, the American and the Vietnamese pilot on his right, dropped their bombs into the jungle west of the perimeter. The shock from the noise and concussion kept the men's heads buried in the sand as the planes made another circle, setting themselves up for a third pass. When Leary and Folger pulled their heads out of the sand, they saw what they had feared. Two of the tracks had been blown into unrecognizable hunks of burning metal. There were burning pieces of men and metal raining down on everyone throughout the perimeter. Some of the men close to the tracks were killed and wounded by the falling and flying debris.

The three planes came in for a third pass. Still in perfect formation, they approached the perimeter. The men on the ground did not communicate—they didn't need to. They grabbed their weapons and rolled over onto their backs, waiting for the Vietnamese pilot who had dropped his bombs short.

As the three planes made their approach to the perimeter, they flew low and smoothly at first. The men on the ground waited patiently, their weapons tracking the Vietnamese plane. Then, all of a sudden, about a half-mile before reaching the perimeter, the planes began to shudder. They shook and vibrated in the air as the engines were pushed to full emergency power. "They're trying to get away," someone screamed. The pilots had either seen what was waiting for them or, more likely, the ground-to-air coordinator had warned them off. Much to the disappointment of the men on the ground, the planes managed to get enough altitude and distance away from the perimeter so that no one had a chance to shoot at the Vietnamese pilot. Some men fired anyway, knowing that they'd never hit him, but trying to feel better.

Five minutes later, Carson came by. "How many did that gook get, Sergeant Carson?" Folger asked.

"I hear twelve dead. More wounded. Any of our people hit?"

"No," Leary said, "too far away. Small pieces, like rain, though."

"Thank God for that. Choppers are on the way. Headquarters says it was an accident, wants us all to try and put it behind us."

Leary remained silent, but Folger couldn't. "Not possible, Sarge, just not possible. Someone should tell headquarters that we just can't forget something like that. We don't trust those South gooks anymore than we do the North gooks, and this is just another example of how right we are. Hell, I take that back, we do trust the North gooks; we know they're out to kill us. But those gooks from the South, they're supposed to be on our side. I got a grudging respect for old 'Charlie Cong,' but I got nothing but bullets for these southern boys, and I don't have any intention of changing it."

"What about you, Sergeant Leary? What do you have to say?"

"Nothing, Sergeant, I've said it so much, I just don't feel like repeating worthless statements anymore. I don't even like our own people in the rear. I couldn't even get along at the hospital. I'll tell you this much, though, like Folger, I'll let my rifle do my talking for me. If headquarters doesn't want us to shoot any of these so-called 'friendly forces,' they better keep 'em away from us." He paused for a minute to look Carson in the eye. "It's just that simple; nothing more to say."

"Okay, I hear you, men. I'm getting the same answer right down the line. I feel the same way." He paused to consider his next words. "But I'm a career soldier and I was told to tell you men, so I did. See you later."

"Later, Sarge."

"See ya, Platoon Sergeant."

An hour later, after the choppers had come in to haul off the wounded and dead, they rotated the perimeter. Like turning a huge wheel.

Where the Second Platoon had been responsible for defending the west part of the wheel, they were now responsible for the northeast part. A needless move, the men thought. They could see no strategic importance to it and saw it as just another stupid order from bored minds. Tooley commented, "It was so those men in the unit hit by the Vietnamese bombs who were not wounded or killed would not have to occupy the area where the blood of their friends stained the ground."

When night approached, Leary and Folger were about twenty meters from Patkins and Marlin. There was a machine gun nest on each side of them. The interval for all groups on the line was twenty meters. The third squad was tied in with the machine gun on their left, as was the Third Platoon with the machine gun on their right. Tooley, Carson, and Nash were about thirty meters to the rear, toward the center of the perimeter. About twenty meters behind the platoon CP was the company CP. And behind the company CP was the battalion CP, which was in the hub of the defensive perimeter. The battalion executive officer was the man in charge. He was a major by the name of Miles and, when the battalion was in the field, he spent the night at the battalion CP. The men rarely saw him except at a distance and, on the whole, they didn't believe he was with them by choice. He would, whenever possible, fly in on the colonel's chopper, spend the night, and fly back out soon after first light.

There wasn't any cover for any of the men on this perimeter but most of them had a large open space in front of them so they could see and fire on the enemy before he could get close. Clear fields of fire were everywhere in the clearing except in front of the second squad's new position. The circle had rotated east once again. This last rotation had placed the second squad a meager fifty meters from an old cornfield. Leary, Folger, Patkins, and Marlin discussed the cornfield just as the sun was setting brilliantly at their backs.

"Damn, Patkins, I wish we'd had time to destroy that cornfield. It isn't much, skinny shoots of dried corn but, still, when it gets dark they could sneak up and get real close," Leary said.

All three of the men lay flat on the ground. Folger and Marlin were on the outside on their sides, and Leary and Patkins were on their stomachs—all looking out to their front. "Yeah," Patkins said, "the moon has been getting darker and darker every night, and the shadow cast by the old cornfield, especially with the jungle behind it, will probably make it impossible to see into it tonight."

"No doubt, and that means the little gooks who are all around us will probably be able to get in grenade range before we see 'em."

"I have the claymores out, one trigger for you and Folger and one for Marlin and me. If we see anything at all, we'll give 'em a five-hundred-pellet blast." It was quiet for a few minutes, all four of them thinking about the situation, looking at it, soaking it all in. "Either way, we'll have to be extra alert. If we can make it through the night, we can stomp the corn down tomorrow. Too bad they moved us so late tonight. It was our third rotation since the bombing and damn sure a late one."

"Damn," Leary said, "we don't dare go out there now. The shadows are already forming. One of our own people might shoot us. Looks like we ride it out till morning."

"It's always some damn thing," Folger said. "They not only rotated us late, but they shoved the whole circle over. I'm for getting away from the blood and all, but not at the expense of our lives. Hell, we live with blood on us and around us. Whoever made the decision to keep moving away from the blood must not be one of us. Speaking of blood, how you doing, Leary? Any pain? I see you have bloody pants. They give you any medicine?"

"Gets better every day. They did give me some shit to soak my ass in, but I threw it away."

It was dark so they quit talking and spread apart. Patkins and Marlin went back to their position twenty meters to the south. They took turns staying awake, and it wasn't until Patkins and Folger were on guard that it happened. It was unbelievable, even for these men.

38

A Prayer

The sun rose slowly, illuminating the shadowed cornfield area. As the darkness receded through the cornfield and into the jungle behind it, a wide path around the perimeter was visible. Four helmets lay where they had fallen. Seven grenades were strewn about the path, but no men. In the center of this path was an ominous Chinese antipersonnel mine still looking as if it would explode at any moment. Even though probably out of range, the platoon, company, and battalion command posts had moved out of its lethal path.

At first light, Leary and Patkins inspected the Chinese mine and, by 0900 hours, most of the men in the First Division had seen it.

An hour later, while heating water for coffee and hot chocolate, the men of the second squad, joined by Tooley and Carson, discussed what had happened.

"Damn, that was close," Patkins said. Though shaking in his ever-thinner body, he wasn't afraid. The old fearful Patkins was long gone.

"Shit," Marlin said, "I waited for hours. Thinking every minute that damn thing was going to explode. Especially before we rolled over. I just knew it would make Swiss cheese out of me any second. I hope I never have to wait for death like that again. It seemed for-goddamn-ever."

Carson and Tooley were quiet, just listening. "Well, if you hadn't thrown that grenade, Patkins, we'd all be in body bags now," Folger added.

"Life is a fragile thing," Leary reflected. "Who would've guessed that one piece of shrapnel, out of the thousands that missed, just one piece, would cut one of the two wires going to that Chinese mine. I mean, think about it. And that was the one pointing right at us, too.

The other one, the one that went off, was tilted too much toward the ground, and the last pellets hit about a meter from Folger and me."

"Yeah, well, the pellets hit about two meters from Marlin and me. But that other one would have done us all in."

"I think it was a good thing we decided not to shoot at it or throw any more grenades. One bullet through the front and into that blasting cap could've set it off or even a piece of shrapnel from another grenade," Leary said.

"I almost tried shooting low, maybe knock one of the legs out from under it to topple it over, but decided against it, with the poor light and all. Finally, especially after we'd rolled away, I decided it was just too risky. Still, it was the shits waiting all night for it to go off," Folger said.

"Yeah, that was torture." Patkins nodded toward Marlin. "I even thought they were doing it on purpose. Making us sweat it out. They must have pulled that trigger a million times during the night, trying to get it to go off. They probably tried the trigger from the other one. Must have screwed with their minds, too."

"What we humans do, trying to kill each other," Tooley said. "But you men did the right thing. That's why we can all enjoy the coffee this morning."

"I wonder if your grenade got one of those gooks?" Marlin said. "I'd like to think so." No one commented. "Even if it didn't, they at least had a bad night too." Nervous laughter broke out at the thought.

"Well, there won't be any cornfield tonight. Know anyone who has a machete?" Leary asked.

"No need," Tooley said. "The new campers will be here about noon and we'll fly out of here."

"We going back to base camp, Lieutenant?" Marlin asked.

"No, not right away. We'll go into a place called the Lo Bo Woods, which is just south of where we landed that first time we went to the C." Everyone groaned, except Carson, who already knew. "Shouldn't be there but a couple of days at the most. Battalion thinks they have a 'hot tip' about a small special intelligence unit working in that area."

Marlin sighed and Folger said, "Hot, my ass. They haven't had a real tip since we've been here. In fact, we should always go where they say the gooks aren't. That's the place they'll be. Of course, I keep forgetting they really don't want to go where we know they are. So it makes sense."

"Well," Tooley said, "they want us to try and take some prisoners for interrogation. I told them if they wanted any live enemy they should send someone else. They didn't think that was funny. I got my ass chewed out over that statement."

"Screw prisoners," Marlin said. "It ain't what we're about."

"Well, since there won't be anyone there, we shouldn't have to worry about taking any of 'em alive," Carson said.

"But just in case, try and take one alive, you know, if you can do it without any risk," Tooley said.

"No risk, hell," Folger said, "letting any of the little bastards live is a risk."

"Well, try if you can," Carson added and, with that, he and Tooley left to brief the rest of the platoon.

⌘

The next day, after a short stop for lunch, Leary was on point once again in the Lo Bo Woods, leading the battalion through an old rubber tree plantation. Their landing the day before had been uneventful. No enemy in the LZ, no enemy last night, and none so far this morning. The brush had grown up between and around the rubber trees from lack of attention over many years.

Suddenly, Leary felt that old, and ever stronger, feeling that the lieutenant hated. Automatically, he halted the column. Folger was back one rubber tree and to his right. Next was Patkins, a tree farther back and on Folger's left, then Marlin, and on the formation went all the way back through the entire battalion. Leary's intuition directed his eyes to a clump of struggling new bushes under a rubber tree thirty meters down and to his left.

As he looked, he thought he could detect a hint of a different color—a minute difference in color visible through a small gap in the bushes. Leary fired two rounds through the bushes at the place he believed would flush the man out. It worked. A small Vietnamese man in the uniform of a North Vietnamese officer made a run for it.

He charged out of the bushes carrying a small pack but had no visible weapons. The man ran directly across the line of fire when Leary opened up and fired three quick rounds from the hip. The first bullet struck the earth three meters in front of his enemy, the second a meter in front of the still-running man, and the third passed less than a foot in front of his chest. By the third round, the North Vietnamese officer had come to a sliding halt. Leary didn't fire again but commanded, "Drop your pack and keep your hands up." *I'd better stop Folger. I can feel him getting ready to shoot this man. Not that I really give a damm but something's different.* "Folger, hold your fire. I want this son of a bitch."

When the men behind Leary heard his shots, they automatically widened their formation in a defensive move, and then the whole battalion watched and waited for information to come back from the point.

"Everyone hold your positions. I have a prisoner. Alert the colonel and watch your flanks. No known danger yet. Stay alert. Could be more of 'em." Leary said, and then nodded okay as he heard the information being passed back. Ordinarily, the lieutenant or Carson would have moved to the front immediately, but Leary was on point and he had said to hold, so they did.

"There is no one else out here. I am the only one," the prisoner said in English.

"So you say," Leary said, almost shouting. "If you lie, you die. You got that?"

"Yes, I understand."

"Good," Leary commanded, "now get your clothes off. Go on, do it, right down to your bare little ass." The man didn't hesitate and quickly shed his clothes. Dropping his pants, letting them wrinkle around his cheap black tennis shoes. Then, almost ripping it off, he dropped his shirt on the ground. He had no hat, and the pack was still at his feet.

"Now, open the pack very slowly and show me what's inside it, from where you are. You move towards me. Move too quickly and you die." The small man did exactly what Leary told him to do. "Good, no grenades, pistols, or explosives. You might live after all. I really haven't decided yet. Now get your pants up and your shirt on."

The prisoner did what he was told. "That's good. Now come toward me, slowly."

When the short-haired, dark-eyed, clean-looking little man was about ten feet from him, Leary said, "Okay, stop. Toss the pack at my feet and be careful. You twitch wrong and I'll kill you." The NVA officer gently made a perfect toss, the pack landing quietly at Leary's feet. "Good, now turn your pockets inside out."

"There is nothing in them. My things are all in the pack."

"You're starting to piss me off. Now turn your pockets inside out and shut the hell up. I'll say when you're to talk."

The man obeyed, as ordered. Now he silently squatted under a rubber tree, watching as Leary went through his wallet. He pulled the money out, thirty dollars in South Vietnamese currency, and handed it back to Folger, who moved up to get it. "Split that up with the squad; we'll have some beer with it when we get back. Just for the hell of it." Then Leary pulled a picture out of the worn black leather wallet. It was of this man in his North Vietnamese uniform standing next to a woman and a young girl, who could have been any age, from six to thirteen. Leary couldn't tell; to him, the Vietnamese looked young until they reached about thirty, and then they looked old.

"That is my little girl and wife," he said.

"I don't give a shit who they are. I told you to shut up," Leary said, but it had gotten to him. *Jesus, the little shit isn't any different than any of the rest of us. I wish I hadn't seen his family,* Leary thought, as he angrily jammed the wallet and a few toilet articles back into the pack.

"Why did you let me live?"

Oh, what the hell. I'm tired of all of this hate and killing. This is just another guy like me. Still, don't slack up too much. "I don't have the foggiest idea, and I'm still not sure I'm going to."

"Why you fight us? Why you come here?"

"Well, we're here to help stomp out you Communist bastards. Help keep South Vietnam free from people like you."

Then Folger said, "Leary, word from on high is hold the prisoner. Platoons in the rear will sweep ahead of us and set up a perimeter. The colonel is looking for a place to land."

"Okay, thanks, Folger."

Only Folger, ten meters away, could clearly hear what they were saying, and he acted as if he couldn't.

"I was in France studying at university," the Vietnamese man said, "when you Americans entered the war on the side of the South. They called me back, said I was needed more at home."

"We don't exactly like it over here, either." Folger was listening and thinking, *Shoot him and shut him up.* He didn't say anything, but knew that that was exactly what he would do if it were up to him.

"What happens if you desert?"

"Me?" Leary asked. "Desert? Where would I go?"

"Maybe Saigon. Catch a plane, go home."

"It's not worth talking about. It's not in me."

"What happen to your family if you desert?"

He thought about it a minute. *I don't know why I'm bothering to have this conversation with this guy. Yet, it's kind of interesting.* "Nothing, really. Embarrass my mom, dad, and family, but nothing else. Why?"

"If I desert, my wife and child are dead." The look on Leary's face encouraged him to explain. "We are from a small village outside of Hanoi. Communism is everything to my people. It is our only way to get our own country back. Foreigners have always owned us. This is civil war to us. If I desert, my wife and child will be killed."

Trying to understand, Leary said, "You mean they would shoot them? What kind of people do you fight for? The South government is surely better than that." *Shit, you don't even believe that. Remember Gaip's situation.*

"No, but the word would spread. It would be said I am traitor to my people. Anger would build until they wouldn't get their food ration, people would call them traitors and begin spitting on them. And then, sometime later, a mob would kill them, maybe at night. No one would care; it would be an example to other Vietnamese. That's the way it is. South Vietnam is worse, no chance there for Vietnamese at all. We can be slaves to the United States or the French, or we can fight to the death for a Vietnam without foreigners."

"So what happens now?" The NVA officer looked puzzled by the last question. "What will happen when they take you prisoner?"

"Oh," nodding that he understood, "I have six month, maybe, to come back my side."

"Well, you are an optimistic son of a bitch, if nothing else."

"Please excuse my English. I have studied it much, but not used it much lately. And when I am nervous, or scared, like now, it is harder."

"You're a hell of a lot better at English than I am at Vietnamese. But get on with it; the platoons have passed our position and we don't have much time."

Feeling more at ease, his English became almost perfect as he spoke. "Simple, I think. We have people in every rank and occupation in the South Vietnamese Army. Your people will take me to the South Vietnamese government. You beat me, they beat me, but when that is over, they re-educate me. I am officer. They will teach me democracy and in a few months put me in the South Vietnamese Army. When the time is right, I'll come back to my side. It is that easy." He saw the frown on Leary's face and thought for a minute that he had said too much.

Folger turned toward them, twisting at the waist with one knee in the dirt, and said, "Christ, Leary, do him now. Shit, he'll probably come back and shoot one of us. Hell, get out of the way and I'll do it." He got up and came over next to Leary, raised his automatic rifle and, snapping the safety off, pointed it at the NVA officer.

Leary did not take his eyes off the prisoner. He put his left hand on Folger's rifle and said, "No, he lives, Folger. He might have a gun over in the bushes, probably does, I don't care. He didn't try to shoot any of us and he damn sure could have. He's my prisoner and I say he lives." He was relieved to hear Folger snap his safety back on. "Thanks, Folger."

"Okay, Sarge. I hear you and I'm not mad. If you want to let the little son of a bitch live, I don't agree but it's okay. I'll stand by you, even if it gets us killed."

Folger had no sooner finished speaking when they heard the colonel and a Vietnamese interpreter approaching.

"Good job, Sergeant," the colonel said as the interpreter started a rough verbal interrogation of the prisoner. Both were speaking in Vietnamese. "Sergeant, didn't I see you talking to the prisoner when we were approaching?"

"Yes sir. I tried, but I couldn't understand a word he was saying," Leary looked at the two Vietnamese just as the interpreter slapped the NVA officer. "Hey, you shithead. Keep your fucking hands off of him. He's my prisoner, and I'll knock the shit out of you if you do that again."

"Leave him alone, get him out of here. The sergeant is right. Still, Sergeant, I could have sworn I heard him speak English," the colonel said as the two Vietnamese passed them. The interpreter pushed the prisoner roughly and glared at Leary as he passed.

"I was trying, sir. You know, to find a few words he might know. The only words I know in Vietnamese are, 'Raise your hands or I'll shoot.' "

"Yes, I remember, we all learned the phrase on the boat. Is that what you used to get him to surrender?"

"No sir, I used the M-14 language and he raised his hands."

They found a nice chopper-friendly clearing right after the colonel left with the prisoner and, within an hour, their choppers came and took them out of there. They had gotten what they had come for and then went to their base camp for a rest. After they landed and were back at the big tent, Folger spoke derisively. "Typical, they send hundreds of men to capture one prisoner. Then once we get one, they're through. They don't even wonder if maybe he gave himself up to keep us from finding fifty more just like him, or a large arms cache, or God knows what. No, they just say okay, we got one, let's knock off for the day—usual stupid thinking. I'm embarrassed to be an American soldier." Though everyone agreed with Folger, they were all glad it was over.

For several days, nothing was asked of the platoon. The second squad played cards, slept, and drank all of the time. Even though it was against regulations, many of the Christmas packages had contained bottles of booze and, as a group, they stayed drunk during the days and hung over during the nights. They just didn't care anymore.

On the third drunken day, Leary sat out on the bunker in front of their tent, pulling guard as the sun rose. None of them had shaved and they had all given up going to the company CP for meals. Even Tooley and Carson had only shaved the first day. They stayed pretty intoxicated, too. As Leary sat on the bunker, his feet dangling over the side, he felt lower than he had ever imagined he could. His head hurt from the alcohol abuse, but mostly he was sick of the killing. *God help me, I just can't see any reason or purpose for it any longer. It never quits, and it's going nowhere, just killing and more killing. God, I've got seven months left over here and I can't do it anymore. The kids, that's the worst, and the women. Every time we come back here and go to the village, there are more orphans roaming the streets. Little boys and girls taking care of each other the best that they can, just trying to survive. When we first got here, I didn't see any orphans, now the place is full of them. Orphans and women crying, that's all I see anymore.*

He rubbed his temples hard with his fists, more in a destructive way than trying to stop the pain in his head. *As much as my head hurts, it's nothing like the pain in my heart.* Almost on an impulse and with a need for relief from his agony, he spoke out loud, "God, whoever you are, whatever you are, I'm so sick of this needless killing. What's to win? Who wants to win? Not the South Vietnamese, that's for sure." He realized that he was praying out loud and, with no shame or embarrassment, he paused for a moment to gather his thoughts. He knew that he was going to ask for something and felt that by asking God out loud, he would not be denied. *I need to get this right, be clear in what I want and what I'm willing to pay for it, because what I ask for will be granted. I just know it.* "Get me out of here,

God, please. I am so sick of the blood and killing that I am afraid I will lose my soul if I stay here. I will fight for my friends; I will kill for my friends because that, too, is what I am. My life is not important to me anymore. I don't want my life if it means I have to keep on killing in this corrupt war. Kill me, God. Get me out of here any way you have to. I am through." Then, after pausing to make sure he had said it all and said it correctly, he whispered, "Thank you."

A Prayer

39

A PRAYER IS ANSWERED

Later that morning, the battalion was told that a convoy was coming up and they would have to guard it. The still-grubby lieutenant and platoon sergeant told an equally grubby platoon that they would set up at the bridge that night and that the convoy was due up from the south the next day.

"What's the matter," Marlin whined, "don't the damn airplanes carry enough candy for these REMFs?"

"Guess not," Tooley said, no longer interested in much of anything.

That night, they camped along the bridge. There wasn't much conversation, no fires were lit, and they all kept to themselves. Many of the men, including Leary and Patkins, had letters back at their base camp that they had received two months earlier but still hadn't opened. The next morning, Leary and the boys patrolled, making a full swing. Folger carried the grappling hook, though they never used it anymore. Leary found booby-traps, but they just went over and around them. He said, "Don't see any use in getting rid of 'em. They'll just be replaced the next day."

Two hours before dark, Leary and the squad came back in. The convoy was held up an hour waiting for them. The last truck in the convoy had been assigned to pick them up, and it was parked in a clearing by the bridge. The rest of the trucks were strung out along the road, all the way to Ben Cat. As Leary and the patrol crossed the bridge and approached the truck, Tooley said, "Where the hell have you been?"

"Pulling our patrol, Lieutenant. We went in over there by the fort, and we came out over there," Leary said, nodding behind him, "down the valley."

"The captain has been all over my ass and the colonel is going nuts. We've held up this convoy waiting for you. Everyone is tired, and the convoy needs to get to Lia Kae before dark."

"Well, Lieutenant, you can't rush some things. You can quit doing some things, but you can't rush them."

Tooley shrugged and said, "What the hell. Load up. Let's get out of here."

The platoon started leaving their positions and heading toward the empty truck as Leary said, "Hold it." Everyone stopped. He walked up to the truck, its engine idling and its tailgate flopped down in the loading position. "Is this the truck we're supposed to ride in?"

"Hell, yes," Tooley said, "it's the last truck in the convoy, and it's been waiting for you."

"No, sir, we can't ride in this truck."

"What in the hell do you mean we can't ride in this truck? It has seats along the sides, though you never seem to sit on them. You always need to stand in the front and direct the driver. Its motor is running, so it works. It even has a spare tire leaning against the front cab in case we have a flat. What more do you want? For Christ's sake, load up." The platoon started to move towards the truck again.

"No, sir, not in this truck," Leary said, as the platoon halted. "What's wrong, sir, is that there are no sandbags in the bottom of this truck. A truck without sandbags is not supposed to haul troops." Speaking faster now, since he could see Tooley's temper rising, Leary said, "If this truck is hit when there are no sandbags to absorb the explosion, it becomes a huge fragmentation grenade. A damn bomb blowing metal, bolts, and wood into us. No, sir, not this truck." Still no one moved.

Tooley knew that Leary was right and, resigned, said, "You're right, Leary. I didn't even notice. I must be losing it."

"I didn't notice either, sir," Carson said. "But the facts are we're late, this is the last truck in the convoy, and we'll have to risk it."

"No, we don't," Leary said. "Send the truck to Lia Kae empty. We'll all go and stay in Gaip's fort tonight. Tomorrow they can send a truck with sandbags to pick us up. Besides, sir, I know you don't like to hear this, but I got a bad feeling about this truck."

"Feeling, no feeling, sandbags, no sandbags, Leary, I can't go back and leave you men here." Tooley's voice sounded defeated as he said, "I can't go back without my men. I can't just decide to stay here. I don't give the orders around here." He had his palms out and his feet apart in a pleading posture as he continued, "Please, Leary, get in the truck. I'm going to get in the truck." And he waited for what seemed like an eternity. Still no one moved. Then finally, Leary gave in.

"Okay, sir, it's wrong, God, it feels so wrong but, if you're willing to ride in the truck, I'll ride in the truck."

Tooley sighed with relief as he ordered, "Load up, men."

Carson climbed in the middle of the cabless truck next to the driver and Tooley rode shotgun. Leary went up to the front of the truck bed, where the spare tire was lightly tied against the wood rails separating the cab from the bed of the truck, and leaned over the spare tire. He was right behind Carson and close enough to touch him. The lieutenant glanced up at Leary and said, "Let me know when they are all in." Leary nodded in the affirmative.

In about three minutes, the whole platoon finished loading. There was no order to it. Some sat on the floor, and others were on the wood benches along the sides. Folger, Leary, Patkins, and Marlin leaned against the wood boards at front of the truck bed when Leary said, "Okay, sir, we're all in."

Tooley yelled over his shoulder, "Nash, call battalion and tell them we're ready." Then he leaned slightly across Carson and said to the half-asleep driver, "Let's go, driver. Pay attention. We're late now. As soon as that truck ahead of us pulls out, follow him, but keep your interval."

The driver was obviously new to Vietnam; he had unfaded jungle fatigues and the manner of a lazy, sluggish bus driver.

Finally, the truck fifty meters in front of them pulled out on to the road and stopped. Their driver pulled out on to the road too but didn't stop. To Leary's horror, he drove right up behind the truck in front of them before stopping directly over a washout in the asphalt road. He stopped their truck over one of the few places on the highway where the enemy could bury and disguise a bomb.

Leary yelled down at the driver, "For Christ's sake, get the hell out of here. One firecracker can blow us all to hell."

Tooley, realizing the danger, screamed, "Back up, get back on the pavement, get us away from that other truck." The now-horrified driver ground the gears as he tried to get the truck into reverse. But it was too late.

Gaip and the old cook were in the east machine gun position on top of the fort. They watched Leary and the platoon come out of the jungle, load into the truck, drive over the land mine, and explode.

Gaip watched the old man rubbing his crippled hands in apparent pain. "Are your hands especially sore today, Father?" Gaip asked in Vietnamese.

"Yes, son, some days are worse than others. It's okay, though. When your mother and baby sister were killed by Japanese artillery, my heart hurt for years. Then, after years of carrying heavy ammo boxes and digging tunnels, my heart ceased to hurt and the pain in my hands began. I think it was the ropes they put on those wooden boxes that did the most to destroy my hands. The boxes were always heavy, and I couldn't even guess the miles I've carried them. I'm sure all the digging didn't help, that and poor nutrition. But like I said, better the pain in the hands than in the heart. Of course, they've been a bonus, too. Many times I've been mistaken by our enemies for an old rice paddy peasant."

"Well, sir, I guess they got 'em."

"Yes, my son, we got them."

"I didn't know you had ordered it, Father."

"I knew you liked the young sergeant, and I wanted to spare you all that I could."

"They didn't even suspect you are my father or a Vietcong colonel from the Iron Triangle."

"It must be that way for now, son."

"Yes, but why didn't you kill them in my fort?"

"I considered it but, to assure your loyalty, the South Vietnamese army has your wife and my grandchild held as hostages."

"Is that the only reason?"

"No, but it is a good enough one. Of course, if I had them killed in your fort, then our excellent cover would be over. There would be an investigation, and maybe the Americans would attack the fort and kill you, or perhaps we couldn't have gotten them all and that spooky man of Leary's would have killed many of us."

"Folger."

"Was that his name?"

"Yes, a tough man, too."

"Well, he is the one blown west of the truck. He appears to be bleeding severely. I think his leg is gone."

"Yes, and Leary is the one on the asphalt in front of the truck. He is also missing a boot and is bleeding profusely. Was it necessary to kill them, Father?"

"Yes, my son, but you tried to save them. You taught Leary how to find our booby-traps, and he was good at it."

"I did try and save him. I don't feel bad about it, but I just delayed his dying."

"That and you made it possible for him to kill more of my men. He was a good warrior. He had to go."

"I get sick of playing my role sometimes. With Leary, I felt some shame at being deceitful. I stuck as close to the truth as possible to make my position believable but still, acting like a coward hurts."

"It's too bad, but it must be that way. Many men have worked hard and taken great risks to get you here as commander of this fort. If it's any consolation, you are good at it."

"Oh, I don't mind doing my duty, it's just that Leary and I looked into each other's eyes and talked—man to man. Sometimes I feel like I'm not doing my part, and playing a cowardly South Vietnamese officer doesn't make me feel that good. Enough of that, but why did you allow me to explain the booby-traps to him? Surely not to save any of their lives."

"No, their lives are nothing to me. I have lost your mother to the Japanese during the second world war and been shot three times, once by the Japanese and twice by the French, so I have no feelings for these foreigners. The elders and I discussed the role you should play with the Americans thoroughly. It was decided that you should tell them about booby-trap detection to see if they could grasp it. In the past, traitors have told them and still they come over here not seeming to know. We had our best booby-trap people trying to blow the sergeant up after you explained it to him."

"Well, he learned, and it was costly. He killed a lot of our men over this experiment. Seems a shame."

"This whole business is a shame. But you are right. We played with him too much and it cost us. I have many loved ones crying over the men he has killed. He learned so well that we couldn't get him in the jungle, but he had to die. You don't leave a cobra in your mother's garden. Leary and his people are cobras in our gardens. We must kill them."

"Yes, well, they came out of the jungle and you killed them on the road, a place where they least expected it, a place where Leary could least control their environment, but even then I tried to warn him. I told him when we first met that if he killed the men of the Triangle, they would kill him. He didn't listen."

"Oh, I think he heard you, son, but what could he do? He had to fight. He had no choice. Besides, he and all of them were marked for death. We had orders from Hanoi, and it was even announced on the radio and known in all of the villages. I knew he was a dead man when he first came through your gate. And there he is, lying dead or dying in the road."

Gaip handed the binoculars to the old man. "Yes, that's him all right and, in a way, he was my friend. I did like him."

"Nothing wrong with liking him, son. You did your duty; you kept your mouth shut about this fort being a guard post for the Triangle. Of course, you couldn't save him. No one can save anyone in our country, not really."

"I suppose that's true. Still, I wish I could have saved him. I liked him."

"Like doesn't have much to do with anything in these times. In my twenty-five years at war, I have liked many people. Most died."

"They're working on him now. Maybe he's not dead."

"Yes, son, he's dead. Maybe not his body, but who he was is gone forever. Breathing or not, the man they sent over here is dead."

"Yes, of course, you're right as usual, Father. How long has the bomb been there in the road?'

"Only a week before Leary got here. It was one of their own 155 artillery shells, buried in the ground with a blasting cap in it and wires running up to the village. The old man on the bike signaled the boy with the battery when the truck was in position. They waited all day for Leary to come back so they could blow up his truck. Ironic, their own artillery shell."

"Why would men like him even come over here to kill our people?"

"That is puzzling. The Japanese wanted our rubber, the French as well, but these Americans claim that they want freedom for us. What a silly notion. No one can get freedom for another person. Freedom is a state of mind. Leary and those men come over here because they are told to. Our being a threat to them is just a sick lie. Can you even imagine Vietnamese going to America to kill Americans because we think they have a bad president? Absurd."

"How long will this killing go on?"

"Until only Vietnamese are left in Vietnam. All that happens until then is just the cost of war, nothing more."

EPILOGUE

Jimmy was wearing his Western Union pants. George was concerned. Jimmy wore the shirt and a hat as part of the uniform. He was supposed to wear the pants too but, in the two years Jimmy had worked for George, he had usually just worn his jeans with the shirt. At first, George had mentioned it a few times and Jimmy would wear the uniform pants for a couple of days and then go back to the jeans. George had finally given up and hadn't mentioned it for the last year.

He had been working for George since he had gotten his drivers license. George had come to know and like the boy over the last couple of years.

George's heart sank, now. He had been watching the boy closely. It was supposed to be an easy job. Most days it was. Most years it was. Not this year. He had sorted them by best route in post housing and put them on Jimmy's desk. Now he waited.

He could feel it just before he heard it. It was like a heavy wet blanket of despair enveloping him from behind, then the weeping.

George reluctantly turned his office chair around. "Jimmy...I know it's a lot; you've got to detach."

"Yes sir, I know. I didn't want to care. I can't be the messenger of death, George. Not today." he sobbed, utterly breaking down. "Not this many. I can't look another widow in the eye. I can't. I'm sorry." He sobbed uncontrollably.

In all the time he had known him, George had never touched the boy. He had never had cause. Now he put his hand on his shoulder.

"Watch the office for me, son." George put his Western Union hat on, picked up the telegrams for the wives and widows of Fort Riley, Kansas, and walked out of the room.